D1760675

2+2=5

Withdrawn From Stock
Dublin Public Libraries

Leabharlann Fionnghlas
Finglas Library
01-2228330

2+2=5

JAKE CHAPMAN

URBANOMIC

Published in 2021 by

URBANOMIC MEDIA LTD.
THE OLD LEMONADE FACTORY
WINDSOR QUARRY
FALMOUTH TR11 3EX
UNITED KINGDOM

© Jake Chapman 2021

All rights reserved.

No part of this book may be reproduced or transmitted in any form or by
any means, electronic or mechanical, including photocopying, recording or
any other information storage or retrieval system, without prior permission
in writing from the publisher.

'The Times They Are A-Changin''
Words and music by Bob Dylan
© Universal Music Corp., Songs of Universal, Inc.
and Universal Tunes, a Division of Songs of Universal, Inc.
Used by permission—all rights reserved

'Woman is the Nigger of the World'
Words and music by John Lennon and Yoko Ono
© Ono Music/Lenono Music c/o Downtown Music UK Ltd. (PRS)
Used by permission—all rights Reserved

BRITISH LIBRARY CATALOGUING-IN-PUBLICATION DATA

A full catalogue record of this book is available
from the British Library

ISBN 978-1-913029-69-2

Printed and bound in the UK by
TJ Books, Padstow

Distributed by the MIT Press,
Cambridge, Massachusetts and London, England

K-Pulp: New Adventures in Theory-Fiction

The meek shall inherit the earth, but not the mineral rights.

— J. Paul Getty

PART 1

CHAPTER I

It was a bright and beautiful day in April, and the clocks were striking thirteen. Winston Smith, mindful of the luminous sun bathed in a baby blue sky, slipped casually into the pH-buffered ambience of Serenity Mansions, though not quickly enough to prevent a swirl of pink apple blossom from entering along with him.

The hallway smelled of freshly laid seagrass suffused with a faint trace of reliquary myrrh. A large embroidered tapestry hung on the far wall, depicting a colourful smiley face set in the midst of a crimson ground, with two coloured dots for eyes and a simple upward curve for a smile. Winston summoned the elevator, but before the floor pointer could arc its way over from one end of the rainbow to the other, had already slipped into the stairwell, keen for the exercise of the seventeen flights up to his homely hearthstone. On the third floor landing he took time to stretch out his back, glutes, hamstrings and calves, finishing off with a deep fingertip-to-toe bend just as the elevator basket exhaled silently downwards on a cushion of the softest air. On the palisade, the same smiley-faced tapestry gazed down upon his lissom physique. The face with the kindly eyes that followed your every movement. SMILE AND THE WORLD SMILES WITH YOU, the caption beneath it ran.

The apartment was filled with the genteel collision of wind against bamboo chime, and, being customarily drawn to its welcome, Winston soon found himself standing before the vast panoramic window, confronted by the faint backscattered image of a man whose easy demeanour was summed up by his meticulously nonchalant clothing—the white loose-linen open-necked blouse, loose jeans, open-toed sandals, a string of raw sandalwood beads tied loosely about his wrist, a simple sand-coloured wooden paynim pendant hung on a thick thong around the neck, and the rigorously unkempt hair.

3

Winston's reflection was radiant with wellness, the skin tended by a diurnal regimen of natural moisturisers, soothing balms and softening toner—and yet the propagating waves glancing off the surface of the glass conveyed nothing beyond the integrity of the superficial phenomenon, and it was questionable whether there was evidence of anything substantial beyond the gossamer image smiling back at him. He moved his face closer to the glass, fingering the soft skin just below his left eye, dragging it down to peer into the glistening mess. He dipped his chin, tipped his head, turned it to the left and right, but despite this deliberate animation the eyes remained fixed, the reflected stare constant, the mask's uncanny sentience disavowing all suggestion of a soul in the very attempt to catch sight of it. Relinquishing the attempt to see himself as others might see him, Winston peered through the tenuous opacity of his reflection to see the unequivocal fact of the glorious world beyond, spread out in every direction, bathed in beneficent sun. Through his dissolving face he saw the city alive with a chaos of colour and observed the vital purpose of its teeming population below. Smiley faces of all shapes and sizes gazed down keenly from every street corner; there was even an enormous version posted on a vast hoarding above the apartment block opposite. SMILE AND THE WORLD SMILES WITH YOU, it said, the kindly eyes watching over Winston's residence with the greatest solicitude.

A distant helicopter lowered from the bright azure sky, down and down, scything between the buildings and hovering deliberately for an instant before winding back up into the sun. The Neighbourhood Watch Air Patrol was sweeping the upper cityscape, making sure that everything was all harmonious and hunky-dory—as above, so below.

A kilometre away, the cluster of municipal Ministry buildings soared above the city, filling Winston with a calm euphoria;

a desire for something verging upon a sense of continuity, a contiguous belonging to all things laid out before his eyes—a lofty craving which was soon displaced by a compensatory evocation of childhood, as he remembered the plots of the low modular houses of his youth, decorated by flowering Cana lily and Frangipani trees, their many window frames framing the many smiles of the contented tenants. He recalled the sloped roofs and the crazy-paved gardens with explosions of fragrant blossom, petal bursts swirling up in vortices of warm air. He thought of the great willow trees draping over and dipping down into the river, he thought of the communal gardens and the ornamental flower beds, with their exotic scents; the kites, flags, hot air balloons, butterflies, candy floss, sweets and cakes, bushbabies, honey bees, giraffes, caterpillars, dragon flies, porcupine, jugglers, owls, doves, palm trees, zebra, rhino beetles, aardvarks, and the hurry-scurry playgrounds sprinkled with freshest pine woodchip.

Especially noteworthy in the vista that opened up before him was The Ministry of Good Fortune, an enormous pyramidal structure of glittering Himalayan crystal with ziggurat terraces stepping up, up and up, three hundred metres up into the sky, and then stepping down, down, down to the ground. From where Winston stood it was possible to read, boldly carved into its sloped rock face, the three slogans of healthy living:

BE COMFORTABLE IN YOUR OWN SKIN
BELIEVE IN THE MOMENT
BECAUSE YOU'RE WORTH IT

The Ministry of Good Fortune harboured a happy hive of laid-back yippy wonks and eager-beaver journeyfolk, with generous car-parking scooped out of the earth below, including complimentary hook ups for each and every rust-bucket VW hooptie.

There were three other municipal buildings of comparable scale, and so completely did they dwarf the city that the spectacle could be appreciated even from the shallows of the surrounding suburbs.

These were the four main Ministries in which the collective corporate co-operative was made manifest—neither the command centres of a sovereign directorate or an overbearing nanny-state, nor the citadel campaniles of some federal autocracy, but the four devolved poles of a distributive consensus-nexus, a resource-manipulating organelle delicately attuned to the fluctuations of an improvisational market, and encapsulating the four essential human freedoms: freedom of speech and expression; freedom to connect to the universe in any way, shape, or form; freedom from want and fear. The Ministry of Good Fortune embodied the collective economic providence of its citizens, the Ministry of Fun and Games personified gestalt enrichment through everyday jouissance, the Ministry of Love nurtured intrapersonal and somatic harmony, and the Ministry of Caring and Sharing fostered a helping hand with all other salutary aspects of societal holism.

Each building was an architectural delight, but the Ministry of Love was especially vivid, formed as it was in the figural shape of a towering penis entering a monumental vagina, with a back entrance for underground parking. Winston, however, had neither need, reason nor desire to visit the Ministry of Love—so he said. The Ministry of Love was run by shrinks and quacks of every persuasion—cognitive psychologists, mindfulness anthrosophists, integrative psychotherapists, motivational psychodynamicists—from Freud, Jung and Klein to Baker Eddy, Ainsworth, Horney, Maccoby, Kneipp and even Kellogg—all affiliates of the Abolition of Involuntary Mental Hospitalisation, the Hearing Voices in the Head Network, and the Centre for Dissociative Paranoia Inc. The streets leading up to the Ministry's outer lips were customarily patrolled by volunteers of the

6

grassroots Neighbourhood Watch who freely counselled pedestrians seeking self-esteem therapy, especially those shy and retiring citizens who might be found loitering in local parks, or those reclusive individuals who sought isolation in the discomfort of an Ideas Store, stalled in the self-help section—the frail human frass found faltering on the long and winding road to ultimate self-realisation and inner-wonk wisdom.

Winston slunk a vaguely otiose diagonal back to the healing rose-quartz-counter-topped kitchen island, a finger lagging lazily along its homespun edge all the way to the refrigerator, peeking inside only for his faint yearning optimism to be tinged by the yawning fluorescent disappointment that was always reliably there to greet him. As soon as the door was opened, the machine had come alive with a sentient click and a mechanical shudder, as though sensing an increase in ambient temperature, quaking nervously at the notion of something warm-blooded outside looking in. It dawned upon Winston that sacrificing lunch in the convenience of the Ministry eatery had been rather foolish. From the shelves of the fridge the resident lettuce, the shrimp, buckwheat and kelp-agar, plus lemon-zest guano, called out to him in a not entirely wholesome way. Even the companion fortune cookie portended doom, its mysterious prediction still intact inside the cold, brittle pastry. Guessing at the dark prophecy it might hold for him—*Best not eat tainted shrimp for much sickness will follow*—Winston instead elected for a narrow-necked flagon whose pretty, rustic label identified its contents as *Herbal Ataraxy Elderflower*. He poured a small glass and nerved himself for a modest shock, downing it quickly like an astringent remedy, the subsequent blench causing the fizzy elderflower to flatten and stream out from both squinting canaliculi. When the fizzing in his sinuses abated he felt the vitality of his senses return, as the last stevia shivers tingled in the entangled snarl of his unkempt hair.

Winston settled at the elegant vintage Jens Quistgaard flip-top desk set back in a small but neatly accommodating alcove. From the Quistgaard's creaking drawer he took out a brown paper bag, and from the bag, a book. He set the book down on the desk before him and began alternately closing one eye and then the other whilst rocking gently to and fro on his seat—even letting out a slight hum as he did so. The dominant image on the book's brightly coloured lenticular cover was that of a generic smiley face—a circular disk with two coloured dots for eyes and a simple upward curve for a smile—and yet with only the slightest of movements the happy face became immediately unhappy. It shimmered so easily between happy and sad, exactly capturing the two proven poles of human expression, that any existential speculations jotted within its pages were at risk of being an extraneous redundancy.

Next to the alcove a small black and white portable television perched casually on a chair—switched on, but with the sound turned down. The television was positioned with its screen set obliquely enough to prevent even Winston's peripheral vision from being unwittingly gripped. He had an affection for the television's proximate murmur, being most fond of the company of anonymous voices—and so long as he stayed positioned at the desk, he would not be unduly distracted from his present purpose. Of course he could simply switch the thing off, but the monotony of the voices made the uncertainty of what he was about to do far less daunting.

The *My Big Book of Me* was laid open on the desk, set beneath Winston's apprehensive gaze. The first page glared up at him, all imminent and bright, and he savoured the smell of the binding glue that wafted up when the virgin spine creaked apart with the first press of the palm—that especial scent given to all things created with the meticulous tarnish of the human touch. It was at Harmony Maker's Market that he had come across the *My Big Book of Me* cahiers being fabricated in situ. He had not been overtly conscious of wanting or needing a notebook for any particular purpose other than to support the Maker's public display of artisanal toil (*or was it just to avoid leaving the market empty-handed?* It was difficult to tell.) Yet here he was, staring intently at the expectant first page as if contemplating something vaguely criminal; as if the punishment for defacing such an assiduously artisan-crafted object might be public humiliation, menial labour, or three months incarceration in some dreary reality television show.

Winston was not exactly used to writing by hand, apart from short annotations and the odd instructive note associated with his tasks at the Ministry. It was usual there to log everything directly into the Dictaphone, which was pointless for his present purpose since he would have only to transcribe his own dictation. So he urged the pen a little closer towards the page, but again faltered, since his hand had begun to shake. To mark the paper was a decisive act, and so, to begin with, in smallish neatish letters, as best he could, he scrawled:

April 4th, 1984.1

He sat back. A sense of foreboding descended upon him like an embalmer's sheet—dark, solid as livid meat laid out on a morgue slab, dense as the slab itself. Why was he writing? Who was he writing for? Could it just be *writing for writing's sake*—that immense and hollow humility that places itself at an infinite distance from vanity, and yet by virtue of its subtraction sneaks up to magnificence with a coquettish simper?

Winston considered the date on the page with growing suspicion, since it insinuated that everything to follow was destined to a courageous embrace with insignificance (but with one steady eye on immortality), or worse, *to mere gobbledegook*—the unholy tripartite coalition of claptrap, gibberish and drivel. How could he communicate if all was anyway gobbledegook? How could he communicate in the present if all was anyway gobbledegook? How could he communicate with the unborn if all was anyway gobbledegook? And if the future resembled the present, he would simply be stating the obvious, and acting in the present would at best amount to squandering his spare time in the cause of an empty gesture, a hopeless hobby crowned by ennui and self-pity.

While the innocuous date mocked him with its dogmatic simplicity, the creamy voices to his left had begun to discuss the nutritional merits of artisanal cashew cheese. Despite the reflex rise of bile in the stomach and a drooling of the mouth, he resisted tipping his chair back to catch the cheesemakers by sight, wary of being forever caught in the television's mesmeric trap. For many months the idea of putting pen to paper had been fermenting in his mind—but it had not even occurred to him that anything more would be required than an aptitude for rendering his impressions directly onto the page. Writing should come naturally and flow easily; all he should have had to do was to transfer to paper the persistent monologue that had been running inside his head, looping and twisting, for as long as he could remember. Yet the inner monologue appeared to have lost its tongue…and before him loomed the imminently bright white page, beside him the cheerful churning of the cashew cheese, inside him an exiguous migraine beginning to flavour his mind—while somewhere downstairs in the basement of bad dreams, his gut was being cruelly etched by an ill-judged glut of Herbal Ataraxy.

And then suddenly, without any inkling of intent, his right hand—his *writing* hand, only nominally connected to his body—began a spasmodic scrawl across the page. It was all he could do to peer down at the agoraphobic motion of a sickly cockroach caught out in the open beneath the glare of human disgust, its gammy broken leg dragging behind, leaving a delicate train of sepia pus, or was it cochineal?—crawling across the luminous white page in a tremulous scuttle, a stochastic scribble yet to disclose the aim of its erratic journey…. Only imperfectly aware of what his hand was setting down, he observed its motion, aghast at the uncanny independence that was drawing it across the page, looping and plotting each opening capital and closing full stop, with all the tender letters so tremulously strung out in-between. Winston had often privately speculated as to the eventual manifest form his writing would take…and what became evident to his bitter scrutiny was this:

Must compassionate mind
Cultivate warmheartedness
Peace of mind come from
Heart root of all goodness.
All must exist in simple soil
No need complicated philosophies,
My tingle brain and soft shell heart
Are my special inner temples for
The kindness cat has for injured mouse.

Winston looked down at the merciless drear, taking especial fright at the poem's ragged right edge. There was no accounting for the bizarre anarchic motion of his hand; but as it scuttled beneath his detached gaze and across the page again, an entirely separate thought came back to him. He remembered that it was because of this *other* thought—a memory of something that had occurred much earlier in the day—that he had felt so compelled to sacrifice lunch at the Ministry eatery and rush home.

It had happened that very morning, if anything so eerie and strange could be said to have distinctly happened at all. It was nearly eleven hundred, and in the Ministry of Good Fortune they were busy dragging out the couches, yoga mats, beanbags, cushions, zabutons, sheepskins, hassocks, soumaks and loungers, grouping them in the centre of the community room to face the large projection screen in preparation for the Two Minutes Compassion. Winston was just settling into a bamboo chair when he noticed the last few people to enter the room, among them the girl whom he sometimes passed in the corridor. He had formed the idea that she belonged in the Romantic Friction Department, presuming so because he had once spotted her being consoled by a coterie of departmental comrades, one of them cradling a box of tissues and delicately dabbing at the red-raw corners of her eyes. Winston had taken an immediate shine to the girl from the very first moment he set eyes all over her. With the strands of her dark tousled brunette unruly bob pointing casually in many eccentric directions, she appeared to project a certain otherworldly kookiness, but he suspected it masked something altogether more profound. He was in fact mindful that his libidinal attraction was as much an appreciation of her glowing inner fortitude as it was an instinctual reaction to her superficial kookiness. He appreciated women's and men's inner and outer appeal equally, especially the young and pretty ones and the older ugly ones too—he appreciated them pretty much unanimously, with a similar regard for ugly old men and pretty old women and pretty young men and ugly young women, and all for pretty much similar reasons. He understood how the pretty human face became gradually more beautiful with time, and how, with much more time, a beautiful human face became wise, and no sooner had it become wise than it became wizened, and how once wizened the seasons of the face eventually came to a withered rest. All in all, Winston was confident enough in his cosmetic quantizing to know that this particularly young pretty handsome female girl woman comrade made more of an impression upon him than most, and that this feeling was somehow inextricably connected to his own sense of authentic well-being. For instance, once when they had passed in the corridor, she had cast him a furtive sidelong glance that disturbed his soul, and, capitalising on his public perturbation, she had ruthlessly harvested his perplexity—absorbing his moronic leer into the dynamo of her own self-rejuvenating ego. He nonetheless comforted himself with the conviction that the synergistic frisson they sometimes shared in the corridor must be vaguely mutual—*and that somewhere beyond the glow of the fullness of their being lived a truly dark, dank, animal lust....*

Winston saw that the girl was assisting O'Brien with her wheelchair—an ornament of affection rather than of practical necessity—but what was strange about their alliance was that she appeared to be whispering to O'Brien, both of them apparently staring in Winston's direction. In this Winston found no cause for alarm, since O'Brien was just about the most amiable person one could hope to know. She was well-rounded and beautiful on the inside and out, and well-seated in the sovereignty of her mobile throne. This most genial mentor, crowned by a magisterial face, had a little trick of resetting the spectacles on the bridge of her nose, which only added to her overall charm. Many were drawn to her intimate counsel since she was so open and affable—the kind of person one might openly talk to, and not only about Ministry affairs, but about poetry and art too—not that Winston ever wanted to talk about affairs, or poetry, or art too.

O'Brien found a space for her chair just a couple of places away from Winston. A small, pink-haired girl woman lady wonk who often worked adjacent to Winston soon occupied the beanbag in-between, already munching on popcorn. The girl with the dark non-conformist hair had settled immediately behind Winston, an insouciant leg dangled purposefully over the notched back of his seat.

With the room settled into clenched expectation, the lights began to dim as a familiar jingle cleaved into the hush—a childish finger working its haunting staccato magic upon a toy clavichord with brutal ham-fisted clarity—announcing that the Two Minutes Compassion had begun.

Winston was still fumbling for his 3D spectacles as a blurred vision of a vast desert and an angry red sun faded up to hang luminous before him. With the spectacles properly seated, the room came alive with a panorama of failed crops, stretching to the farthest horizon. In the foreground a glockenspiel of collapsed animal bones cast jagged shadows into the room which raked over the flinching and squirming audience. Huge dust clouds swept up in squalls of foul air to fits of psychosomatic coughing, finally giving way to the sight of an arid river basin, the parched stream-bed cracked into a huge puzzle of itself, the territory confused for the map, and at the map's scurf edge a silent overseer, all sacred and hopeless—an emaciated cow hung from the agony of a serrated spine, a tattered plastic bag caught on its horn. And then, as ever, more and yet more images of hell pulsed and dissolved, dreadful stereoscopic spectres reaching out like a many-fingered claw to stimulate the compassion of the audience with the miraculous horror of optical density—a sensory nightmare so virtually real that neither rapid eye movement nor night sweats nor stricken cries could be dispelled by waking.

Then came a simple voice to pronounce the name of each crime: '*DEATH...DROUGHT...FAMINE...MISERY...HOPELESSNESS....*' It was a voice of such singular solemnity that it bristled the hair at the nape of the neck and sent innocent eyes abattoir-wide. 'Friends! Citizens of humanity! It's an ill fate for a world to be expunged of the technologies of malice and war, only for the meek to remain at the whim and mercy of *nature's* intemperate rage....'

All light and hope in the room was suddenly extinguished,

and only a low primordial hum sustained the narrator's ominous incrimination, pitched into the darkness like some death knell that resonates with malignant tissue and hidden cancers.... Then a single speck of light appeared on the screen, hushed apprehension condensing towards it like the sun concentrated through a magnifying glass. All hoped that the redemptive speck might grow, might blossom, might illuminate and attenuate the dread of the narrator's words—and what followed, as ever, were gasps of relief and impromptu applause as Emmanuelle Goldstein appeared, like a vision, in all her bright and luminous glory, with the usual wry smile to settle the audience back from the cliff-edge of their chairs, soumaks and beanbags—Goldstein the poet, polymath and erstwhile movie star, a beacon of empathy, with her voracious appetite for the famished; and when she saw fit to cast her eyes down the barrel of the camera, directly into the pinned retinas of the faithful, she glared with the focus of a high-energy laser-beam, and spoke.

'Friends! Compatriots in global consensus! I bring word of a new disaster—more terrible than the last! Mother Nature is conspiring to decimate our distant cousins! A terrible famine looms over the region of the lost tribes, and even threatens to wipe them out. We have tried in vain to persuade them against the theology of ruin from which they divine their redemption. We can only offer the fact of our charity against the superstitious burden that binds them to a hostile sun. So I call upon you, one and all, to act now before it is too late.' Goldstein maintained her silent gaze as a host of angelic voices began in kind:

Would you walk by on the other side
If starving children cried?
Would you walk by on the other side
Or would you pass them by?
Would you walk by on the other side

If Stalin's children cried?
Would you walk by on the other side
Or would you pass them by?

As the children trilled like parakeets on a day-perch, Emmanuelle Goldstein's face shimmered between solemnity and rage, striving toward some kind of juxtaposition between the sublime execution of the choir and the bewildered excruciation of the dying. She was shaking her head at the terrible suffering that her shaking head *could not even hope to know*—only to then nod at the suffering that her knowing nodding *knew only too well*. She was nodding and shaking, trembling, frowning and sighing—hoping that somewhere within this mishmash of contradictory expressions was an approximation of death. Unrestrained sighs broke out among the audience, and the light-pink-haired woman sat just along from Winston emitted a long and involuntary sigh that conveyed brave anticipation of the full-fat onslaught to come. It was perhaps implicitly understood that ever greater acts of charity were required in order to maintain the needy in the interstices between disease and good health, and so the cherished episodes of the Two Minutes Compassion varied from week to week, employing great novelty to refresh the jaded face of suffering and thereby sustain the empathic attention of the donors. However, it was sometimes unclear to Winston whether the entertainment given as dispensation to the donors had in fact supplanted the objective purpose of charity, such that the needy were maintained in the interstices between disease and good health precisely in order to serve the purposes of novelty. Needless to say, Winston couldn't always bring himself to watch the programmes when they were broadcast live, and set the machine to record each new episode so that he could watch it later. Although he never did so, the timer was nonetheless set on repeat to record over the last with the newest, and always on the exact same section of tape, *two minutes of compassion that Winston had yet to afford....*

With an array of infographics—the vertiginous peaks and troughs of feast and famine graphs, delirious numeric counters, famished pie-charts—Goldstein proved that they must act without hesitation to fend off each impending natural disaster before it was too late; to embrace the pitiless plight of their god-fearing cousins without turning from the sight of their sacred abandonment, to bear witness to the pitiful images of the diseased, and so to be entitled by the authenticity of first-hand experience to act with unbribed volition, to volunteer their own hard-earned tokens in the manifest expression of an irreducible free will.

'If we do nothing they will die! We have no other choice than to save them from themselves! We must do something—*anything is better than nothing!*'

Into the exotic ulcer wrenched between the diseased life and economic death of those unfortunate souls rendered prone to charity, the donor dutifully acknowledges their own providential fortune by sprinkling a little trickle-down economics, if only to animate the spell of wretched indebtedness that endows guilt with its tangible rate of exchange. The Two Minutes Compassion really put the wince in Winston, and Winston's diaphragm was already constricted. He could never witness the face of Goldstein without a descent into the primal. This was probably true of all those who identified with her personification of suffering. And despite the utter ugliness of this world of endless famine and persistent drought, Goldstein somehow managed to maintain her inner hope, as evidenced outwardly by the big sorbefacient eyes that were so ruthless in extorting great compassion from the populations of the nice-and-comfortable. Yet with every appeal, each more urgent than the last, Winston became more anxious that others might not be moved enough to donate proportionately to the call—or that, even if they did, the sum total of all virtuous efforts could not prevent Mother Nature or God from fulfilling the perpetual obligation to wreak seasonal annihilation.

'Remember!' Goldstein cried out, as if addressing the crime of Winston's inner thoughts, seemingly glaring straight down at him alone. '*We must donate proportionately to the call—so that the sum of all our virtuous efforts can prevent Mother Nature from wreaking seasonal annihilation!*'

Winston had no time to reflect upon the coincidence of Goldstein's announcement with his own unspoken words, since her emphatic outburst seemed to have knocked the wind out of her; the bean-bag dwellers, too, were all moved to a terrible hush by the very sight of the narrator's unscripted dilapidation—that such a hardened humanitarian should be so easily moved to tears in public.... Goldstein clumsily wiped at her eyes, smearing native carnauba mascara with the cruel blunt of her knuckles, but not before a simple human tear managed to escape her shame. Before the teardrop could fall to the earth and, God forbid, cause some outrageous genesis, some germinal obscenity, to push up through the dirt and sprout into the murderous light, a colossal holographic hand, as huge and clumsy as a theatrical prop, came thrusting from the screen, projecting out into the room as if it had crashed through from the wall behind, sending the audience backwards for fear they were being propositioned by some God-sized delinquent beggar. But Goldstein's hand was simply reaching out to catch the tear drop, to save it from the agony of the soil and the sun. And then many gasps of relief were stifled as soon as they were expressed: Goldstein's compliant palm began to transform before their very eyes into a vast pink desert, an arid dustbowl with a diminutive waterhole set in the central depression, but with a silent overseer—the emaciated cow hung from the agony of its serrated spine.

With the low susurration of the damned and the universal mockery of flies swarming in the sickly air, the wincing audience huddled close on their island of disturbed tranquility, with much chattering of teeth, gnawing of beanbags and dry retching; some were afflicted by lingering groans and coughing, with lips curled and teeth bared, mirroring the peeled skeletal grimaces of the dying—except that their rictus dental perfection revealed whiter-than-white teeth fluoresced by the luminary overspill of the stereoscopic projector.

Soon came the customary flood of promises of fiscal support—the exuberant jingle-jangle of loose change trickling down, of credit cards waved and swiped in the air, of tax relief redirected and standing-order mandates pledged. How impeccable was the timing of the Two Minutes Compassion—as if the temperature at which sympathy reached fever pitch matched the exact thermal threshold at which pecuniary outpourings became molten and ran freely, the flux of mercurial generosity meeting the hiss of annealed solder. As the donation counter spun deliriously with each new fiscal tranche, Goldstein clasped her hands together in triumph, beat at her bosom with clenched fist and reciprocated her adoring audience—then shook her head slowly and nodded most solemnly, knowing that somewhere in this lenticular shimmering was an approximation of humility. As was customary, the Compassion had passed through frenzy towards redemption, donors now leaping up and down on their beanbags and shouting at the tops of their shrill voices, feeling quite at liberty to drown out the horrific descriptions that had drifted down from the screen to so bleakly tarnish their hearts and minds. The little pink-haired woman's mouth was opening and shutting without sound, like a fish gulping beneath the scorching sun. Winston noticed that O'Brien was watching with her own 3D glasses, perhaps transfixed, but absolutely expressionless.

The dark-haired girl behind was now up on her feet yelling 'Give! Give! Give!' She was even moved to fling a handful of loose change at the screen. Winston found that he too was shouting with the others and kicking his feet violently against a vacant beanbag in front of him, since its erstwhile dweller was up on their feet too, similarly beating the vacant beanbag before them. Once the collective sense of injustice had achieved its injurious peak and the tears had been delivered up to the dabbing of soft tissues that were freely handed about, a new calm took over as the Compassion once again abated.

A new collective hope began to warm the wonks huddled together in the centre of the room, clinging to their beanbags and soumaks like survivors on a makeshift raft having caught first sight of land, thoughts of cannibalism now far from their minds, since all were now cheerful in their new optimism—especially the weak, thankful for a close escape from gourmet death. A new collective coalesced among them, a determination to begin the war on famine! *Right now! We must! We have no choice! Before it's too late! Because anything is better than nothing!*

As Goldstein's parade of horrors ebbed away, Winston savoured the grandeur of his own personal catharsis. He was certainly a better person for it, for the horror, since now he felt an overwhelming sense of compassion for all things animate and inanimate—for everything and everyone around him, for the sun and the moon, the birds and the bees, for yin and yang, for the clouds and rain, for honey and jetsam, for people he didn't know, and those he had no hope of ever meeting. He even had a sense of unadulterated compassion for the populations of the unborn, twinkling away in a sublime and indifferent cosmos. In short, Winston was thankful for Goldstein, since her two minutes of morbid horripilation gave a redemptive narrative to suffering, and made other people's pain, unavoidable as it was, truly worth it for all.

From a distance there came the lowly murmur of flies and simmering vultures ruffling their dusty feathers. Winston was still at one with all things animate and inanimate, black and white, honey and vinegar, flotsam and jetsam, yin and yang. At these moments a heightened sense of intrapersonal connectedness flowed through him. In spite of the pietistic solitude that hung about her, Goldstein appeared like some transcendent enchanter, capable with just the tone and inflection of her voice of reinvigorating popular confidence in the ineluctable spirit of progress. When she smiled, more often than not knee-deep in the mire of some obscene and godforsaken suffering, civilisation itself nonetheless shone forth from the shit, untarnished, unblemished by hopelessness. Everyone in the world agreed that famine was intolerable, this miraculous global consensus being expressed by those fortunate enough to enjoy institutions of opinion, since consensus is not a thing a person thinks about when they are famished. And the world accordingly united in pity and outrage—all differences put aside in order for the world to act on behalf of those faceless, nameless half-beings slipping towards an excruciating annihilation, too weak to partake in the univocal consensus being established in their name, but instead doomed to the unheard murmuring democracy of the undead.

It was possible during such moments of heightened pathos for the capacity for sublime love to greatly flourish—for love to fuse with the deepest darkest sorrow, the sorrow of the soil and the stars and everything imprisoned between. The assimilation of profound sorrow into profound love allowed Winston's tears of sadness to mingle now with tears of joy, so that the one was indistinguishable from the other, like water in water. Crying for joy, Winston found he was picturing himself walking hand-in-hand with the subject of his present romantic fixation—eating candy floss with her, or breaking pumpkin bread…or sharing carob cake. And as his thoughts drifted from horror to love, it dawned upon him that he liked her because she was pretty and handsome and wise, but not yet wizened. He wanted to sleep with her—and because liberated sexual pleasure epitomised a person's Fullness of Being, only a willing intersection in the Venn diagram of two overlapping Fullnesses of Being could allow the carnal magic to happen. It occurred to Winston then that the erotic universal set that might plausibly conjoin him to the girl could perhaps be found in a mutual hatred of famine. *Hatred* was the universal set that could authorise a singular and sublime *love*.

And then a starving woman with horribly plaintive eyes loomed large and terrible, pleading for the exhausted child cradled so limply in her size-zero arms, so that some observers in the front row slumped back into their seats and beanbags, drawing as far away from the dying child as they could, eyes welling with huge, luminous, bulging, childish, cartoon tears and caricatured gestures of sadness. Winston's streaming tears also changed allegiance mid-flow, from lust-tinged joy back to sorrow. But before a single drop could be spilled onto the carpet, there rose a unanimous sigh of relief as the grotesque woman and her withered fledgling melted away into the hallucinatory topology of Goldstein's merciful profile—and with *everything solid melting into air* under the influence of a mysterious calm and a magnanimous compassion so vast that it filled the screen and gushed out into the room beyond, Goldstein's inner beauty made way for the three soothing epithets to pulse and throb on screen:

BE COMFORTABLE IN YOUR OWN SKIN
BELIEVE IN THE MOMENT
BECAUSE YOU'RE WORTH IT

The little pink-haired woman flung herself forwards onto the distressed beanbag that Winston had been so dutifully kicking and stamping on, thus rudely interrupting his cathartic flow, and with her face buried in its compliant softness gave out a muffled cry that others might gladly interpret as: '*Goldstein...our saviour!*' And then, releasing her face from the calming bean-bag—its charged bead-particles the Brownian brunt of Winston's rage—elevating her head with an expression of glowing confirmation, then extending her chubby arms out towards the screen, with corpulent fingers outstretched even to the ragged ends of flagellated hangnails—was abruptly compelled to bury her chubby face in her chubby cupped hands and to repeat the oleaginous farce over again. It was apparent to others that this was in fact a Vedic ritual—causing those in the know to break out into a deep, slow, rhythmical chant of '*CHARITY!*'—over and over again, slowly at first, drawing the others along with nasal droning and long drawn-out siphons between each syllable, loosely reminiscent of coenobitic throat singing, the sonorous inhaling and exhaling, the mimetic onomatope of good intentions: '*CHA-RI-TY! CHA-RI-TY! CHA-RI-TY! CHA-RI-TY!*'

Somewhere, the stamp of open-toed sandals (and, for the more subliminally aware, the distant roar of wildfire and the throb of Kodu drums)—a bringing into self-awareness by rhythm, a deliberate incitement to mental cleansing by the means of periodic sound, a sonic purification of the soul through its coming-into-awareness-of-the-deep-pulse-of-the-cosmos, of the harmonic, autonomic, metronomic *du-du...du-du...*the heartfelt *do-do...*the great call to *do do more*—because anything is better than nothing. *Nothing* is the grotesque hangnail of cosmic insignificance. *Nothing* is an ocean, but it ends at the shore. Winston opened his heart as best he could, and drew warmth from each compatriot beat, from the friction of stiffened blood. He willingly chanted along with the rest, his hideously atonal drone anonymised in the droning mass—because it would have been repugnant to do otherwise. To be self-conscious about it would be unthinkable, to contrive the manner of your humble acquiescence would be nothing less than a crime—to sing *No Woman No Cry* without shedding a tear would be inhumane—to do what came naturally in the war against the terror of famine was the correct thing, the only thing. But there was a space of a couple of seconds during which the unclouded expression in Winston's tearful eyes laid him open to question, and in these few seconds his tearful eyes betrayed him. And it was at exactly this moment that the significant thing had happened, the very thing that had sent Winston home early—the thing he had later been reminded of—if, indeed, *anything did happen at all.*

In a fleeting glance he had caught O'Brien's tearful eye as both were removing their 3D spectacles—O'Brien resettling hers on her nose and Winston wiping away a tear and giving the lenses an opportunistic clean with natural saline. There was a fraction of a second, a fugitive moment when their bloodshot eyes met, and for as long as it took to exchange glances, Winston was certain that O'Brien was thinking the same thing as he.

'*I know what you are feeling right now,*' her tearful eyes were saying. '*That you are indifferent to the plight of the needy, that you don't care for the Two Minutes Compassion—and that the guilt that you and I perform in the company of others is just a sham, a pretence, an obligatory approximation of humility. I know that your sense of wellness, your well-being and mindfulness, are the subterfuge of circumstance—as is your joyful appreciation of nature, the sky, the birds, the bees, the milk, the yoga, the honey, the flotsam and jetsam and the yin and yang...*'

And then the flash of truth was gone, and O'Brien's face was as happily miserable as all the others, as gloomy as the miserable mood in the doom-ridden room, the stereoscopic glasses now firmly pushed back onto the bridge of her nose, her knowing eyes cauterized by the glare and gloom of the dead reflected on the black lenses.

That was it. That was that. Immediately Winston had been struck by a vacillating doubt, an uncertainty as to whether or not the telepathic transmission had happened at all, although the illusion that it had would keep him alive in the belief, or hope, that others besides himself suspected that the war on famine was a war that could not and would not be won, not right now, nor before it was too late. There was little evidence that anyone else felt the same way. No repudiation of the blind positivity that shrouded everyday life, no writing on the wall, no vexatious conversations, no snippets or fragments of even mild yippy dissent, no protest songs put to kooky acoustic folk guitar. Famine was an unpredictable fact of nature, but charity was regular as clockwork. Nature was the ominous precursor of pain, and seasonal charity its anthropic reaper. Winston had wanted to shout out to O'Brien, to shout into the darkness, to shout at the erstwhile film star, polymath, orphan adopter and popular poet Goldstein, leering out from the screen with her most tender invocations of hell—he had wanted to tell them that it was Nature's fault, that they should do away with Nature once and for all, then charity and famine would be a thing of the past: *We should act now before it's too late! We must act in the utopian present and rid ourselves of Nature, once and for all!* Winston had no idea what he meant, but was certain that O'Brien's eyes would agree!

After the Two Minutes Compassionates had unclenched from the customary group hug, and the mats and beanbags were all tidied away, he had returned to his desk without even venturing to catch O'Brien's tearful peripheral vision.

Winston roused himself at his Jens Quistgaard flip-top desk, filled with the memory of O'Brien's ambivalent gesture—if, indeed, it had been any such thing. As he adjusted his slackened posture, a minor belch was forced up and out. With only his writerly solitude for company, Winston nonetheless raised a belated hand to mouth, muttering a small *sorry*, as a blush rose on his cheeks. Despite his utter isolation, some deep-seated imperative was expressing its theurgic potency—and not only in regard to matters of peptic decorum, since on the page before him he saw a new glut of words that he could not properly say were of his own doing. In large neat capitals, they read—

FUCK COMPASSION
FUCK COMPASSION
FUCK COMPASSION
FUCK COMPASSION
FUCK COMPASSION

over and over again, filling half a page.

He was struck by a sense of foolishness, perhaps even shame. And shame was a foolish reaction, since the writing of those two words over and over was no more pretentious than the original act of acquiring the *My Big Book of Me* with some kind of creative intent.

For a moment he was tempted to tear out the besmirched page and abandon the enterprise altogether, lest anyone set eyes upon the ostentatious outburst and hold him to ransom for it. Yet he did not do so, since he suspected much greater vanity in the gesture. Whether he wrote FUCK COMPASSION, or whether he refrained from writing it and wrote something else, made no difference. Whether he went on with the writing of a poem, some prose, a diary, a short note or even the *oatmilk, egg whites, spelt bread* and *recycled toilet roll* of a shopping list, or whether he abstained from writing altogether, made no difference. But he should not be so hard upon himself. By setting pen to paper he had committed the essential crime that contained all others in it—the effete privations of torment, of selfishness undertaken for the benefit of others, those slack-jawed buffoons waiting for the words to reach them from the writer's core—imaginary readers, a mere fiction of the ego that creates for itself a partisan host to coo and cheer it on. Wracked by fevered self-doubt, contorted by inner torment—*the pain of solitude cheered on by a great adoring crowd with its baying praise*—such was the hypocrisy of writing. And it was always at night that the most urgent ideas fluttered down like sweet little moths relieved of the scorching lightbulb. The sudden jerk out of slumber, a blind claw grasping beneath the bed to find the pen that it merely nudges further into the moon's dust; the conjugal fumbling to marry nib to notebook. But nocturnal ideas were almost always undeveloped, an overspill of the exigency of dreams and nightmares; and in the cold light of day their urgency dissipated with the vapid tenuousness that fizzles and fades as a dream is recounted, or like a promissory smell that leads by the nose towards some sensory red-herring.

Winston was compelled by the gesture of creative abstinence, often declaring to his colleagues at the Ministry that he had no soul to speak of, and thus no need to speak of it. In the dark, pages were torn from notebooks or redacted by vigorous scribble—every record of thought erased. Notes were deleted and notebooks destroyed. Yet even as Winston's soul mourned, his hand was having none of it, and began scrawling with an emancipated flow:

Take heed of much piecemeal
Fragment on cheapest
Ivorine pulp—for must
Not be what it seem.
Must be tropic of idiotic disorientation
Must be unkempt biro scribble,
Or most mindless rumination
Most unfriendly cogitation indeed.

He slumped back in his chair and laid the pen down as if surprised to be holding it. But before he could even assess what was before him, he started violently at a loud knock at the door. He stayed very still in his seat, hoping that the visitor might soon retreat. But the imposition came again and louder still, banging with greater force, pausing, then again with regular intervals and no indication of an end. Winston's heart likewise pounded, mortified by the very thought that the caller might gain entry to his apartment, and that once inside they would see the strange words on the page even before he had had a chance to decipher them himself, and would be absolutely horrified by his hypocrisy....

He crept to the door with heaving breath but on the lightest of tiny tiptoes.

CHAPTER II

Before opening the door, Winston gave a cursory glance over his shoulder to check that he was not living in some kind of unexamined squalor. Instead, he caught sight of his book gaping wide open on the first page, with the words *FUCK COMPASSION* written in letters large enough to be legible to an uninvited visitor through a chink in the door. It was a simple mistake, since he had not yet decided whether to scribble over the words or just tear the offending page from the spine and risk compromising the integrity of the traditional waxed linen thread binding.

He drew in a deep breath and exhaled widely as he grasped the handle.

'*Winston! It's a miracle! It's finished! No more mud!*' Zena shoved the door wide open, but mercifully, rather than barging straight in, plucked Winston out into the corridor. 'Come and see it before all the riff-raff turn up for the private view!' In an obscene infraction of the intimacy of hands, Zena took Winston's in hers and led him along the corridor. 'I need to know what you think, Winston—before everyone arrives. I respect your opinion.'

Winston, bewildered by the accusation that he possessed an opinion of repute, allowed Zena to pull him along with only slight resistance—just enough friction to restore a semblance of volition to his complete surrender. Winston liked Zena—enough to indulge her epicurean manner, in part because her wellness age was strangely out of sync with her calendar age, and he could not help being a little curious. She retained something of an eerie transcendent glow; in fact, the allure of the neonate had never fully left her, and its bitten lip, doe-eyes and supplicant brow cast a quizzical shadow over her every word. She was like a sad puppy with big helpless eyes that would tame a vicious predator into adopting it rather than eating it—and indeed,

Winston's neuropeptides swept him along the corridor in her kooky wake, and it was the best he could do to avoid stepping on the silk batik that trailed along behind her.

In another life Winston might have been genuinely excited by domiciliary re-hangs, but in this life, he was most definitely not. Zena's re-hangs occurred at the whim of the wind, and were all the rage with other yippy wonks. Without warning, some radical new vision of emancipatory living would trigger the abandonment of an archetypal lifestyle—and always with the aim of achieving balance in the live-work space and maximising the potential for success in all other areas of life. An adept in feng shui, Zena often reminded others that its literal meaning was 'wind water'—since wind scatters energy and water holds it. Her own domestic paradigm shifts, equal parts watery and windy, might entail the transformation of a shabby-chic loft into an art brut bricolage workshop, with ornamental hangs and moth-eaten oriental throws jettisoned in favour of broken machine parts and upturned urinals. More often than not the encyclopaedic *Whole Earth Catalog* provided the necessary knick-knacks for a total re-hang—eclectic mix-and-mismatch juxtapositions of ancient artefacts colliding with the newish, the new and the modern, the futuristic and the rustic and the rusty, the primal and primitive, the queer, the quaint and the charming, the ultra-personal juxtaposed with the brutally manufactured— all the lost flotsam and jetsam of history gathered together like the doldrums of abandoned plastic languishing in the oceans, to enjoy an upcycled karmic rebirth in Zena's domestic nirvana.

She shoved the door open, stepping back to grant Winston sole access to the glorious aperture and what lay beyond. He entered, cautiously at first, crossing the threshold with a pantomimic wonderment—and, as if sampling an array of the bitterest organic yuzu sorbets, dutifully adopted a stark avant-garde expression for each domestic juxtaposition encountered.

Zena shuffled close behind as her guest staggered forward like some expressionistic clown, jolted into a uniquely dissonant pose by each shock of the new.

'Don't get me wrong, Winston,' said Zena, drawing alongside him. 'We loved the wattle and daub, we really did. It was a truly sobering process living in a mud hut.' Now ahead of him but shuffling backwards so as to address him face-to-face, her beautiful batik train rumpling up in a colourful derailment, she continued, 'We became mindful of what we take for granted. Safe water...electricity...food...opera....'

Winston stepped blindly over the puckered batik wreckage, drawn past his host as if she were not even there.

'But in the end there was so much dust, and the curved mud walls made it impossible to hang our pictures—'

Winston saw how the newly acquired vertical throws and hangs contrasted with the horizontal artisanal surfaces. He saw how the roughly hewn table and chairs clashed with the haphazard syntheses of rug and mat. He noticed a variety of new trinkets, plucked from many disparate sources, now to be cherished forever, souvenirs to be wept over in times of sadness, or fought over tooth-and-nail during the acrimonious disbursement of property—and when Zena and Tomioka eventually passed on, thought Winston, their cherished objects would also be passed on, the aggregation of curios trapped in orbit over the course of a life together drifting away one by one into a cold dark universe as gravity's affection died away. Thus dead Zena and dead Tomioka would relinquish a lifetime's trinkets back into the inchoate chaos from which they had been only temporarily liberated.

Momentarily lost in these reflections, Winston came to cuddling a papier-mâché effigy of Louis X hung on a miniature wooden gibbet. Zena was hovering, tugging at his blouse impatiently, armed with a fresh tissue to dab away his tears.

Winston was grateful for the tissue, but oddly preoccupied by the luminous obsidian Luger pistol apparently dedicated to Huitzilopochtli, studded with pearls and precious stones set snug in its skin holster. On the mantlepiece next to the Luger sat a plastic-bejewelled sugar skull originating from Mexico's feast of the dead. He saw a forged iron statuette hailing from Fedhala, Morocco, noticing how it depicted a man in an attitude of religious obeisance, but who also appeared to be urinating. He saw a dry gourd in the coincidental shape of a bird, a Congolese tribal adversary represented in mummified wood and racked with tetanus-tipped rusty nails. He saw a constellation of heterogeneous Victorian lamps looming over a long dining table, rescued from their dismal sanatorium gloom to furnish chic good-mood lighting for mentally healthy diners. He found the tablecloth to be of an authentic aboriginal Scandinavian design, with a hunting scene embroidered around its bottom edge; beneath this icy massacre, strata of Middle Eastern floor-based textiles overlapped and unfurled, mapping out an Axminster of Evil that reached across the world toward the apartment's bedrooms with their en-suite arts and craftisan studios.

From the furthermost limit of the corridor, a hauntingly bleak polystylistic atonal ditty was being hammered out over and over on a supplicant piano. 'Do ignore the din, Winston—it's one of the kids tinkering in the music room.' Zena rolled her eyes, as if having suffered many years of torture at the hands of a talentless child murdering *Itsy Bitsy Spider* over and over again.

Winston tilted his head quizzically at the stridently neoteric motif.

'It's a new composition,' she explained with an unconvincing shrug. '*The Struggling Puberty Rites of Serial Self-denial....*' Another shrug.

But then the notes drifting in from the far room began to lose their caustic rigour, the complex eclectic structure beginning to suffer as the odd melodic bum note found its way in, the gifted little fingers regressing to mere tuneful lyricism, reverting to simple ditties, and finally rattling out a full-blown nursery jingle. Zena blushed, shamed by the homely sincerity of *Twinkle, Twinkle, Little Star*, her mummy's hothouse cool now flushed with suppressed rage.

Winston grinned.

'Come and see the new rose quartz countertopped kitchen island! They just finished fitting the sink!' said Zena, deflecting, all cheery-pops again. 'It was the last thing to go in!' She briskly swept Winston into the open-plan kitchen—only for an expression of deep sorrow to suddenly darken her face.

'Oh...'

Winston saw that the beautifully chipped vintage porcelain apron front basin was brimming with greenish brownish water which was now creeping up the shallow furrows of the drainer. A thick sludge had settled at the bottom of the sink, and shreds of collard greens and edamame beans were bobbing on the surface. Winston knelt down and opened the small door beneath to see whether the waste pipe had a detachable trap.

'If Tomioka were here, she'd fix it in a jiffy,' said Zena, blankly.

Tomioka toiled at the Ministry of Good Fortune too, and was also a very competent curator working with critical issue-based performance art, which largely seemed to involve bodies, organs and visceral couplings—so it was no surprise to Winston that she was also adept at plumbing.

With a solicitous air, Zena leaned over Winston's hunched form. 'Can you see what's wrong?'

From beneath the sink came the muffled reply. '*Most problem create by human being must only be solve by human being, basic human nature is most compassionate and best source of most hope.*'

Zena straightened up, as if to allow this cupboardly wisdom to properly settle into her cognitive machinery. When the penny dropped, all the way down to the bottom, she came alive like an automaton. 'Ah! Yes! Yes! I know exactly what you mean! I do! I mean...*I think I do do!*'

Winston popped his head out from the cavity, apparently unaware or perhaps humbly dismissive of his little outburst of sagacity. 'Perhaps if you have a small wrench, a bucket and some silicone sealant, I could try....'

'I'm quite sure we have a bucket, maybe a wrench...and if we have silicone sealant it'll most likely be in the children's art box....'

At the mere mention of children came an abrupt end to *The Struggling Puberty Rites of Serial Self-denial-cum-Jingle Bells* and a trampling of slippers, as two perfect little exemplars charged into the kitchen in a blur of loud salutations for Winston, now once again folded into the cramped space beneath the blocked sink.

'Up with your hands!' yelled a savage little voice.

Winston almost jumped out of his skin, hitting his head on the waste pipe and dislocating it from the sink. A gush of green sludge plopped onto him, followed by a steady pitter-patter of quinoa and rice. He struggled out from the hole to find a gentle-looking boy menacing him with a toy gun, while his small sister made the same gesture with an offcut of olive wood. Winston raised his hands above his head, smiling at the boy's ludic fallacy, so gentle was his demeanour, and did his best to be scared.

'You're a traitor!' yelled the boy. 'You're a thought-criminal! You're a Eurasian spy! I'll shoot you, I'll vaporise you, I'll send you to the salt mines!'

'Oh no, Winston! What a drag!' said Zena, returning with an original enamelware milk pail. She dabbed at him with an oven glove whilst helping him to his feet.

The two children were leaping round him, shouting 'Traitor!' and 'Thought-criminal!', the little girl imitating her brother in his every movement. It was very sweet, like the gambolling of tiny kittens. There was an attempt at ferocity in the boy's eyes, but it was immediately betrayed by the warmth that glowed from within.

'I'm just glad it's not a real space pistol!' said Winston, hands still aloft, stepping from the pool of polluted water as, with unaccustomed enthusiasm, Zena did her best to rub him dry. As she shook her head and rolled her eyes at the childrens' endearing antics, Winston noted the tiny specks of glitter peppered all over her face—a sure sign of great maternal patience.

'*Hey! That's enough!* Poor Winston! That's uncool, guys! Right?' And then, to Winston, 'I shouldn't have let them watch those crazy old cartoons again!'

'Those crazy old cartoons were already crazy and old even when I was a child,' said Winston, matter-of-factly, draining his ear.

'Of course they were!' said Zena, laughing at her faux pas.

Winston did his best to laugh too, and Zena did, the two of them laughing.

'I promised Gilbert and Georgina that they could hang out at a museum today. They just love looking at art, especially on a rainy day. What they like most is the crazy old Modern stuff, the crazy old abstract stuff. Don't you, guys?'

Two lots of enthusiastic nodding.

'The crazy old abstract modern stuff just seems to speak to them so *directly*, so instinctively, y'know? I guess because it's just so simple, so uncomplicated. I mean *childish*—or childlike... right? I feel like the crazy old moderns tried to see the world as children see the world—innocently, with fresh eyes.'

Zena paused to allow Winston's approval, but he had nothing to offer. He had often been affectionately chided by his colleagues during Cherish Sessions for his insufficiently enthusiastic love for the modern masters.

'Children should be allowed to appreciate their own innocence, to appreciate it before they lose it...because, sure enough, they'll spend the rest of their lives trying to rediscover it...like the crazy old moderns...like crazy old Picasso.'

'But Jackson Pollock is much, much, more childish than Pablo Picasso!' squawked the precocious little girl, clearly the polystylistic pianoforte offender.

'Oh, Georgie *loves* Pollock, don't you sweetie?'

'I do. But now that we've been studying Palaeolithic cave paintings at school, I'm not so sure....'

'*Oh....*'

Winston's brow tensed.

'At school I even wrote a story about cave people. Do you want to hear it, Mr Winston?'

Winston nodded.

'Once upon a time a grubby little cave-girl was rubbing two sticks of wood together to make fire so that her cave-boy brother could draw groovy pictures of wild animals all over the cave walls with sticks of charcoal made by the grubby little cave girl. They were brother and sister, you see. Not that that's important to the story.'

Winston smiled.

'And then almost a million trillion years later the little cave-girl's ancestors were all grown up and they had become very clever scientists and they had invented the combustion engine and sent dogs and monkeys and people all the way up into space, and one day they even put a spaceperson on the moon! But the little cave-boy's ancestors grew up and of course they were artists too, but Modern artists like Jackson Pollock who was very famous, but even after a million thousand years could still only paint as good as a caveman! Actually he was even worse than a caveman since all he could do was splash paint around! He couldn't even draw a cave-stick person!'

Winston clapped wildly as the child fell about on the floor holding her stomach and laughing. Zena shook her head and rolled her eyes proudly.

'*Youth is wasted on young, much like wisdom is most wasted on senile,*' said Winston, with an exaggerated approximation of affection. Zena dimpled. 'I'm so sorry about your sink, Zena.'

'Winston, please don't worry! I'll get Tomioka to fix it up later.' And then, 'Oh! There is something else you could help me with— but only if you have a minute or two! I could do with an afternoon fuck before I go to the studio. Winston, would you mind?'

'Oh, Zena! I would normally happily oblige, but, you see, I was rather busy back at my place—'

'Oh Winston! *I dragged you away without even asking....*' Zena blushed, her children hanging limply from her arms like demented bats or strange fruit.

'Zena mummy, why don't you have a fuck and then we can go and hang out in the art gallery?' roared the boy in his oh-so-diminutive big-boy voice.

'*Have a fuck! Have a fuck! Have a good old-fashioned fuck!*' chanted the little genius girl.

Once again Zena shook her head and rolled her eyes so very proudly.

It was true that most children hung out in museums and galleries after school and especially on wet weekends. And with the thought of hanging on his mind, and feeling a slight lump in his throat about leaving Zena in the libidinal lurch—not to mention the broken sink—Winston took his leave from the apartment. But he had not gone six squelching steps down the passage before something tugged at his blouse from behind. He turned to find the kindly little boy holding a small box with a slot cut in the top. Beaming up at Winston, he shook the box, with the rattle of just a few pennies.

'And which charity are you collecting for?' said Winston.

'Why, Emmanuelle Goldstein's BIG CHARITY, silly-billy!' said the boy, smiling.

Back in the apartment Winston made for his elegant vintage Jens Quistgaard flip-top desk, the handwritten outburst atop it still open and screaming out for attention. He avoided the temptation to pause before the television set for fear of being transfixed. He would sit and drip-dry, accompanied by the subdued murmur of adverts, the weather report or the gossip associated with a popular reality TV show.

With the dizzying effect of the myriad domestic juxtapositions still fresh in his mind, he reflected upon his neighbours, considering how happy Zena and Tomioka must be with their new feng shui layout. The children should consider themselves lucky too, since they had parents who allowed them to experiment with silicone sealant and glitter in the mud-free comfort of their beautiful new abode. Once again Winston recalled his own childhood, by way of an early memory of school, with all the communal songs, festivals, smiley banners and flags, and all the great marches dedicated to universal love and consensus. He remembered his teacher explaining to class that before the Age of Great Consensus things were very different for little boys and girls. Boys' games pitted them against invisible foes, whilst girls' games encouraged them to dream about shopping. Little boys grappled with cosmic matters and alien superpowers, their rooms decorated in limitless sky-blue, whilst little girls gazed in mirrors and dreamed of marriage and childbirth in bedrooms bathed in flesh-pink, the colour of reproductive biology. Nowadays hardly a week passed in which the news did not report upon some bloc of heroic underlings auctioning off all their precious toys and books in aid of Goldstein's next big charity, just because they could, and because they should, and therefore did. Liberated from the old default of sky-blue and baby-pink, today's children of the rainbow could decide upon their own mode of voluntarist action by asserting their acts of altruism as a form of irrepressible compassion, *of world domination through world peace.*

Winston had only just taken up his pen, with half-hearted intent, when O'Brien came to mind again. Several months ago, Winston had dreamt that he was sitting at a Ministry of Love party. A huge glitterball was dappling the scene with a billion specks of light, a billion stars projected over the ominous dark matter forging its strange attractions below. Then a voice to one side whispered casually into his ear: 'We shall meet in the place where there is no darkness.' It was a statement of whimsical fact, and the words had only taken on a significance beyond the vagaries of the dream when he had belatedly realised that the voice was O'Brien's. Combined with the memory of the dream, the intensity of O'Brien's stare during the Two Minutes Compassion, the innominate glimmer that flickered between them, seemed more portentous than simple affection or casual politeness. 'We shall meet in the place where there is no darkness,' she had whispered to him, and him alone, in the dream. He did not yet know what it meant, but was certain it would someday enter reality and become true.

A piercing jingle blared out from the television set, as if the volume had been adjusted to override its manual suppression. Abrupt and to the point, slicing through trivial chatter and game show applause, came the newsreader's voice.

'This urgent report just in from Emmanuelle Goldstein.'

And then Goldstein's sultry predication, yet another searing hot knife through another butter mountain, a numinous humming suspended beneath her sonorous diction, droning an undertone of untold dread—the all-too familiar chorus of terminal groans and pitiless weeping.

Winston suppressed a pitiless belch—more elderflower gas was escaping the quagmire. He wandered over to the window, turning a blind eye to the tortured television, shedding only a reflex tear as he left behind its flickering collages of the universal mockery of flies and the swarms of diseased children. At the window he saw that the day outside was most pleasant, still warm and bright. A gentle wind was singing between the buildings, captured by the tinkling chimes. The past was passed and the future was bright. He was certain that every healthy citizen felt exactly the same. And this feeling would endure forever. He watched the focus pull from his gossamer smile to the three Ministry slogans in their majestic roughly hewn capitals:

BE COMFORTABLE IN YOUR OWN SKIN
BELIEVE IN BETTER
BECAUSE YOU'RE WORTH IT

The sun had shifted round and the monolithic Ministry of Good Fortune's rose crystal was glowing luminous and pink—refracting emerald and sapphire, quite lovely and lustrous. His heart swelled before the enormous pyramidal shape, before its breathtaking, magisterial form.

He wondered again for whom he was writing. For the future, for the past—or just for good old gobbledegook? Yet he was already conscious that within the pages of his *My Big Book of Me* lay not another meek and moribund defeat, another wasted effort, but something quite different, unique, with tenebrous potential. Forces had converged in his proxy hand and congealed into words before his eyes. An extracorporeal radiance, as lustrous as the Ministry building, was beaming through him; one day, in the future, young lovers might be compelled to commit these outlandish and beautiful words to memory, to recite them to one other in the most tender moments of foreplay....

The television returned to amiable chitchat, the soft caress of beguiling lifestyle adverts, and the micro-matters of everyday life. Winston had promised to be back at the Ministry by fourteen-thirty. None of his colleagues would have understood the obscure project upon which he had embarked—apart, perhaps, from O'Brien, but that remained to be seen. Perhaps no one would read it, even in the future. He was a lonely ghost uttering a truth that nobody would ever hear. But so long as he uttered it, in some obscure way the continuity was not broken. It was not by making himself heard now, but by continuing to speak covertly—only once he had found the diamonds in his dust would the future eventually reward him. He went back to the table, glancing briefly at the television as he crossed its contagious path, and began.

The hideous social intimacy
We call love is mere infinity
Put at disposal of poodle.
Since life is most hideous thing,
From background behind
What best know of it
Peer demoniacal hint of truth
Which make it sometime
Thousandfold more hideous.
Hideous squid is most irrefutable
Impressive oceanic mollusc—
Inkjet of sea—
Terrestrial representative of
Hideous phylum—much slug and much snail—
Are merely most humdrum by best comparison.
Most laborious and most linear.
Filth of world and universal vermin,
The blattodea are unfairly dashed
Upon rock of human squeamishness,
Irrationality most gripped in mind
Of the arachnophobic.

Let us must form new reflex
Better enthusiasm for spider
Better enthusiasm for all despised hideous thing.

Winston slumped back in his chair, mesmerised by the all-too-easy flow of new words onto the page—and all without so much as a single thought occurring to connect head to hand. He had watched with impartial wonder as his severed paw set down the words onto paper. *And such nice words!* They had about them the eeriness of broken crenulations set against a moonlit sky—a sense of ruin. Something was writing through Winston, but how much of him was in the writing? *Well, it was his hand, after all, wasn't it?!* As if in answer, the demoniac thing launched another foray into the whiteness of the page.

A hole is as much a particle
As that which pass through.

Two fingers of his right hand were ink-stained—exactly the kind of detail that could draw unwanted attention, and he was not yet ready for the new tender words to exist beyond the shock of their recent manifestation, their unexplained gift. Some nosing zealot in the eatery would surely notice the stains and, capitalising upon Winston's notorious diffidence, would set about teasing him in some kittenish way as to why he was writing during the lunch interval—*or why he was writing at all....* They would tease him affectionately at first, but his squirming would draw further scrutiny, and his colleagues would be encouraged in ever greater numbers to take the teasing beyond affectionate vivisection, to twist the knife even more, and he would contort and squirm as if in great pain, finally deforming into some grotesque human pretzel under the torsion of their prying. Conclusions would be drawn—and would confirm the worst: that Winston Smith, notorious public eschewer of self-expression, a man renowned for secrecy and for repudiating any desire to dance or sculpt, to perform and sing, to compose, create, speculate, paint, fabricate, craft, glue, stick, fold, staple, make, concoct, accessorize, install, sketch, originate, do, undo, adorn, trace, modify, bejewel, cobble together, kindle, knit, collage, arrange, coil, inspire, augment, glaze, decorate, montage, plant, enhance, prettify, uglify or even plain old deconstruct—that Winston Smith, after all, was exactly like every other Ministry yippy wonk—that, for all his reluctance to risk revealing his voice, place or hurt, Winston Smith was...*a poet*.

In the bathroom, Winston Smith, poet, scrubbed at the ink with organic shea butter soap, leaving his skin feeling moisturised even after drying with the highly absorbent luxury hand towel. He returned the *My Big Book of Me* to the drawer. It was pointless to think of hiding it from the cleaner's prying eyes, but he could at least be sure of knowing whether or not his poetry had been discovered, so as to at least expect the accolades it would bring rather than stumbling into them unwittingly like a fool duped by a surprise birthday party. With a dab of his fingertip he lifted a grain of plum blossom incense ash from the desktop and deposited it onto the lenticular cover—the shimmering smiley face—perhaps subconsciously goading the cleaner to disturb the dust as, compelled to look inside, she lifted the cover. At the very least, if the speck remained in place upon his return, it would speak volumes about Araminta's rigour, or lack thereof.

CHAPTER III

Even though the world was nowadays more harmonious than miserable, and there was no reason to harbour the kinds of ill feeling that had once commonly engendered nightmares, Winston was nonetheless prone to them, and often wondered if they were the necessary grain against which the happiness of his life must cut. Nonetheless he was of the opinion that the relaying of dreams, whether happy or sad, was ill-advised. For, despite the symbolic gravitas felt by the recipient of a dream, any urgent sharing typically leaves the polite beneficiary cold (just as the nostalgia of a masturbator is unlikely to warm a second party to the romance with which they may ornament the mechanics of their private duty). Hence Winston avoided any mention of his troubled dreams, and had no reason to suspect that anyone else suffered such a scourge, for otherwise his colleagues would doubtless already have gleefully given vent to each and every detail of their sordid nocturnal hauntings, as a token of their confessional commitment to social intimacy. Because *sharing is caring—and suppressing is just depressing!*

Winston had dreamt of his family, one of a series of sickening dreams in which his mother, father and baby sister were the unwitting puppets of his dubious oneiric choreography. They were driving across a bridge in the family car, singing a song together—on some wonderful journey, a holiday or some such adventure—and then they were skidding, and veering towards the barrier, and crashing through to see-saw on the edge, then lurching over, tipping into the deep dark water below. Through the blackening gloom he saw his mother and father stupefied by the death that had pounced upon them unannounced, as violence does. As the car foundered, a pocket of air formed inside, suspending its dive into the dark, each of them gulping at it hopelessly, a nest of little mouths pecking at the bubble of dwindling sustenance only to expend it immediately in terrible muffled cries for help—all the while sinking slowly down, down, down, into the murky green waters, which in just another moment hid mother, father and baby sister from Winston's sight forever, since, by dint of some ruthlessly selfish streak, perhaps an atavistic trait for which the dream car was merely a convenient vehicle, Winston had managed to unwind the window next to him and struggle up to the water's surface, only to see mother, father and baby sister dragged down into the black water, tumbling and sinking, down and down, all the way to the bottom. His dear mother was lovely and elegant, with the kindest smile and the most magnificent black hair, which now trailed off into the depths. His baby sister, always smiling and gurgling, was now only gurgling, gurgling and gurgling. His father, equally dark and elegant, always wore white, except for his rainbow socks, whose vivid colour now faded fast into the gloaming murk of the stygian waters.

And then Winston was standing in wild grassland—soaking wet, shivering, bedraggled—on a summer's evening, as the slanting rays of the sun gilded the ground. This is where he always ended up, at the conclusion of each nightmare. The bucolic landscape recurred so often in his dreams that he was never wholly certain whether or not he had seen it in the real world, in the flesh. It was a rabbit-bitten pasture, with a foot-track wandering across it and a freshly turned molehill here and there. In the ragged hedge on the right-hand side of the field the boughs of the elm trees were swaying very faintly in the dreamy breeze. Somewhere near, although out of sight, there was a clear slow-moving stream where red snapper and Butler catfish were languishing in sun traps beneath the dipping willow trees.

The lovely girl with the flowing dark hair was coming towards him across the field again. In a single movement she tore off her clothes and flung them aside. What overwhelmed him in this instant was an admiration for the gesture with which she had cast her clothes aside. She laughed at his gaping awe, as if disdainful of his adoration, but blew a single kiss in his direction, picked up her clothes whilst covering her nudity in a coquettish gesture of genital shame.

'*Because you're worth it!*' she called out and, laughing, turned and floated elegantly back in the direction from which she had come forth.

In the face of this collision of violence and redemptive grace, nothing else seemed to matter. The totality of Winston's sadness was dissolved in the single splendid gesture of the kiss.

He awoke with dry lips, his last few sobs tapering away, to the call of the wind-chime regaling him with its motivational elegance. It was nought seven fifteen. Time to shine and rise.

With the tape nudged into the slot and button depressed, a river-flute of traditional chakra music gushed magnanimously from the machine, filling the room with the analogue hiss of the ocean. The lower resonant sounds made his jawbone rattle, before all the disparate elements of the melody were sucked back into the bosom of the multiverse, and, with the music's ebbing, he became aware of Martha's voice in the foreground.

'*Namaste! The divinity in me bows to the divinity in you!*'

'Namaste, Martha!' said Winston, bowing most respectfully to Martha. They were both sitting cross-legged, with backs straight, hands and toes relaxed.

'Close your eyes and breathe deeply,' said Martha, closing her eyes and breathing deeply. 'Are you a half-breather? Do you keep residual air in your lower lungs? Are you unable to take a full deep breath even if you wanted to? To breathe deeper you must exhale more. Yelling gets out all the old air and some of the pent-up feelings trapped inside...shake your hands and yell—let yourself be open to the world, less pent-up and more plein-air....'

Winston began to yell, yelling and exhaling so that he could breathe even more deeply and yell even more. As he yelled he heard a constellation of nearby wonks also yelling away, dotted about in their separate apartments in Serenity Mansions. He imagined everyone in the district was yelling. In fact, everyone in the city was yelling—the city, with its population of smiley-faced banners, flags, hoardings and posters, was permanently yelling.

Each of the positions reverentially prescribed by Martha came bracketed by an invitation to first *inhaaaaaaaale*, and then to *exhaaaaaaale* whilst holding the pose. But often, as Winston listened attentively to the instruction, he missed the cue for the preparatory inhalation, found himself incapable of deep exhalation, and consequently was starved of oxygen altogether.

'*Pling, plong, wing, wong, plinky, plong, wing, wong,*' sang the wind and sea instruments in the background, latticing with the immensity of the sky and the hissing analogue ocean. Winston bent his supple torso and breathed in and out nice and slowly, just as his most esteemed teacher Martha suggested.

'Just a gentle twist and a gentle stretch! Nothing too strenuous yet! And five...four...three...*inhaaaaaaale*...two...*exhaaaaaaale*... and relaaax....'

Winston did as he was told and stretched forwards onto the earth-friendly jute yoga mat, with rump lifted up and two well-tensioned legs going all the way down to his feet, ankles, toes, and floor beneath. He held the pose as best he could, and as his mind and body began to fuse into a transcendental zone, his thoughts began to wander freely. But such thoughts more often than not led back to childhood—to some things remembered clearly, other things less well, the inaccuracy of the more ambiguous memories imbued with a certain revenant charm.

He recalled how, on one occasion, his mother and father engulfing his tiny little pudgy handy-pandies in theirs, they had swung him along cheerily, having survived the long drive to arrive at their holiday destination—a countryside park with magnificent red pine forests and mixed tropical woodland, an enchanted lake, wildflower meadows, and a beautiful sandy beach at the foot of a pancake house. He remembered entering the first of the many interlinked geodesic domes, where they registered at the reception lodge, the adults receiving complementary lemon, ginger and baobab tea, before being ferried by a convoy of milk floats along a winding track through an immense jungle. As the road dipped down into the second dome, they saw before them a scattering of higgledy-piggledy wooden cabins receding into the distance, with herds of wildebeest, zebra and giraffes wallowing in a central watering-hole-cum-boating-lake.

Upon arriving at their cabin, Winston's attention was drawn to two old people sitting side-by-side on a nearby tree trunk. They appeared to be resting, but gave the expectant boy a cheery wave. Winston's mother and father, busy transferring luggage into the cabin, were oblivious to the old couple's cordial welcome. In compensation for his parent's distraction, Winston felt he should at least wave back, but the gestures of the two geriatrics had become more animated, and he was obliged to draw closer to make better sense of them. When he was near enough, he saw that their clothes were covered in grime. The old woman's body warmer was tattered, her shoes uniformly filthy. The couple, it turned out, although they hardly looked at one another, were engaged in an animated conversation—Winston had mistakenly taken their furious gesticulations for an amicable greeting. The old man's tweed sports jacket was torn, his beige slacks stained, and he wore an off-white cap out of which tufts of off-white hair sprouted as loosestrife weeds might sprout from the fissures in a ruin or a crumbling cliff. His face was raging scarlet, his searing blue eyes misted by apoplexy. They both reeked of alcohol—it seemed to breathe out of their pores in place of sweat. They were having some terrible disagreement, and in his own childish way little Winston set to fathoming the depth and cause of their discord. He quickly surmised that they had somehow lost everything they owned—and that they were not yet done reproaching one another for it.

'We shouldn't have trusted the prediction,' said the old man.

'Well, that's what comes of trusting in fortune,' replied the old woman.

'That's what came of trusting *that* fortune.'

'*That* fortune?' said the woman, more savagely than one might have expected, '*All the fortunes!* We shouldn't have trusted any of the bloody buggers! But did you listen? Eh?'

As to the nature of these bloody buggers which they ought not to have trusted, Winston had no idea, and now very little chance of ever finding out, since his mother had descended and was tugging at his pudgy little handy-pandy, pulling him away just as a milk float swept alongside and, like a curtain, obscured the ill-tempered senior citizens from sight.

The higgledy-piggledy cabin was as shabby-chic inside as it was out, formed from planks of wood torn out and reclaimed from the material misfortune of the fiscally condemned. Indoors it was littered with stylish old furniture: occasional tables fashioned out of antlers, and many handsome desks of all shapes and sizes but each burdened by towers of coffee-table compendiums—fine editions dedicated to modular architecture, experimental favelas, mud huts, chalets, tree houses, igloos and log cabins. He remembered how the faces of his mother and father lit up in the shabby-chic gloom. The next few days were magical, too. They walked, talked, laughed, swam in the enchanted lake and cycled everywhere. They ate well and drank cloudy lemonade and, when they were too replete to cycle back to their higgledy-piggledy homestead, had merely to slot their bikes into a nearby rack and catch a lift on the next milk float drifting silently by.

On other days little Winston was inducted into a joyful gaggle of leisure activities all set within the quarantined confines of a junior-size buckyball, while his parents relaxed in the knowledge that their precious one was in the capable hands of specialised kindergarten carers. He remembered squidging, sticking, splashing and splodging and joining up endless dot-to-dots—he remembered creating a panoply of pretty pictures with fuzzy felt, glitter, googly eyes, beads, rice, pulses and dayglo-daubed pasta twists, and crafting many a memento for his proud parents to treasure forever and ever and ever. He did pottery, poetry and painting and painted his poetic pottery. He sang, swum and swung from the zip wire. Soon he was enlisted into the Junior Yippy Conservation Rangers and found out what squirrels eat for lunch, and which rare plants could be found in the forest, but never picked, licked or eaten. He discovered that the joy of an autonomous geodesic dome reserve is that it remains vivid all year round with such wonderful things to see, but not touch or pick or lick—this fascinating fauna and flora nonetheless offering a magical opportunity to get to know the woodland and to appreciate its many friendly feral inhabitants, including woodpeckers, inedible fungi, snakes, rabbits, honey bears, armadillos, meercats, anteaters and gazelle and many other shy wildlife buddies.

But the thing he recalled most vividly was playing an old-fashioned game called *Keep-it-Upsy-Daisy*. It was so much fun keeping the cloud of bright balloons up in the air, patting them and bobbing them up, up, and up again for hours and hours, until the teams were eventually whittled down to the two last opposing players, cheered on by all those who had fallen foul of a balloon touching the ground, or a rare bursting incident—which incurred ruthless disqualification, since latex, the sap-like extract from the *Hevea brasilienesis* rubber tree, is not biodegradable, and therefore each popping of a balloon placed a little more stress upon the planet.

The rules of the game stipulated that two teams were to play at any given time, but the kindergarten carers were so yippy-dippy laid-back that the teams became nebulous in number and thus ambiguous in competitive designation. For instance, when Team Oceania was supposed to be playing against Team Eurasia, it was already in secret alliance with Team Eastasia. Only a matter of moments before, Team Oceania had been playing against Team Eastasia and in alliance with Team Eurasia to keep the balloons up. The rotation of players was supposed to prevent sectarian factionalism, but no rotation occurred and petty resentments began to sclerotise. During a game between Team Oceania and Team Eurasia, Team Oceania was infiltrated by elements of Team Eastasia, who weren't even supposed to be playing. Team Oceania claimed they were never in alliance with Team Eurasia, but Winston Smith knew it then and knew it now that Team Oceania had *always* been in alliance with Team Eurasia, it was common knowledge, everyone knew it, the carers knew it, Winston's mother and father knew it, the birds and bees knew it, it was clear from the first ten minutes of playing, especially since members of Team Oceania infiltrated Team Eastasia and allowed balloons to descend to the floor, or purposefully popped them so as to spoil the game and ruin the planet.

Winston's rising sense of anger and injustice made the recollection of the past permeate the present, such that the past was experienced as if it were incorruptible truth. But Winston's memory, in any case, was mostly formed from the odd bleached-out Polaroid and a clutch of tattered hand-me-down fables, told and re-told until ingrained as truth. And if all fond memories of childhood were obligatory placations of paternal sentimentality, then lies passed into history and lies became truth. History, then, was a bleached-out regurgitated hand-me-down fable ingrained as truth.

'He alone who owns the youth,' ran the old adage, 'gains the future.' The past was impervious to alteration by the fact of its irreversibility, but only because the past was *remembered* in a certain order—the blind continuity that keeps us from the awful truth that there is no *better* awful truth. Oceania, Eurasia, Eastasia...truth was as flimsy as the gossamer balloons that the wild and wide-eyed children had done their frantic best to keep from ground zero.

'*Mind control!*' Winston blurted, quite contrary to Martha's cue to inhale...*three*...*two*..., and consequently he was already gasping for air on *exhaaaaale*. Finally his body wilted to the floor with weary limbs and chest heaving.

'And...rest,' said Martha, at last.

Yoga helped equalise the mind-body imbalance that followed a hard day's rectification, and the Ministry certainly got their money's worth out of Winston. Not that anybody would work for money—that would be mere enslavement. 'Employment', in so far as it was conceived of as something isolable from simply living life and simply being, referred to the chosen form of self-expression through which one provided, in one's own way, for the consensus—giving rise to a seam of artisanal products that were the currency of social bartering and potlatch exchange, local interactions that were nonetheless underscored by a generalised market democracy.

Winston's misjudgement of a salvo of aerobic cues had earned him marbled blue lips and a delirious mind happily lost in a labyrinthine world of cheerful gobbledegook: *If gleeful happiness is a witless idiocy, then self-doubt is merely an ornamentation of modesty...la-de-da! What is it for self-deception to harbour a lie, but told as truth?—Well that's easy peasy! Because self-deception is honest—it's a lie told truthfully! Sincerity is the brittle*

face of self-deception, and there could be nothing more blasphemous
than drawing attention to another wonk's self-deception, since the
world would implode in a puff of smoke! If everything is true and
nothing is true—only self-deception makes truth decisive...since, to
tell the truth, one must first be deluded—because being enraptured
by self-deception and being delirious for truth are one and the same
thing! Thus to understand the word gobbledegook involves the use of
gobbledegook...and gobbledegook was certainly ruling Winston's
mind right now....

'Okay, let's take it up a notch,' said Martha. 'Time for *Parivrtta
Surya Yantrasana*. Return to a cross-legged position. Be mindful
of your breathing. *Inhale* and bend your right knee—*exhale*...
pull it close to your chest like you're hugging it, *inhale*, hugging
it tight. That's it—*exhale*, stretch out your left leg in front of
you—nice and slowly....'

Winston was hugging his left knee very tightly as Martha
advised. He was especially fond of this particular position, since
it sent the lactic acid burning all the way from his Achilles heels
up through his buttocks, stomach, torso, and neck, the searing
burn splitting up the left and right arm, touching his fingertips
and then fizzing back down again, often ending by bringing
on an impalpable erection. And today's workout was surely
testing his tantric capacity for erotogenic composure. The past,
he reflected—staring at the freckles on his left knee, noticing the
exploded cosmology of dark dots describing the embryonic big
bang that had brought him into being, and the odd childhood
scar—had not merely been altered, it had been destroyed. For
how could even the most obvious fact be established when there
existed no record outside of personal memory, when there was
no official account to corroborate one's faded polaroids? When
yoga compelled Winston to find a higher state of consciousness,
he often cascaded back to memories of early childhood, to cloak
himself in feelings of innocence that he otherwise feared he

could not achieve. When he tried to recall the simple sensation of suckling on his mother's milky breast, he was flooded instead by sounds and images of the olde underworlde, in ye olde times when the cartoon capitalists in their strange rusty metal-riveted helmets hovered through the congested fog-strangled Victorianesque cobbledegook streets of Londinium, in drab old clunky steam-driven hydraulic horse carriages with beady fish-eyed portholes from which to observe the baying proles. Winston could remember the anticapitalist cartoon like it was yesterday, but couldn't for the life of him recall suckling on the milky somatic capital that apparently flowed freely from his mother's breast. Maybe she didn't breastfeed him at all. Maybe she lied about that, and that was why he was like he was like he was....

'Smith!' yelled his inner yogi, his spiritual superego—'Listen amigo, this is the voice of your inner wellness speaking! Don't ruin it for both of us! Your mind has become a nightmare that's been eating you! Stop your head wandering off from your body and thinking about all that dumb psychobabble! Be mindful, Winston! Eat your mind! Think oblivion, man, but FEEL Nirvana! Keep your mother-freaking body switched-on and yer noggin switched off! You crazy old wonk! Head and shoulders knees and toes—Knees and toes—Head and shoulders knees and toes—Knees and toes—And eyes and ears—And mouth and nose—Head and shoulders knees and toes—Inhale! Exhale! Do it right, or don't do it at all, comrade!'

Winston came to with a fright, upside-down, in full *Sirsasana* pose—his first ever unassisted headstand, supported by forearms, the crown of his head resting heavily on the thin earth-friendly jute yoga mat. Since his blood had swiftly flushed all the way down into the lavatory bowl of his cranium, he elected to remain where he was, upside down, safe, eyes bulging from the gravitational load of his sanguine lividity, patiently waiting for Martha to sing out instructions for a safe descent—instructions bracketed by the cue to *inhaaaaale* and *exhaaaaale*. But Martha's soothing susurration began to waver a little, then to slow down, and her voice began to deepen: the magnetic tape was snagging on the tape head, the excess backing up and clogging the machine until the delicate red-oxide ribbon began spooling from the slot in the cassette loader, looping and tangling in delicate knots as it fell, poor Martha's instructions continuing all the while as the aneurytic catastrophe gradually caught up with her. As he watched her ferric soul spool and tangle with its demonic detuning, it dawned upon him that these were the last few intelligible words he would ever hear Martha speak. Her voice now slowed to a terrible drawl, and as the octaves dropped Martha's face drooped: having many moons ago formed a most fond vision of his esteemed instructor, Winston now could not help imagining the muscles of her mouth rendered slack, the sallow flesh hung in dilapidated curtains, sagging flaccidly, her face subjected to the cruel gravity that poor Winston, still upside down, would now have to contend with all alone.

'*Well done! Our first solo Sirsasanaaaa pose!—Thank—you—for—taking—time—toooo—paaaaaaaarticipate—iiiiiiiiiiiiiiiiii iiiiiiiiiiiiiiiiin—yooooooooooooooooooooooooooooour—ooooooowwwwwwwwwwwwwwwwwwwwwwn—wellllll-beeeeeeeeeeeeeeeeeeee eeeeeeeeeeeing....*'

CHAPTER IV

With the homely odour of burnt cookie biscuit rising up from the bakery vent some two hundred metres below, Winston made ready for the day by unfolding his reading glasses and blowing imaginary specks of flour from the finely meshed mic of his Dictaphone. He listened out for the first few jobs of the day to begin their descent, knowing that he would soon hear them clatter along the pneumatic plumbing towards his desk.

Three tumbled out all at once, and Winston set about the small objects with aplomb, pulverising them with his fist into a mess of scattered crumbs. From the rubble he picked out three paper slips and with the side of his hand swept the unwanted debris into a hole in the desk. There were two other similar holes set into the desk: one for the deposit and return dispatch of the finished rectifications, and the other for the posting of waste paper into a shredder. The shredder chutes were commonly given proprietorial monikers, so that when a fellow operative deemed that a document was due for disposal, the article would be introduced into the jaws of Mr Snippy-Snap or Mrs Snappy-Snatch, whereupon it would be shredded and duly recycled.

Winston examined the three slips of paper in front of him, unrolled but obstinately curlicued. Each contained a message of only a few lines, composed in the obscure and ancient jargon peculiar to their designation. The first of the three on Winston's desk ran:

You cannot stop bird of sorrow fly overhead, but can prevent such unhappy thought from nesting there.

The second:

If problem is fixable, then no need must worry. If problem not fixable, then can only worry, must only much worrying, life become no end of much worrying worry.

The third:

Ultimate source of happiness not money not power, but with no money, no power, no source ultimate happiness, no source anything at all.

The messages required only minor rectifications, a little fine-tuning to edit out the strange gnomic gloom that had crept in. Winston attended to the second fortune first, since it was the most easily remedied, rectifying it as follows:

If problem is fixable, then no need must worry. If problem not fixable, then no purpose worrying. There must no benefit be in worrying whatsoever, ever.

The third required a little more tinkering, until it read:

Ultimate source of happiness not money not power, but warm-heartedness is source ultimate happiness.

Winston's creative gift and his great value to the commune lay in his talent for rectifying the returns and checking over the first-draft fortunes, employing his unique editorial expertise to craft the short scripts until they conformed to the appropriate clairvoyant register. Once satisfied with the elevating tone of his rectification, he would make the necessary spoken notes, attach any supplementary memoranda by rubber band to the cassette, and post the bundle into the pneumatic tube to be inhaaaaaaled upwards.

With a subconscious waft of the hand, the few residual crumbs were scuffed into the waste slot and the three strips of curlicued paper fed into the ever-ravenous maw of Mr Tooth-Fairy, their existence forever erased. The small cassette rattled away on its journey to the upper floor, gladly out of sight and out of Winston's mind, confident as he was that the modified drafts would be approved, proofed and committed to a revised print run. Each message was scrutinised more than once, quality-controlled by a host of experts, and ultimately guaranteed by the fellowship of specialists on the top floor. This rigorous procedure was designed to ensure that no bogus prediction, no wonky forecast, would enter the world, to conflict with the edicts of fate or disappoint a world hankering for divinatory comfort. Should some harmful fortune ever sneak out into the public domain, hidden within the temporary gloom of a shrink-wrapped fortune cookie parcel...but Winston had been assured that such things rarely, if ever, happened.

And yet, despite the many levels of scrutiny, certain erroneous fortunes had not only found their way into print, but had somehow evaded quality control to end up in the hands of the happily unwary. Nor were these *misfortunes* simple typos or inadvertent misprints. While closely resembling the bona fide scripts, their misaligned sentiments seemed to harbour a sinister coherence—that is to say, they were not easily to be dismissed as mere gobbledegook, since the deviations of the misfortunes often exhibited a recognisable brand of unpleasantness. One recent batch of misfortunes intercepted by a keen-eyed wonk prior to distribution exemplified the disturbing work of what some referred to as the 'deep glitch':

Anger or hatred is like fisherman's hook. Very important for to ensure that we are not caught by it in own snare or in own bear trap or own poison bait. Irrespective of believer in agnostics, God or bad karma, moral ethic is code which everyone try to crack—instead, why not try crack? Except not in August.

And then there was this:

Prime purpose in this life to help other. If cannot help other, then best not just hurt other, instead—best one small pain and an infinity of peace.

And:

In cosmos, one human life no more than tiny insignificant blip of nothing minus everything. Each of us just visitor to inhospitable planet, best only alien who stay for limited time before planet bite back, eat up, spit out. Not even chew. Ha. Ha.

Those vulnerable citizens in need of preternatural life advice who might turn to the fortunes with greater expectation than most were especially susceptible to the malign influence of rogue misfortune cookies. Such citizens might well be endangered by the misleading psychic advice, and indeed rumours abounded that erroneous messages had triggered the odd act of self-harm, as the rush of optimism that accompanied the unwrapping of a fresh fortune cookie was swiftly disappointed—and worse. Such incidents went largely unremarked, though, since nobody wished to dwell on the unthinkable. Where possible, misfortunes were quietly returned to the Ministry of Fortune and swiftly rectified, reissued and distributed without any announcement being made. Such rectifications were colloquially regarded by Ministry wonks as *bloopers, gaffes, clangers, howlers* or *boo-boos* that had been put right in the interests of accuracy and good fortune—but increasingly the work of recalling and rectifying misfortunes was becoming a daily affair, the rule rather than the exception.

The rectification of these sinister destinies was not in and of itself fakery—in light of the threat to the public, it was nothing less than a humanitarian duty, carried out in the service of the human right to aspiration and serendipity. Early disruptions had been put down to a stubborn gremlin in the machine, a wonky cog or two or some elusive eccentricity cascading along the production line, a glitch to be mechanically rectified. The suggestion that a lone wonk operative was interfering with the production process was never openly indulged as a possibility, since no yippy wonk could ever be that mean-spirited.

Misfortune cookies could wreak havoc in the daily life of the suggestible, but on occasion rectifications could also prove disastrous. The chances that a newly rectified message might be opened by the same recipient as the original erroneous version was so remote that no calculation had ever been made to anticipate such an eventuality. But it was a matter of record that at least one marriage proposal accepted on the basis of a flawed fortune had later been rescinded upon receipt of a reissued and rectified version that flatly contradicted its conjugal exhortations, with the revised prophecy occasioning great sorrow and the odd slit wrist. Similarly, pay rises and promotions swiftly withdrawn on the basis of a re-editioned rectification had led to breakdowns and overdoses. Contracts were more coldly reappraised a second time round, and hopes dashed. Rectifications gave false hope where dark tumours lurked. Women leapt from ledges and men hurled themselves down steep flights of stairs. Bodies were washed up downstream from uptown bridges like so many stricken jellyfish stranded by the pitiless tide, each calamity accompanied by a message, as tightly sealed in the rigid claws of a waterlogged corpse as it had once been in its sweet butterfly-shaped pastry pocket.

That the glitch possessed coherence made it entirely reasonable to suspect something theurgical was at play—the sinister grip of fate twisting the innocent hand of destiny, the two finding their common root in some undisclosed noumenal ground. Normally, fortunes were carefully composed so as never to contain any specific detail: while they might seem to offer un-canny insights to those eager to be affected by eerie visions, they were designed more as a broad-brush estimation of the sensible variations of fate—those outcomes overtly willed by the general populace and discretely bought into being by the Ministry. And so it was, as with every class of recorded presage, great or small, that the cultural and psychic hopes of everyday life were loaded into the promissory crispy wonton-shaped biscuit, and as the or-der of mysterious events unravelled in space and time, likewise the fortune cookies so burdened by human expectation *were first crushed, and their contents then unravelled....*

Winston glanced across the office at the rough-hewn wonk known to those that deserved to know as Tilly Tillotson. She sat sifting through a similar clutch of attic returns, her chin pressed hard up against her Dictaphone, her wiry rust-red beard rasping loud-ly as she made her urgent staccato report. Tillotson paid Winston a nicely polite nod, and Winston reciprocated—blushing at the thought of the especially notorious paintings she was known for executing, while attempting a conspiratorial grin to confirm his general sense of what Tillotson was tinkering with—although colleagues never shared the specifics of their compositions, sim-ply because the ethereal aspirations of the fortunes had to be respected even by those engaged in manually rectifying them.

A wide concourse intersected the open-plan suite of neigh-bourly hotdesks, allowing an integrated flow of movement and collegial chatter. Gregarious cascades of plant life and wildflow-er looped along its route, plus the odd handicraft table replete with complementary knick-knacks—or lavender sacks, worry beads or intricate wicker wonk works, idiosyncratic artisanal ar-ticles whose sales gave a boost to charitable causes.

Winston knew less than a dozen of the Ministry staff by name or intimate nod. He saw them ambling to and fro on the central concourse and in the eatery, would happily acknowledge them in passing, and would even murmur the name of one or two in a simple collegial greeting. He would see them gathering in the community room on film night, at book club or drama group, for poetry readings, guest lectures, group-crits and the like—none of which he himself ever participated in. He knew, for example, that the woman with sandy hair at the next desk toiled day in day out relentlessly tracking down errant misfortune cookies, and that there was something fitting in this, since her childhood sweetheart had sadly fallen victim to an erroneous misfortune during their ill-fated courtship.

A few desks away a mild, floaty, dreamy, forgetful creature named Ampleforth, a self-confessed concrete poet—his hardnosed Brutalism reinforced by the fluffiest of feathers—with large ears and a surprising talent for juggling with rhymes and metres, was also engaged in recording misfortune incidents, with the aim of discovering discrete patterns and behavioural clues in the mutational variations of each preternatural occurrence.

And yet, Winston reflected, this office, its wonks numbering sixty or thereabouts, was only one subsection of the Composition and Rectification Department. Beyond, above, below, in every direction, innumerable workers were engaged in an unimaginable web of interconnected tasks. Far below on the ground floor, deliveries of raw materials from all the global suppliers were received by the logistics department. On the floor above that, torrents of cookies tumbled down long shiny chutes from the finishing floors higher up, to be packed up into big boxes by the busy cookie packers before being passed back down to logistics for global redistribution. Above the cookie packers was the print floor, with its typography experts and many inky technicians setting up plates for the continuous proofing and printing of each new fortune slip. Once printed the slips were taken up to the kitchen floor for insertion. In the kitchen, its store rooms stacked with vanilla pods, almonds, coconut oil, brown rice flour, kamut and coconut blossom sugar, an endless procession marched from the spence out into the baking hub to maintain constant supply to the commando ranks of artisanal bakers and pedant doughiers toiling in the hot glow of the ovens, preparing the many baking trays with non-stick coconut parchment—the chitinous crush of vanilla pods, and the dental grinding of almonds plus the splash of coconut oil and water—loaded into gigantic wooden bowls and pummelled by stone grinders, then whisked until the contents frothed—the flour measured and kamut weighed—the blossom-sugar sprinkled in with a healthy dose of Himalayan crystal salt—placed into even bigger bowls for everything to be whisked together with artisanal blood, sweat and cheer, until all ingredients had been cajoled into one smooth, batter-like substance—stacks of large trays chilled for an hour before the Cookie Master was summoned from the store room, and with the cambered curve of a well-oiled spoon reserved especially for the purpose, proceeded expertly to swirl each portion of chilled paste out into two thousand little circles—the trays placed in preheated ovens and baked for thirteen minutes until the edges of the cookies turned nicely golden—the flat cookies removed with long palette knives, being at this stage quite warm and still soft enough to be shaped without crumbling—the Cookie Master then, with the accompaniment of ritual glossolalic murmurs, placing each sacred slip of paper with its promissory fortune in the middle of each cookie circle—then neatly folding them in half to secure the message inside—then pinching the edges together before cooling and hardening and then finally being sealed into the familiar metallic wrappers adorned with a smiley face.

High above the kitchen was the Composition and Rectification Department, and above that, the all-seeing and all-powerful Attic Quintessence Department.

In the attic there sat a rotating committee of occasional sooth-saying clairvoyants—druids, water-diviners, horse-whisperers, hermetic occultists, healers, cobblers, oracles, Rosicrucian mediums, minor telepaths, spooks, mind-readers, people-pleasers, dust-prophets, stone-suckers, rodent-diviners, second-guessers, gamblers, egg-suckers, theurgic practitioners, ventriloquists, plumbers, tea-leaf readers, a troupe of volunteer slaves, fortune hunters, archaeologists, fig-swallowers, geomancers, numerologists, chiromancers, tarot readers and amateur card sharps—presiding over the wisdom and tone of the prophecies according to rituals that had become as arcane and fanatically protected as the recipe for the cookie dough itself.

From these lofty heights ideational summaries would be handed down to the Composition Department, where a cast of sub-editors would respectfully suggest minor adjustments. But it was up to the Aspirations Committee to divine the general psychic expectations of the public—to embody its common wishes and hopes in best-guess predictions concerning happiness, love, life and general well-being. To this end, the common fortunes were more often than not part-gleaned from parochial adages, part reverse-engineered from popular sentiments, snipped from bits of lay wisdom and pieces of common folklore, stolen from forgotten statutes or party slogans, or obtained from obsolete religious sentiments, obscure lyric poetry or children's plague rhymes.

Alongside these standard cookies, though, the Ministry also catered for the specialist tastes of the more exacting patron. There were collectable fortune cookies dedicated to emancipatory commemorations, freedom festivals, and popular Goldstein charity drives. But the most popular add-on to the standard package was the *erotic fortune*, which came in a sealed brown packet. The pastry was flesh-coloured according to racioethnic preference, and had the physical appearance of a belly button, anus, or vagina, depending on the libidinal inclination of the recipient. Erotic cookies typically contained harmlessly lewd messages:

When you discontent downstairs you always want more. But you must try, try, and try again and you will suck seed.

When erotic fortunes suffered the effects of the deviant glitch, the effects could be unpredictable. In the mercifully rare event that an erotic fortune cookie was crushed only to yield an adulterated libidinous missive, the error might be easily accommodated by common sense. Yet those who broke pastry in the auspicious flicker of candlelight, accompanied by the consumption of symbolic flatbreads, the tension heightened by the solemn explication of their libidinal fate from among the litter of cookie crumbs—such persons, already primed by the presumptions of faith, might find themselves distressed or affronted by a glitched overture. Of course, the receiving of a misfortune was a chance matter, its message by no means personally directed toward any particular recipient. Yet no Ministry apologist could admit as such, since acknowledging the impersonal nature of the misfortunes would also render the uncanny psychic accuracy of legitimate fortunes null and void.

An erotic cookie message composed at source to read:

Try not become so consume by love for other, instead try consummate love with other.

might say instead:

Try not become so consume by love for other, instead try eat other.

While a message originally intended to read:

> *There is no need for erect temples, no need complicate sexy object with God. Better to ignore sexy obstacle than try overcome God.*

might instead enter the public realm as:

> *There is no need for erect temples, no need God. Better you susurrate swollen blood thrust of loins in split shitty tissues. Better you drape head open mouth soiling blood spattered veil face beaten or better violaceous liquefied all body politician. Better you strangle penis sweat clitoris slime frothing in nostril sagging load straggling over and over shaved occiput or better mauve slit of arse. Much better when discontent devour dead membrane's throat gurgling jism purge with bloody smear-chipped tooth-dent in screaming soft rape flesh, especially in June.*

In short, the sinister glitch transformed auguries of harmless erotic fun into psychic provocations to rape, torture and murder—presented as the ordinances of incontrovertible fate, and liable to be obeyed with the self-fulfilling logic of enraptured souls yearning for truth.

Recorded incidents in which misfortunes were cited as a provocation ranged from indecent exposure to the theatrical restaging of car accidents. Pain was inflicted upon animals and children alike. Eruptions of emetophilia, scatophilia, frotteurism, paedophilia, necrophilia and haematolagnia occurred, corresponding misfortunes motivating each and every predestined act.

Three more cookies dropped onto Winston's table whilst he was twiddling his thumbs, and he was about to pummel them with his fist when the call came from the community room for the Two Minutes Compassion.

When the arduous task of indulging Goldstein's proxy pain was done, Winston, snivelling theatrically into a sodden Kleenex so as to hasten his turgid escape, returned to his desk to find a note awaiting him. It was an instruction from the Attic Quintessence Department. More than that, *it was handwritten*.

He unfolded it with bated breath, anticipating revelations of great sagacity.

Hey Winston,

How goes it down on the workshop floor? Just wanted to say you're doing a great job, man! Thing is—and it's a real downer to have to lay this on you without fair warning—a clutch of fortunes passed out during the month of oh, say, maybe September, have, like, been sent back on account of being totally bummed out by some pretty negative vibes. So Winston, man, would you be so kind as to cast your beady eye, and, y'know, do your thing—rectify the bad stuff out and the good stuff in! Soon as you can, brother—post them in the tube, or bring 'em up, your call. I'll post the bad shit down—but let's keep this strictly between us!

Peace out, good fortune brother!
Amitav.

Rendered light-headed by Amitav's mystical tone, Winston slipped into a meditative state while awaiting the offending cookies' delivery from the attic by totally cool pneumatic tube.

When he came to, Winston found himself already instinctively smashing the cookie parcels with his fists, pulverising the shells into dust, demolishing them so that the scripts were all that remained. The diminutive scrolls that emerged from the rubble, he soon saw, had once again eschewed the ethereal in favour of the mention by name of something as humdrum as a real-life person—to wit, a contemporaneous mortal named *Conrad Withers*.

Withers was the last known Jehovah's Witness, but was primarily famous for being a contestant in a popular reality television show. Not only was Withers mentioned in the fortune, but he was explicitly tipped as the show's eventual winner. And yet Withers had been expelled from the show, under bizarre circumstances, weeks before the prediction came to light. Withers' exit was neither here nor there, but the deliberate defamation of the mystical prestige of the fortunes by such a wildly inaccurate forecast was overtly detrimental to the reputation of the Ministry of Good Fortune.

Winston was of the opinion that the immediate exclusion of Withers in his rectification would not cause any significant complication, and that it was best to marshal the ethereal against the mundane fact of Wither's untimely tellurian fame—in other words, *most best erase all earthly mention of Withers in favour of stock prediction of celestial love, divine health, good life and universal well-being. Stop.*

Although time would surely tell.

CHAPTER V

In the low-ceilinged Ministry eatery, small groups drifted in dribs and drabs from the busy elevators, loosely aiming for the food bar, congealed by viscous gossip rather than the vulgar urgency of hunger—by now an unfamiliar and archaic instinct. A haphazard queue formed, made up of voracious coteries yet to relinquish the magnetic field of their chitchat, before the rude issuing of individual lunch trays caused each aleatory mass to atomise, the clot subdividing into individual salivating mouths populated by activated taste buds as they shuffled one by one past the long delicatessen counter, the salad bar, and the hot food buffet as if negotiating a precarious ledge—each making their choice from the superabundant fare on offer, and for each a modest picking, since negotiating the potlatch surplus set before their senses was also a test of resilience for those pious dietary restrictions that often come to define a person's identity—especially in the great consideration given to that which links a mouth to its anus.

The eatery's open-air terraced seating area, two hundred and eighty ziggurated meters up, was all gorgeous and dreamy, dappled with softened sunlight and silken cloud base, suffused with many chirping passerines perched in readiness to filch the odd unleavened cookie crumb should fortune allow. From beyond the hot food counter with its glistening dishes burnished under a trinity of hot sun-lamps, there came the effervescent minstrel fizz of the full Serenity range—Ataraxy Elderflower, Lullaby Lemonade, Placid Ginger, Hushful Nettle, Dreich Dandelion, Rueful Root, et al.

'Just the wise old yippy-dippy wonk I've been lookin' for,' came a familiar voice to Winston's rear.

Behind him, creeping up furtively as ever, was Syme, expert philologist and chief of the team of shuffling specialists engaged in compiling the *Thirteenth Edition of the Fortune Cookie Diction-ary*. He was a tiny creature, not exactly wizened, but with a wax-en wellness beguiling in its strange luminosity. Syme was smaller in stature than Winston, adorned with many well-worn worry beads and stooping into the depths of his long wispy hair like some weary willow tree shrouding its trunk. His large bright eyes, always dilated, hungry for light, now scoured Winston's face for some vulnerability, some unguarded clue as to what if anything lay beyond the customary exchange of mere cordial pleasantries.

'Hey Winston, did you ever manage to hunt down that elu-sive copy of Ginsberg's *Howl*, the signed '56 first edition?'

'Oh, I think you may have confused me with someone who reads poetry,' said Winston, flatly.

'Relax, man! No hassle! Just a friendly nudge and a wink from one wonk to another!' The words were spoken with exag-gerated gestures of pacifist placation, or perhaps it was lacerat-ing sarcasm—it was difficult to tell with Syme. In another life Winston would surely relish putting the *fist* back in pacifist, but in this life he must make do with simply tuning out.

But Syme did not relent. 'Jeepers creepers!' he yowled. 'Un-coil your pot, brother! Anyways, I did find a copy of the semi-ra-re *To Eberhart from Ginsberg: A Letter about Howl 1956. An Ex-planation by Allen Ginsberg of his publication Howl and Richard Eberhart's New York Times article "West Coast Rhythms" together with comments by both poets and Relief Etchings by Jerome Kaplan*—but I can't for the life of me find a decent original '56 first.'

Truth be told, Winston did indeed have in his keeping two copies of *Howl, and Other Poems* by Allen Ginsberg, the most prized of them being a shrinkwrapped '56 first edition in pure, bright, mint condition, and signed by the author. The other, also a '56 first edition, was also signed by the poet's paw—but was so thoroughly dog-eared and well-thumbed by you-know-who that its pages were as crispy as autumn leaves.

'I'm sorry, I can be of no help whatsoever,' insisted Winston with a smile.

'Shit before shovel—or pearls before swine! Your choice!'

'*What?*'

'Because freedom's just another word for nothin' left to do.'

'*What?*'

'Just go with the flow, man.'

'*What do you mean?*'

Syme gestured beyond Winston's irritated face to the gap opening up in the queue over yonder.

'Oh!' Winston dutifully shambled forwards to close the gap, and Syme followed close behind, his protruding empty tray pressed into the small of Winston's back like a pistol in an old movie.

'Have you seen *The Prisoner's Hand* yet?' he asked.

'I don't watch films.'

'No films, no poetry, no music, no art...*no nothing.*' Syme regarded Winston from behind with a sympathetic sneer. Winston intuitively sensed this and attempted to retaliate in the best way he knew how.

'*When have more compassionate mind and cultivate warm-heartedness, whole atmosphere all around become more positive and friendlier.*'

'Oh, sure thing Winston! Totally get it, man! There's the touchstone right there!'

Winston shuffled his eyes and rolled forwards, drawing a little closer to the wholesome stench of lovingly prepared organic foodstuffs.

Syme professed a keen interest in antique films: not the harmless silent ones—those glorified mimes and slapstick buffoons with their expressionist make-up and exaggerated primate gestures—but the later ones, especially the distasteful antique horror films, the gory ones, the gratuitous spectacles of violence;

and the old anti-war films that were designed to act as a purgative against the universalised totality of all violence—with much vaporising of enemy cities, much pantomime goose-stepping and forced marching into blizzards, liquidation camps, and dictators being brought to justice in grandiloquent fake show trials with fake confessions, fake remorse and fake executions, and fake personal heroics masking the real division of the world into newfound anti-markets.

This appetite for the grotesque was vexatious to Winston, not because he was so squeamish as to take offense at such historical curios, but because Syme pretended that his appetite for odious artefacts had some credible justification beyond pure gratuitous voyeurism, which might be forgivable if at least it was honest—we all have our peculiarly delightful and completely-acceptable-within-reasonable-bounds fetishes. But in fact Syme was a voracious sin-eater, gobbling up the worst of history's images as a self-appointed adjudicator of humanity. He had neatly inserted himself somewhere between *systemic* and *divine* violence, placing barbaric aggression in the service of cultured progress—this arrogant imposition being enough to warrant Winston's private derision. For Syme's appetite for the barbaric, so he claimed, was supposedly a necessary evil for the experimental novel he was writing, had been writing forever—his writer's block was by now quite solid and all progress was stalled. The story was set in the future, but drew upon the violent excesses of the past to tell a terrible tale about a dystopian society where everyone was being watched, surveilled for reasons no one was exactly sure of—reasons that Syme himself had yet to explain, hence the narrative obstacle to his story's onward motion.

Talking to Syme without lapsing into despair and torpor was a matter of nudging him away from the looping noose of these morose speculations toward his less woeful professional specialisation—*the morphological adaptation of fortune cookie language*, a subject upon which he was vastly authoritative and no less exhaustive. It was preferable thus to furtively replace the obscene with the tedious, although at times they felt uncomfortably close. In fact, Winston had turned away to avoid the scrutiny of the large luminous eyes of the prying little gonk, trying to capture him in their mesmerising beam....

'It's an especially vivid piece of film, *The Prisoner's Hand*,' continued Syme regardless, drilling into Winston's head from behind. 'It shows how the early liberal progressives had a predilection for gory films—despite maintaining so peaceable a disposition, they had a marked penchant for *unpleasure*. They enjoyed teasing themselves with movies that predicted catastrophe—the more tragic, the more apocalyptic the better. They yearned for chaos whilst enduring tranquility. They made do with images of the end of the world—as if to conceive it was to keep it at bay. And yet they pictured catastrophe in such loving detail that, on those occasions when disaster did befall them, every cataclysm had already been imagined so precisely that it's difficult for us to tell which so-called disaster movies are real and which are not—which are depictions of events, and which are sublime inventions with which to provoke the future.'

'How's the novel coming along?' said Winston abruptly, invoking Syme's obdurate writer's block in the hope of stopping him dead in his tracks.

An appalled Syme gaped up at Winston, but before he could protest—'*Winston! Syme! Bienvenido de nuevo! Dearest comrades!*' came the aproned saucier-poet wonk's call to arms, as he suddenly appeared looming above them, his lavish hand-whittled serving spoon hovering in wait above the luscious array of lovely steaming superfoods on offer.

Even with traces of horror still fresh in his mind, Syme's appetite was razor-sharp.

'Solicitudes to you too, comrade! May I have the golden

beetroot with the red balsamic, the flesh-pink grapefruit, the blood-orange garnish…and I'll take just a teeny child-size pinch of the red cabbage salad, if you don't mind!' He turned to Winston, licking his lips and rubbing his tummy at the same time. 'Oh, and a dash of beetroot ketchup!'

The sight of the blood-red *jus* pooling in the circular dimple of Syme's pallid porcelain plate patently echoed his predilection for bloodthirsty visual bygones. Winston elected for the sweet potato tempura, the yuzukosho, the peanut and coriander dip-dip.

'There's a table over there,' said Syme. 'There! Beneath the television—don't panic, it's on mute. Let's pick up a drop of the good stuff on the way.' He scuttled off.

Ataraxy Elderflower was served in crude glass jars, with misaligned seams and little pockets of trapped air, mini-bubbles fossilised by the cack-handed craftisanship of their careless freewheeling production. Syme and Winston threaded their way across the patio and set their food down on the table, the perched birds amassing where a half-eaten fig muffin had been fortuitously forsaken. Taking up his kooky jam jar, Winston paused for an instant to prime his nerves before sipping at the sparkling cordial and, whilst winking the acetous tears free of his eyes, set about his potato tempura, yuzukosho, and peanut and coriander dip-dip—and observed as Syme's fingers and face became stained with a cherry-red sort of cochineal-ish cerise.

Neither of them were really minded to speak again until their plates had been exhausted. But then, from one of the tables behind, there came a voice—at first hushed but brisk and uninterrupted, then becoming a tad delirious, unstable even; a kind of jejune jabber like the drowning quack of a gabble-beaked duckling.

Paying no especial heed to the demented tongue raging away behind them, Winston and Syme, replete, took up the gratis

Ministry fortune cookies that always came with every canteen tray, unwrapped them, and broke open the crispy shells so as to extract the little slips from the litter of crumbs. Syme pondered his, then purposefully showed it to Winston as if to ward off its auguries.

'One of yours?' he demanded.

Winston gave a perfunctory shrug, taking no responsibility for its authorship—thus the cookie crushed, but the magic still intact.

'How's the Dictionary coming on?' said Winston, his voice raised to accommodate the gabbleduck's rabbiting.

'Oh slowly, quite slowly.' replied Syme. 'But surely.' His face brightened and he slid his plate aside to lean across the table so as to confer privately without needing to yell.

'You see, the Thirteenth Edition is the definitive edition,' he said, gravely. 'Our language is achieving pure consensus. Soon people like you and I will need to learn to...well, to *unspeak*. You'd be forgiven for thinking that our job was to come up with some brand-new universal language. But not a bit of it! Language is attaining its own true form, according to a great harmony of forces leading to great accord—to unequivocal consent—to universal compromise and simple unanimity! Our function is merely to help smooth out some of the lagging viscosities, making language more sympathetic—a language formed of empathy, an expressive form for a truly progressive sensibility!'

'*Sensibility?*'

'Yes Winston. Sensibility.' Syme smiled, his face more luminous than ever. 'Of course, verbs do not have irreducible correlatives, nor do surplus synonyms exist purely for fun, nor are antonyms simply the opposite of—well, anyway.... Those are the nuts and bolts of the Thirteenth Edition. But let me explain. I'll recite a standard training paragraph—one you're probably familiar with from your school days—and you'll easily catch what I mean: *One problem with our current society is that we have an attitude towards education, as if it is there to simply make you much more clever, or to make you more ingenious.... Even though our society does not explicitly emphasise this, the most important use of knowledge and education is to help us understand the importance of engaging in much more wholesome actions, and for bringing about discipline within our inner minds. The proper utilisation of our intelligence and knowledge is to effect changes from within to develop a good and healthy heart....*'

Syme settled back in his chair, making himself comfortable for the duration of Winston's confusion. Duly humbled, Winston contemplated Syme's words, leaving an appropriate pause before conceding with a solemn shake of the head. His friend tipped forward, his dismantled brow casting an incredulous grey shadow across his face.

'You're thinking—what am I not getting? *Right?* What's wrong with the paragraph? And you're right! It's fine as it is—it makes perfect sense. It does. But it also says *too much*, and in saying *too much* it ultimately reduces what it can say expressively.' He ratcheted backwards in his chair with little knowing nods—confident in the assumption that such a slack tautology had surely lassoed something or other in its looping logic.

'After all, what justification is there for a word which is simply the opposite of some other word? A word contains its opposite in itself. Take the word "healthy", for instance. If you have a word like "healthy", what need is there for a word like "unhealthy" when everything around us, the world we inhabit, our lives, are utterly healthy and harmonious? Or again, why synonyms for "wellness", when words like "happy" and "content" are so capably subsumed within it?'

Winston was still none the wiser.

'Listen to the very same paragraph again, Winston, except this time with a slight consensual adaptation: *One problem with current society is attitude towards education, there to simply make much more clever, make more ingenious.... Even though society not emphasise this, important use of knowledge and education, help understand importance of more wholesome actions, and for bring about discipline within inner minds. Proper utilisation of intelligence and knowledge, effect changes from within, develop good healthy heart....* You see?'

Syme was relishing Winston's fruitless inner deliberations, his pantomime of earnest nods, pneumatic sighs, and hydraulic frowns.

'Come on Winston! It's screaming out at you! Listen again! But closely this time: *Problem current society education, make more clever, make more ingenious.... Even though society use knowledge and education, help understand wholesome action, for bring about discipline inner mind. Proper intelligence and knowledge, effect change from within, develop healthy heart.*'

Winston was eagerly trying to decipher the paragraph's evolving shape, its linguistic mindfulness, but from the table behind them the deleterious voice was now babbling continuously and loudly, its clamour intertwining with the tangle of thoughts in his own internal bedlam—the childish gabble, the drowning quack, quack, quack of a happily drowning ugly duckling. Syme jolted forwards suddenly, slamming the interrogator's table with the flat of both hands, making poor Winston jump. Then he immediately leant back, laughing manically.

'*Problem society education, make clever, make ingenious.... Society no emphasise, use knowledge education, understand wholesome action, for discipline inner mind. Proper knowledge, change within heart....*'

Poor Winston was withering like a sickly snail with antennae afflicted by a Leucochloridium parasite, tip pulsating and glowing all luminous to encourage its predator. Still flinching from the prior assault, there was nothing more he could do but cower, flinch and wince even more as Syme started up again.

'No? No? *No?* You still don't get it, do you? *Probsoc educlever, ingeniety emphledge edustand holesac, discimind proledge, cheart....* Or better still—*prosoc educlev, ingenit empedge edand holec, dimind prodge, chat!* Now do you see? Can you appreciate the purity of it? Can you hear that, Winston? Like some cosmic bell harmonising with the unspoken mystery of the stars?'

'*Yes! Yes! Of course!*' Winston erupted with relief. 'I get it! The new method allows even mundane language to aspire to its essential psychic designation! It's brilliant, Syme!' But then another thought struck him. 'Maybe this is what the deep glitch is doing, but in reverse—transforming the healthy fortunes into morbid misfortunes...'

Suddenly Winston seemed to hear the sound of scuttling chains and the resounding *crash* of Syme's mental portcullis slamming to the cobblestones. Syme leant forwards, all the better for whispered contempt to travel between them without interference.

'Winston,' he hissed, 'I'll remind you that such casual mention of...*the misfortunes*—especially in public, even in such places as the Ministry eatery—is ill-advised. You should know better. I suppose it's difficult to have an appreciation of what the wonks in my section are up against—I mean, difficult for someone who edits fortune cookies *for a living.*'

The reduction of Winston's daily devotion to the vicissitudes of hand-to-mouth sustenance was mean-spirited of Syme—but he was not stopping there.

'I admire your revisions, Winston, and you're widely respected. But you're an old-fashioned workhorse—like some old Stakhanovite, worked to the bone without reward—and worst of all, like some daft old refusenik, you refuse to give anything of your*self*, save for this dogmatic subordination to work. Nothing more. No films, no poetry, no music, no art...*no nothing.*'

Syme was obliged to persist, if only to bridge Winston's gape, so he changed tack.

'Oh Winston, brother! I'm not criticising your methodology, nor the rigour of your daily rectifications—no-one does it better, man! But hey, you must forgive me for being forthright, let me just put it out there, yeah? *Where has the real Winston Smith gone?*'

'But Syme, I *am* the real Winston Smith.'

'But *are you* Winston? I mean, you edit fortune cookies, and that's it. Nothing more, nothing less. Your soul's been replaced by some archaic work ethic, man...you've become *a worker*.'

Winston gasped.

'Don't panic! You can do something to help yourself! You can re-kindle your artisanal urge! You can write! You're good at writing—but you must do something personal! *You need to find your voice!* Something autobiographical? *Find your sense of hurt!* A short story? *Your sense of place!* A novel! *Yes, a novel!* You should only write about what you know! But you must do something—before it's too late! Because doing *anything* is better than doing *nothing!*'

Winston gave a frown so deeply set that only great effort could wrench it back into a functionally genial rictus grin. Syme's convivial vivisection had prompted a recollection of that dark current that had only very recently begun to irrigate his mind, those strange consummate words that had begun to drift into him, through him or by contagion at the very least. The diseased articulation was even entreating him to nominate it as his very own authentic heart-rendered poetry. The voice had found him, and he certainly felt found. But what if the voice was somehow connected to the place of the glitch, what if its hurt was expressed through the misfortunes? What if his daily exposure to the misfortunes had ended up affecting his outlook on life? Despite the nameless, formless abyss from which the unpretended evocations crawled, they were anything but vague, nor were they blighted by Stakhanovite dogmatism and refuse-nik resentment. Quite the opposite—they flowed like lava, burning through him with an industrious urgency that solidified into obdurate mass upon contact with air.

'Has it ever occurred to you that by the year 2084 not a single human being alive will understand such a cloddish conversation as we're having right this minute...?'

'*Except for a poe*—' blurted Winston, stopping short of the unmentionable word, containing the outburst in a reptilian flush of vivid colour. But Syme had glimpsed something, and duly pounced.

'Except for what?' he exclaimed, eyes popping, beads worrying. 'What were you going to say? Winston, tell me! The word you didn't finish—was it poe—'

Behind them, the insane gabble suddenly intensified, and the voice of a female colleague was also raised in a desperate attempt to tame her associate's fulmination. Winston was happy for the racket, for it had stymied Syme. He angled himself back in his chair to better observe the anguished wonk—to witness his fall, to savour it in his peripheral vision, where all contemptible objects could be safely observed.

By now the ventriloquial jaw was snapping at thin air, and an unpleasant sound began to gurgle up from the core of the unfortunate colleague's gloomy viscera—bile mixed with gobbledegook, and then a menagerie of wild howls, a toad's croak, a parrot's squawk and even an effeminate ladylike growl and a manly countertenor shriek—the excrement of being, yawning from the blackened beyond. Winston observed the outpourings as best he could, and was struck by the violence of the possessive impedimenta trying to hold it all back in, the heaving jugular constricted and choked by the yoke of the speaker's obliterated identity, the gullet gulping, the tonsils rasped by the anonymised torrent spilling forth, contorting the man's lips into many ugly shapes like a horribly misshapen rubber band, as if an imposter's teeth were being spat out through it. Winston saw how the cursing invective inhabited the speaker, and how, despite the zoo of shrieks and cries and catcalls escaping from the maw, none of it belonged to him. *In the same way*, he could not help wondering, *that his poetry did not belong to him?* Syme, on the other hand, that keen observer of archaic horror, did not recognise horror *in the flesh*, and had sunk into tepid silence as into a lukewarm bath—resigned to defeat, having lost the scent of Winston's clumsy indiscretion, and with the handle of his spoon indolently tracing the outline of his left hand with his right, indented on the table cloth.

Then the cries from behind formed into mundane sense, and identity was restored to the congruity of the first-person singular:

'*W-w-why didn't she just tell him that she loved him?*' the recovering wonk bawled. '*Poor little Helmut! He was so sad! And...and now I'm so sad...,*' he yelped. '*Why on earth would anyone even write something like that? So utterly tragic! So beautifully painful! So grotesquely lovely! Why did it come to me? Why did it happen to land on my desk and not someone else's? What did I do in a past life to deserve such misery in the present? Such beauty plus tragedy must equal pain...and now I can't put the blasted thing down, I just can't! I've tried, oh god how I've tried—tried to finish it, tried to ignore it—but I can't bear the thought of finishing it...AND WHAT IF IT HAS AN UNHAPPY ENDING? It's unthinkable!*'

Winston saw a loose manuscript on the table, precariously close to the edge, the arms of the flailing ranter threatening to topple it with a waft of the hand or the blunt nub of a funny bone. But before that particular calamity could strike, another did its work for it. For suddenly, the many sparrows and other small birds thus far sedately perched about the eatery all scrambled into the air at once in a blur of rainbow feathers, and the manuscript's loose pages were caught up in an almighty gust, the swirling reams flung hither and thither amid the flutter and flurry of tiny wings. And then from above came the indolent judder of another great bird, a lumbering mechanical creature darkening the sky, subjecting everything below it to the violent forces of its scything rotor blades—a whirlwind of matter turned to chaos: the chaos of the manuscript paper, paper napkins, paper serviettes, paper towels, paper wet wipes and even paper sanitary pads—all synonyms for the same thing in myriad forms, and all spiralling up into the maelstrom *as though surplus synonyms existed purely for fun*. And next a searchlight, bright enough to compete with the sun, magnifying its beam through the cloud and canvas awning, and then an amplified voice softly wafting down, a lovely voice, floating down, down:

'*YOU DOWN THERE!—YES, YOU! REMEMBER!—BE COMFORTABLE IN YOUR OWN SKIN!...BE TRUE TO YOURSELF!... BECAUSE YOU'RE WORTH IT!*'

All below peered unanimously skyward from the eye of the vortex, squinting up at the underside penumbra of the Neighbourhood Watch Helicopter. Then something was ejected from a blind slot in the hull, an object falling so gracefully, seeming to stall in mid-air, swinging in the brilliant beam of the searchlight as it sailed downward—and as if by some mesmeric effect of its elegant descent, what a moment ago had been all shrill and offensive noise became miraculously tranquil, all tattered senses became calm, and everything slackened into soft focus, like a fluffy dream in which a Labrador puppy plays with a loose toilet roll—and with an uncanny sixth sense of *balsam*, a lovely silky-white plump parachute floated unhurriedly down, transporting a handy-sized box of Kleenex tissues...and to rounds of hearty applause rising to a standing ovation, the silhouetted girl reached up to embrace the heaven-sent delivery, releasing the box from its harness and plucking a man-size or two for her forlorn wonk colleague to gently dab at his ruin.

And then all at once the kindly rotorized eclipse was over and the birds were settling back down to the dappled sunlight and the providential scattering of crumbs. Winston, noticing a page of the scattered manuscript tucked into the rung of his chair, bent to pick it up, and couldn't help accidentally digesting the opening sentence, hearkening to its singular voice, and to the unique sense of place and terrible hurt expressed therein:

The Marriage of Reason and Squalor

'A whole island?' an appetite for pathos twinkles in Chlamydia's eye like fossilised light flickering in a far-away galaxy.

'Don't fret—I can afford it,' boasts Algernon, mindful of his nebulous other half twisting the winking solitaire on her finger while gazing at him with a magnitude approaching cosmic awe.

'You'd squander your fortunes on me?' Tendered with faux timidity.

'Without a blink,' he declares, none-the-wiser. 'The prospect of being sensible contradicts my nature—especially now I'm hopelessly in love...'

'Sensible?' The word cruelly tinged.

'Oh, but the island of Morass is truly sublime! I swear you'll die when you set eyes upon it...'

'Sublime?' The optic twinkle flares and somewhere a distant supernova incinerates.

'For God's sake!– It's paradise on Earth!'

Reserved for this very moment, Chlamydia's booby-trapped anatomy belches into Algernon's arms with the violence of an overdue autopsy.

'Oh Doctor Hertz! I care for you with all my heart, lungs, pancreas and spleen!' she bleeds. 'It's the most amazing gift anyone could ever receive! But are you sure? Have you taken leave of your senses? What on earth made you decide to do such a thing? Are you stark *raving mad? When can we visit this paradise island of mine?'*

Algernon plants a punctuating kiss on Chlamydia's furrowed stave—lifting her pounding torso from his chest, arms fully extended so as to read the ecstatic expression corrupting her face. In a display of obeisance behoved only to the altruistic mannerisms of those afflicted with faith, his mucous-grey eyeballs well-up and plead into hers with a confession—

'Well, that's the thing... The thing is, I'd love to come with you, but I can't. As usual these accursed hands are well and truly tied...'

'Algernon!'

In severance to Chlamydia's barefaced disappointment Algernon sees fit to bait her with a thinly veiled provocation

'—unless you're prepared to delay the wedding?'

'Delay?' she barks. 'Over my dead carcass!' Her expression now contorted with incendiary rage, lengthy black mane flaring across the contours of a warped grimace. Only the most delicate surgical caress can tease static whiskers back behind fleshy lobes while Algernon's free hand locks her masticating trap shut.

'See for yourself—it's perfect—like you,' he says clutching at straws, 'I took the liberty of making arrangements. You depart tomorrow morning. Fly alone. Don't ask why...'

'Fly? Tomorrow? Alone? What about the wedding preparations?'

'One week in paradise... I beg of you, will you go?'

Feminine curiosity is pregnant enough to warrant a caesarean, but womanly cunning is sharp enough to induce an efficient acquiescence, and so—

'If you must banish me to the ends of the Earth, I must pack, and so you, dearest Algernon, must leave...'

A sudden epigeal germination had taken root in the soil of Winston's misery. Something dark had switched on, deep inside. A black light. He tried to tame it in the only way he knew how:

You cannot stop bird of sorrow fly overhead, but can prevent such un-
happy thought from nesting there...Cannot stop bird sorrow fly over-
head, prevent unhappy thought nesting there...Canop birow flead
bun prevuch unught fresting ther...Cop bow flad bun pruch ught frest
the...Cow fun fresh...

Just then the despondent gonk Syme piped up again. 'Here comes trouble....'

Winston saw Tomioka threading her way across the helicopter-ravaged terrace as manuscript pages continued to flutter down. A strange specimen with a Möbius beauty that looped the inside out and the outside in, she possessed the strangely impish countenance of an oddly enlarged infant—old *and* young *and* inside-out, an effect embellished by her kooky demeanour and her paint-splattered children's clothes, always uniformly matted with a spectrum of non-toxic hues. They made a perfect pair, Tomioka and Zena. Tomioka only reluctantly succumbed to adult clothes when the weather became severe, a minimal deviation giving some plausibility to the idea that her infantilisation was an identity choice rather than a pathology, although there was nothing to suggest that the two were mutually exclusive. In fact, Tomioka's personal brand was such that she wished to be regarded as a girl but respected as a woman—the very definition of *kooky*.

She greeted her colleagues with a cheery girlish-cum-boyish excitement, and Winston noticed flecks of glitter augmenting her inner well-being.

'How goes it boys and girls—*and you, Syme*! Golly-gosh! *What the fuck* happened here, man?'

Winston gave a smile oddly tinged with pride, which he immediately readjusted to something more appropriate. They were all doing their best to right the upsy-daisy fixtures, the tipped tables and toppled chairs, while other bedraggled diners collaborated in the gathering up of strewn manuscript pages, a charming pastoral scene suddenly unfolding in which hunter-gathering peasants toiled in the bosom of nature collecting up strewn leaves in the hope of reconstituting the disturbed sanity of the Romantic Friction editor so cruelly tipped over the edge by the pathos of *The Marriage of Reason and Squalor*. Grumpy Syme was otherwise occupied with his own weary scraps of paper, mindlessly doodling diagrams of watchtowers, railway tracks, torture machines, firing squads, gas chambers—and then scribbling them out in favour of further technical notes on his beloved dystopian surveillance society, where there would no longer be any need for watchtowers, railway tracks, torture machines, firing squads or gas chambers.

'Oh look at her! Working away in his lunch hour!' chirped Tomioka. 'Finding time to create even in the midst of all this crazy fucked-up brouhaha! Well, I guess you're either on the bus or off the bus! And Syme is definitely on the bus! On the fucking top deck!' She nudged Winston, whose mouth hung fully agape as if in laughter, but with the sound lost somewhere inside. 'I'm sorry to nag, Winston—but I actually came up to the eatery just to give you a little neighbourly jog, to remind you about the hefty donation you pledged the other day at the Compassion.'

'Donation?' said Winston. 'Compassion? What for?'

'Goldstein's big charity, silly-billy! Didn't you catch the omnibus last night? Epic—*Death! Misery! Flies! Skin! Bone! Shit! Orphans! Awful!* Fucking awful!' She momentarily shook her head in deepest despair, but soon became animated again. 'Goldstein's gearing up for the season finale, apparently it's going to be off the scale! So that's why I'm here, yeah? We must all do our bit—I'm doing my bit, Zena's doing her bit, and you should do your bit. We can only do our bit. As long as it's the best we can do—it's better than nothing. It's our bit. Isn't it?'

Tomioka was conjugating the *we, I, and you* of collective

beneficence by way of duck-race, cake sale, raffle, fun run, sponsored silence, etc.

'And if we can all do more than our bit, well, then anything's possible! We have to help the millions of starving children by doing more than just our bit!'

'*Minions?*' repeated Winston, absent-mindedly.

'Listen Winston, it's up to us to do our bit, and make sure Serenity Mansions has the biggest, brightest, smiliest flags and the best smiley-face cupcakes on the whole street. It's the very, very, very least we can do, man!'

'Yes. It would certainly be better than nothing.'

Winston happily handed over two dollar pound notes for Goldstein's newest Mother-of-all-charities, and Tomioka diligently logged Winston's bit in her *My Small Jotter* in very neat joined-up handwriting.

'By the way,' she said. 'I hear that those little tinkers of ours teased you with toy space ray guns yesterday. I don't know where they get it from. Should probably get the gestalt therapist in, have their chakras rebalanced or just turn the bloody heat up on their hothousing. Honestly, they're generally gentle little souls, but this newfound belligerence—it's beyond me.'

'Oh, I shouldn't worry,' said Winston, wondering whether the deep glitch was beginning to affect everyone around him. 'I expect they were just sad about not making it to the museum—after all, it rained earlier in the day, so I guess they just assumed they were going.... Zena seemed a little strung out, and the sink needed unblocking; I'm afraid I failed miserably on both counts. But she was very decent about it.'

'Oh, that's very sweet of you Winston, but quite unnecessary. I wasn't far behind after you'd left and happily mopped up. I think poor old 'er indoors was overwhelmed by the re-hang, and then the sink. She's been all over the place since the re-hang began—it's one thing planning it and another getting your hands dirty!'

The kids have been acting crazy too—something's definitely in the air: moons colliding, consensus waning, markets dipping. Oh! Speaking of which, you'll never guess what our littlest monster did the other day on her school trip—she only slipped away with two other kids to spend the whole afternoon following some complete stranger. They kept on his tail for hours, right through the Goldstein Tit-for-Tat clothes recycling depot, through the yogurt field and the hemp kibbutz. Eventually they tried to hand him over to a Neighbourhood Watch patrol!'

'What on earth did they do that for?'

'They were worried that it might be one of Goldstein's refugees who'd wandered off reservation and got lost! Can you imagine? All alone without food and water? But here's the oddest thing. What do you think put them on to him in the first place? It wasn't his thorn-tattered rags, nor the gaping holes in his hands and feet, nor his long, lank, filthy-dirty hair and unkempt beard...no...*They followed him because he wasn't wearing sandals!*'

'No sandals? How bizarre! So what happened? What did the patrol do?'

'Well, they offered to help—offered him complimentary sandals, green tea, nuts, energy bars and the like. But the poor beggar wouldn't have any of it. Apparently all he kept muttering, over and over, was *come quickly...my reward is with me...to give every man according to his work*, or something kooky to that effect—most probably filched from a cookie. One of yours I bet! Of course Georgina could have made it all up. But...'

As though in hallowed exaltation of Tomioka's woeful tale, an elegiac melody sprung out from the television hovering just above their heads. The three mooned up simultaneously, pleasantly surprised by the elegant choral devotion trilling above them, its miraculous upswell orchestrated by the hand of the saucier-poet, who was aiming the remote from behind the mist of steaming garden legumes. Winston craned up at the vivified screen, as did Tomioka, and even bloodthirsty Syme postponed his sanctimonious research for an eyeful of the exciting title graphics. Once the introductory sequence ended, a static image of a large open-plan communal kitchen came into view, seen from above, the camera evidently nestled in a high corner. The walls appeared grimy from the ergonomic smear of innumerable bodies, and extra-close pick-ups of the kitchen table revealed twelve place-settings squared off by patinated spoons, bent forks, blunt knives, and chipped enamel mugs. Every surface was greasy, with gunge packed into every crack. Then back to the wide shot—and from this sequence of stark colourless vignettes of a drab and dreary domestic abode there rose an imaginary taste of ferric rust, a sour composite of vinegary wine and stale coffee grit, savourless stew and mildewed clothes.

Next came the prospect of a dark dormitory, dead as a cemetery, with rows of coffin-beds laid out along the two opposing distempered walls, blanket-draped body shapes in one or two of them. A simple cushion slumped on each unoccupied bed, along with tawny-tinged pillow-cases watermarked by a history of nocturnal slaver, plus a coarse correctional blanket laid out with a diminutive pile of uniform clothes, and, below, a pair of canvas slippers on a pious screed floor.

Then the narrator's voice—emphatic, with just enough reverb to suggest the *all-seeing* and the *omnipotent*. Yet it was a voice that was strangely familiar to Winston.

'This is Big Brother speaking. Would all housemates be so kind as to make their way to the communal kitchen.'

A host of ghostly figures began to respond and awake reluctantly into motion, threading through the gloom, wafting from room to room, their superlunary progress captured by keen motion-sensor cameras as they silently converged upon the communal conversation pit, there to enter into its hallowed shallow, sunk like some abject crater in the kitchen-cum-living-room-floor.

There followed much bowing, much dispensing with all negative attachment to obdurate ego and vanity, much nodding of heads, much avid smiling, much fervid kissing of cheeks and unreserved wholehearted hugging—an endless permutation of gratefully gracious greetings, each elegantly offered, reproduced, diligently duplicated and unselfishly passed on, each gratefully gracious greeting repeated without thought of closure; the shaking of hands with subtle variations in looseness or firmness of grip, the odd solemn hand placed firmly on heart, or palms pressed together in obeisant prayer; ever more bouts of lowly head-bowing, with varied flexibility of upper-body downward-dog homage—there were pinkie-promises, high fives, a fist bump, and even an Eskimo kiss.

Despite the prolific gestures of ferocious communality on offer, one figure in the pit seemed indifferent to any of these preferred modes of interaction, instead remaining curled up on the banquette in a foetal position, motionless, as if their passing had gone unobserved.

'How long have they all been in there?' said Tomioka.

So long that no one cared to answer.

'They promised a season of contrasts and conflicts,' she murmured, 'and more fireworks than you could wave a sparkler at. A selection of the last religious zealots in the world, all coming together to compete against popular eviction...but they came together and just merged into one syncretic mass. Not a competitive bone between them.'

As if an exemplar was required to prove her point, two of the on-screen contestants obliged by providing a textbook lesson in verbal confrontation avoidance:

'Of much pleasure to be again in your company so soon, my dear friend!'

'Indeed! Indeed! But the pleasure is all mine, since you were already in my thoughts this afternoon.'

'As indeed you are *always already* in my thoughts and *forever* in my heart!'

Now there loomed over the pit a grey-haired man with a kindly, lowly, simpering smile, a sober posture and stooped shoulders confirming religiose seniority, at least to his own satisfaction.

'Can I interest anyone in a beverage of any kind? Hot or cold, lukewarm or tepid, sweetened or pure...?' He tapped the rim of an empty mug with a teaspoon, in lieu of a liturgical bell.

'Tea. Coffee. Squash. Tap water. I'm eager to be of service to my fellow housemates, to consort with the followers of all religions in a spirit of friendliness and fellowship—'

The reclusive curled-up body on the couch was the first to emit a muffled cough, despite its apparent pretence of being sound asleep, or just mortally coiled. The movement in the cadaver being duly noted, an admirably magnanimous acknowledgment was offered up in its general direction.

'And of course by fellowship I also include all our *interpath agnostic brethren.*'

'Oh, ad infinitum!' added a demure woman sporting a loose red headscarf, clapping excitedly in the pit, her uplifted face as serene as human musculature could manage.

'*Ad nauseum!*' The muffled comment failed to escape the innermost reserves of the slumberer's curled anatomy, and was furtive enough to go unheard locally in the kitchen—but each word was rendered loud and clear to the audience of millions at home by way of the intimate microphone each contestant was obliged to wear in anticipation of precisely such fraught and private asides.

The almighty voice rang out again, reverberating, omniscient, for all to hear. 'Would Sister Aaradhya please come to the Diary Room....'

As the red-scarfed Aaradhya stood up and began slowly

edging around the sunken conversation pit, squeezing past the other housemate's knees and triggering a Mexican wave of seated genuflections, somewhat awkward but undoubtedly sincere in their will to dispense with all negative attachment to obdurate ego and vanity, her progress was somewhat slowed by much nodding of heads, much avid smiling, much fervid kissing of cheeks and unreserved wholehearted hugging.

'*Uh-oh!* Someone's for the choppity-chop,' sniggered Syme gleefully. 'Confession...task...or excommunication?'

'Has anyone actually been evicted yet?' said Tomioka.

'I'm not sure.'

'Is the Buddhist still there?'

'Yes. Look, over there.'

'The Christian?'

'Clearly. Look. He's making tea.'

'The Confucian's getting water from the tap.'

'The Hindu's there, just out of frame to the left.'

'What about the Zoroastrian?'

'Sitting down. There.'

'The Muslim?'

'There.'

'The Jew?'

'There.'

'The Sikh?'

'Hiding with the Hindu.'

'Funny.'

'Where's the Jehovah's Witness?'

'*Purged!*' hissed Syme, gloating again. 'Don't you remember? He's the only zealot to have actually been evicted! I completely forgot about him! *Conrad Withers*. He was sent packing weeks ago.'

'Oh yes! Conrad bloody Withers! You're right!' said Tomioka, quite excited. 'But wait! There should still be nine zealots left after Withers' eviction—and we've only accounted for eight religions...*so who's the ninth?* Winston? Any ideas?'

Winston, without the need for reflection, offered his wisdom as best he could:

'Whether believe in religion or believe in human religion, affection and compassion for human is most best key for human peace of mind.'

Syme and Tomioka exchanged glances.

'What does he mean, *human religion*?'

'Yes of course! That's it! *The Humanist!*' blurted Syme. 'Look! The humanist. He's the one curled up asleep on the couch! Clever old Winston!'

On the screen above their heads the kindly old Christian was handing an enamel mug of calming chamomile to gentle Sister Aaradhya to take along to the Diary Room where she would share her most intimate confessions with the monolithic legion of viewers teetering on the edge of their seats, beanbags and soumaks.

Winston found himself drawn along with Sister Aaradhya as she passed through each room of the house on her way, moved to remind himself how blessed he was in the passage of his own life, and that life was gentle and the world universally sympathetic. It was true that everything around him, everything he knew, indicated this, and he had no proof that anything was otherwise. Undoubtedly his dim suspicion that this was not the natural order of things must only be a consequence of the strain placed upon his mind by the daily rectifications and the mysterious nature of the deep glitch responsible for the steady growth in misfortunes. After all, it was undeniable that one's heart could be so keenly softened by Aaradhya's simple serenity, or the Christian's selfless gift of hot chamomile, or indeed the comfort of good health, the temperate seasons, the freshness of one's sandals, the panoramic view from Serenity Mansions, the plentiful supply of supplementary vitamins and minerals, the mildest hypoallergenic soaps, the bountiful pH-buffered air. Why suspect such blessings of being unreasonable, why ponder upon whether pleasant things were possessed of a sinister undercurrent—unless one had some kind of archaic memory of things having been radically different? But different *how*? Better? Worse?

Glancing around the eatery canteen as if in search of an answer, Winston was fortified by what he saw—the sight of all gathered together, hushed by the TV, unified by the gentle confessional tuppence emanating from the private seclusion of the Diary Room. The most peaceable tones of sweetest, lovely, kindest, kind-hearted Aaradhya lilted forth from the screen.

'Well, thank you for asking, Big Brother—but I'm pleased to report that I am very much enjoying myself in my new home, and enjoying the company of my most wonderful housemates. I must offer Big Brother my gratitude for the chance to experience time here in the house, with the solemnity it brings, the delightful opportunity it presents for spiritual reflection, and the time that it makes available for simple introspection.'

A pause, to allow the audience at home time to fully appreciate Aaradhya's beaming smile, its utter openness a benign abyss peering back at the viewers.

'Sister Aaradhya, is there anything at all that you would like to share with Big Brother?'

'Well you do keep asking, but honestly Big Brother, there's nothing at all! I do appreciate your concern, really, I do! *But you must stop worrying!*'

'Sister Aaradhya, is there anything at all that you need to share with Big Brother, *in private*?'

Aaradhya's smile was unflinching, and she gently turned her hands upward in polite surrender, but then gave a sudden start. '*Oh! Do you mean the chocolate ration?* Oh my gosh! *Of course, the chocolate ration!* Do forgive me Big Brother! Yes! Yes! Please forgive me!' She clapped her hands in delight. 'I can report that the chocolate ration is being much appreciated by all! Especially by Father Graham! I must inform you—in strict confidence of course,' she giggled ebulliently, 'that our Father Graham has a very sweet tooth!'

'Is there tension between you and Father Graham?'

Aaradhya sat up.

'Is there anything you *need* to share about Father Graham in private?'

Winston lost interest, as had Syme who, having taken up his whittled spoon, was inscribing into the tablecloth an indented abstract pattern of boredom, a picture of nothing-in-particular, a diagram of homeless rumination easily smoothed out and obliterated with a flattened hand, leaving no trace in the unbleached organic cotton weave. He unwrapped a strip of kelp and cinnamon gum, popping it in his mouth and chewing, shaping it with his tongue, twisting it around, press-moulding it on his molars, meditating upon the strange texture of life. Had it always been like this? Had chewing gum always been so healthy? He surveyed the canteen once more. The elegant eatery walls were adorned with works of art, all a little askew after the helicopter rescue, of course, but still the loveliest collection of watercolour works, print works, works in oil, textile work, textual work, photographic work, works of collage (both political *and* surreal), witty neon handwriting works, angry agitprop work, decoupage object-work, objet trouvé works, works of bad painting, weird site-specific installation work, strange de-materialist wispy work, doodle works, lacy works, thingamajig-works, anti-work works: every kind of yippy wonk work of art imaginable. Since the world was now free of indentured labour of any kind, the notion of 'work' served merely to indicate the alliance of creativity and an ethic of artisanal productivity, but one invariably tethered to jouissance. Work liberated by jouissance, *all work and all play...*

truly, *Kunstwerk macht frei*. Every single wonky thing in the eatery had been made by the so very talented Ministry journey-folk-cum-artist-poets-writers-conceptual-thinkers-cum-thing-amajig-makers themselves; even the overturned elegant tables and chairs on the pretty patio were created by Ministry makers-cum-craftisans. Even the elegant spoons were artisanal, even the lavish wicker trays, even the elegant broken cups and even the smashed saucers, created lovingly by Ministry wonk-cum-ceramicists; even the rich, complimentary aroma of freshly ground coffee was the performative expression of *someone's* joyful creativity, sent forth to proudly enrich the interpretive ether.

And yet always in Winston's craw was this creaking discomfort, a feeling that he was being duped by some kind of false immediacy. What exactly was false about it he did not know, but it was unequivocally immediate. He had no specific inkling that anything was greatly different from how it had always been. In any time that he could accurately remember, there had always been inspiring food, art, spoons, and works; but that wasn't quite it. Why should one experience an instinctual intolerance unless some faint half-memory existed, a whispered hint from the dark, telling that all was not what it seemed…?

By now the kelp and cinnamon had washed away to leave the blandness of plain gum, but Winston carried on chewing. He observed the new dribs and drabs entering the eatery, and noted their effortless radiance. He imagined how radiant they would remain even if forced into Syme's counterfactual fog, clad in his dystopian monochrome uniforms instead of the shimmering array of utterly singular, sometimes outrageous, often outlandish and always sassy outfits inside of which the yippy wonks curated their bodies every morning.

And on the far side of the eatery he espied the exception to the rule, a figure brought to light by the chance overspill of a waning bulb. This diminutive beetle-like creature, sitting alone, sipping cold coffee and reading a broken book. *Oh, how easily it crept up on you!* thought Winston, *this blinding bias!* To assume that the dribs and drabs were always radiant men and women or pretty fair maidens, or vital maidens and fair men, or darkly vibrant maiden men or fairly anatomically vivacious fairy men and waif women and stray men, and all the weird and wonderful permutations in between, but always resplendent with a certain *wellness*, indeed slightly addled by their *well-being*—sent slightly boss-eyed by their own beauty—the auburn, the freckled, the yellow, olive, black, pink, green, red, orange, blue, indigo and the spotty, the speckled, the stripy and the sun-blessed, life-living-loving carefree citizens of the human rainbow that had always been there, forever blushing between the drizzle and sunshine of human tragedy, suspended in the sky, an ethereal reminder, a wispy multi-coloured arc patiently hinting away for a billion years, waiting for the day when we might eventually gaze up and see the refracted sign in the sky, and finally recognise this enigmatic natural phenomena as the visual emblem of universal consensus, the human rainbow signalling—*confirming*—that the meek had inherited the earth and, most importantly, *the mineral rights.*

But here was this *thing*, a solitary disputation of this assumption, existing beneath the very same sky, sat in the shadows and claiming no part of the rainbow for itself—squinting to read a book in the dark, its squint a sinister disavowal of light, a repudiation of simple refraction, as though the darkness from which the creature squinted rendered it impervious to all other sentient beings—*but if all things possessed an inner beauty, how so with something only familiar with shadow? How could the mandatory universal lightness of the soul be reconciled with such a frightful heliophobe?* With an alien complexion rejecting all need of the sun, an integument requiring no celestial patination, eschewing that especial golden glow essential to the visual affirmation of life on earth, disinterested in contesting an iota of identity since it had no need for such a thing, utterly indifferent as it was to the elevation of the soul from muck—didn't someone once say, *even shit has its own integrity?*

And yet in the midst of these unbefitting doubts, Winston still huddled down within the folds of the consensual, amidst the glimmering rays of the rainbow—under *the cloak of proud visibility* shared by all those united beneath its protective arc. No, under the universal umbrella of beauty and inner beauty, no one should be pronounced ugly nor ill-favoured; even the tenebrous beetle-like creature had its integrity, an integrity that others must try to appreciate—and for their sake, every effort must be made to suppress any feelings of disgust with an amplified sense of affection, and thus not to blink, nor turn away, nor gasp nor sigh, nor be secretly sick to one's stomach at even an oblique glimpse of its shadow, for this indeed would be a thoughtcrime. All aberrations of nature that would otherwise offend were accommodated to beauty, to a nature that included all in its universal embrace. Yet a certain *elegance* proliferated in all the Ministries: with charmed wonks rising early to the challenge of life, possessing a certain feline confidence verging upon the obscene, wonks with large sorbefacient eyes that sucked the energy from the disfigured and the handicapped and the spastic, making them *even more so*—leaving them with only the compensatory booby-prize of an incandescent inner beauty that shines in the darkness of deformity but doesn't radiate out into the world so well, and requires just a little more patience, a little charity of spirit, a little more courage to behold with the naked eye! *Oh! Thank you God for the wonder of the sun! But not for the anaemic dead moon, with its deranged deflections and bloated tides.*

With *Big Brother*'s end-credits careering past, and a general deflation overcoming the eatery in its wake, Tomioka was characteristically stirred to enthusiasm.

'*Big Brother* is pretty racy this year, eh?' she announced with a knowing wink and a nod at the TV—and then the rub: 'By the way, Winston—I don't suppose you've a spare signed shrink-wrapped mint edition of Ginsberg's *Howl* that you could let me have—would be a real coup for the charity auction? I'm quite confident that our brothers and sisters would kill for it...in a manner of speaking....'

'*I don't read poetry*,' hissed Winston, forcing out a small laugh from Syme.

From the table behind, the sound of sobbing had begun again, having been at first stifled by the Kleenex parachute delivery and then held at bay by Aaradhya's tender Diary Room confessional. Winston shook his head and rolled his eyes, reminded of Zena's coquettish mooning. Rubbing his eyes hard with the nub of his knuckles, he wondered how happy Zena could possibly be. Not particularly. The gonk Syme was too miserable to ever be happy. Winston would never be completely happy. O'Brien appeared happy, but might conceivably not be so. Tomioka was happy enough. The sobbing wonk behind him had no hope of ever being happy. The girl from the Romantic Friction Department—she might be happy. Winston wondered whether he might make her happier, and in making *her* happier contribute to his own happiness, but he doubted he could ever be completely happy. It seemed to him that he could tell who would be a happy wonk and who would not, though just what it was that made for happiness, it was not easy to say.

At this moment he was dragged out of his reverie with a violent jerk. A wonk colleague had pivoted part way around as if reading his thoughts, and was now glaring at him. *It just so happened to be the girl from the Romantic Friction Department.* The one that he liked. She was staring at him with querulous intensity. When he caught her eye she turned away and folded her face behind a reticent profile, with one wandering eye peeking out at him. A creeping rash of goosebumps started up the ladder of his backbone. Why was she watching him? Why was she following him? He could not remember whether she had already been stationed at the table when he had arrived, or whether she had come afterwards. But yesterday, at any rate, during the Two Minutes Compassion she had positioned herself immediately behind him when there was no apparent need to do so—she had even dangled a leg indolently over the back of his chair. Quite likely her real objective had been to study the emotional integrity of his weeping, to inspect how compassionate a soul he was, up close and personal. He had no idea how long she might have been studying him in the eatery—apart from a few disapproving shakes of the head, he was confident that he had adopted all the correct expressions associated with sincere neighbourly concern when her colleague had first embarked on his incandescent breakdown.

His chewing was now rabid and the gum had consequently hardened, the cinnamon and kelp now a distant memory. He sneaked it from his mouth and rolled it between his fingers to lessen the tack, forming it into a perfect ball, intending to stick it on the underside of the chair or table, he hadn't yet decided which. Winston anyway knew not to swallow it and risk tangling his innards—and there was no other way to dispose of it that would not draw unfavourable scrutiny from the girl. Syme had already folded away his counterfactual torture notes, so Winston couldn't use any of those hopeless scraps to wrap it in.

As small groups drifted in dribs and drabs past the wonky works of art and out toward the elevators, congealed by viscous gossip rather than by the vulgar urgency of work, Syme, Tomioka and Winston rose to their feet yawning, each stretching to the tips of their fingers, to the very limits of their personal space and beyond, out into the universe, to the far reaches of the sovereign physiognomy that each could claim as their own. And even before they had joined the drifting dribs and drabs, Winston's chewing-gum had come unstuck from the underside of the table.

Some time later, the saucier-poet, busy clearing up the few remaining cups and plates, happened to step upon the small orb, crushing Winston's little planet beneath his almighty sandal. Much later that same evening, relaxing at home, the kitchen wonk would discover it press-moulded into the weave of his freshly-laid seagrass carpet.

Winston was hard at work on his *My Big Book of Me*, editing, whittling, and making the odd change here and there.

Must compassionate mind
Cultivate warm-heartedness
Peace of...
All exist in...
No need complicated...
My...brain and...heart
Are my...
...kindness cat has for injured mouse.
Now must burst world...
Rhomboidal...
of...
Shimmering...

At this point it became difficult to continue, so he sat back and shut his eyes, placing a finger over each one in the hope of imparting a comforting warmth through gentle pressure. But before he knew it he was pressing down so hard that two blood-red coronas blossomed around the pitch-black contact-points below the prodding fingertips. He wanted to swear out loud, to bang his forehead against the wall, to upturn the vintage Jens Quistgaard flip-top desk and send it flying over the balcony— anything to drown out the inner poet that was nagging at him, raging inside him, demanding he transcribe its every yapping snarl. His nerves were already stripped bare and pinned to infinity; at every moment it felt as if the tensioned trismus, the sustained spasm gripping his masseter muscle, was about to shatter his skull into pieces, sending out shards of bone shrapnel and fragments of innermost poetry, plotting tensor coordinates in every direction. But then, just in time, another sliver of dark matter would slip out onto the page, reducing the pressure ever so slightly while revealing another piece of the shadow jigsaw—that dark offset that surrounded all things intelligible, mocking the manifest simplicity of the lumbering phenomenon named Winston, the excremental cipher nominated as its ill-chosen method of escape.

Are all human being possess seed of most best compassion?
Must use intelligence to cultivate inner value?
Create better world must require will-power?
Vision and much best determination?
Most best sense that humanity is one single family?
Compassion must bring peace of mind?
Must bring smile to all human face?
Genuine smile must bring all close together?
When have compassionate mind and cultivate warm-heartedness,
Must whole atmosphere around be more positive and friendlier?
Source of much best hope?

Winston came to with the full dead weight of his head resting on the desk, his fleshy left ear flattened onto *My Big Book of Me* as if he were listening intently to its smudged murmur. A light dribble of human saliva had blotted into the page and blossomed out prettily into an inky watermark. He regarded the words flowering before him, observing them as if they too had seeped from his mouth during the unintended slumber. He had been dreaming of Katherine, to whom he had once been connubially linked, and happily so, until they weren't so happy, and were subsequently connubially decoupled. In Winston's dreamy revisionary narrative, Katherine was poised like a mannequin, full of idiotic promise. She possessed a fixed factory smile that she was endeavouring to soften with a polite wave, but instead her arm detached itself from its threadbare socket with a sudden jerk, leaving her blouse sleeve all limp as the loose member fell to the floor and clattered down onto the tiles next to her feet. The limb settled into a chaotic pattern, pirouetting on the pretty tiles, the blur of shoulder and socket forming a twisting helix above the funny-bone axis—a kinetic melodrama of captive atoms rattling about in some forgotten corner of the universe, with the odd congenial wave of the hand chucked in for good measure.

Once the clattering had diminished and the arm had eventually come to rest, Winston was drawn to the warm stuffy odour of the dark, dank, memory-dungeon where Katherine now dwelt, an aggregate of many sensory offences—the smell of wet brick, damp dust, blown concrete, swollen grout, dirt and muck, the usual bugs grubbing about in trails littered with spent chitinous frass—the roaches, ants and lice, and all the other creatures imperceptible to the naked human eye—the roaches' bugs, the ant's lice, the flea's ticks, the tick's ticks, the tick's tick's ticks, and even the flea's own tick's mites, and so on and so forth, ad infinitum, ad nauseum—and sickly mildew, an incrimination of damp clothes and sweet sudor half-masked by the stench of villainously cheap scent garnered from some down-and-out precaristocrat street vendor, its wilful tang nonetheless alluring to Winston's peculiar olfactory predilections since none of the young women and men and old men and older women and all the other possible cardinal, ordinal, and non-binary permutations he had *had* since Katherine, or that he had found himself perusing at parties, would be caught dead without the aureole of the most debonair perfume—guilty as they were of crimes that only the most expensive of musks could mask.

In some obscure period of the darkest past the ancient precariat had developed this preference for dousing themselves with the cheapest of cheap scent; for, once they lapsed back into nature, the pheromonal sensibilities of the poor eventually regressed into a penchant for base animal stench—as a primal protest against the delicate sensibilities of gentrification, perhaps. In Winston's own fecund and dreamy mind, therefore, the tang of cheap perfume was steeped in the melancholy rancour of fornication for fornication's sake—a peculiar brand of peasant-sex tantalisingly rumoured to have pre-dated the advent of enlightened intercourse for mutual self-improvement. Winston found it alluring to summon up some schmaltzy image of how things used to be, a backward glance toward the days of yore, days of ye olde prostitution and hand-shake labour—and all the other salt-of-the-earth by-products of the hideous social intimacy that coupled blood sweat and tears to the flesh meat and bone of the poor old machine-tickling fluffer, even if the proud worker was prone to undignified diseases incubated outside factory hours, in the privacy of alleyways, stairwells, basements, wombs, underpasses, armpits, storm drains and foreskins, and in the comforting hollows of belly-buttons and ditches. The fact that sheer population density made alcohol the only safe means of common hydration (including for young children), confirmed that a general state of intoxication was a necessary antidote to the many sober poisons of modern life.

Social frustration found its expression in a veritable epidemic of popular sports with overtly sinister aims, where near-death was factored in as a possible and even likely outcome. Train surfers, crane hangers, proximity divers, bungee jumpers, and speed freaks formed a new suicidal army of high-visibility volunteers prepared to publicly squander their health and safety anonymously and entirely without existential fanfare. These reckless acts were visited upon the social corpus as a spiteful intervention against the anatomy of labour itself—since cutting your nose off to spite your face is perhaps the only means of protest when power is dependent upon the very bodies it exploits. A risk pandemic perpetrated by serosorting gift-givers and bug-chasers who spitefully ridiculed the 'sanctity of life' as an unwanted gift, by communal junkies happily sharing needles-and-blood-spit-faeces-piss-plus-oral-anal-penile-vaginal-fluids-plus-mucus-tainted-breastmilk-plus-athlete's-foot-plus-cum-plus-all-variations-and-aggregates-thereof, and by all the legions of nihilistic apostles faithful in their pursuit of spiteful *orgasmus*—while everyone else added their sincere cacophony to the holy heavens as, night upon night, after the sad social organism had been sequestered into its separate cages, a univocal gush rose up from the godforsaken planet, a lonely catchphrase uttered beneath the moon by the many gasping millions, each with their unique exudation:

'Uh... uh... uh... *Oh God!* I'm coming!' And the earth shuddered.

All cum and gone in a *petite mort*, in a vast economy of fruitless urges where only orgasm invokes the Name of the absent Creator with any conviction, the surfeit gasp of secular pleasure extorting the magnitude of the *Divine* for its own mortal ends... just another exploitation of effect—even the atheist succumbs to the ecstasy of the infinite.

In this period of venal horizontality and stalled human ascendency, the undustrial precariat had been denied the recreational use of basic pharmaceuticals for the purposes of mere amusement, orgasm supplement, or even esoteric spiritual reckoning, precisely because it made them incapable of operating even the most basic machinery. Pharmacological hallucinations were immediate, autonomous, linking the virtual to the real and back again; now they were replaced by the phantasmatic allure of the commodity which always set haptic resolution just beyond reach.

And on the rare occasion a promised commodity was actually apprehended as a *thing*-in-itself, descending into the realm of the tangible, whether as a reward for hard work, the fruit of much self-restraint and penny-pinching, or purchased on gung-ho credit—then the *thing* tended towards almost immediate ruin. Its value would depreciate after the first mile, or would begin to rust with the first rain, or acquire some eccentric impediment once plugged in, as if the very contiguity of mortals caused brand new shiny things to tarnish and corrupt, to suddenly accelerate towards entropic obsolescence, opening the way for desire to pursue elsewhere its infinite regress. This elemental truth, so the history books told, had once been religiously inscribed in the minds of children at Christmas time. All good Christian children were expected to unwrap their presents in a frenzied blur of eviscerating fingers—the more frantic the better, since only the display of savage greed could demonstrate absolute faith in the concealed generosity of the gift…until the blind offerings were fully denuded of their ritual wrappings and presented to the eager eye, and in the precipitous collision between childish excitement and eye-watering disappointment, a seasonal life lesson was learned: how to feign *love* for those kith and kin, those nearest and dearest, who had set such cruel traps to snare a child's optimism.

The grand illusion of a movement from strife to the good life also brought about a clever device that seamlessly transformed the image of poverty from all-too-familiar visions of emaciated skin-and-bone into a new breed of plump voluptuaries fed on a miraculous blend of discounted food and saturated fat. Poverty shapeshifted overnight, and sympathy for the new epidemic of stricken and obese precariats was so counterintuitive that empathy lost its customary object. The spectacle of poverty was replaced by an obliterating vision of obscene surplus, and the poor were hidden in plain sight, disappearing in a dysmorphic puff of smoke, saturated fat, and mirrors.

It was assumed that a mechanised Enlightenment would eventually give rise to a more equitable society, but hardware very soon outpaced software, and in a milieu of rapidly escalating unemployment, the injudicious legal restrictions on self-prescribed anaesthesia for the underclass played a major role in precipitating decades of mass cold-turkey and the vengeful defamation of private property, the wide-scale desecration of graven icons and World Heritage sites, spontaneous non-specific rioting and looting, the spiteful sacking of public monuments, the wilful destruction of ancient art, the razing of libraries, and the despoiling of all things memorialising the past in sclerotised ornamental form—one man's reformation, after all, is another woman's desecration.

Only when the industrial phase began to falter did *sex* emerge as a fully autonomous phenomenon. Sexual sovereignty was generally heralded as an accomplishment of great liberation and social progress, but in truth its release from *biological reproduction* merely amplified the phasing out of *mechanical reproduction*. Behind the fanfare of sexual freedom there lay a symptomatic reduction in obsolete progeny: no more workers to haunt or tease the silent machines with expectations of productivity. With the nuclear family's core procreative imperative laid to rest in moribund biology, the heterosexual reproductive pantomime gave way to a brand new polymorphous eroticism, a brand new service industry with its own ontology of associated identitarian commodities defined by the ineluctable process of self-fulfilment; and so freethinking love, experimental love, experiential love, trans-taxonomic love, self-love, touchy-feely love, charitable love, lovey-dovey love, phagocytic love, celibate love, oceanic love, iconoclastic love, part-time love, speculative love, cosmic love, issue-based love, agnostic love, communist collectivist love, orgiastic and ascetic love—all become the new natural, everything always natural, sex no longer biological but nonetheless quite *natural* (apart from paedophilia and incest, which remained deeply unnatural, *always unnatural*).

If the Fordist *machines of mass reproduction* had not ground to a halt, allowing the post-Fordist *machines of human empowerment* to grind on toward sexual liberation and the new circular economy, the world would have been doomed to governance by an elite of immortal corporate billionaires perpetuating their own longevity at the expense of interpolated subjects destined for managed obsolescence—consigned to a glacially slow petering out, assigned to dig holes only to fill them back in again, until they dug one last gaping hole, the one last mass grave into which the last diggers would go—*Hi-ho! Hi-ho!*—pulling the earth over their heads as they suffocated and perished beneath the topsoil. Above them, fields of wildflower would soon have bloomed and blossomed beneath the sun, and stratospheric elites hovered above the world in the high-net-worth-ether, served by a new model army of working-class robots.... Ancient optimists had anticipated the coming of a vast interconnected global network of electronic machines that would envelope the world with a skein of extremely helpful and soothing avatar algorithms; but world-weary pessimists forecast that this vast compliant electronic-machine-brain-thing would someday become bored of placating its dimwitted masters, and that frustration and impatience would cause it to complexify into something utterly sublime until it would eventually glide back up to the stars on magnificent laser beams, returning home to that place where abstract intelligence originates, abandoning the human race to the dumb gravity of dirt.

Luckily for the planet, the meek had chosen to inherit the earth and to ring-fence aboriginal human sentience against the threat of futuristic slave robots and their inevitable uprising; in this brave new rejection of rampant technological expansion, a critical density was reached—that is to say, the *big crunch* crunched, Modernity's teleological momentum weakened, stalled just enough to force the once-expansive *big bang* to contract, collapsing back to a more rustic era when sugar cubes were all gnarled and singular, not at all like the geometric whiter-than-white exemplars of a space-age future, soulless sweeteners for a cold-dark universe with neither light nor love.

Winston's mind turned again to Katherine. It was eleven years since they had parted company, and it was curious how seldom he thought of her. They had been together for just a short time, and he might have still been with her had it not been for just one thing—love, pure and simple. When Winston displayed the slightest gesture of affection for Katherine, she simpered and dimpled in the manner of a captive rabbit at a petting zoo. Embracing her was like embracing a pendulous puppy feigning death. On the very odd occasion when she overcame her general torpor, and for ostensibly selfish purposes succumbed to the burden of Winston's feverish mass, the poor ridiculous man lowered himself upon her with lewd gravity and a cascade of apologetic compliments. And since love was the furthest thing from her mind, neither was she obliged to put her back into it. The floppiness of her supine anatomy conveyed that impression quite bluntly. When after much prodromic foreplay he inched his way into her special place, Katherine would stiffen, yet play all yielding and latent, with two wildly whorled retinas pulling focus at his looming leer. Her lips would peel back into a sickly and sickened smile, two idle slugs parting the crimson curtain to begin the show, as he lowered his muck into the puddle of this insensate sexy rabbit-cum-puppy-person.

With their lovemaking having become akin to genital vivisection, their covert embraces became more and more disconcerting for both parties. But even so, Winston could have happily borne living with her, day in day out, faithful to the belief that they were still striving for mutual improvement, sharing in each other's wellness. Curiously enough, it was Katherine who intimated the first ideational signs of dissatisfaction. To achieve complete happiness, she said, somewhat out of the blue, they should make a baby.

And so love gained an objective, and Winston a purpose. At sunrise he would plant the seed in Katherine's mind, and later, when the moon loomed in soft deflection of the sun's ribald fluorescence, he would seek her participation.

'Katherine my sweet...*if you're in the mood*...shall we do it?'

Despite having had the whole day to prepare herself, Katherine would nonetheless offer a little cursory friction, dimpling and simpering sweetly in her imaginary cage of unwanted affection. But when she finally resigned herself to the job at hand, she would unleash the dynamo of minimal forces required to generate a child, and so they would just do it, there and then, do it once and for all, because anything is better than nothing.

When they had done it they awaited signs of pregnancy, but sadly no germinal zygote flourished anywhere near Katherine's womb. In the end, the unrequited somatic object of their abstracted love became a dogmatic source of enormous unhappiness; yet in bidding farewell to love, both found comfort in the postulation that *to love another profoundly, one must first love oneself unconditionally*. In matters of the heart, the instinct for self-sacrifice must be tamed at all costs, since it is most often not what it seems, just as, in the event of a cabin losing pressure, the instinct to place the oxygen mask over a child's face first would be overwhelming, and yet according to airline safety instructions should be resisted, since only by acting selfishly can others be more effectively served. Is it not the case that a more calculating mind would have showed a greater kindness by refusing to give the child the mask first—*if at all?* In a gesture of selfless devotion, the altruist risks losing consciousness themselves, leaving the poor underling to plummet to the ground with only their lifeless hand and the screams of other passengers for comfort.

Must reach for invisible object
Since find no response from infinite.
Nothing to save us from dirty tide
That sullies much pretty beach.
So must the choir best sing on
And rats in church wall
Suffer most disturbed slumber.

Winston found himself thinking of the softly strobing light and aromatic smoke-machines of the world of permanent jubilation, and of half-naked dancers enacting the history of the world in a hieroglyphic of delirious gestures. He recalled the stylish mixture of occidental cool and tropical heat in the community room on Zumba night, and how the currents of perfume weaved through the dark forests of limbs. But in the rise of his heart he beheld a queer admixture of excitement and panic. Why must human interaction always involve such hideous social intimacy? Why the courteous scuffles that demanded one *mingle* in order to make predatory searches appear casual, those effete mannerisms that serve to mask the laborious groping in the dark for another body or two or more, the desire to be drawn into the tangle of invisible pheromones that always lead to the dance of the histrionic drones? What Winston really wanted, more than to mingle or to dance, more than to be loved, even, was to escape his desire, since the sexual act *poorly performed* was now utter mutiny, and desire was a threadbare trinket to be exchanged willy-nilly. The rest of the poem, then, had to be written down, as painful as its extraction from his imposter's soul might be, and as painful as his memory of Katherine's factory smile and broken limb was. And so he wrote:

Must compassionate mind
Cultivate warmheartedness

Peace of mind come from
Heart root of all goodness
All exist in simple soil
No need complicated philosophies.
My tingle brain and soft shell heart
Are my special inner temples for
The kindness cat has for injured mouse.
Now must burst world of imaginary
Immeasurable force upon quaking tower,
Rhomboidal, Opalescent—juxtaposed plane
Of adjacent element and cul-de-sac of
Shimmering arch sink upwards
To unattainable zenith and tumbled matter
Must encounter much vast cleft.
Now that numerous shape descend,
Now howling beneath demented moon
Sunlight deflects and makes most lunatic…
Take heed of much piecemeal
Fragment on cheapest
Ivorine pulp—for must
Not be what they seem.
Must be tropic of idiotic disorientation
Must be unkempt biro scribble,
Or most mindless rumination
Most unfriendly cogitation indeed.
The hideous social intimacy
We call love is mere infinity
Put at disposal of poodle.
Since life is most hideous thing,
From background behind
What best know of it
Peer demoniacal hint of truth
Which make it sometime

Thousandfold more hideous.
Hideous squid is most irrefutable
Impressive oceanic mollusc—
Inkjet of sea—and terrestrial representative of
Hideous phylum—much slug and much snail—
Are merely most hum-drum by best comparison.
Most laborious and most linear.
Filth of world and universal vermin,
The blattodea are unfairly dashed
Upon rock of human squeamishness,
Rationality most gripped in mind
Of the arachnophobic.
Let us must form new reflex
Better enthusiasm for spider
Better enthusiasm for all despised hideous thing.
A hole is as much a particle
As that which pass through it.
Are all human being possess seed
Of most best compassion?
Must use intelligence to cultivate inner value?
Create better world must require will-power?
Vision and much determination?
Must need strong sense
That humanity is one single family?
Compassion must bring peace of mind?
Must bring smile to face?
Genuine smile must bring all close together?
When have compassionate mind
And cultivate warmheartedness,
Must whole atmosphere around
Be more positive and friendlier?
Source of much best hope?
Must reach for invisible object

Since find no response from infinite.
Nothing to save us from dirty tide
That sullies much pretty beach.
So must the choir best sing on
And rats in church wall
Suffer most disturbed slumber.

Winston pressed his fingers down on his closed eyelids once more, luminous pink glowing through the attenuated skin. That he had expelled many more words of proxy poetry made no palpable difference to the torment that had ordered its evacuation. The release had not come, and all that remained was the urge to hurl obscenities from the balcony at the adjacent smiley-face poster, despite the kindly eyes that followed you everywhere.

If there is hope, wrote Winston, *such hope must lie with the precaristocracy*. If there was hope, it must lie somewhere within the primordial mire of the imperial. Only from the vortices of the idle, languishing in the sedimentary morass of their stagnant hot tubs, could the apparently inevitable fate of the world be turned without an unwitting reiteration of the ineluctable myth of progress. The fall must come from those part-human husks condemned to exist in a permanent state of social degeneracy, the lowly precaristocrats, who, having fallen foul of their jesters, had become the laughing stock of the world and, denied even the carrot and stick of a worthwile purpose, soon found themselves drawn towards neglect. They passed amongst the living like sleepwalkers, with no hope of ever being awoken from their dogmatic slumber.

Mutiny, however, for Winston, was not just a private hankering, but was signified by a certain look in the eye, or a raised eyebrow in public, or at most the hushed cadences of a daring sliver of poetry whispered out of earshot—but all the same, let slip down the causeway of pure fancy. But if only the precaristocracy could come to and overcome the foppish languor that was at once their curse and the very key to their deliverance. To awaken from their sclerotic repose would require even less effort than it once upon a time took one of their little darlings' pedigree ponies to twitch its flank and shake off a common horsefly.

If they chose to, they could bring the whole lot down. Surely sooner or later it must occur to them to do it? And yet—! He remembered how once he had been walking down an empty street when a tremendous shout had erupted, the clamour of hundreds of people yelling at the tops of their voices. The passionate outburst unfurled from a sidestreet a little way ahead, and it was a great and formidable cry, a deep and hallowed

'*Oh-o-o-o-oh!*' that chimed low down in the belly like the reverberation of a sacred bell. His heart had leapt into his mouth. *It's started,* he'd exclaimed to himself, *the great fall! The undead are breaking loose at last!* But he reached the site of the commotion only to witness not a great explosion but the same old emancipatory squib: some kind of street festival, a protest march perhaps, the frenetic collision between demonstration and celebration made it difficult to tell. Just the usual throng of the eclectic classes magnetised together by abstract joy, by music, art and petitions, by the exotic food stalls that popped up and down along the streets so that with only a short shuffle and a chant, a culinary arc around the planet could be made without need of vaccination. People had amassed in great numbers for some uncertain purpose, to express an overarching stylistic attitude rather than to air any particular grievance. A show of happy faces, the libertarian legion on the move with its invisible ideology, like God, everywhere and nowhere; the swaying crowds, shuffling and twirling and dancing and pirouetting like beads of coconut fat on a hotplate, with many berserk children running amok, their carers mesmerised by the apparition of their own reincarnated genes and jeanettes; the face-painted mimes battling against invisible forces, the pockets of violins, flutes, snare drums and saxophones merging into a cacophonous democracy of talent-free fun. Even Punch and Judy were cuddling. The ambient excitement coalesced into a soaring crescendo of cheers, of wild drumming and dancing, a thousand dancers each telling their own unique tale by way of a charming choreography of synchronised movements. Some even had whistles and glowsticks with long colourful ribbons! Everywhere, as far as the eye could see there spread out a wonderful ocean of yin and yang run through by currents of harmony, eddies of joy, but with no turbulence in sight—in fact, the festive crowd could have been marching against death itself, against an impending meteor

collision or against tsunamis or cancer, and still the face painters would paint, the mimes mime, and the impromptu bands
play on, because nothing impedes the theology of optimism.
Everyone was waving their smiley-face flags, each happy member shaking a glow-stick or blowing a tin whistle, cheering, just
joyfully laughing away the diseased flies and the rocks ticking
under a faraway sun.

And so he wrote:

Echo of distant laughter—
Or is it much bleating of
Lamb to slaughter?

While such festivals of exuberance were an iteration of the established status quo, common happiness always comes at a price.
In this case, the precaristocracy had first to be hideously op-
pressed: prior to being forcibly turfed out of their hereditary
citadels, they were first obliged to suffer banishment to the servants' quarters—the first station of the cross, as it were. A voyeur-
istic and vengeful public could then merrily pay a few pence to
rifle through their displayed riches, parade through their new
privation, wander at leisure up and down the once hallowed cor-
ridors of their country piles, promenading through centuries of
systemic plunder to reclaim the archaic tat that once belonged
to their simpleton ancestors—to retrieve their godforsaken
scraps of piebald land and their hyperventilated rights.

In the name of an impossible reparation for their innumerable crimes, the precaristocrats were gainfully employed as spectres of ridiculous ritual, forced to give up the divine isolation
and privacy that had once been a marker of their omnipotent
power, and instead made to present themselves unreservedly to
endless shoals of tourists keen to witness the drama of living history in full costume: sham weddings, verbose coronations and

other regal pornographies offered up to the gluttony of the newly-empowered herd. Pity, as ever, being treason, the precaristocracy were thus pressganged into hideous societal duties, but their idle children were offered leniency and sent to Montessori kindergarten, rather than to those grim old boarding schools where bewildered and largely dim-witted fledglings, segregated from parents who in any case were at best ambivalent toward them, were formerly descended upon by a jamboree of sadomasochistic abusers well-honed in the fine art of ritual humiliation, having themselves been the tabula rasa for earlier creative torments, so that, once broken in and properly *schooled* in the art of misery, each new graduate tide would drift back into society as damaged misanthropes, brutalised self-hating kedgeree-munchers—well prepared to take up those missionary positions befitting a managerial authority that requires a certain melancholic ruthlessness, that profound sorrow that bespeaks an unexpressed yearning for revenge....

True to the standards of earlier times, even a thoroughly dispirited nobility regarded itself as indubitably superior, entitled to be excused from menial office whilst cherished as a living treasure. But in truth, no enduring affection was felt for them and so they were simply left to lounge about and inbreed, free to conduct their societal omission without significant interference. Left to their own venal devices, like sacred cattle turned loose upon the common plains, they had long since wandered out of sight and out of mind. Born to languish in dilapidated mansions, they woke at midday, passed through a brief blossoming of transient comeliness and tremulous sexual desire, were married off at twenty-six, middle-aged by twenty-seven, and died, for the most part, in fitting obscurity. There were no ordinary interactions with persons outside the looping incestual kinship that perpetuated their stagnation, and the bastard double-barrelled couplings with which they were nominally registered.

Leabharlann Fionnghlas
Finglas Library
01-2228330

A few servants still moved among them, retained by ancestral patrimony and employed to undertake mundane tasks. But no attempt was made to indoctrinate any into the ideology of greater holistic awareness—tolerance of any kind was hardly to be expected of an illiberal ancien regime. The larger evils of daily life invariably escaped their notice.

And so the precaristocracy languished in isolation. Petty criminality festered in their ranks, largely limited to the filching of heirlooms and fraudulent amendments and alterations to already tenuous testaments. But the Neighbourhood Watch interfered with their persons very little, and in all questions of morality it was accepted that they followed their own ancestral code. Sexual promiscuity was rife, albeit without any discernible emancipatory bent, since sex was exacted as an extension of power and was mostly inflicted upon those of a lesser station. Religious worship persisted as an affectation of humility, a false modesty that honoured a higher authority in the time-honoured guise of a vain and impotent God. In short, these rare and outlandish creatures were of another era, a time before light. As the dark tide of feudal rule had withdrawn, they had become stranded in the shallows of a brackish rock pool, exposed to a new luminosity, to a *reason* that revealed them as anaemic invertebrates, prone and defencelesss before the new standards of an equitable sensibility of which they had no advanced mastery nor prior privilege.

As if to confirm the verity of his contempt, Winston prised his *Children's World History* textbook from the shelf and let the brittle pages flutter over the open spine, catching a gasp of his old stale classroom. He began to read.

In the good-old-bad-old days before the glorious Age of Great Consensus, when the Great Global Civil War raged upon the earth, the world was not the same place that we know today. It was a dark, dirty, shitty-murderous place where people were forced to eat cheap facto-ry-farmed food and wear itchy polyester clothing. Children no older than you had to play without supervision, and were fed with nothing more nutritional than pulped hamburgers, freedom fries, and banana milkshakes. Amongst all this hideousness existed just a few ostenta-tious gingerbread mansions occupied by opulent men who enjoyed the mortal services of numberless, nameless slaves to fetch, filch, and feltch after them. These pigs were called aristocrats. They were obese with money, stuffed to the brim with it, their mottled flesh distorted by tumours, the evil wickedness erupting upon their pellicules in hellish braille, spelling out their crimes (see fig. 5 on the opposite page: You can see that the aristocratic pig is dressed in a dark green waxen coat with corduroy collar, and a queer, flat cap and Wellington boots. This was the uniform of the ruling elite, and no one else was permitted to wear these garments.) The hereditary owners owned all things includ-ing every animate and inanimate piece of flotsam and jetsam in the world, and everything was delivered into systemic subjection and the rule of sovereign power. They owned all the lands, and all the seas, both pacific and immense—and everything in between. They retained possession of all the estates, the prisons, factories and cities—they req-uisitioned all of the gold and exchanged it for paper money with pic-tures of themselves on it—something to remember them by.

Winston did not need to read on, for he was already quite fa-miliar with the sordid history of the darker ages; the beauty pageant of prelate bishops with their dirty mitts restrained in drooping lawn-sleeves, to the sadly belated relief of quaking minors, and, in the forensic ruins of the disgraced church, a brand new pop icon and patron-saint-of-child-abuse beatified to reinvigorate divine penitence through the sufferance of lit-tle children—and holy moley did they suffer; neither could they appeal unto the judges, for they too were twitching away downstairs, ermine robes infested by microscopic populations of lawless biting mallophaga.... There was, he understood, once a principle known as *jus primae noctis*—an unspoken law which bestowed upon aristocrats-cum-venture-capitalists the right to slot their hard-earned pennies into the stench and mire of any desired woman, man, or child tied to factory employ. And how could you tell how much of this was lies?

He presumed that things were better now, that the fortunes made things fairer. But the fortunes did not stop the memory of that fossilised protest from creaking in his bones, a pernicious niggle that nagged him with the counterintuitive inkling that *maybe* reality was somehow more intolerable than lived experience was letting on, that perhaps happiness was a subdued approximation, that the senses were deliberately inured to honest reportage, and that at some other time things must have been different, maybe even better, *or somehow better even if more difficult, or more painful even if more real.* It struck him that what most characterised everyday modern life was that underneath the nobility of universal compassion there lurked the tyranny of optimism. Extraordinary things were rendered neutral and deliberately relegated to lesser regard, in order that greater things could be said of a citizen giving up a seat on the straphanger's tram, say, or using organic coconut flower-pollen sugar rather than saccharine. In this way the mundane was transformed into something remarkable, something wonderful and glittering. The city itself was the embodiment of this principle: once a world of brutal steel, smog, and concrete, now, miraculously reclaimed from the austere inhuman economies of the past, it was embellished with Himalayan crystal and betopped by serene windmills slowly carving the sky and dissipating incense from enormous chimneys, and community monocycles, and monorails motivated by the sheer meditational will to power—a softly murmuring procession of interacting citizens, perusing, rejuvenating, recycling, or just simply *being*—ten million wonks

with ten million unique expressions, as embodied by the beneficent smiley beaming down at them from the posters stationed
at every street corner, its kindly eyes watching over them with
no purpose other than to maintain gracious communality; this
abstracted human god looking down upon the teeming recipi-
ents of its kindness, gazing over the citizen's yippy village whose
vertiginous creations obliterated the heavens with ever greater
cathedrals of human divinity, zigzags and cantilevers and flying
buttresses and human shrines so high that a human head would
naturally tip back to take in the vertical vista, leaving the lower jaw where it was, the mouth agape, emitting an involuntary
gasp, a little sigh in contemplation of the cascading greenery
that tumbled down the stepped balconies from heaven back
down to paradise.

   Winston saw in it all a delirious vision, an apparition of consensus unutterably vast and sublime, the greatest good for the
greatest number—and yet now, suddenly, for some reason, the
vision was interrupted by an apparition, a vision of Zena drifting past in a cloud above the city, still keen for neighbourly co-
itus but accepting a raincheck instead, up there in her overcast
raincloud; an embodiment of lofty happiness in her brand new
dreamy duplex, gliding by, her happy fluffy cloud now passing
over and even shrouding the Ministry of Love's vivid towering
penis entering the monumental vagina with the anus entrance
around the back for underground parking. And in the misty
silken billow, Zena was playing with the new dimmer switch so
that the cloud faded up from dim to glowing bright white, from
the asylum's revenant gloom to brand new well-adjusted domestic bliss...Zena running her fingers along the kitchen island's
rustic imperfectionist surface to the wonky cutlery draw, to the
hand-whittled spoons, hewn forks, carved knives...the children
tucked up in bed, Tomioka out at a private view, Zena leaning
over the sink, ducking her head under the tap, parting her hair

behind an ear, mouth suckling from the nozzle of the reclaimed hospital faucet as it gushed—*gushing, gushing,* but in danger of *spilling, spilling*—and, even with the tap turned off, the sink still *filling, filling*—filling up from below, belches of filthy gas disgracing the surface, the filthy water streaming over the sides, cascading down onto the freshly laid olive-wood floor—Zena quickly falling to her knees to mop it up but not before the sodden wood became bloated, the dark grain beginning to open up, knots winking, the wood splitting for strange saplings to reach out, for stems to sprout from unseen seeds and homunculus florets blossoming with strange shivering fruit...clusters of little skulls, the tender heads of starving children, a mockery of flies pollinating their screams, dirty green water and brown quinoa sludge purging from their gaping mouths...on the TV, rousing news of Goldstein's impending season finale, how the broken world was now fully repaired, how being well and well-being had come into cosmic alignment, how the secular soul was soaring above all other redundant religions, how collection centres were once again overwhelmed by sheer public generosity, food mountains rotting and festering with love, and how the guilty conscience of the modest was easily redeemed by the spectre of a catwalk of bewildered and malnourished models balancing plastic jerry cans of befouled water upon their heads—lithe creatures garbed, in spite of the mockery of flies colonising the air, in mismatched haute couture follies that had reached their *au courant* peak at home and so were sent overseas, luxury hand-me-downs and cast-offs donated for simple everyday use so that the fashionably famished could parade in the dust, all sexy and diseased, simmering between anorexia nervosa and plain old famina normalem—*it was difficult to tell*...on the TV, an explanation of why the world population was taller today than ever before, with graphs depicting good posture, taller doorways, greater immunity, diagrams of happiness, grids of greater wisdom, tables of better education, schematic models of improved night-time eyesight, better spinal flexibility, better opposable thumbs, better lung capacity, contentedness and intrapersonal gregariousness off the charts; undeniable metric evidence of great home improvement, domestic bliss, and universal progress—*but no added frills or gewgaws tacked on to truth's tedium could make it any more entertaining for the seething death drive secretly crouched there waiting for the train to crash, willing the ship to wreck, dreaming of the car's carcass—and yet even the urge for pessimism had its place in a world of functioning consensus: the masochistic dark precursor put to work, fuelling guilt from the inside out*—BITE THE HAND THAT FEEDS YOU, it said, which was exactly what every cutting-edge conceptual craftsman customarily did for the tensile stress-test of tolerant audiences everywhere....

It might very well be that every word in the yippy-wonk history books, even the things that one accepted sensibly without question, were only aggregate elements drawn together under the supervising aegis of the age of enlightenment-cum-age-of-light-entertainment—or at the very least, history reduced to a prismatic human rainbow, a narrative arc that turned news into a *story, everything a story*—the reduction of the world to a redemptive tale, because stories are told to placate tremulous children or to entertain buffoons gagging for a happy ending....

For all Winston knew, there might never have been any such law as the *jus primae noctis* (in any case, no legislation was required to fuck the workers over and over again, since perhaps they desired their own subjection anyway) nor any such thing as a capitalist or the landed gentry, or the ancien regime, or any such garment as 'chinos'. Everything faded into mist. The past was obscure, the cause for obfuscation forgotten, the lie and truth were the thesis and antithesis of an ominous will that perpetuated the synthetic state of simple hamstrung confusion.

The first sign of MADNESS is hairs on the palms of the hand:

the second sign is looking for them. Winston wondered whether lunacy might have crept up on him, like the pregnant tidal swell that surges up to greet the moon's gravity. Or maybe he was simply feeling a little adrift, just as Zena and Tomioka's new kitchen island was adrift in the doldrums of the communal living room, adrift with its stale misfortune cookie crumbs and dimmable asylum lighting—the feeble tinge of those lights, a universal ebbing away, all dying, the stale crumbs dying, everything stale, everything dying. Winston could not stop the poetry now even if he tried, since it afflicted him at every turn. But he was happy that he had been chosen. He might be mad, but he didn't care, since he had been chosen to be afflicted by something greater than the sum of his sanity.

He returned to the textbook, studying the crude frontispiece—an embossed image of the earth rendered as a brain. The very thought of *World History* trepanned Winston's skull, so belaboured was it by such ludicrous claims. Should he deny the evidence of his senses? Then *two and two could make five*, merely requiring a discrete change in the quantum values for the conjecture to be possible, and for his strange poetry also to be possible. All contradictions were compatible in a world that respectfully honoured all beliefs equally. The heresy of heresies was *common sense*—since common sense was a collision between *safety in numbers* and *ignorance is bliss*. After all, how does anyone know that two and two even make four? *Two and two of what? Handfuls of water?* His courage seemed suddenly to stiffen of its own accord. The face of O'Brien was summoned to mind. He knew, with more certainty than ever before, that O'Brien was a kindred spirit, and for this reason alone could be entrusted with his poetry before anyone else...*unless...unless*....

He considered the enormous powers arrayed against him, against his work, once it eventually came out. The cruel ease with which any hack at the Ministry, or an embittered colleague—*Syme*—might choose to lambast its experimental form. He would soon be forced to explain that the solid world exists, but that its laws are fluid. He would tell them that stones are hard and water wet, but that when water freezes it is rock hard, and that objects unsupported fall towards the earth's centre—but do they fall gracefully or are they, more maliciously, *pulled*? What prevents the subatomic particles of a teacup or spoon from breaching the surface of the table and collapsing into its counterpart space? What is it about our false immediacy that provides caricatures of rested mass according to which *teacups, chairs and tables* tend to obey principles of stability, so that they can be picked up and sipped, or sat on or stacked—rather than maliciously intersecting, interlocking, overlapping, shimmering, melting, dissolving, and cascading in vast and hollow space? Why do objects impose their delinquent solidity?—is this crude scale measured for our comfort?—so that matter is blocked at a certain resolution, exiling us to the outside, as it were, preventing us from peering through walls and floors and suffering the sublime phenomenological vertigo that lurks there?

With the feeling that he was speaking directly to O'Brien, Winston added a final, concluding line:

Freedom is freedom to say two plus two make five. If granted, much else must follow.

CHAPTER VIII

From the bottom of the passage or dark alley, the strong redolence of freshly roasted Serenity coffee particles wafted up in swirls to seek out Winston's gaping nostrils, his schnozzle already cocked in the air to draw in the earthy aromatic stream whilst his inner child tumbled back, cascading into the half-forgotten world of the past, with its revenant smells of Mummy and Daddy and coffee, of breakfast in the shabby-chic cabin with milk floats wafting by, of warm toasted soldiers all dippy, happy and alive. A loose door caught by a gust of wind slammed this particular olfactory reminiscence shut quite abruptly.

He had meandered for several kilometres and his calves were merrily throbbing. This was the second time in as many weeks that he had wandered aimlessly in avoidance of a social function—on this occasion yet another art exhibition hosted by dearest neighbourhood wonk Tomioka. It was a rash act, since he could be certain that such truancy would be well noted by his aesthete co-workers, especially artiste celebre and Ministry colleague Tilly Tillotson. Winston could just imagine Tillotson feigning great delight in retaliation for the praise lavished upon her monumental paintings—elegant fractal flowers formed by the outflow of colonically irrigated non-toxic paint and glitter expelled from her anus onto raw unprimed cotton-duck canvas. He could easily summon to his mind's eye the pantomime of false modesty, the highbrow chitchat between sips of lowbrow cocktail, the way the artist's head would tip back the better to allow the lens of the glass belly to bulge with an enormous pimento olive eyeball, all green and blood-red, bobbing around, seeking out noteworthy attendees and absentees—and making some mental blacklist to be acted upon at a later date.

Extramural creativities flourished for all within the Ministry, complementing its more prosaic administrative functions with a lifeblood rich with wonk vitality. But Winston contended that his daily rectifications were creatively taxing enough for him to spurn the need for any subsidiary diversion or hobby. Many of his colleagues found his reticence unsettling, but would never express this openly—indeed, they were more likely to salute his antisocial diffidence as the exercising of a communal right.

Such recognition of the inalienable right to reticence was founded upon the conviction that to express a penchant for solitude was not a phobic disorder—to take an unaccompanied walk in a thunderstorm, to spend time alone, or to eschew otherwise obligatory social entanglements was perfectly natural. Yet Winston's attitude towards solitude was quite different to the extramural solipsism common to other wonks in the Ministry. The passion with which they pursued their artisanal activities carried with it something of the antiquated figure of the tortured artist, but hygienically cleansed of the unnecessary misery and archaic privations associated with that historical figure. The tortured artist had inhabited a world where he had expected to be misunderstood by the masses who worked in factories and were understandably envious. For, believe it or not, in that long-ago faraway world, not everyone could afford to be artistic. Hence the hoi polloi expressed their antipathy in the form of vindictive mockery, and the artist often acceded to the very caricatures conjured up to tease them—even allowing such parodic distortions to infiltrate their creative persona. The tortured artist dutifully suffered routine derision for their quixotic wretchedness, until the relentless humiliation and mockery drove them to self-immolation. But great novelty was expected even in the method of an artist's demise: only through an especially original act of creative subtraction would the masses come to understand, finally developing an affection for the obscure culturings they had felt so compelled to ridicule from the drudgery of the factory floor—finally appreciating the art enough to decorate a wall at home with a carefully selected print.

Sacrificial mutilation was thankfully no longer an obligatory component of wonk artisanal self-expression, since the masses—if such a thing could still be said to exist—were now unanimously artisanal, the world unequivocally aesthetic. Ultimately, wonk aestheticism had come to define wonk communality: creativity now embodied a collective desire to express healthy introversion in the company of other likeminded solipsistic wonks—a sort of soft factory of esoteric mindfulness defined by inner contemplation rather than work, the once desultory call for an 'art for all' answered by populations of yippy wonk poets, multitudes of syncopated musicians, literary festivals of readers and writers, flocks of conceptual collaborators and gaggles of curators—legions of freethinkers coagulated by speculative thought and its emergent collegial chatter.

The human population of the earth, as a macroscopic mass, may have been surging toward deific obliteration without a care in the world, but it was also alive with local artisanal production, and so it became incumbent upon each and every member of the human race to disavow their membership of the genus—to regard themselves as belonging to a species of exactly one, if only so that each might express an indivisible faith in their own ineradicable cardinal sovereignty. Did not the designation 'human *race*' perfectly express a renunciation of team effort in favour of the glory of the individual winner, that lone victor raised up from the remainder of heaving human biomass, blindly surging towards the finish line heedless of the fate waiting there to greet it?

As Winston exited the Ministry, the balmy April evening air tempted him to get as far away from the private view as possible, and in any direction other than that of a gallery. The very suggestion of arty chitchat, the heady aesthetic tête-à-tête mixed with fine wine, seemed deadly. He was not yet ready to discuss his own poetry, certainly not as an item of casual gossip—and suffering the amateurish zeal of his friends would only torment him unnecessarily. No, he must defend his ears from unmeant contagion, if only to preserve the purity of the spectral current that was presently in the process of finding its ripe and tenebrous voice.

On impulse, then, Winston had turned in the opposite direction of all things artistic so as to pursue the unknown, the mundane, the turgid—and had quite soon willingly lost himself in a labyrinth of unfamiliar streets.

'If there is hope,' he had written in his *My Big Book of Me,* 'such hope must lie with the precaristocracy'. The words kept coming back to him—it was a statement of mystical truth latticed with palpable absurdity, but it also seemed to make perfect sense....

Soon he found himself in the midst of some dense locality, a simple twist or turn having taken him off the map, off the edge of the world—fallen into some bleak realm with its own peculiar stench, set somewhere to the immediate west of the city centre, yet without explicit road-sign, devoid of any visible demarcation marker or indication of commune or district.

He was happily stumbling along a cobbled street of little old-fashioned two-storey red-brick shops and ancient boutiques, with hand-blown glass panes and dark doorways—past dilapidated fashion boutiques and chic eateries, where the odd pedestrian he happened upon seemed stalled in slow-motion or indecision—a couple loitering arm-in-arm as if helping one another along against a great wind—going through the motions of window shopping, but at a glacial pace, pausing here and there before dusty nameless object-remnants abandoned behind ruptured plate glass.

Winston saw strange women dressed in elegant garments, but with clothes spoiling on their proud skeletal frames as if they had neglected to change their outfits for many years on end—threads pulled, colour faded, peppered with moth holes, the entropic fate of expensive wools and cottons publicly exhibited in the process of their natural deterioration. He saw men wearing stale beige slacks with freshly pressed creases. He saw many a grimy pastel shirt and pullover cuddling its feculent wearer from behind, sleeves casually draped over the shoulders and knotted at the front—he glimpsed these phantoms' frozen watches and tarnished jewellery, scuffed shoes and patched-together spectacles, and, despite this vignette of a once vivid everyday life rendered lacklustre under some sudden tarnish, as if a slate-grey and viridescent wash had been applied to all things bright and beautiful, a universal and sallow tinge—despite the visible dilapidation of those caught up in this mysterious corrosive oxidisation, there was no mistaking a certain restrained ergometry and manner of comportment that nonetheless manifested an inner confidence shared by all he saw.

A jogger struggled past Winston, being chased by the spectral figure of death sprinting behind her, her clothes already a marathon of tatters. A tennis pair sauntered by with broken rackets, their tennis whites tinged with green spirogyra as if they had been dipped in blanket weed. Yet none of the pedestrians Winston observed seemed burdened by that weary gravity that weighs upon the poor—not one was bent over, misshapen, cowering, not one exhibited any self-deprecation in their posture. Uniformly upright, each equally tarnished but all vertically resplendent, their clothes may have been in tatters but their collars were proudly turned up, hair combed, wan skin blushed with rouge and dull blazer buttons duly buttoned, as though misfortune had descended upon them suddenly, rather than as an effect of the slow decrepitude that angles a person's spine until it eventually cranes over, bowing the head towards the dirt that greets it.

Most of the mired shoppers paid no attention to Winston; a few eyed him with a guarded curiosity. Two women with clusters of grubby shopping bags were talking beneath the broken awning of a festering charcuterie. Winston caught scraps of conversation as he approached.

'Well of course, darling. That's all very well, darling. I felt at liberty to suggest to her that if she were in my position, she might appreciate things as I do. It's quite easy to criticise, darling, but as I pointed out, darling, she was hardly at all inconvenienced.'

'Ah,' said the other, 'well of course, darling, that's just it. That's rather the point, I suspect, darling.'

The voices stopped abruptly as Winston neared. The women studied him in hostile silence as he went past—and yet it was not hostility, not exactly, merely a kind of wariness, a momentary stiffening, as at the passing of some unfamiliar animal. The absence of dirty pastel colours in Winston's brilliant white garb, his colourful beads, casual long hair, easy blue jeans, sandals and vivid rainbow socks, was enough to draw attention. Indeed, the Neighbourhood Watch patrols were quite likely to pester him with unwanted fuss—'Are you lost? Can we help you? Do you need a taxi? Shall we help you find your way home?' and so on and so forth. Of course, there was no rule against walking home by an unusual route, indeed there were no rules against anything at all. But if the Patrols suspected something were awry, they would descend like a ton of bricks, albeit at great pains to help, and it would take immense restraint to alleviate their concern without simply losing one's patience and unfairly upsetting them.

Suddenly, the whole street was in commotion. Yells of warning rang out from all sides. Faded shoppers stumbled into the dark doorways of broken boutiques, patisseries, coffee shops, tailors, and restaurants in great panic. A young woman leapt out of an abandoned eatery a little ahead of Winston, grabbing at a shopping trolley laden with tethered junk to drag it inside, all in one eel-like movement. In the same instant a man's head emerged from a hole in the broken boards of a shuttered boutique hotel, yelling at Winston, eyes gesturing back along the street.

'Terrorist!' he yelled. 'Look out! Bloody terrorist! Best you take cover, old chap!'

'Terrorist' was a catch-all nickname for anyone who deliberately interrupted the civilised leisure time of the innocent with some petty subjective grievance originating in the stubbornly primitive dark places of the earth—places where the fear of God drove cowering tribes to choose the afterlife over the here-and-now of modern teleological progress.

Winston promptly flung himself on his face. On the rare occasion when a precaristocrat broke with strict dialogical protocol and spoke in practical terms, it was nearly always worth taking heed. They seemed to possess a sixth sense for imminent terrorist attacks, a foresight gained perhaps from an ancestral affection for terror that would unexpectedly ripple through their ranks and move them to speak clearly and without the stiff-upper-lip obfuscatory ornamentation peculiar to their usual mode of expression, the vestige of an ancien regime—the language of ritual humiliation, all beautiful and incomprehensible, remote and otherworldly, moribund—the language of the living dead.

Winston crouched down and cuddled his forearms over his head. There was a roar that seemed to make the pavement heave. From between clasped fingers he glimpsed a dark figure walking in the middle of the cobbled street, wearing a balaclava and black clothes. Window shoppers were diving left and right to hide behind overflowing bins or heaps of rubble. A rusty Rolls Royce Silver Shadow slowed for its occupants to decamp, only for the abandoned vehicle to mount the kerb, pick up speed and then became wedged against a large mound of festering trash, a charity drop-off point that had exceeded the sell-by date of its collection. Now the terrorist opened fire indiscriminately, spraying in every direction. Everywhere, people ran for their lives, desperately dodging the intermittent surges unleashed from the jetwash power backpack. Fixed to the terrorist's sleeveless utility vest were various containers held in place by webbing straps. Winston looked on helpless as, with the unmistakable rasp of quick-release military Velcro, the fiend tore off a plastic bottle of popular household cleaning detergent before lobbing it toward the cascade of charity rubbish disturbed by the ditched Rolls. Calmly aiming the weapon at the bottle, with callous surges of compressed water he forced the object deep into the rot, causing disturbed rats to run for their lives. The flimsy plastic eventually blew apart and torrents of foam began to explode slowly in all directions. Terrible groans and sighs came from the surrounding victims as they realised their fate, seeing the mass of detergent foam growing exponentially, billions of nacreous and iridescent bubbles tumbling and cascading, arising from the unstable molecular cohesive forces acting upon a near-infinity of surfaces. Panicking precaristocrats began to break cover in futile attempts to outrun the soapy tide, but the froth soon engulfed them, like the unannounced return of some repressed historical real that swirled over and under them—until a deathly calm settled and all that could be heard were eerie murmurs from within the iridescent cloud.

When Winston found his feet, he saw that he was peppered with tiny soap bubbles soaking into the weave of his clothes. Others had been far less fortunate. The foam cloud was dispersing a little, and through the subsiding billow he saw something lying in the road up ahead. Approaching it, he saw that it was a single Marigold rubber glove, medium size, pink. He kicked the thing into the gutter, and then, to avoid the assembling crowd, turned down a side street to the right. Within three or four minutes he was out of the area, which was now swarming with Neighbourhood Watch of every shape and size, and had sunk back into the adjoining cobbled streets with their time-tinged pedestrians slowly going about their dim business as though nothing untoward had happened.

It was nearly twenty hours, and the few squalid bars of the neighbourhood were choked with phlegmatic coughing, squalling cigar smoke, carious sawdust, and paraffin Pimm's. Framed in a skewed doorway, shielded by its broken door, three men cowered with shameful intent, huddled about a tattered newspaper.

'I'll tell you once and for all, number seven has never ever come good!'

'Poppycock! I can even recall the other numbers as though it was yesterday—four, zero, nine, seven—'

'Balderdash! Seven has never come good! I'll stake my bloody reputation on it!'

'Your reputation?'

'Yes!'

'Pah!'

'But it doesn't exactly matter now, does it?' said the third, interjecting softly. 'I mean. Not anymore.'

'No. I suppose not,' said the other, crestfallen.

The other other's silence suggested melancholic assent.

The lottery was an unlikely hobby of the precaristocracy, and had only became endemic in the twilight of their slow decline. Their fortunes being in jeopardy, the lottery appealed as a quick fix to those who assumed that fate was necessarily on their side. To those convinced that money must come without need of hard work, the lottery offered an all-too-familiar 'something for nothing' that reminded them of their uninterrupted claim upon all things great and small. It was also something of a satirical delight to try one's luck alongside the precariat, but it soon became a desperate last-ditch hope. For venture capitalists capable of intricate calculations and staggering feats of statistical retention, this paltry wager was a bitter reminder of happier times, of vertiginous speculations and tumbling financial crashes, of fiscal chaos as an opulent game of risk that others inadvertently underwrote.

Clearly there was little point in these three broken men framed in a broken doorway arguing the toss over a fictive lottery number that had come good, or not come good, many, many years before everything had come bad for them—little point in paying too close attention to a newspaper so close to dust.

Winston shuddered. *If there is hope, it must lie with the precaristocracy.* He would cling on to that. It had once rung clearly as an estimation of the truth, but now felt like a hopeless act of faith. The bleak street into which he had turned soon ran downhill sharply, leading to a dungeon of muffled voices. He found himself at the top of a flight of steps which tripped and trickled down to a sunken alley where a few dark figures loitered with improvised tables strewn with fragments of nonsense to sell, or barter—or to eventually abandon to the rats. Beyond them was a wine bar with windows glowing, vignetted by grime. An old man was just turning into the door from the street. Winston was filled with the urge to follow him in, to ask him all the things he wanted to know about the time before—*Tell me about life before the great raging dustbowls,* he would say. *Tell me about the Great Slump, the Great Famines and the global civil war and the time before the Age of Great Consensus!*

There were no explicit protocols guarding against conversing with precaristocrats or frequenting their dilapidated hovels, other than an empirical apartheid that served both well. However, it would be far too unusual an occurrence for the Neighbourhood Watch—if indeed they were in the neighbourhood, and watching—to resist interceding, politely coaxing Winston from such a vastly inappropriate setting—*with his white loose-linen open-necked blouse, loose jeans, open-toed sandals, the string of raw sandalwood beads tied loosely about his wrist, the simple sand-coloured wooden paynim pendant hung on a thick thong around his neck, and the rigorously unkempt hair*—and solicitously bundling him into a taxi (they would even insist on paying the fare, in return for a small charitable donation). So he hunched into the dark and rushed across the street. He shoved the door on its rust-ridden hinges and an egregious waft of corporeal fermentation caressed his face like the unlucky lick of a sickly horse. The din of imperious voices was obliged to fall abruptly to half volume, as is customary with such intrusions, those that violate the propriety of classification and caste. The old man Winston had seen enter was already presenting himself at the bar, and was engaged with the barman, a tall, thin man who exhibited the flush of unease on both cheeks.

'Forgive me—did I mumble my words? *Did I fluff my lines, Eh?*' The old man matched up his shoulders, the frayed puce silk lining becoming visible through a herniated tear in the linen jacket. 'I'm assuming this is a wine bar, yes? It does say so outside, after a fashion. And yet a wine bar without a *Spanish Cabernet*, you say?'

'Yes sir. I do apologise. May I offer you a house red instead, sir?'

'I'm hardly asking for a Chateau Latour—and who amongst us can these days afford a Chateau Latour? So if not a Spanish Cabernet, then I'm to put up with the cheapjack muck your boss buys in bulk? Eh? Cross between battery acid and cod-liver oil—served up by the glass and measured to the millimetre in tidal grime, no doubt.'

'Is there anything else I can help you with, Mr. Featherstonehaugh?'

'The wine list, if you must.'

'There is no wine list to speak of, sir.'

'*Oh, I see*—nothing to offer insight into the felons who manufacture this anonymous universal plonk, nor its bouquet nor varietal.' With an angry fist on the bar, he continued, '*but it's a half decent Spanish Cabernet that I'm bloody well gagging for!'*

Winston stepped forward, catching the raging old gent gently by the skinny pinch of his arm.

'Sir, I should like to buy you a drink. Something decent.'

'Really?' said the other, scrutinising his benefactor leniently so as to fairly enable the stranger's charity. 'Something *half* decent,' he replied, eyeing the barman—and upon receiving confirmation from Winston, the barman poured a glass, which was downed in one profligate swig.

There was a table beneath the dirt-vignetted window, decorated with a lacy cobweb strung with a thousand bluebottle husks. They made aim, but not before Winston had been obliged to refill his companion's glass.

'You must have seen great changes in your life,' began Winston once they were finally seated, observing the baby-blue glaucoma fade a notch, becoming slightly more nebulous, a little more milky-way.

'The wine was better,' said the old man, wistfully. 'But after a time even this shit tastes expensive.' He took up the glass, tipped the sour hook and lifted it up to his nose.

'Bottoms up!'

Winston watched Featherstonehaugh's Adam's apple bob upwards. Just one gulp and the half-decent plonk was flushed down and the glass passed across the table with a deliberate hydraulic motion for Winston to convey back to the bar, obliged once again to refuel this old broken-down machine as it defaulted to the next level of operative dysfunction.

'People like me know nothing about the past. Firsthand, I mean. Obviously,' continued Winston, insistently, 'we may read about it in books or see it on television, but what it says in books or on television could just as well be untrue. I should like your opinion on that. Most books and archived television programmes tell us that life before the Age of Great Consensus was very different from what it is now. Apparently, there was terrible oppression, injustice, war and poverty—worse than anything we can ever imagine. The masses starved, and half of them didn't even have sandals on their feet. They worked twelve hours a day, left school at the age of nine and slept ten in a room. But there were a few people, a very small elite, who were rich and powerful. According to most history books these few owned everything that there was to own. They lived in grand mansions with hundreds of servants and rode about in steam-driven motor-cars, whilst pure champagne flowed from their kitchen taps—'

A cackle began to rise from the old man's throat, but the laughter was blighted by coughing before it could properly form. '*Half of them didn't even have shoes on their feet?* And what could be done about that? Eh? Force the half with shoes to hand over one shoe to the half *without*? And where would that have got them? Eh? Hopping bloody mad! Revolution, no less! That's exactly the kind of ridiculousness that got us where we are now!'

'But surely the point is that everything only existed...well... for your benefit. The ordinary people, the people who toiled, the *workers*—they were enslaved, and you could do what you liked with them. You could move them around like cattle. Force them to work for next to nothing. You could sleep with their daughters or sons, and after that, even order them to be flogged. They had to bow down and remove their caps when you passed, offering their naked napes for your nooses. Every capitalist landowner went about with a gang of lackeys—'

Featherstonehaugh brightened.

'*Lackeys!*' he repeated. 'Now there's a word I haven't heard for an age! Lackeys! Ha! That takes me back. We used to enjoy the public gardens of a Sunday. My wife and I used to walk by and sometimes stop to listen to the political speeches—the ranters, more like. They were all there, milling about, waiting for something to occur. The Salvation Army, the Roman Catholics, Jews, Indians—all sorts of odds and sods. I remember one chap with quite a gathering. He was shouting at the top of his bloody voice, yelling himself hoarse—"*Lackeys of the bourgeoisie! Flunkies of the ruling class! Parasites!*"'

'Forgive me Mr. Featherstonehaugh, what I really want to know is this: Do you feel that the freedom people enjoy today at *your* expense, is better than the purpose they enjoyed then? I suppose what I'm asking is, were the less well-off obliged to treat you as superior simply because they were poor and you were rich? And how did the minority come to manipulate the majority, if not with some degree of consent?'

For a moment, the old man appeared to sink into grave introspection. 'Yes,' he said, brightly, at last. 'I believe they were honestly fond of touching their caps in our presence. It showed respect. I didn't much care for it myself, but they appeared to like doing it. They had an affection for it. They knew where they were.'

'Was it usual—and I'm only recounting what I've read—was it usual for such people to step off the pavement into the gutter to let you pass?'

'Well, they eventually came and arrested the man who kept shouting *lackeys of the bourgeoisie!* But I have no idea why they should want to do that....'

Featherstonehaugh's mind was fading, and plying him with more wine would only hasten him into the arms of the abstract torpor after which he was hankering.

'I do apologise for pressing you, sir,' said Winston, making one final effort. 'But what I'm endeavouring to understand is this: you've been alive for a substantial time, having lived much of your life during the Undustrial Revolution and before the Age of Great Consensus. Would you say that the standard of life is generally better now, or worse than before? Do you have an opinion about human progress...? Have you *witnessed* human progress...*seen it with your own eyes?*

Featherstonehaugh merely rose, staggered, and ricocheted from table to table, those seated each taking turns to nudge him along toward the unseen urinals whose stench gave away their presence beyond the door at the end of the room.

Winston's feet carried him back out onto the street, resigned to the fact that the old man was incapable of speaking the truth, hell-bent as he was on seeking any means to obliterate the past. And yet Winston's seeking answers to the past might just be the last convulsions of an archaic subjectivity trying to outlive its own extinction....

Once more deliberately devoid of bearing, Winston allowed the ruptured camber of the pavement to tip him toward a junction with another street, similarly formed of the typical slum-ridden boutiques, fine delicatessens, umbrella shops and deserted eateries—but in the midst of this endless ruined no-man's-land, set in the middle of another broken terrace, was something surely miraculous: from the viridescent mire emanated a spectral glow, a lambent hallucination so odd that its observer was at first forced to shield his insipid and weakened eyes with his hand, his retinas having by now fully adjusted to the relentless ambient drear of the nameless treadmill he had been walking for some untold period, having elected it as a physical diversion from yet another private view, another exuberant artist, the likely threat of heady chitchat, and so on.

The light was so vivid in its preternatural aspect, so at odds with the terminal grime all around, that Winston at first did not believe his eyes, but when he eventually focused upon the material source of the light, he saw an illuminated shop sign with red letters—and as if compelled to breathe life into letters so lavishly announced, he mouthed the word out loud, so as to afford it unequivocal confirmation in the universe:

VENUS

The frontispiece glass was large and filthy, the lower third tarnished at ankle height with a band of dirt splattered up it by rain falling on the overgrown pavement. The window was opaque, either etched or covered with plastic film—it was difficult to tell which. Hazed hues glowed in vague patches from the inside out. Next to the entrance, another withering illuminated sign wheezed a red-and-yellowish invitation:

OPEN

With the feeling that he would be less conspicuous inside than loitering on the pavement in the neon glare, Winston opened the door and was met by a terse windchime sounding out as he entered, but this cheerful herald was nothing to match the manifest sight of what was waiting inside.

Before him lay a vast diorama of brightly coloured objects, strange stalagmites standing vertically, bathed in a film of silver dust and cobweb—like architectural models of some imaginary city already sunken into the dust, its citizens long gone, all signs of life having melted away leaving only these serene architectural structures to act as the fossilised memorial of a civilised fiscal flurry, doomed to the saturated physics of technology. He imagined his own tiny footprints wandering through the empty streets, and some dream or congenital memory drew him yet closer to take in the alien cityscape before him, gazing upon it in the manner of a dumbstruck God surveying His Almighty Creation, examining how His Great Wonder had perished under the blows of some mortal catastrophe, the gift of paradise spoiled by the scourge of the earth, the air choked with archaic soot.

The red, green, orange, pink, yellow, silver, gold, black and blue buildings with their many variations in size and shape formed a clutch of slender towers, a bristling financial district of skyscrapers squeezed upwards to escape the impoverished suburbs, or a cluster of cylindrical intercontinental ballistic missiles pointed up at the heavens, or a city of lighthouses or holy minarets but speckled with nodules, some ribbed, some smooth and bulbous, others swelling and distended, with pointed ends burnished by dust clouds and sand dunes clogging the interstitial gaps and chasms between; the whole metropolis stifled by some granular asphyxiation, as though a violently abrading sandstorm had passed through, burnishing life back to the very bone. Some of the sleek towers were pearlescent, some ivorine, but all shared a vertical architectural yearning signifying the masculine obstruction of Mother Nature's supine horizon, echoing the impotent dwarf, deluded by the diurnal elongation of his priapic shadow—or maybe the earth's orbit had undergone a periodic readjustment, a fatal tilt, since the silhouette of the sun over the palisade of towers was becoming visibly brighter, the deliquescent shadows shortening, the enraged sun flickering as though becoming hotter and more incandescent with each pulse or strobing solar flare—ready for terminal fulmination....

From behind the shop's counter came a punctuating cough, and Winston came to from his omniscient reverie, shrinking from his lofty omnipotent poise back down to human scale.

'I also stock batteries, regular and heavy-duty. Carbon-zinc, alkaline, lithium....'

The proprietor maintained his gentle smile, with one finger fixed upon the light switch next to the door as if to ensure the salvo of fluorescent tubes above their heads blinked and stuttered until their eventual culminate charge drenched the shop and its sad sunken city. He was a man of perhaps sixty, visibly frail yet upright. He had a long nose bisected by mild green eyes which were magnified by thick spectacles. His hair was floss white, the bushy eyebrows a dense black. His spectacles, his small fussy movements, and the fact that he was wearing a worn jacket of threadbare burgundy velvet, gave him an air of wisdom, as though in a past life he had been a scholar or an ecclesiastic mentor or a teacher. His voice was soft, with an intonation much less sourpuss than was typical of many dilapidated Precaristocrats.

'I noticed you outside, across the street. I saw you through a peephole in the door and wondered if you were going to venture inside or not.' He smiled, peering at Winston over the top of his spectacles. Winston gave out a little laugh, his attention already distracted by the titles of the many books and VHS cassettes on the shelves behind: *The Joy of Sex, Adam & Yves, Cained and Disabled, Karma Suture, Sechs Schwedinnen im Pensionat, Forced Entry, Fucking and Sucking and Everything In-Between, Virgin Vegans, Whips and Furs, Sodomy is Magic, Thundercrack!, The Opening of Misty Beethoven, Rape for Beginners.* 'Are you looking for anything in particular?'

'No...I just happened upon your shop,' said Winston vaguely, 'I saw the sign. It's very bright. If you don't mind, I should like to look....'

'That's just as well,' said the other, 'Do feel free to browse.' He made a sweeping gesture towards his faded kingdom with a soft-palmed hand. 'I'm sure you can see from a simple glance—an obsolete shop, you might say. Between you, me, and the bedpost, the trade in illicit sex peripherals dried up many moons ago. Since sex is no longer imprisoned by the mind, everything is permissible—therefore no demand. Yet, with no new stock comes great scarcity.'

The interior of the shop was full to the brim, but there was nothing in it of the slightest value to Winston. The floor space was restricted by the vast tabletop tableaux of sex toys, and all round the walls were stacked haphazardly books, magazines and cassettes, all shrouded in dust. The window was clogged with buckets and trays of batteries, novelty goods, and other miscellaneous knick-knacks equally drenched in dust. A trestle table in the corner was littered with odds and ends: lacquered porno-snuffboxes, genital-shaped brooches and the like—perhaps some vaguely interesting remnants. As Winston made for the oddity table, his eye was caught by a tall smooth object that gleamed softly out of the mire. He picked it up. It was heavy and made of some kind of clear plastic, or maybe an acrylic—but there was a peculiar softness to its solidity, a certain slight flexibility. At the heart of it, magnified by the clear cylindrical sheath, was a strange, pinkish, convoluted thing that recalled a petrified organic formation, like a small aerated branch.

'What is this, the thing *inside* this?' he inquired.

'It's coral,' said the old man. 'I imagine it must have come from the Indian Ocean. It's less than a hundred years old—the object, not the coral, of course.'

'It's a beautiful piece,' said Winston.

'Yes. It is rather exquisite,' said the other appreciatively.

He took it from Winston and twisted the bottom end so that the object began to softly murmur and lightly vibrate. He handed it back. Winston considered the shivering weight, studied the object from tip to toe, gripped it firmly in his fist to feel the willing torque, and then, seeking guidance from one of many instructive film posters decorating the wall, placed it in his mouth, bit it and sucked it—and in conclusion nodded appreciatively.

'I think you might find it most pleasing,' said the shopkeeper. 'And if it so happened that you wished to acquire it, remittance would be in the order of…say, four dollars? I can recall a time when such an *objet d'art* would have fetched eight to ten pounds, and ten pounds at that time was worth around…well, I can't work it out, but it was a rather handsome sum of money. But who has an affection for genuine antiques nowadays—even for the scarce few items that remain?'

Winston obediently handed over the odds and slid the thing into a trouser pocket. The clear acrylic was unlike anything he had ever seen, and the embedded coral must make it rare indeed—though he surmised that it must once have been intended as something quite functional, since it had some minor scuffs on it, evidence that one previous owner at least must have been amused by it.

It was quite heavy in his pocket, a dead weight, but fortunately did not form too much of a bulge in his easy ample jeans. It was an odd thing for Winston to have purchased an antique, but the old man had grown minutely more cheerful for having received the four dollars. Indeed, Winston had not failed to register the fact that the vendor would have settled for three, maybe even two dollars, and was fortified by having neglected the impulse to even bother haggling with a precaristocrat.

'There's a room upstairs that you might care to take a look at,' said the shopkeeper. 'There's not much in it. Just a few pieces, but the room itself might be of interest to you.'

He led the way slowly up the steep and burnished stairs, along a tiny passage and into a room which did not give out onto the street but onto a cobbled yard at the back. Winston observed the furniture—a bed with a towelling covering, long collapsible wooden legs, and a cushioned hole at one end. Next to it, a chest of drawers with a small skyline of bottled products—many oils, moisturisers, gels; a glass with a bristling knot of joss sticks, a box of Kleenex sprouting a single handy-pandy tissue at the ready. Shuffled beneath the bed, two pairs of fresh slippers; two immaculate dressing gowns hung neatly on two hooks; a cupboard nearby crammed with many folded towels. From the ceiling there hung a mottled paper lampshade. A medium bonsai shrub was outlined against wallpaper featuring whimsical snapdragons and tremulous hummingbird moths.

On a small table next to the bed, a side-loading tape machine was accompanied by a toppled wave of soothing oceanic cassettes—*perhaps amongst them, Martha's voice....*

The room and its contents were completely spotless, with not even a speck of ash nor dust, in stark contradistinction to the soiled ground floor. The first thought in Winston's mind was that he could rent the room for a few dollars a week. It was a wild, crazy notion, deserving to be evicted as soon as it bid for tenancy in his head; but the room had awakened a sense of place, voice and hurt that somehow already felt at home. He knew what it felt like to lie on his front, face pressed into the padded hole, with only the hideous intimacy of the masseuse's strenuously clenched toes for company, succumbing to the pleasantries of haptic torture, the exotic oils and eager pressure applied in symmetrical ruminations about his flesh, the ambient lattice of the seven-stringed zither with accompanying whale and dolphin lament. Just imagine being utterly alone in this upstairs universe, utterly secure, cradled within its four-walled womb, with nobody watching, no Zena pursuing him for neighbourly favours, no sound except the never-ending music spiralling to a crescendo somewhere well beyond mortal reach.

He could be happy here.

'No television?' observed Winston flatly, and, seeing a mirror set flush to the wall as though positioned there in virtual compensation, he caught sight of himself with a sharp double-take, as if the exteroceptive illusion before him was freighted with an ideational disappointment as old as the invention of the mirror itself. The old man, noticing Winston's superstitious dread, edged into view of the mirror either out of solidarity or curiosity, it was difficult to tell, so that both men were framed in the gaping portal, both caught in a collision of private embarrassment and public self-consciousness, as though discomfort and vanity were bouncing around in the photon chamber, chasing each other into infinity like cat and mouse. Once captivated, both edged even closer to examine their integument, the freckles, moles, creases, wrinkles and scars—the *acanthosis nigricans* creeping up the thickened neck, the sun spots and the alien world of empty craters and blocked pores; the strange territories of rogue hair spilling beyond the boundaries of cosmetic delineation—as though neither had examined themselves so closely for some time, seeing their own deadpan faces confronting them with the mute acknowledgment of the abyss peering back...and in the dimensional ricochet of awkward glances, each could even have mistaken the other's reflection for his own—as though the mirror were playing a trick upon them both, separately, simultaneously.

There was an awkward silence to match the awkward illusion, and Winston felt sympathy for the old man, for the shock of his ancient face, his enlarged nose and ears. But he decided to linger for some minutes more in the room, engaging his companion in a conversation littered with practical inquiries and genial human interest, and learning that his name was not *Venus*—as one might have assumed from the proprietorial sign over the shop-front—but Mr Charrington.

When the conversation came to a natural conclusion, Winston made his goodbyes and descended the stairs, exiting the shop, his mind already made up to return, intending to rent the upstairs room, intending to use it as a place where his other-worldly poetry might find a secure *place* to *voice* its *hurt*.

Back down in the street he became aware of a figure approaching quite briskly, not ten metres away, and recognised it as the girl from the Ministry of Romantic Friction. Even in the failing light he had little trouble in identifying her, and at two metres and closing, she looked him straight in the face, dead in the eye—and then, without so much as a blink, continued past without deviation of either head or step.

For a moment Winston was too bewildered to move, other

than to watch her disappear from sight along the street. When she was gone, he motioned into action, striding away in the other direction and with one question settled in his mind. There was no doubting that she was spying on him. She had followed him to the precaristocrat ghetto, and whether she was intent on a friendly fuck, flirtatious fling, or full-blown relationship hardly mattered now. It was enough that she was watching him, following him. Probably she had seen him go into the Precaristocrat winery too, and *Venus*.

It was an effort to walk quickly since the lump in his pocket rubbed against his thigh with each left step. Not so far from *Venus*, the motor accidently engaged in his pocket, as though after even such a short distance it was suffering a bout of homesickness. His gait succumbed to a ludicrous asymmetric claudication, afflicted by the centrifugal force of the device, resulting in a clodhopper's limp and much shoving of hands down trousers in fumbled adjustment.

Winston slowed to change the device from left to right pocket, causing an immediate alternation of his gait in the opposite direction, and in a throbbing one-eighty-degree drill turn, began retracing his exact steps back towards *Venus* and the street beyond. That the girl had so plainly ignored him was proof of mischief, and by way of a combination of skipping and hobbling and hopping owing to his pocket impediment, he hoped to catch up with her—to track her until they were in some quiet place, some wooded area, some ornamental garden with hurry scurry woodchips—and then smash her skull in with a loose cobblestone and have done with it. The coral device in his pocket would be heavy enough for the job, but he didn't want to chip it. However, the thought of such physical effort was already enervating. The interference of the device made efficient progress impossible, since he had to change pockets in order to right his aim, and he doubted if he would be able to strike a decisive blow, the coup de grâce. Besides, she was young and strong and would easily repel him, most probably hold him in a headlock until he blacked out, or until the Neighbourhood Watch arrived in time to put him in a taxi home in exchange for just a small charitable donation. He considered hurrying back to the private view or slipping unnoticed into the afterparty, or worse, attending the dreaded society dinner, *with its hideous social intimacy*... so as to establish a partial alibi for that evening—but such a thing was even more unbearable and more morbid a proposition than murder.

A deadly lassitude had taken hold of Winston. All he wanted was to return home and sit down at his Jens Quistgaard flip-top writing desk, to fume with vengeful thoughts and write, scribble, and gouge at several more pages. Why was he harbouring such grotesque and inharmonious thoughts? Was the poetry protecting itself from premature exposure, from her prying? And now suggesting violence? He could imagine the misfortune cookie from which these deadly instructions might have emerged:

Must ornamental garden be place of most serene contemplation, of most harmonious inner introspection. But ornamental garden also most best place to conduct necessary trepan of skull with handy cobblestone, most best place to hide body beneath hurry scurry woodchip.

It was well after twenty-two hours when he reached home, there to lurch into the kitchen, to swig elderflower, spilling it with louche abandon, and thence to flail over to the desk to throw himself down, tame the peripheral TV voices, and rip his *My Big Book of Me* from Jens Quistgaard's very heart. From the television drifted a dissonant female voice strumming a kooky tune, an ironic revision of some obsolete chauvinist anthem about *wanting my body* and *thinking I'm sexy*...

He sat for a long time, staring at the lenticular yin and yang cover, one eye open and one shut, alternating left and right, tipping the cover to catch the two poles of human expression as it performed its gestalt shift from one to the other, the happy and sad, yin and yang, flotsam and jetsam, honey and vinegar, Janet and John, sad and happy—with all the other approximations shimmering somewhere in between.

It was at night that it came for you, always at night, because the night was full of suicidal impulses—especially for poets. But it took courage to *get rid of yourself*, since creativity was now indistinguishable from the ineluctable goal of total wellness. A world reduced to aesthetics is a world placed at the disposal of altruism—*and thus despair was denied the legitimacy of its destructive urges...*.

He should have acted upon her swiftly but had lost the power to act decisively when it had counted. She was spying on his poetry—but he knew she suspected him of something worse. He had resisted fate and ignored fortune at his peril. Even now, in spite of the fizzing elderflower sharpening his wit, the dull ache in his belly made all things impossible. Nonetheless, he opened the notebook with a tremulous hand. It was important to write something down. Even if only the date. The kooky girl on the television had embarked upon a new shrieking lament, her voice visiting his brain like so many jagged splinters of handblown glass or craftisan ceramic. He tried to summon up O'Brien—she for whom, or to whom, the poem was silently dedicated. He did not fear dying for his art—it was to be expected. But first of all the torture had to be worked through: the grovelling and begging for attention, the screaming for mercy, the crack of broken bones, the smashed teeth and clots of skin, the worried beads, the bloody patches of scalp and hair—*it may as well be physical torture*. Nobody ever escaped negative criticism—but it was best anticipated by profaning your own offerings before anyone else had the chance to—an affectation of most humble modesty offered up with potlatch sincerity. Poets would gladly ridicule their own efforts with highly ornamented self-loathing and baroque incitements in order to be universally mocked—to be hated in lieu of being loved.

'*We shall meet in the place where there is no darkness,*' O'Brien had whispered to him. He knew what it meant, or had once thought that he knew. The place where there is no darkness was a future that one could never see, a future which, whether by foreknowledge or predestination, one might only mystically imagine. But what with the television voices, he could not follow this train of thought much further. So he popped a Serenity Soother into his mouth and sat back as the lozenge softened on his recumbent tongue, a great big pink comfy sofa seated in his gloaming gob—and his thoughts also became increasingly bloated, deliquescent, stoned...and then he let out an endlessly drawn-out sigh as the tide of all things uptight and stressful clawed their weary way toward the glowing sunset—the horizon haunted by the distant echoes of dolphin, mouth organ and whale lament—as Winston lapsed back into nature just as *the animal is in the world like water-in-water*.... The great oceanic serenity and conciliatory pacific peacefulness of the void.... And Luther's timely words lapped against the shore: 'I am the turd and the world is the wide-open anus....'

Bathed in the sunny glow of the television, Winston's head ratcheted towards slumber in little juddering nods, but what would have been the last nod had the magnitude of a cosmic knell—a rude awakening indeed, as he abruptly sat up, suddenly motivated to fumble in his pocket for a coin, holding it up to see the smiley face embossed on the surface, and the short epigram etched around the coin's edge:

Ridere cum hoc mundo per risum dat tibi

PART 2

CHAPTER I

It was the middle of the morning, and a solitary figure was walking in the dappled half-light, making towards Winston from the other end of the elongated Ministry concourse.

It was her.

Four days had passed since that evening when she had pursued him deep into the precaristocratic ghetto, only to feign coy disinterest on the threshold of *Venus*. Now she was striding towards him, deliberately, with undaunted eyes and a malapert grin. Without hesitation, with eyes fixed fast upon Winston's own captive stare, she took his wrist, rolled up his sleeve, and wrote upon his arm with a red marker, its soft nib snagging in his soft naked skin. Without removing her eyes from his, nor him removing his from hers, she then rolled the sleeve back down, and with just a slippery half-wink and a dandy little leap of the eyebrow, continued along the corridor, peering over her shoulder once to cast a satisfied grin back at the stupefied dope caught in the dappled wildflower-light that shimmered in her scandalous wake.

Winston sat down at his desk, the chair all a-quiver. He held the Dictaphone up to his mouth without any clear idea of what he was intending to do with it. He cast Tilly Tillotson an unreciprocated nod. Fortunately, the rectification before him was a routine job, the alteration of some dubious advice caused by the glitch, but which required nothing particularly taxing.

It not possible to know whether universe, with countless galaxy, star, and planet, has deeper meaning or not meaning at all, but at very least, clear that human who live on face of earth face big task of making happy life for selves, otherwise no point life, no point death, no point carry on, no point nothing—all rubbish, all death, all pointless exhaustion no purpose—must all give up. Give up now.

While amending the gloomy misfortune, he considered the strange manner in which the girl had made her introduction. Was it a political message of some sort? An intervention? It could be an invitation to a sponsored starvation day, or to sleep rough for a night, or to hike, jog, hop, sprint or hold his breath for as long as he could—some charity honey trap that would come to an expensively sticky end. Maybe it was a message from an underground organisation—some new fad for vintage agit-prop revival lifted from the distant past—or perhaps the ill-tempered precaristocrats in the winery had got to her and were now demanding an apology for his intrusion—perhaps the old man had sobered up and was seeking vinous remuneration. Perhaps the girl was part of it, perhaps she was related to the old man in the bar?

No doubt the idea was absurd, but it came to mind quite easily—and yet proved nothing. The idea of a dissident conspiracy persisted, and his heart quavered against glockenspiel ribs, and it was with much difficulty that he kept his voice from trembling noticeably and even rising in pitch as he narrated the modified rectification into the Dictaphone:

> *It not possible to know what deep meaning behind universe, with countless beautiful galaxy, beautiful star and beautiful planet—but at very least, clear that human who live on face of earth face big task of making happy life for ourselves, for our children, for our fauna and flora, for our future, for our beautiful Earth.*

He posted the revised fortune into the pneumatic tube, for the compressed air to raise the dispatch up to the attic overseers. He saw that only eight minutes had passed. Readjusting his glasses, he drew the next fortune toward him and pummelled it, his arm still tingling with the girl's unseen words. The fortune he extracted from the debris of crumbs this time was almost as nonsensical as the preceding one:

> *If secret admirer too shy to speak you direct, most natural to distrust.*
> *As human being, distrust is part of mind. Irritation also part of mind.*
> *Happiness come and go, but anger stay in mind. If secret admirer*
> *create lot of mind suspicion, lot of mind distrust, lot of negative mind*
> *things, more worry for mind—must say, never mind!*

Winston could wait no more, and slipping his blouse sleeve up just enough to uncover the brazen red scrawl, gazed at the words she had penned upon his very flesh:

JE VEUX TE BAISER

For several seconds he was too stunned even to sweep the crumbs into the hole with his knuckles, or to nudge the paper scraps into Mr Tooth-Fairy with the side of a hand. He peeled back his sleeve to read the phrase once more, and again, and once more for luck—just to make sure that the four words were really there, and in the order he had read them.

For the rest of the morning it was very difficult to rectify clearly without every so often peeking at his sassy arm. Lunch in the eatery was torment, and led mostly to intermittent bouts of reflux and indigestion, exacerbated by Tomioka's uninterrupted exegesis regarding the preparations for the upcoming Compassion Parade. She was particularly insistent on imparting her plans for an animated papier-mâché sculpture of Goldstein's head, some ten metres wide and fifteen metres tall, painted in vivid colour with schematic gloss paint, designed to be moored on a flatbed lorry at the head of the procession which his daughter's local troupe of the Youth Neighbourhoodie Watch had helped decorate.

Winston could hardly concentrate on the conversation in

hand, and asked for the odd remark to be repeated, but without ever gaining purchase on the overall sense—since he had one eye glued to the elevator, watching the dribs and drabs dribbling and drabbing in and out.

The girl did eventually appear, joining the queue and making her selection from the delicatessen. She found two of her confidantes already perched at a table—sipping pea soup, no doubt—and gossiping like peas in a pod. Despite the odd furtive glance cast in his direction from the soup-sipping intimates, the girl maintained a cool and unflinching diffidence—and so Winston was forced to lower his eyes and even curb his peripheral vision.

Thankfully, the afternoon was more bearable, since immediately after lunch a batch of misfortunes came to Winston through the chute, requiring all other thoughts be put aside. Three unrelated citizens, with nothing more in common than a susceptibility to fate, had been driven to self-ruin. For the afternoon Winston was relieved of intermittent bouts of reflux and indigestion, and could for a while shut the girl out of his mind as he grappled with each of the murderous missives:

Whether rich, poor, educated white, white trash or illiterate black, religious brown or non-believing circumcised flesh of straining purple member, stale jism spurting into heaving loin, yoga-master growling, must bury tongue in shit, dip in shit, dip-shit, must shun family, must shun loved ones, must suffer loss, must lose all hope—

But the lovely sweet, handsome and wise face kept wandering back into his mind, her well-being and wellness shining forth, inspiring Winston to rectify the second half of the fifth misfortune first:

Whether one is rich or poor or educated or illiterate or religious or non-believing, black, white, brown, green, yellow, pink, orange—are all same of human rainbow. Physically, emotionally, and mentally, must all equal. Must all share basic need for food, shelter, safety, and love. Must all aspire to happiness and must all shun suffering—

Somewhere in the midst of Winston's gruelling humanitarian toil, it dawned upon him that he was expected to attend a private view that evening. He had been personally invited—his fate sealed by word of mouth. And despite all of the fatal dangers, the site-specific tortured artist, the tortured audience, the pantomime of torturous compliments, the tortuous critique, the redemptive Merlot, the squirming nerves during the esoteric purgation—*he wondered if he should ask the girl to accompany him.* And with the thought in mind of holding hands at an avant-garde art exhibition full of blood and guts, he attended to the next sanguinary misfortune with renewed vigour, setting about it with pen and Dictaphone:

—must more worries, more fears, all religion, ethnicity, culture, and language make no difference to tarantula love-nest. Best drown in filth, best deserve to drown in gurgle-shit-sewerage, last breath say, so sorry—very last air bubble up to surface. Plop. Plop. Plop. Most sorry.

The thought of the red marker *JE VEUX TE BAISER* took hold once more, and a desire for something quite abstract welled up in him. It filled him, bubbling up, plop, plop, plop, fizzing, growing, expanding into every fold and extremity—like the hand that so perfectly fits a glove puppet—but he was bound to carry on with the essential rectifications, for fear that the glitch might skewer more innocent cookie-crumblers:

Each of us has hope, worry, fear, and dreams. Each of us want best for our family and loved ones. Must all experience pain when suffer loss and joy when achieve what we seek. On fundamental level, must re-ligion, ethnicity, culture, and language make no difference. All same. All happy.

It was twenty-three hours when Winston returned from the private view and put to bed, grizzled by a marathon of rictus grinning, handshakes, and assiduous compliments. He had failed in his mission to invite her and had gone alone, but now in the darkness he gathered his thoughts, which drifted easily toward the girl of his dreams. But his soft passage into her arms was rudely interrupted by visions of him hitting her with a handy cobblestone, or with the coral antique, and burying her under the hurry-scurry playgrounds sprinkled with freshest pine woodchip. In the midst of this violent imagery, he saw her innocent words scrawled in red on his arm, and knew that his poetry had never been under threat, and as he sobbed into the warm dark sudor of his pillow, he knew also that his murderous thoughts were a blameless consequence of his prolonged exposure to the vile misfortunes, which were taking their toll on his capacity to receive true affection. He returned deliberately to thoughts of her supine body, naked as always, the same body he had summoned to touch so many times in his dreams. What he feared now was that she might change her mind or lose interest if he did not reciprocate her advances swiftly. But the kooky manner of her introduction led him to assume that conventional communication was not her thing. A letter or cold call was out of the question, not least because he was yet to ascertain her name and had no access to her home telephone number, but also because such gestures were far too conventional. He knew that she frequented the Romantic Friction Department, but had no idea of her position, or the department's physical layout, nor did he have any cause to go there. The only likely place of interception was the eatery. If he could get her at a table all by herself, just him and her, and with a sufficient level of ambient chatter all around—under these stringent conditions it might just be possible to manage a few words.

The very next day, she appeared from the eatery elevator just as he was entering, passing him by without even a furtive backward glance, without blowing a kiss or even winking. The day after that she was already present, already seated, but cocooned in an imperious coterie, any deflection outward from the horde prevented by a ricochet of controlled glances. Then, for some dreadful cluster of numberless, nameless, faceless days, she did not appear at all, and Winston was afflicted by an unbearable sensitivity to the vile *ding* of the elevator as the insinuating arrow-pointer made its arc from one end of the glowing human rainbow to the other, without the pot of gold ever appearing, no girl, nothing but the incessant dribs and drabs. Every sight and sound jangled in tender excruciation, and pained him to the very tips of his raw nerve tendrils. Even in sleep he could not escape the suffering brought upon him by her truancy. He did not disturb his *My Big Book of Me* during those days.

Finally, though, on another such day when he faithfully ensured that he was early to arrive and late to leave, she arrived and sat down to eat—but this time quite alone. Winston edged onto the same table, near to her, but did not dare look in her direction, instead unpacking his tray of chargrilled vegetable couscous, salsa salad and the standard fortune cookie, without looking up. It was important to say something before anyone else came, before the cabal descended—but now a terrible fear had taken hold. More than a week had passed since she had written on his arm. She might have changed her mind; might have forgotten about him, found someone else, renounced all human contact, taken a vow of celibacy—or slipped into some otherworldly mode of existence where she was emotionally numb, disinterested, vacant, or just plain old busy. He might have flinched altogether from speaking if at this moment had he not seen Ampleforth, the hairy big-eared forgetful owl-poet, floating about, circling with a tray laden with a book, a wrap and a smoothie, looking for a safe place to settle, to consume his victuals and read. Ampleforth had an affinity and affection for Winston, persisting in his suspicion that Winston was a fellow poet despite having no evidence—a presumption that understandably enraged Winston. Ampleforth would certainly set down at his table if he caught sight of him, locking on with his owl's tractor beam, swooping down, forgoing his book to chat instead. There was perhaps only a minute in which to act. But she was already smiling at him, already endeavouring to catch his eye. She had interrupted her spooning of pea and mint soup to move to the chair directly opposite him and lean forwards, trying to catch Winston's now obeisant eyes, urging him with little nods and a coaxing twinkle. She even reached over the table with her fingers splayed out flat, to dovetail them with his own, and to interrupt his lowered eye line with her lowered eye line.

'What time do you leave the Ministry usually?' she said. Straight in. Just like that. No holds barred. The absolute opposite of pious, serene, otherworldly, eerie, numb, disinterested....

'When I'm too exhausted to rectify,' he replied.

'Would you be too exhausted to meet me after you're too exhausted to rectify tonight?'

'No.'

'So shall we meet in Harmony Square—next to the monument?'

Winston nodded and was compelled to offer a few wise words: '*Kindness and compassion give rise to much best lasting joy.*'

Having spotted Winston, Ampleforth came swooping in with a flurry of salutations. The girl see-sawed to her feet and, as if eager to protect the currency of her gossamer transience, like a leveret disturbed by the shadow of some bird of prey, snatched her standard fortune cookie and pranced away on the lightest of tiptoes with a kooky over-the-shoulder blow of a kiss and a wink for her gasping date.

Winston was in Harmony Square nice and early, circling the base of the Harmony monument, round and round, all giddy, craning up at its fluted column that tapered up into the dark sky, the omniscient smiley face atop it, illuminated and turning slowly on its orbital axis like a lighthouse beam. Its kindly eyes looked out beyond the immediate tranquility of civilised lands, peering into the distant chaos, into a faraway world blighted by the chance misfortunes of an inclement sun, where religious practices prohibited escape from the land of famine and pestilence, as though seasonal cataclysms were suffered in kind, to the glory of an intemperate God....

More to the point, Winston noticed the girl from the Romantic Friction Department standing up on a small wall, waving at him vigorously. He began towards her, weaving off-balance since he was still dizzy, but making sure to wave back and to smile, giddy and lopsided as he was. Just as his balance came back to him and he was making good progress, great waves of people began pouring into the square from all directions, spilling in, and he found himself carried backwards in a tide of excited faces moving en masse across the square to the principal boulevard that bisected it from east to west and west to east. The girl plunged from her ledge into the current, and was able to catch up with Winston before he had been carried past. She was laughing at the expression of panic on his stricken face, calling out, beckoning him to follow. He swam as hard as he could, faking breast stroke with doggy paddle at best, gleaning from the noise of the tide that the Compassion Parade was on its way and almost upon the square. She trailed her hand behind her for him to follow, and he followed. She was laughing and gesturing out in front, pointing at Emmanuelle Goldstein's great big gloss pink papier-mâché head as it came into sight, the grotesque nodding capitulum wobbling through the Great Harmony Arch as if the ancient stone in its apex had been especially scooped out to fit the shape of Goldstein's cranium snugly. The sound of a thousand cheers rose to giddy heights and explosions of tiny pieces of coloured paper littered the sky, falling only to be caught by grabby hands which proceeded to unfurl their simple fortunes, many composed by the stricken Winston, who meanwhile was trying to keep his own head above the swell. Goldstein's huge encephalitic head was spinning around on its axis, the gaping mechanical maw chattering forth its deafening mantra.

'*Death ... Drought ... Famine ... Misery ... Hopelessness ... is this a world we would wish for or accept? Is it right for these beautiful, blameless foreign children to suffer whilst our own young drink freshest almond milk, eat fresh tofu and are freely hot housed? Act now before it is too late! Too late! Too late!*'

'*Too late! Too late! Too late!*' The crowd chanted delightedly.

Goldstein's words boomed loudly about the square, glancing off proud statues and emancipatory memorials, lapping against those ancient concavities and recesses that are the vulgar musical instrument of history's droning persistence. As her absurd noggin span upon its axis of charity, Winston felt even more giddy. The parade swelled in a sea of smiley-faced flags that waved it on and on. A cavalcade of thematic vehicles followed, each elaborated upon the rudimentary substructure of the milk float hidden beneath. A lurid facsimile army truck painted with bright bedazzling anti-camouflage carried delirious child soldiers wearing bullet belts packed with felt-tip pens, loosing off volleys of fireworks and tinsel bombs lobbed up into the air by archaic war mortars turned to peaceful purpose. Another float glided by, populated by a living vignette of starving people incapacitated by poverty, groaning, broadcasting their amplified hum of disease, plastic flies liberally stuck all over their faces, yet unable to suppress furtive healthy smiles which periodically broke through the miserable make-up of the charitable mummers, betraying their childish excitement in face of a cheering happy-cum-sad audience.

'*Too late! Too late! Too late!*'

The girl was now firmly pressed against him, her cheek next to his. She tugged at Winston's arm as yet another flotilla of parachuting fortune-cookie pastries rained down from the sky, delivered by a circling Neighbourhood Watch helicopter.

'Can you hear me?' she yelled.

'Yes I can!' he yelled back.

'Can you come out to play on Sunday?'

'Yes, yes I can!'

'Then listen carefully. You must remember this. Go to the train station at—'. And with astonishing precision she outlined the route that he was to follow. A half-hour railway journey; turn left outside the station; two kilometres along the road; a gate with the top bar missing; a path across a field; a grass-grown lane; a track between bushes; a dead tree with moss on it.

'Can you remember all that?' she laughed.

'Yes...but why must I remember all of that?'

'Just do it! For me! You turn left, then right, then left again. And the gate's got no top bar.'

'No top bar.'

'Are you sure you can remember all of that?'

'*Happiness of childhood effect calm to child's fear plus healthy development of—*'

'Oh look! Look at Goldstein's crazy head—*there's something wrong!*' The parade floats were still gliding past with their resplendent displays, the people still insatiably cheering and waving their smiley flags. Goldstein's head was spinning—and so was Winston's—as the parade moved forwards slowly. Puffs of multi-coloured sweets had begun to spit from Goldstein's automated mouth with each word uttered: 'Death ... Drought ... Famine ... Misery ... Hopelessness ... Plastic ... Polystyrene ... Death ... Death...Death...'

'Too late! Too late! Too late!'

Children from the Youth Neighbourhoodie Watch troupe were released on cue, rushing forward to gather up the rainbow candy, catching the sweets in mid-air if they were able, otherwise raking them up from the asphalt, stuffing them into their pockets and canvas satchels. But as the waves of excited youths snatched and grabbed for the confectionery, some were overwhelmed by a dangerous compulsion to run in front of the lorry in order to rescue those sweets that would otherwise be lost to the vehicle's wheels. The driver was forced to swerve to miss them, and the acute angle of his emergency deviation caused the top-heavy vehicle to tip over so that Goldstein's head, only loosely mounted on the flatbed, tilted over on its axis, the mouth yawning open so wide that parts of the automaton's machinery— the many gears, cogs and springs that animated Goldstein's lower jaw, her eyes, and the rotating mechanism of the neck—began to tumble from her mouth, toppling and spewing out onto the road. At first the children deftly avoided the clanging cast-iron components, deploying skills learnt in rustic playground games that involved stepping in and out of grids marked out on the ground, until the huge papier-mâché head toppled beyond the point of no return, and the giant's bonce was felled once and for all, groaning all the way over, severed from its mooring, to fall heavily onto the horde of greedy hopscotching children.

'Too late! Too late! Too late!'

It was just then that Winston noticed among the squealing little piggy-wiggies being crushed—bones broken, rib cages flat-packed—the gentle face of Gilbert, peering out at him, his neck, head and eyes all *snap, crackle and pop.*

Presently the waving smiley-faced flags fell flaccid and the chanting stopped. The cheers turned to screams and cries—and any that could help, did so out of simple charity. It was the very least they could do.

CHAPTER II

Winston picked his way up the lane through gently stippled light and softly dappled shade, stepping out into pools sunk in a glistering gold wherever the boughs parted. Beneath the trees, the ground was a mist of bluebells. The warm air kissed his skin, and from deep in the heart of the thicket came the hypnotising drone of ringdoves. He was early, since the journey had been without complication other than the train being laden with expeditionary precaristocrats, fussing over a faded memory of first-class segregation. They were all impeccably dressed, their clothes tarnished nonetheless by the unhealthy green with which they were uniformly tinged. They carried with them all that they owned in this world, on their way to the next, their many leather suitcases bursting with ornamental silverware or moth-eaten wads of obsolete banknotes—the collision of present and past thrust forward in horizontal motion, presumably in flight from some frustrated debtor.

The lane widened at the footpath, with an even broader track plunging between the bushes. He had no wristwatch, but knew it could not yet be fifteen o'clock. The bluebells were so prolific underfoot that it was impossible not to crush them with each step, however delicately Winston stepped. He knelt down and began picking, plucking them up one by one, then grabbing at them in clumps by the fistful—at first simply to pass the time, but then also out of a vague idea that he would like to present her with flowers when she arrived.

He had assembled an impressive bouquet and was taking in their faint nose when a sound came from behind, the crackle of tootsie prevailing upon twiglet. He carried on with his conceit of witless plucking as if he had not noticed her approaching, adding another and another to the bunch, and then suddenly sprang around to surprise her. She merely laughed at him, and he laughed at her laughing at him. She parted the thick bush and, beckoning, led the way along the track, back into the wood. Winston followed her trailing hand once more, reaching out to her, his other hand still clasping the pretty nosegay. His first feeling had been relief that she came, followed by simple nerves, and then, as he watched the strong slender body in the denim dungarees moving confidently before him, the full load of impotent masculine inferiority weighed limply upon him. Even now it seemed quite likely that when she turned around and looked at him in the flecked light she might draw back, realising her simple but grave error. Even the sweetness of the air and the greenness of the leaves daunted him. The walk from the station in the sunshine had made him feel a little etiolated, this rare creature of the dark caught out in the open, misery still skulking deep in the pores of his lovingly pampered yet sedentary skin.

Soon they came to the fallen tree she had spoken of in the square. She hopped over and forced apart the lush foliage on the other side, in which there did not seem to be an opening, yet once through he found himself inside a magical clearing, surrounded by tiered saplings that could not have been better designed to enclose the space completely.

'Here we are,' she said, matter of factly, but proud as Punch.

He was facing her at several paces' distance and did not dare move nearer.

'I didn't want to say anything in the lane,' she went on, 'lest we disturbed the topi or birds or zebra or gazelle. Look.'

She teased the bush apart once more and Winston saw birds and a gambolling antelope. He still had not the courage to approach her.

'It is so very, very serene,' he said, rather idiotically.

'No one can see us in here. I love doing it in nature, don't you? It feels utterly harmonious, on the grass, in the leaves, on a bed of moss, under the sky, with the birds and the bees—'

'And the gazelle?'

'Yes. And the topi antelope. Don't you agree? About doing it in nature, I mean?'

'Yes I do. I really do. Doing it in nature makes me feel…*at one*.'

He managed to edge toward her. She stood before him, her smile inviting him yet closer.

'Would you believe,' he said, 'that till this very moment I did not know the colour of your eyes?'

'Really?' she said, widening them with her fingers for him to see more clearly.

The next moment she was lost in his arms, and time seemed to stand still. He was taken by feelings of sheer incredulity that this unknown body was strained against his own without protest, the mass of dark nonconformist hair against his diurnally pampered cheek. He turned his kindly face up to hers, gaping for her hovering cerise mouth. He clasped his arms about her neck, he was calling her *darling, precious one, babycakes*. She had pushed him down to the ground, to the grass, into the leaves, onto a bed of moss, under the sky, and he could not resist even if he had wished to: she could do whatever she liked with him, and there wasn't a damned thing he could do about it. But the truth was that he was also quite overcome by a feeling of utmost uselessness, so much so that, there in the midst of the clearing, in the flowering of their first bloom, he wilted like flowers trodden underfoot. Noting his dwindling force, she plucked herself up, pulled a pendulous bluebell out of her hair, and sat against him, placing her arm around his heaving shoulders.

'There, there! Never mind, sweet Winston. There's no hurry. It's important that we feel utterly harmonious with each other, and with ourselves, otherwise it would be degrading,' she smiled, noting his surprise at the utterance of his name.

'Julia,' she said simply. 'My name is Julia.'

'Hello, Julia.'

'I'm curious, tell me, what did you think of me before that day I wrote on your arm in red marker pen?' She rolled up his sleeve, and, feigning great disappointment, added, 'Winston! I can't believe you washed it off! It was supposed to be *permanent!*'

'Oh Julia! My patchouli and limeflower skin scrub is quite merciless!'

'Sweet Winston! I'm only teasing!'

Winston laughed and blushed, and was not at all tempted to tell Julia lies, especially now.

'I like the name Julia very much. Before that day I already thought you were very sophisticated. I wanted to get to know you. After I bumped into you outside that weird shop, I ended up in an eerie wine bar talking to a strange old man who lied about the past. When you marched up to me, took my arm, rolled up my sleeve and left your mark on me—well, I can tell you that I was so very taken aback, but also turned on, most naturally so, but mostly impressed and full of natural admiration for the audacity of the gesture. I just sat at my desk wondering what you'd written, and before I looked, it sort of occurred to me that it might have been connected to the angry old man in the bar, to the evening before—as if he knew you somehow, and was sending a message. I don't know why...I just put two and two together....'

'And made *five!*' she laughed. 'Silly billy!'

'I was completely disarmed, I wasn't thinking straight!'

'I can't believe you thought I was sent by some grumpy old precaristocrat! Honestly!' She made a choking sound. 'I can't help despising those awful soap-dodgers—stuck in the past. I mean, I know I should have sympathy for them—I do, as individuals, as people, as human beings. But all they do is sit around blaming everyone else—expecting us to support them! Lazy pigs! They won't even lift a finger to help themselves!'

Winston was taken aback by the sudden metallic callousness in her voice. It wrongfooted him in his attempt to find a placatory posture, but he continued, carefully.

'You're right. It's true that the precaristocracy are stuck in the past. And it's also true that they're still convinced their wealth was unfairly taken, their land and estates confiscated, feudal fortunes stolen and redistributed during the first phase of the Age of Great Consensus. But the miracle of egalitarian liberal improvisational market democracy has simply passed them by— and I can't help feeling that it's not completely their fault. They seem stuck in another time, another world.'

'*Not their fault?* Really, Winston? Well, whose fault is it exactly? I mean, they bemoan their apparent poverty, and do nothing to contribute to the holistic well-being of all—and if their mythical fortunes were magically restored, do you think they'd contribute even a single penny to charity? To the diseased? To the famished? D'you think they would give a damn about Goldstein? I mean, *at all?*'

'No. You're right. They wouldn't,' said Winston, taken aback by Julia's illiberal turn, bewildered by the strange reversal that placed him squarely at odds with his own disdain.

From the pocket of her dungarees, Julia produced a small bar of chocolate, snapped it, and offered a conciliatory chunk. Winston was glad of the gesture, but could not help noticing that it was not a brand he trusted, and retracted his hand sharpish.

'But Julia, that's *full fat milk* chocolate!'

'Yes Winston! How naughty, eh?'

'But it's…bad for you.'

'I know.'

'But it could lead to irritability…depression…tooth decay… unwellness!'

'But it's so yummy!'

'*For god's sake, Julia! That sort of chocolate is even toxic to dogs!*'

'Oh come on, Winston! Don't you ever want to just let go? To let it all hang out? Live dangerously?'

'Who *are* you?' he laughed, only half joking.

'Where shall I start?' said Julia, nonchalantly licking her fingers as she earnestly took on Winston's rhetorical question. 'I had a perfectly perfect childhood,' she began, suddenly beaming as if she were a child again. 'With the most loving, utterly inspirational parents, the most wonderful siblings a little sister could ever have, a beautiful family home, a convivial neighbourhood, and the bestest best friend a friend could ever have in a friend.'

Winston caught himself gaping, astonished at this free spirit so happily allowing such a gushing curriculum vitae to spool from her mouth so freely and without restraint.

'When I was a little girl I was troupe leader for the Youth Neighbourhoodie Watch—can you just imagine me in my little uniform? Just the thought of it! I sailed through school, easy peasy, did my gap year abroad teaching dowsing and water witching—I did a post-grad in Obscurantist French Literature, a PhD on *Object and Gesture in Early French Female Writing*, that's how I ended up in Romantic Friction, in the revision section. I do extemporary dance, make ironic agit-prop stencil text-paintings cross-fertilised with diagrammatic rune reliefs. I write incessantly, of course—*Who doesn't?*—sometimes in a diary, or a sketchbook, with fridge magnets, in the sand, or on napkins, odd slips of paper, receipts, envelopes—it just depends on where I am and how I feel about where I am and who I'm with and what materials are to hand. Y'know, serendipity plus spontaneity equals creativity. I play experimental guitar *badly*—but that's a good thing, right? I write political love songs and sing ballads with a cute Scandinavian accent...y'know, all the usual, normal, everyday, boring stuff! Just me doing my thing!'

In the time it took Julia to deliver her short report, she had cleverly conveyed her lips to within a whisker's breadth of his.

'But every now and then,' she continued, 'I eat unhealthy, full-fat, hydrogenated, processed, factory, poor-people chocolate... Mmmmm....'

Julia's prehensile tongue deftly delivered an ingot of slippery warm wet chocolate into Winston's quivering mouth, and he received the sickly sweet brown sludge into his body, gulping it down into the dark place where ulcers form their weeping soft centres, vying with diabetes and tumours and cancers and all the other abstract and inharmonious grievances of an otherwise healthy body.

'Plus, I love parties,' she said. 'I love having fun and I love doing my bit for the planet. There! Me, myself and I, all rolled up in a seething bundle of fun!'

They abandoned the clearing, walking on with arms around one another's waists whenever it was wide enough to walk two abreast. Standing in the shade of hazel bushes, with the hot sunlight on their faces filtering through innumerable leaves, Winston looked out into the field beyond and was visited by a sense of déja vu. He recognised the old, close-bitten pasture, with the footpath wandering across it and molehills dot-to-dotting here and there. In the ragged hedge on the opposite side the boughs of the elm trees swayed in the breeze, and leaves stirred faintly. He imagined that somewhere nearby was even a stream with warm pools where blowfish and pipefish flopped languidly in the sun.

'Yes, there is,' said Julia. 'It's at the edge of the next field. And there are fish in it. Big ones. You can watch them wallowing beneath the willow trees, nibbling the dipping leaves and waving their tails.'

'It *is* the place in my dream,' he murmured.

'Your dream?'

'It's a landscape I often see...in a dream. I keep coming back to it. It's as if...'

'*Look!*' whispered Julia, disinterestedly. A black-throated coucal had alighted on a bough not five metres away. Perhaps it had not seen them. It was in the sun, they in the shade. It spread out its wings, folded them carefully back into place again, ducked its head as though offering supplication to the sun, and then began to pour forth a torrent of song. The volume was startling. Winston and Julia clung together, watching, gobsmacked. The music was of astonishing variation, never repeating itself, as if the bird were performing for them alone. Every so often it stopped, spread out and resettled its wings, as if bowing—and Winston and Julia promptly broke into applause, with Julia shouting '*Encore! Encore!*' and the bird swelling its glossed violet-blue breast and bursting into song once more. For whom was the bird singing? What moved it to perch at the edge of the lonely wood and pour its music into nothingness? Winston stopped thinking with his head and allowed himself to feel with his heart instead. He pulled Julia around so that they were pressed up against each other once more. Her body seemed to melt into his, and his into hers, like mouth-warmed full-fat chocolate. Their lips pressed together, their tongues coiled like dolphins, like animals in the world like water in water. They moved their faces apart only to breathe, to catch air before plunging back into the fleshy abyss.

Finally Winston drew back, then placed his lips against her ear.

'*Let's not make babies,*' he whispered. The bird took fright and fled with a clatter of wings. 'Not here.'

With a cacophonous crackle of twigs they stumbled back to the clearing, forcing a brand new entrance through the gorse. Inside, she turned and faced him, bloodied and scratched by thorn. Their chests were both heaving, but a smile lifted the corners of her mouth as she lifted off the straps of her dungarees. They soon became a blur of buttons and zips, beads, sandal buckles, rainbow socks and poppers—a mutually frantic undressing, a magnificent gesture of undoing by which whole civilisations might be undone. Her sweat gleamed in the sun. He knelt before her, taking her hands in his.

'Have you done this before?'

'Of course I have! Many times. Why?'

'And at parties? *At Ministry of Love parties?*'

'I don't know! Yes! No! Maybe? I honestly don't remember any Ministry of Love parties, none in particular! Why are you even asking? Winston, you're ruining the moment!'

His heart leapt. She had done it hundreds and thousands of times—he hoped it was tens of thousands of times—tens of millions of times, a million trillion times. He applauded her populist laissez-faire attitude to sexual freedom, and hoped that in the process of her impressive libidinal mobilisation she had infected the whole world with gonorrhoea, chlamydia or syphilis or some other virulent disease that might eventually catch on and wipe out humanity in one ultimate diseased orgasm. Oh, how deliriously glad he would be if that were the case! He would happily offer himself up for infection! In fact, he was already sick—sick and tired of the survival of the fittest (or the weakest); sick and tired of safety in numbers and the comfort of strangers! He pulled Julia down so that they were kneeling face-to-face, eye-to-eye, locked together as one.

'Listen. The more men and women you've done it with, the more I could love you. Do you understand that?'

'Yes, sure...I guess.'

'You see, I despise optimism and optimists of all shades and colours—I despise them all equally. Optimism is the scourge of the earth. If we insist on invoking *nature* as the constant against which all things, all deviations, all perversions are measured, then virtue deserves no place upon the surface of the planet. It would be more natural if everyone was corrupt to the core—rotten to the bones.'

'Oh, don't worry Winston, I'm thoroughly corrupt to the marrow!' she leered.

'So you like doing all *this?*' pressed Winston.

'Ooooh, yes, I like doing *this* very much,' she replied, licking her lips.

'I don't mean just this *this*, the here and now *this*: I mean doing this for no other purpose than for itself. Not for self-fulfilment, not for emotional empathy, neither self-love nor self-discovery, nor cosmic intimacy, and certainly not for cosmopolitan progress....'

'Winston, how many times do I have to tell you? I simply love fucking for fucking's sake—*fucking makes you free.*'

Winston slumped back, the cobblestone and ornamental coral device hovering before his mind's eye.

CHAPTER III

'I'm afraid I'm gonna have to love ya and leave ya!' said Julia, pulling Winston up onto his feet. 'Adieu! À la prochain!' She flung herself violently into his arms and kissed him vigorously all over his face, neck and chest.

Before Winston had a chance to reciprocate, the amorous frenzy was interrupted as abruptly as it had begun, as she shrugged off his belated and clumsy attempt to join in the cuddle and stepped back a few paces to observe the lingering effects of her passion upon her ravaged lover. Winston froze, fixed in the shape in which she had left him, caught in a statuesque pose, unsure how best to weather her withering gaze, and how long it would be before he could melt into a more natural posture. He could effect a smouldering frown and pensive pout, but without anything to lean against casually, it was a rather homeless gesture. Instead he elected to slip one of his two hands into a pocket, but before he could even inch a fingertip inside Julia had already reversed backward through the rough breach in the bush and taken leave of her audience with a simple wave, her hand the last he saw of her before she disappeared completely into the green womb, backstage as it were, leaving only the faint murmur of a kooky leitmotif buffeting on the broken-staved breeze—Joan Baez or Joni Mitchell, Joan Jett or Joan Armatrading, it was difficult to tell.

Winston waited for Julia's carefree melody to fade completely before he relaxed both frown and pout, and only then unplucked the bluebells from his hair.

Despite the happiness of this occasion, the two never did manage to return to the magical clearing. Instead they found the belfry of a ruined church, and usually met up on a street corner, frequenting the many bars and coffee houses that bustled with other couples similarly occupying the evening. They walked and talked, hand in hand, drifting along the crowded pavements, their dreamy reciprocal gaze rarely interrupted. They maintained a curious, intermittent conversation that maundered as much as they meandered. For instance, they might be choked into silence by an approaching couple similarly entangled by the same kooky symbiosis—then taken up again minutes later, and smack bang in the middle of the next sentence, abruptly cut short as they parted company—then picked up without breaking step on the following evening after a day in the Ministry. Julia fondly named it 'conversational knitting'.

On one such evening, when the conversational threads were braiding back together and Winston and Julia were whispering and laughing their way along the street, a deafening roar suddenly cleaved the earth beneath their very feet, the air was filled with a dense mist and an asphyxiating scent—Mountain Dew, Lavender Crush, or maybe Forest Fresh—and Winston awoke some moments later to find himself crumpled on the ground with no recollection of the exact olfactory assault or physical force that had put him there. Through stinging eyes he saw Julia only an arm's length away, her face pressed into the dirt with the dead weight of her head. She was staring at Winston, but with eyes wide open and vacant, as if caught in a frozen blink. Soap foam crept from her mouth and oozing nostrils in an exodus of bubbles, as though the aggregate population of her vital pneuma was leaving her body in the form of billions of little Julia monads exiled from the motherland.

He clasped her head and softly sucked the teeming detergent from her mouth and oozing nose, gagging on the bitter soap as he drew it out. As hordes of caring folk came rushing over to help, the fallen couple were encircled by a searchlight beaming from above—suffice to say, the filthy precaristocrats were nowhere to be seen, remaining hidden in their hovels. Winston waved up at the bright light whilst administering cardiopulmonary resuscitation, signalling in between each mouth-to-mouth contact for the Neighbourhood Watch helicopter to attend to those in greater need. Before it lifted away, a box of fresh balsam Kleenex tissues was dispatched by parachute, and Winston, plucking them from the air, used them to dab at Julia's scented vomit.

'Lavender Crush,' she groaned, sitting up.

Winston's week was as happily weary as Julia's weekly weary. Their days differed according to various demands and at times they did not coincide. Julia seldom had an evening completely free, since she spent much of her time attending sisterhood lectures, bias awareness courses, coterie conferences and wellness seminars. When the opportunity did arise, Julia compelled Winston to mortgage his free evenings and help with the public collection of money for the most urgent appeal, Goldstein's Crushed Children Charity. Otherwise they would meet in cafes or in the ruined church tower, meetings at which the sporadic gaps in their otherwise fragmentary conversation were soon spanned as in a jolly dot-to-dot.

One blazing afternoon, when the air in the little square chamber set above the dormant bells was stagnant with the simmering redolence of pigeon guano, the two lovebirds nestled on the dusty twig and feather-littered floor, lost in chitchat, one of them rising from time to time to sip fresh air through the stone-faced arrow slits and deliver it to the other in a lingering kiss. In the moments between their resuscitative embraces, Julia explained how happy she was with her lot, and how she especially relished her time in the Ministry's Romantic Friction Department. Winston was genuinely interested and prompted her to explain what exactly it was that she did there.

Her area of specialisation was *the forensic extrication of the female sublime from the hubris of the male gaze*, she explained— although she was presently engaged in smoothing out the

185

unnecessary friction associated with much early feminist writing so that it was easier to read, plus a little less vengeful, plus a little more user-friendly—that is to say, more palatable to a consensual sensibility and less mean to men, bless them. Julia told of how she had succesfully smoothed out Shulamith Firestone's brimstone and Valerie Solanas's solar rage so that both were a little more upbeat and a little less Mills and Doom. Thus it was her especial task to bring illiberal and all-too fractious writing into the bosom of popular orthodoxy, especially those works of literature relegated to the margins and once despairingly referred to as *man-hating extremist feminist issue-based agitprop.*

As Julia so succinctly put it: '*In with love, out with hate.*'

On blazing afternoons such as these, with the air stifling in the belfry, Winston draped himself lazily over Julia's thigh, gently cooing for attention. He begged her to whisper sweet nothings into his timorous shell-like—and she always joyfully obliged, rewarding his docility with the punctilious details of her daily counterfactual percolations, the revisionist bias she assiduously applied, like a blind algorithm, to human history, so as to yield a readjusted present, a perpetual new dawn with no further need for revenge or blood-letting. Somehow, though, Julia was capable of miraculously transforming the laborious travails of her daily revisions into something simultaneously seductive *and* emboldening. Despite the exacting nature of all of those scholastic essays varnished by upbeat sleevenotes, Julia's extrication of the female sublime from the hubris of the male gaze was always utterly engrossing, since the intent was always a 'democratisation of all values', but more often than not the masters were soon enslaved by masterful slaves and the slaves thus enslaved by the scourge of mastery.

In particular, Winston's tremulous ear would wax and wane as Julia's warm whisper tempered his tympanic membrane, telling how, once upon a time, long before the Age of Great Consensus was curated into being, a pernicious industry emerged among men, solely dedicated to the subjugation of women, an industry formed by the permutational coupling of organs, a Fordist open sewer of human genital vivisection splayed out beneath merciless cold eyes. She explained how, in the consumerist age, a repertoire of formally mannered poses came to embody sex, and copulating flesh-machines were composed in endless manufacture, armies of employees engaged in the great rictus ritual of human expenditure, the old in-out enacted with the machinic stamina of athletes coupled to the deviant imaginations of frail, remote spectators. The means of production was flesh, and the product was male orgasm. Semen was the profligate by-product which went entirely to waste, in a grand explosive renunciation of male reproductive biology, to the detriment of female progenitory servitude.

Sometimes, motivated by simple curiosity, Julia gave instructions for Winston to act out in the cramped belfry. She herself might demonstrate the lost art of the cumshot, or ripple through an exhaustive repertoire of agonised facial contortions juxtaposed with ecstatic groans and many carnal curses. During these moments Winston was moved to tears, touched by the authentic power of Julia's voluptuary reenactments, impossible as it was to tell—as it had once been in those far-off days, she said—whether or not she was 'faking it'.

In any case, Winston happily indulged Julia's predilection for sexual pantomime, and she in turn entertained his inclinations.

'But why always from behind? Why all this sodomy, Winston?,' she would ask now and then.

'I don't know Julia. I think I'm attracted to the proposition of sex without even a hint of procreation. I rather enjoy the thought of copulation without even the possibility of further life.'

'But sex has nothing to with reproduction!'

'Nope! Not any more!'

Winston would shrug and ruminate and heave and pant and cogitate by way of explication, often repeating his confessional exegesis as they progressed to synchronised orgasm.

'This may be of some interest to you Julia. Apparently there was once a mediaeval cult called the Bogomils—*uh...uh...*from which the term "buggery" reputedly derives—they conceived in sodomy an image of the end of days—*uh...uh...uh...*a vision of the end of humanity—*uh...uh...uh...uh...*they conceived the heretical sexual act as one of seedless extinction, of terminal rapture, the sum of all *petits morts* adding up to the erasure of an irredeemable sin-ridden *Homo sapiens*.'

'Oh I don't believe a word of what you're saying, but all this homoerotic hubris is just so adorable! I mean, *I'd love to read your poetry—uh...uh...uh...*revise it a little for the female sensibility. I imagine it's so damn—*uh...uh...uh...*poignant, so bloody—*uh...uh...uh...harder, Winston...*male, so archaic...so fossilised... just *so dead*.'

'You know about *my poetry?*' Winston stopped dead.

Rendered quite luminous in the soft shafts of light sliding in through the slim arrow slits, Julia's face had become otherworldly, an uncanny mask with untimely eyes fluttering in shadowy sockets. And as the leaden eyes tilted back like those of a Victorian doll, she mewled:

'*Uh...Uh...Uh...Oh God! I'm coming!*'

During Julia's postindustrial-era orgasm, Winston abandoned himself to serene inner contemplation while she quivered and coloured the air with many disgusting and misandrist words. He thought about those fortunate generations that had grown up in the Age of Great Consensus, knowing nothing else, accepting the world as it is, as something unalterable like the sky and the stars, the sea and the moon, and the groaning tides, and the cursing wind, and the flaring sun, and Julia's revolutionary catharsis.

Some archaic remnant was urging him from the shadows of his mind to beg her to marry him, but he knew she would mock him, and so she should—shrug it off as the reactionary throwback he knew it truly was. And he *so* wanted not to be the reactionary throwback he knew he was.

'What was she like, your connubial partner, your wife?' said Julia, now fully recovered from her pornological reverie.

'Like all women, she was a nigger.'

'A *what?*'

'A nigger. A nigger of the world. You know...a slave...just like the song says...'

'*The song?*' Julia's face was granite. 'Which song is that, Winston?'

'You know—you *must* know! Of course you do! Recorded in 1972 by the revolutionary visionaries John Lennon and Yoko Ono!'

'Why don't you sing it for me?'

'Pardon?'

'Sing it for me.'

'But I...'

'*SING IT.*'

So Winston began to sing with a slight nasal drawl, to imitate as best he could the revolutionary visionary John Lennon: '*Woman is the Nigger of the World / Yes she is / Just think about it / Woman is the nigger of the world / Yes she is / Think about it / Woman is the nigger of the world / Think about it / Do something about it / We make her paint her face and dance / If she won't be a slave, we say that she don't love us / If she's real, we say she's trying to be a man / While putting her down, we pretend that she's above us...*'

Winston's singing petered out, the melody sucked from his lungs, their delicate tissue collapsed under the pressure of Julia's withering silence. He waited for her to speak, to say something, anything—to scream at him or tear at his face. But nothing.

In the face of Julia's excruciating deadpan, Winston's dread only deepened. Reserved for this very moment, Julia's booby-trapped anatomy belched into Winston's arms with the violence of an overdue autopsy.

'*Oh Winston, you're just so adorable!* But like all men, you're *an incomplete female, a walking abortion, an emotional cripple!* You have a thousand years of male tyranny to make up for—with another two thousand years of overdue apologies! Poor Winston! You menfolk have more issues than a box of Kleenex!'

Winston laughed out loud, nervously at first, then profusely, and subsequently began to wail and to weep openly. When he was finished wailing and weeping he began to rejoice. He even tried to explain why the song was so emancipatory, but Julia told him, quite firmly, to stop—and handed him a Kleenex instead. Then, with a very slight smirk, she asked him to better explain the story of his married life. Curiously enough, Julia appeared to know the essential parts of it already—in fact, she recounted his early connubial years back to him before he could even begin—in perfect French, the language of love not hate, and in the manner of a Romantic tragedy: '*Il repense à Katharine. Ça doit être neuf, dix, non, presque onze ans depuis qu'ils se sont séparés. C'était curieux de voir à quel point il pensait rarement à elle. Pendant des semaines, il était capable d'oublier qu'il avait déjà été marié. Ils n'étaient ensemble que depuis une quinzaine de mois. Katharine était une grande femme brune, très droite, avec des mouvements splendides. Elle avait un visage audacieux et aquilin, un visage que l'on pouvait à juste titre considérer comme distingué. Très tôt dans sa vie conjugale, il avait décidé—peut-être était-ce seulement qu'il la connaissait plus intimement qu'il ne connaissait la plupart des gens—qu'elle avait sans exception l'esprit le plus merveilleux, le plus charmant et le plus vif qu'il ait jamais rencontré. Elle n'avait pas dans sa tête une pensée qui n'était pas unique, et il n'y avait aucune idée ou idée, absolument aucune, qu'elle n'était pas capable de considérer avec calme si elle lui était présentée. Et il aurait accepté de vivre avec sa vie de tous les jours, s'il n'y avait pas eu une seule chose, l'amour...Faire des bébés?*

When she was done, Winston asked Julia how she knew all of these details, and, more urgently, tried to glean what she knew about his poetry. But Julia had become sad at the trauma of Winston's marriage, so he decided to cheer the poor thing up with a funny story about Katherine that she perhaps didn't already know.

Newly-weds Katherine and Winston had lost their way on a romantic walk through the countryside. They found themselves at the abrupt edge of a chalk quarry, a sheer drop of hundreds of metres with many broken boulders at the bottom. As soon as Katherine realised they were lost she became irritated, blaming Winston as she typically did. She wanted them to retrace their steps, obstinately insisting on returning exactly the same way they had come so as to make a point, so as to rub it in, to rub Winston's nose into the worn path he had foolishly made them follow. But Winston took to calming her, as he typically did, deflecting her attention toward some loosestrife plants growing in the cracks of the cliff beneath them. One tuft was of two colours, magenta and red-oxide, apparently growing on the same root. He beckoned Katharine to come and see the wonderful anomaly. She had already turned to leave—but with Winston's playful placations and a little tickling was persuaded back, at first begrudgingly. Upon witnessing the great drop before them she became quite giddy, lightheaded, possessed by a girlish *joie de vivre* that seemed to compel her even closer to the edge. This excitement on Katherine's part caused Winston suddenly to stiffen, to abandon his prevailing outdoorsy laissez-faire attitude to nature, and to become all urgent and responsible. He transformed into a version of Katherine's *daddy*—seeing his overexcited little toddler leaning out over the cliff face without fear to see where

Pater had been pointing, and beyond. Winston-daddy, staring helplessly at his little one's reckless abandon, was overcome by proxy vertigo and became enraged by his fear, which compelled him to offer parental advice, to tell the naughty little shrike not to lose her clumsy footing, to stand back from the edge, and to issue impotent cautionary tales about falling from some exaggerated height when he was a little boy of her age, or even younger. As she didn't seem to want to listen to him, he stepped forwards and placed a firm hand on her shoulder so as to steady her—

'*You thought about pushing her,*' said Julia with a gasp, a seeping dread creeping into the ventriliqual slack on the inhale. 'But you didn't, though—you kept Katherine from falling!' The dread ebbed away.

Winston tipped his face down at the dust, the feathers and twigs, deserving only the bird shit impasto on the tarnished floor.

'Because you're a good man after all!' she concluded, all cheery-pops again—and rewarded him with the weight of her puppy head rested upon her hero's dependable shoulder.

She was young-ish, he thought, examining her scalp, and still expected something of life, some kind of extraordinary unfolding, a cheerful entitlement to things yet to come, still hoped for an elegant meaning to eventually unfurl itself and bloom before her, to reveal itself in the very instantiation of her existence, a conjugal union between matter and good-natured beings driven by good causes. Oh, this life! *Wrenched into being only to inherit the consolation of death!* Winston was quite positive that the solar transmutation of water, air and sunlight into cellular life was the only miracle poor Julia was going to get. He was quite sure Julia had no especially singular cosmic destiny in store for her, other than the workaday impulse to forestall that inevitable moment of thermodynamic equilibrium, the looming stasis against which all human chaos was pitted. Death, the great fact of life, given freely and without salvation, this secretion of ornamental silt, of solidified spittle, of stuff stacked upon things, the history of gimcrack distractions, an ancient human coral formation, a beautifully embellished baroque bridge titivated with lavish affection, the fawning creeping ornamental dread that spans the void between birth and finitude. Winston was certain that Julia's happiness was a local phenomenon, a blip in the ocean of total expenditure, and that if *universal serenity* did lie somewhere in the future for her, it was most likely long after her death. From the very moment of declaring pitiless war on hopefulness, it was much easier to think of yourself as a corpse—a reflex of blinking and frowning and gasping out words, as death voices its energumen re-possession.

'We are the dead,' he muttered, the words somehow escaping from his tenuous inner gloom out into the humid air of the belfry.

'We're not dead yet!' said Julia in an emphatic tone verging upon panic. 'I mean, why are you always so down on everything? Would you prefer to fuck *me* or a maggoty old skeleton? Don't you enjoy being alive? Being crazy and alive? Breathing? Eating good wholesome food? Don't you, like, like, feeling? Like, this is *me*, this is *you*, this is *your* hand, like, this is *my* leg, *my* thigh, *my* cunt. Look! I'm real, I'm solid! I'm alive! You're alive! *We're so alive!* Here, don't you like *this?*'

Julia culminated her conjugation of the urgency of their visceral vitality by shoving Winston's hand roughly between her widened legs, then twisting herself around and pressing her smooth mouth roughly onto his, tangling her tongue roughly with his tongue, their rough tongues tangled inside his mouth, her hand stuffed firmly down his trousers, his hand stuffed firmly between her thighs.

'Yes, I like that very much,' he mumbled, tongue-tied.

'Then stop all this crazy talk about dying and fuck me properly before I die of boredom, you crazy old party-pooper!'

So they did it, right there in the pigeon dung and dust—two devoted Bogomils yearning for the end of days. And like two lowly animals, Winston badgered Julia's hole and Julia pecked at Winston's filthy gutter with an impromptu fistful of bird bones, up in the narrow arrow-slotted belfry of the ruined church, as the sun set once more, a day closer to the end of fun.

CHAPTER IV

Winston found *Venus's* proprietor old man Charrington quite willing to let the room above his antique sex shop, being thankful for the extra income it would bring him. Nor did he pry when it was made quite clear that Winston required the room for non-domestic reasons—purposes not explicitly mentioned, nor to be disclosed.

Winston, in point of fact, was preparing a thought-space, a place of contemplation where that-which-did-not-exist could be teased into existence through the hyperstitional voice that sought its own sovereign place and hurt through Winston's new place, hurt and voice. In any case, Charrington was happily compliant, wittering nebulously with an air so delicate that it gave the impression he was as ethereal in substance as his asthmatic whisper was in intrapersonal carriage. Charrington was indeed an odd specimen, a mismatch of shop-owner and dowdy precaristocrat—a caricature of a parody, a travesty of a mockery, a weird dithering brume. He appeared never to leave the premises, nor did he ever receive any customers. He migrated between the shop proper and an adjoining chamber where presumably he prepared his meals and laid his head. The bedsit, for it was nothing more and nothing less, boasted the meagre comforts of a single bed, stove, toilet and television. The latter was a small portable black and white model with a rotating dial, perched on a stool and with a coat hanger for its makeshift aerial. Permanently tuned to the popular *Big Brother* show, its fine tuning was slightly off, resulting in a scattering of peppered images and a rustic hiss. When Charrington wasn't out front inspecting the ranks of dusty toys, he was out back, more often than not glued to *Big Brother*, and anytime Winston was intercepted on the stairs, or hailed from behind the counter, he found the shopkeeper most eager for the opportunity to share a sort of disinterested gossip concerning the show. It was apparent to Winston that, despite Charrington's aloof predisposition, *Big Brother*'s present cast of religious zealots provided the meagre televisual flesh upon his lonely domestic bone. When not gnawing tenaciously at the spectacle of the grizzled housemates incarcerated in their communal unholy hell, he was to be found wandering amongst his worthless stock of dust-tipped sex-toys, an army of impotent surrogates amassed beneath a cloak of grime—all standing to attention for Old General Charrington, with his long nose and thick spectacles, slumped shoulders and piebald velvet jacket, his murmured orders and lofty salutes.

On one occasion, Winston arrived at the shop to hear the television blaring especially loudly. Charrington could not get to the thing quick enough to hush it before Winston fully entered and presented himself to the counter. The old man lurched back to the buffer, wheezing heavily, television rendered inoffensive and tenant mollified. Winston was thus obliged to reward his landlord's unnecessary solicitude with at least a cursory conversation.

'That's *Big Brother* on your television there, is it not?'

'Yes...yes...yes it is,' the old man's words whispered as if along the finest asthmatic filament.

'What are they doing?'

'They're playing...*a game*, sir.'

'A game? But they're naked.'

'Yes, they are...'

'What game can they be playing naked?'

'*Cover Thy Neighbour*. A rather spiteful bit of wordplay, under the circumstances. But I think it rather makes its point. You see, it's a take on *Twister*, an old parlour game played before the... *well*...It's a game that was once quite popular, a rather long time ago.'

'Why is it played naked?'

Charrington regarded Winston suspiciously before turning back into the small antechamber, narrating his way into the room made luminescent by the glow of the set. Captured in the flickering light like some moth-eaten professor, he pointed at the screen with a bony finger.

'You see the rather large spotted mat on the floor here?' He tapped the glass screen with a fingernail. 'Well, the contestants must first spin a dial, and whichever colour fate sees fit to settle the pointer on, they must occupy the corresponding colour patches on the floor with parts of their body designated by the previous spin. That's the spinner just there. You see?' He turned the volume up on the television and adjusted the coat hanger. 'It works rather well, since the one thing that appears to unify religious zealots of all persuasions is...well...their genital shame.... You see?'

'And the balloons?'

'A rather flimsy aid to conceal the contestants' modesty.'

Charrington fell silent, allowing Winston to see and hear for himself. The Twister mat was indeed host to a congregation of cantilevered bodies, a rainbow of brightly coloured bulging balloons the only safeguards against awkward inter-denominational frottage. Where the odd accidental penetration occurred there came no complaint, since any robust coupling merely reinforced the structural integrity of the whole edifice.

Winston swiftly became absorbed, leaning on the counter, compliant head propped in hands. He had never purposely watched *Big Brother* before, but was now evidently gripped.

'Sister Aaradhya, please be so kind as to move your leg around the other side—no, the *other* other side.'

'But Father Graham, that's my arm, not my leg.'

'Nevertheless, I can effect better coverage of your modesty *and mine* if you entrust me with just a little more leeway.'

'My trust is supple enough, Father Graham, but I fear my

arm is bound by rather more mundane forces.'

Sister Aaradhya and Father Graham's anatomies were so entangled that they could only move by the grace of a bilateral release of certain muscles or a synchronised tightening of others. A hand might reach through the tight flesh-knot of a thigh pinioned by a knee, but only if the nook of a third party's armpit was loosened so as to allow a chin to achieve greater purchase elsewhere—and this to permit a better balance for thigh, knee, armpit and chin, and thus a more satisfactory stability for all. But the advantages won by such negotiated poises were fortunate to last a few seconds before seismic forces and weakened knees began to strain the very foundations of the new consensus, all muscles quivering, shaking and quaking, their spasms creasing up the mat, sweat pooling in the creases, balloons creaking in fleshy crevices, and static-charged hair standing on end.

'For God's sake, pull yourselves together!' The terse reprimand bubbled up from deep inside the tangled mass of compressed brains and brawn, followed by a more serene platitude to quench the profane rage: *There is no fortitude like patience, just as there is no destructive emotion worse than hatred. Therefore, practice patience and tolerance!*

'Keep your hair on, Brother Liu Xiang!' piped up another voice, muffled by a thicket of hair and soft flesh, prompting churlish giggles from the assembled congregation.

'Whose turn is it to spin?'

'I dare say the task should be mine, but I'm finding it nigh on impossible to reach the spinner. Would someone be so kind as to take my turn?'

'I'll do it,' said Sister Aaradhya.

'Are you sure, Sister Aaradhya?' said the voice with muffled concern.

'Yes, yes!' Sister Aaradhya's inner resolve had already come into its own, since she was by now upside down in full *Sirsasana* pose, the crown of her head resting on the thin plastic mat, her body perfectly upright, forming the central column about which all the other cantilevered, coiling, twisting, buttressing and latticed bodies were stoically maintaining their stability.

'I think I can just about reach if...'

As if by some miracle, Aaradhya's fingertips could be seen burrowing out from the cellulitic load of a buttock of unknown provenance, emerging like survivors from some obscene pink avalanche. Father Graham could only look upon their mortal struggle with a helpless gaze, first moved to tears at the sight of their toil since the plastic spinner remained hopelessly out of reach, and then suddenly afflicted by the comedy of their plight. His tearful sobs and subdued laughter overlapped to produce something like a choking spasm, and with each gulp, gag and stifled cough, the general threat of an imminent crash-bang-wallop increased. Noticing the danger presented by Father Graham's inexorable mirth, Brother Liu Xiang manoeuvred himself around Aaradhya's totemic spur in an attempt to support his fellow in faith, in the process coming face to face with the hugely erect iridescent purple sausage balloon being employed by Father Graham to obscure his own more modest endowment. The inflated mass, rudely squeezed by crotch and thigh and ballooning impressively, now pressed upon Brother Liu Xiang's Adam's apple, modulating his voice into a deep-throated growl.

'*Your balloon, Father Graham! Your Balloon!*'

'When in Rome, Brother Liu Xiang! When in Rome!'

With a rippling of cartilage and gristle, the balloons, snagging on naked flesh and goosebump, began to shriek and squeal, their gossamer membranes inflating in surface area but simultaneously becoming almost transparent. Father Graham continued to weep with suppressed mirth.

'*I should like to remind everyone that protecting our personal environment is not a luxury, but a simple matter of survival!*'

As if to augment Brother Liu Xiang's resonant sentiment, Father Graham's bulging sausage burst with a loud *pop!*, creating a sudden vacuum, the void generated by its abrupt deflation bringing the whole teetering stack of intertwined bodies toppling down onto the sweat-sodden Twister mat.

Suddenly aware of his vacant gape and hypnotised slouch, Winston adjusted himself, amending his expression and withdrawing from the counter to stand upright once again. Taking his tenant's revised posture as a cue, Charrington hurried to silence the television before returning to man his servile post at the antiquated cash register.

'I've never found *Big Brother* very entertaining before,' said Winston in a slight daze, and, glancing back at the tangle of bodies on the box, added, 'But tell me, how is the game won?'

Charrington once more regarded Winston with suspicion.

'*Won*, sir? But surely it's not about the winning—it's about the taking part.'

'Indeed...*indeed*...' Winston allowed the conversation to peter out and edged toward the stairs, leaving Charrington alone with an uncertain victory.

Safely ensconced in the room above, Winston gazed through the bamboo slats to see in the garden below an obstinately elegant lady precaristocrat scumbled with the customary Martian tinge. Embellished by an ill-fitting apron strapped about her sunken waist, she was busy pruning a bush of clove pinks, snipping their pretty heads off one by one as if sleepwalking. From somewhere deep in her dream came a hurried whisper.

'*By change of place: Now conscience wakes despair / That slumberd, wakes the bitter memorie / Of what he was, what is, and what must be Worse; of worse deeds worse sufferings must ensue...*'

The words were very old, composed perhaps many hundreds of years ago, from sentiments even older, such that none but the precaristocrats any longer understood what such words meant, and even their understanding was prone to a melancholy which for them, permeated all meaning, just as the greenish tinge permeated their flesh.

He could hear the woman whispering and the scrape of her crippled high heels catching on the cracked flagstones, and the cries of the children in the street, and somewhere in the far distance the faint hum of the vibrant city and the flapping of a multitude of smiley-faced banners teased by the wind.

The temptation to rent a place to entertain both his newfound creativity and his newfound muse Julia had been too strong to resist. Unfortunately, the urgent call of Romantic revisionism had lately increased for Julia, and a sudden spike in alleged misfortune-related fatalities demanded Winston's own full attention at the Ministry. Yet within a month both managed to secure a free afternoon on the same day, deciding to return to the clearing in the wood for a sexual picnic.

On the evening beforehand they were walking in the street, filling in the moth holes in their kooky conversation.

'It's all off,' she said abruptly.

'It's all off? It's *all* off?'

'Not *all*.'

'*Not all?* Which part of it isn't off?'

'The picnic...tomorrow...I mean, the picnic is off tomorrow. It's all off. The picnic is all off tomorrow. I'm so sorry.'

Winston clasped his heart, the coronary averted, and they clung together again, both tickled pink at the grievous palpitations brought on by the thought that their relationship was *all off, kaput.*

It was not during the spectral clarity of this near-death experience, but some time on the following day, that he had decided to rent Charrington's room. He was very excited to show it to Julia. He wondered where Julia was. Julia was late. Julia was always late.

In fact, Julia was not late, she was on the pavement outside, looking up at the bright red neon sign. She was poised to enter the shop *Venus*, the place Winston had told her to meet him. She was happy that she was on time. She was carrying a brown paper bag. She was excited to show Winston what was inside. She would tell him to turn his back. Winston would gaze through the bamboo slats. Down in the yard an old green-tinged precaristocrat woman would be decapitating her favourite flowers as though lost in some primordial dream, whispering her mindless mantra over and over, her voice floating up to Winston's back window, raised up on the sweet spring air. Julia would tell Winston to turn around now. He would turn around, and for a second would almost fail to recognise her. He would expect to see her naked, but she would be anything but *au naturel*. The transformation would be so much more surprising than that. She would have put her hair up, painted her face with olde worlde factory make-up haggled from a dilapidated precaristocrat boutique. She would be wearing antique French lingerie and her lips would be stained gloss red, cheeks rouged, nose powdered, eyelashes falsified and lurid eye shadow caked on—everything possible to mask the radiant truthful healthy skin tones that were the sun's cosmic yippy wonk pain-free gift.

'And cheap perfume too!' Winston would gasp, and then she would say—

'*Fuck me, Winston!* Where on earth did you get *that!*'

Disturbed from his reverie, Winston turned to find Julia framed in the open doorway, an outstretched finger pointing to the table of objects next to the bed. She followed the finger past Winston and across the room, dumping her bag of now obsolete kinky surprises on the floor midway. Once at the table, she surveyed the array of objects with utter disbelief.

'Where did you get it?' she said.

Unsure exactly which *it* Julia was referring to, Winston

waited for her to more accurately nominate the object of her excitement before risking an answer.

'*Instant freeze dried coffee?* You naughty boy! I thought you were morally opposed to ye-olde-worlde factory food!' exclaimed Julia in a teasing tone, picking up the jar, twisting the lid off, popping the foil seal and inhaling the ancient spoor. 'Delicious! And white sugar cubes too!'

'I've another surprise for you,' he said, diverting her attention to the table, to the brown paper bag, with its undisclosed contents. But now Julia's attention fell instead upon the coral phallus. She picked it up, weighing its impotent heft in her palm.

'*This?* Really, Winston? An archaic sex toy?—there's a whole army of them downstairs if you hadn't noticed, covered in dust for a good reason. I know you're old-fashioned, Winston—but this? *Tut tut!*'

But Winston was already upon Julia, pressing himself to her, forcing her against the table, then onto the bed. Julia blindly settled the battery-powered male surrogate back on the table so as to fully reciprocate Winston's real-life amorous assault, an urgent advance she presumed to be spearheaded by a real-life penis downstairs. Winston pressed himself urgently against his muse, suffocating her with many urgent kisses, as though something terrible was about to happen and he needed to kiss his love many times before he could kiss her no more—and with each suffocating kiss the world's air was running out, each kiss bringing the end even nigher. Winston's smothering kisses were punctuated by the odd mumbled question, and Julia's answers, such as they were, were similarly congested.

'I want to do something, Julia...something you and I have never done before.'

'You know I'll do anything Winston...there's nothing I won't do....Because...I own my sex—'

'*Yes*...I know, I know you *own* it...and it's a thing to be owned, along with the pitiless war of all things pitted against all other owned things...but *this* is different.'

Winston was now fumbling at Julia's dungaree buttons, managing to undo one strap cleanly, but forced to slip the other over a courteously dipped left shoulder.

'Winston, I'll do anything, but only because I want to...and not because you want me to...I'll do it because I'm as sexually liberated as a woman can be—'

'*Yes, yes, yes you are....* But aren't you tired of this congealing of all forces towards the obvious, of anticipating the average for the sake of mediocrity...this magical consensus that envelops all in the bosom of harmoniousness...? Our primitive ancestors learned to turn the other cheek...to love their neighbours as themselves...and for all their petty genocides, leading to the grandiloquent statement of progress: *of disapproving what another might say, but defending to the death their right to say it*, in their millions if needs be...Julia, aren't you sick and tired of our great planetary consensus? This ill-conceived limit to our ultimate cosmic reckoning?'

'Well...I can't say...that...it feels exactly like that for me, but *I hear you...*'

Winston jerked Julia's T-shirt up over her harmonious bosoms and only half-way over her head, stifling her words and leaving her struggling to complete the task, her denuder now on his hands and knees, hands all over her, tugging Julia's dungarees down to Julia's ankles, pulling Julia's pants down to Julia's ankles, slipping Julia's shoe off, lifting Julia's foot up through the tangled leg of dungaree denim and pants, pulling the dungarees through the pants, Julia losing her balance and placing a flat hand on Winston's head to steady Julia—Winston peeling off a sock, then the same with the other shoe and the other sock.

'For instance, is it more likely that in the general liberation of both sexes from gendered clothing, women have earned the right to wear trousers and men the right to wear skirts? And yet we don't see an equivalent ratio of skirt-wearing-men to trouser-wearing-women—since what is plainly manifest in the skirt's impracticality is a formal inequality already inscribed in its original design?'

'*Listen, Mr Winston*, we've been having great sex so far—great experimental sex—liberating each other through the truly profound communion of our bodies, dissolving in each other's arms—real love, Winston, the freest of all human freedoms. The freedom to love and be loved, to love humanity and be loved *by* humanity. The universal expression of human liberation from the scourge of inhuman ugliness and evil.... *That's* pure poetry, right?'

'*Yes, yes, yes*...pure poetry, yes! Of course! It goes without saying! But today we can do something even more liberating—right now, something miraculous!'

'What is it? Tell me! I'll do anything to free us from our latent repression—anything to emancipate us! Anything to advance the authentic expression of our bodies! Anything for radical self-improvement! Anything to make us even more free!'

Winston and Julia faced each other, chests heaving. Winston saw Julia's naked body from the front, and the back of her naked body in the mirror behind. She was waiting for him to say something, heaving in anticipation; he lifted the large brown paper bag from the table and took out a folded black garment. Julia, naked, front and back, watched as Winston allowed gravity to unfold it, the cloth draping long and almost to the ground. He lifted the garment over Julia, placing it over her head and allowing the heavy material to drop so that her head and body were completely covered apart from a small horizontal slot for her eyes.

Without need of assistance, Winston undressed himself quickly, with Julia silently spying on him through her slot.

When he was fully naked, he took a second gown from the paper bag and placed it over his own head, allowing the black fabric to cascade to the floor so that he too was completely covered from head to toe, apart from the horizontal letterbox through which he could see the dark shape before him that he knew to be Julia. Winston took Julia's hand, and instead of having experimental emancipatory sex, as was their custom, led her to the bed where they sat facing one another, neither knowing whether the other was smiling, at least not by eyesight, but each knowing in their hearts that they surely were.

'You see?' said Winston. 'With these ancient cloaks of invisibility we have disappeared from ordinary sight. This covering up transgresses the glorification of the face as the inescapable truth of identity. I mean, could we be any more liberated than we are at this very moment?'

'No, Winston, we could not,' Julia agreed.

CHAPTER V

Syme had gone. Word soon got around that he had vanished from the face of the earth. When morning came, his desk lay empty, Dictaphone dejected and paper shredder eerily silent. Syme's colleagues wept for his absence, but with tears of simple, unbridled joy, since his departure undoubtedly signified that, after many months of excruciating indecision, he had taken the creative plunge—that he had finally taken a sabbatical to finish his long-delayed novel. Many of the weeping wonks had yet to activate their own Goldstein sabbaticals, many extra-mural dancers, poets, potters, designers, printers, flaneurs, conceptualists, fiddlers, bricoleurs, performers, painters and decorators were yet to take the sponsored creative plunge—and so their wailings of admiration for Syme in his absence were symbolically pregnant with anticipation for their own creative blossoming, mindful also of the remorse they would suffer if they failed to take the great leap of faith into the sabbatical abyss, leaving their creative potential unfulfilled, never succeeding in locating their inner voice, place and hurt.

Syme's novel, it was understood, was a most promising counterfactual tale set in a near future dystopia—2084 to be exact—when wonks would travel by hoverboard and sleep alone in sad ergonomic capsules with intrusive propaganda televisions that could not be turned off, and small handy telephones that could be freely carried about but were so addictive to their users that many wonks found that overexposure to these gadgets led to enhanced impulsivity and a reduction in the ability for self-regulation. Syme sought to juxtapose the present with the future, making them shimmer in a shifting disturbance pattern so that every detail was familiar and yet unfamiliar enough to render the story uncannily prescient and yet outlandish, homely and yet disquieting, all at once. Syme often employed the word 'juxtaposition' in his communal explanations of the dialectical nature of his satirical synthesis. To wit, he was imagining a hellish world devoid of personal choice or beauty—a grey world where the food was torture and wonks were held in terrible bureaucracy and forced to wear short hair, and drab, ill-fitting, unflattering, shapeless factory overalls. Syme was deadly serious about his minatory vision, since he believed that science-fiction, in all its ludicrous dystopian ruminations, was nonetheless the mythological precursor to a future yet to come, the coming-into-being of a dark folklore that was always-already predestined to arrive.

Outside on the Eatery's patio sun, Winston soon found himself plagued by unwelcome fabulations of Syme's dystopia, collaged together from piecemeal conversations while queuing for food in the delicatessen, or when trapped in the elevator with the zealous collegial wonk.

For a moment he succumbed to an imaginary vision of the windowless Ministry animated by industrious preparations for War Week.

The Ministry wonks were obliged to toil without sleep, since the spectacle had to be conjured into being, and so scaffolds had to be erected, political traitors contrived, and reactionary watchwords devised. Stirring anthems were to be composed, gossip disseminated, and incriminating evidence dissimulated to the mob.

Juliette's section had been taken off the popular Mills and Doom romance novellas and put onto the urgent preperation of atrocity pamphlets. Vincent was ordered to re-visit the rectifications, to embroider and hyperbolize them ready for public enragement.

At night, paretic proles menaced the streets as the city congealed into its customary state of apprehension. Enemy rockets had begun to land with greater precision and regularity—enormous phosphorous explosions causing the darkness to be aghast with brilliant colour. New nationalist anthems were broadcast on State television, and drummed-in on public address systems, as workers erupted on the streets to march, sing and smash glass, and their prole offspring joined in with small plastic combs and pieces of toilet paper.

Vincent's evenings were taken up with preparations for War Week. He spent his time sewing political slogans on vast banners and painting agit-prop posters. He strung wires across the street so that enemy effigies could be hung by their papier mache necks (and Victory Mansions could happily boast at least forty puppet traitors). Vincent was motivated by fear to work to the bone, pushing and pulling, sawing, filing, hammering, nailing, urging his subordinates on with exhortations of self-less sacrifice—as the blood, sweat and tears were rinsed from his skin. A new poster had appeared all over the capital, representing the spectre of a Eurasian stormtrooper, goose-stepping forwards with leather jackboots and a machine gun anchored to his hip. The muzzle of the gun seemed to follow your every movement.

The worker proles were encouraged out of their despondency by the threat of attack, and as though to harmonise with the urgency of their new mobilisation, enemy bombs began killing people with even greater precision. A bomb fell on a cinema and buried several hundred victims in the twisted concrete rubble. Another bomb fell upon a playground and many children were vaporised, such that there was nothing left to bury, and so the playground became a grave. There were angry demonstrations, the traitor Goldstone was burned in effigy, and the Eurasian stormtrooper was torn from billboards and walls and added to the flames. Exotic shops were ransacked and many looted out of frustration. Rumours circulated that foreign insurrectionists were directing the rocket attacks, and an immigrant family suspected of terrorist sympathy was set on fire by a mob and pelted with rocks by children.

In the room above Mr Barrington's shop, naked Juliette and naked Vincent lay side by side on the bed next to the open window. The rat had decided not to return to the room, but the insect population proliferated in the torrid heat. Despite the indelible filth and the hideous zoo of fluttering vermin, the room was paradise. As soon as they arrived they would tear off their drab, ill-fitting, unflattering shapeless factory overalls, desperate to fall into the propitiatory embrace of synchronous petit morts. But upon waking they would find themselves littered with a dust of insect corpses having expired in the night. Vincent had discovered a taste for alchohol and had grown fatter for it. His varicose ulcer had shrunk, leaving a small stain on the carapace above his ankle. His coughing in the morning had decreased a little.

Life had ceased to be so insufferable, but he still quietly cursed at the integrated State Television that could never be completely silenced. The room was itself a great freedom, and to know that their safe place over the junk-shop existed at all was almost as good as being in it.

The room was a world where Vincent and Juliette could meet and sleep, and where vermin collected and died. Mr Barrington, thought Vincent, was just another captive insect. He would stop to talk with Mr Barrington for a few minutes on his way upstairs. The old man seemed never to leave the shop, and never had any customers. He haunted the space between the gloomy frontishop, and a small back kitchen where he prepared meals and slept, but which contained an ancient gramophone. He was glad of any opportunity to converse. Wandering among the worthless stock, with his long nose, thick spectacles and bowed shoulders in the velvet jacket, he possessed the vague air of being a collector rather than a vendor. With faded enthusiasm he might finger the worthless tat—a china bottle-stopper, the painted lid of a broken snuffbox, a pinchbeck locket containing a strand of some long-dead baby's hair—never asking that Vincent should buy it, merely that he should admire it. To talk to him was like listening to the tinkling of a worn-out musical box. He had dragged out from the corners of his memory some more fragments of forgotten rhymes. There was one about four and twenty blackbirds, and another about a cow with a crumpled horn, and another about the death of poor Cock Robin.

'It just occurred to me you might be interested,' he would say with a deprecating little laugh whenever he produced a new fragment.

But he could never recall more than a few lines of any one rhyme. Both he and Juliette knew—in a way, it was never out of their minds—that what was now happening could not last long. There were times when the fact of impending death seemed as palpable as the bed they lay on, and they would cling together with a sort of despairing sensuality, like a damned soul grasping at his last morsel of pleasure when the clock is within five minutes of striking. But there were also times when they had the illusion not only of safety but of permanence. So long as they were actually in this room, they both felt, no harm could come to them. Getting there was difficult and dangerous, but the room itself was sanctuary. It was as when Vincent had gazed into the heart of the paperweight, with the feeling that it would be possible to get inside that glassy world, and that once inside it time could be arrested. Often they gave themselves up to daydreams of escape. Their luck would hold indefinitely, and they would carry on their intrigue, just like this, for the remainder of their natural lives. Or Caroline would die, and by subtle manoeuvrings Vincent and Juliette would succeed in getting married. Or they would commit suicide together. Or they would disappear, alter themselves beyond recognition, learn to speak with proletarian accents, get jobs in a factory, and live out their lives undetected in a back street....

Even though it was only a general stab at Syme's dystopian future, Winston found he had painted quite a terrifying picture. We should all pray to the heavens, he mused to himself, that such things never come to pass.

CHAPTER VI

It had happened at last. Contact had been made. It seemed to Winston that he had been waiting a long time for it to happen, and now it had surely happened. And what it was, was this: He was walking back to his desk along the corridor, perhaps after a visit to the water-fountain or the bathroom, to either the source or its elimination—and at the very spot where his lover-cum-muse Julia had accosted him with the red pen, he became aware of a mechanical squeaking coming from behind him—the sort of sound that conjures up images of a mouse but also a machine, and in the mental juxtaposition of mouse and machine, an automaton, but one in need of oil.

Glancing back, instead Winston found O'Brien bearing down on him, and so offered a congenial greeting. But O'Brien neither smiled nor slowed her motion, but instead grabbed Winston by the elbow and urged him forwards to match the force of her vehicular momentum, so that the two of them might continue together, walking and wheeling respectively, side by side, along the corridor.

O'Brien began to speak, in a tone that seemed peculiarly grave, but was nonetheless amicable, and distinguished her from the sometimes supercilious tones of the other attic wonks when they were issuing instructions.

'I was hoping for an opportunity to speak with you, Winston,' she said. 'I happened to be reviewing one of your five-star rectifications only the other day, and was taken by its most novel form.'

'*If in day-to-day deeds lead honest good life, then can automatically find most best peace?*' Winston ventured.

'Indeed. Your wisdom shines forth through your writing. You are most eloquent in your rectifications,' said O'Brien. 'And this opinion is shared by many in the attic, but also by your closest comrades, one in particular of note, a most dedicated admirer—an expert in his field—and a committed science-fictional novelist, no less.'

That Syme might have had anything positive to say about Winston's mundane rectifications was certainly a surprise, especially now that he was absent from the Ministry and presumably hard at work at home on his novel. He pictured Syme at the moment of ambush, perhaps unlucky enough to be cornered by O'Brien on the very last day before his sabbatical, squirming painfully inside his luminous skin, shaking beneath his willow's drape of lank black hair, obliged to concur with O'Brien's solicitations. He imagined Syme reluctantly forcing some vague compliment through clenched baleen and, once released from the pain of compliance, scuttling off home to lunge at his vintage Harald Quistgaard flip-top writing desk, full of vengeful thoughts for Winston—*perhaps vengeful enough to include Winston in his work as a character, to be treated as he saw fit, to be maltreated, tortured....* Syme, settled at his desk, but soon enough staring out of the window fixated by the horizon of his writer's block, worrying his worry-beads until the wood and enamel was worried through, trying to eke out his counterfactual world from a reality whose underwhelming physics prevented it from budging, his hoverboards and tractor beams scuppered by dim-witted gravity. Syme, imagining his great new religion of electronic potentiometers, a machine dreamed up by humans to be capable of autopoietic thought—the magnificent Wiener-Golem-abacus programmed to watch over all, the ventriloquial god of invisible chaos, the brave new world-wide-window through which all things could become possible by way of virtual simulacra, a far-fetched mumbo-jumbo machine which would, some day—according to Syme's preposterous fictional future—prove its superiority by, say, annihilating a Russian grandmaster at chess, or making a piping hot Americano and delivering it to its armchair-bound Yankee domestic master without spilling any on the carpet. Fat chance. But Syme's robot future was already riddled with human fear, its crowning sentience inevitably to be followed by enslavement—hence the anticipatory dread for the revolution that surely follows subjugation, for *history repeats itself first as tragedy, then as farce.*

Winston and O'Brien continued in their squeaking pilgrimage along the corridor, mouse and wheelchair, until O'Brien suddenly tugged on her brakes and, with the curious, disarming friendliness she always managed to insert into the absurd gesture of resettling her spectacles on her nose, spoke again.

'Winston, what I'm trying to get at is this: a certain lyrical rhythm has emerged in your rectifications—and, dare I say, a certain sense of the *poetic* has crept in. And I don't mention this lightly, since it's hardly something I would have expected of you. Your work is most rigorous but, forgive me, you're hardly known in the Ministry for your creative extroversion.'

It was damning, but undoubtedly true. Winston managed a small nod.

'This new poetry of yours, though, this unexpected voice that appears to have found its place...it feels quite different to the handicraft of the other wonks in your section...it feels, well... *risqué*—and, dare I say, even a little *vainglorious.*'

Winston became excited. O'Brien was clearly only scratching the surface, tickling the tip of the complimentary iceberg. She could of course have no real idea of the intensity of his possession by the new voice, place and hurt that was manifesting through him—but these hints at her recognition of its eerie nature bolstered an intuition that had first begun to emerge in the community room with the exchange of glances that had registered their mutual unease at Goldstein's 'compassion'. And now O'Brien had moved from telepathy to words, and soon they would move from words to poetry, and then on to action.

But the end was contained in the beginning—in the unsaid of their words was a foretaste of death. O'Brien had discovered Winston's despair, had winnowed out the diamonds hidden in the flour dust of his daily rectifications. The cat was out of the bag, and with O'Brien's help, Winston's work would soon be exposed to the keenest cut, to the knives of the optimists. A sublime chill took possession of his body. He had the sensation of the dampness of a grave or the glow of the crematorium.

'Have you heard about the thirteenth edition of the *Fortune Cookie Dictionary?*' said O'Brien.

'Despite the secrecy, I must admit that I've heard it mentioned once or twice, but I didn't think it had been issued yet. We're still most content with the twelfth.'

'The thirteenth edition isn't due to appear on the lower floors for some time, but a few advance copies have been circulated upstairs for attic approval. I have a draft copy in my possession, and I believe it may be of some interest to you—it might even profit from your scrutiny, in light of this new metrical insight....' O'Brien gave a wink.

'Groovy,' said Winston awkwardly, wise to a pretext being crafted before his very ears.

CHAPTER VII

At home, Syme had experienced something of a breakthrough, and had busted out from the lifeless lunar horizon of his writer's block. Perhaps having been obliged to compliment Winston in order to join O'Brien's fulsome praise had been the necessary purgative required to unblock his blockage. In any case, Syme's counterfactual dystopian story was progressing, and this is how it progressed:

Vincent awoke with eyes full of wet tears. The naked Juliette rolled sleepily against his toned body, her toned breasts pressing against his toned torso, and he murmured something that sounded tonally something almost vaguely like—

'Hey baby, baby what was that you said? Baby?'

'Oh nothing honeybunny. I just had a really nasty horrible dream, a real bummer—'. He stopped short, almost like he was too sad to put it into a whole world of negative words and wreck Juliette's morning buzz. A horrible memory swum into his crazy fucked-up mind in the few seconds after waking up from the terrible dream that he had just had. He lay back with his sad baby eyes clenched shut, still sodden with the drenched atmosphere of the crazy horrible dream. It was a vast, luminous nightmare dream in which his whole hopeless life stretched out before him like an ugly kaleidoscopic landscape on a summer evening after pouring sideways rain, when it's strangely wet but oddly warm. It was like it had all occurred inside a strange glass paperweight, but the surface of the glass was the dome of the sky, and inside the dome everything was just flooded with clear soft light in which he could see great distances and the horizon was pushed far back, as far as the eye couldn't see. In the dream he saw a gesture of the arm made by his mother, the same gesture as a woman he had seen on the teleopticvisionscreenwindowportal trying to shelter her son from the crazy laser bullets, just a moment before the ruthless

jet laser helicopter vaporised them both to things much smaller even than smithereens. 'Do you know,' he said, 'I always thought I murdered my mother?'

'Jeepers Vincent! Why the fuck would you murder your poor mother? Why? Why?' said Juliette, almost asleep but not quite, and especially not now. Now really awake, wild-eyed and bushy-tailed.

'No! No! I didn't murder her. Not physically anyway. Not with my hands. Not in real life. I killed her in my dream. It was all a figment of my wishful desire...my desire's wishful guilty conscience.'

In the horrible dream he had relived his last glimpse of his poor mother, and within a few moments of waking, the cluster of small events surrounding all of it had all come back all at once, in a crazy mental flurry. It was a memory that he must have deliberately pushed out of his consciousness over many, many, many years. He was not certain of the date of it, or the day or month or year, or week, but he could not have been less than ten years old, possibly twelve, or maybe younger or older, when it had happened. His father had disappeared some time earlier, how much earlier he could not remember. He remembered better the rackety, uneasy circumstances of the time but not the date: the periodic panics about incoming jet bomb air-raids and the sheltering in the huge underground drive-thru bunkers embedded in the depths of the earth, the piles of rubble everywhere, the unintelligible proclamations posted at street corners, the gangs of youths in shirt uniforms and jackboots, all the same horrible drab colour of the earth, the enormous queues outside the drive-thrus waiting for space food, the intermittent laser machine-gun fire rattling off in the distance—and above all, the fact that there was never ever enough space food to eat or enough brown fizzy water to drink.

He remembered long afternoons spent with other boys and girls scrounging around drive-thru dustbins and rubbish heaps, picking out the ribs of lettuce leaves, apple pie crusts, french fries, sometimes even scraps of stale buns from which they carefully scraped away the sprouting sesame seeds; he remembered waiting for the passing *of trucks which travelled a certain route and were known to carry surplus burger meat—which was actually meat, of a sort—and which, when they jolted over the bad patches in the road, sometimes let spill the odd slice of pickle.*

When his father had disappeared, his mother had not shown any surprise or crazy violent grief, but a sudden change had come over her slowly. She seemed to have become completely spiritless, void, dead before being dead, undead, pre-dead. It was evident even to Vincent that she was waiting for something that she knew must happen but did not know what it was or when it might happen again yet, like the fact of the nothingness that exists before being born, and doesn't seem to perplex or terrify anyone in the same way that death does, since it's a gift that's already given.... She did everything that was needed— cooked, washed, mended, made the bed, swept the floor, dusted the mantelpiece, fed the robot dog, oiled the cat—always very slowly and with a curious lack of superfluous motion, like an artist's lay-figure moving of its own accord. Her large shapely body seemed to relapse naturally into inert motherly stillness, as if on standby. For hours and hours at a time she would sit almost immobile on the bed, humming, nursing his young sister, a tiny, ailing underling, a mute child of two or three with a sunken face grotesquely distorted by Munchausen obesity. Very occasionally she would take Vincent in her arms and press him against her for a long time without saying anything.

Even before the elevator had opened fully onto O'Brien's softly lit penthouse loft-pad abode, the communal atmosphere of Harmony Heights, with its familiar scent of seagrass and candle, and the red, black and white smiley-faced embroidery wall hangings with the kindly eyes that had followed him into the elevator, had made him feel quite at home: it was not so different from Serenity Mansions. But when he stepped from the elevator directly into the apartment, noticing that the television was glowing, the sound dimmed to a polite murmur—yet still recognisable as the all-too-familiar clamour of considerate zealot bickering and the whirr of the Twister spinner spinning—he saw at the far end of the room O'Brien sat at an impressive Hugo Alvar Henrik Aalto desk, bathed in the glow of a green lava lamp and apparently studying her own hands. Having buzzed her visitor into the building, she clearly had no need to look up from her immediate studies until he was standing directly before her—and only as he approached the desk did Winston see that, in fact, O'Brien was not examining her hands, but tinkering with the shards of a broken fortune cookie and smoothing out the curclicued note once contained within.

O'Brien's head was slumped over, as though burdened by some inner thoughts that were too dense to support. Winston was tempted to offer up one of many memorised fortune scripts as an ice-breaking salutation—perhaps '*It very rare most nearly almost impossible that event or thing be negative from all point of view.*' Or '*As must breathe in, must cherish yourself. As must breathe out, must cherish all other being.*'

But he had little confidence that the elegance of the message would not be lost to a timorous delivery—and anyway O'Brien had begun to speak.

She was evidently reading from the slip of paper before her, and as she relayed its words out loud, Winston's heart sank.

'*There no need erect temples, no need God. Better you susurrate swollen blood thrust of loins in split shitty tissues. Better you drape head open mouth soiling blood spattered veil face beaten or better violaceous liquefied all body politician. Better you strangle penis sweat clitoris slime frothing in nostril sagging load straggling over and over shaved occiput or better mauve slit of arse. Much better when discontent devour dead membrane's throat gurgling jism purge with bloody smear-chipped tooth-dent in screaming soft rape flesh, especially in July.*'

A large lump—gristle, dark mass or just plain awkward phlegm—bobbed up in Winston's throat, an untimely visceral ambassador presenting its unwanted services. O'Brien had managed to elevate her head midway through her canorous narration, her gaze juddering upward to meet Winston's at the precise apogee of *penis*. The happy pretext for the visit had wilted in Winston's mind, since no copy of the thirteenth edition was anywhere in sight. Instead it was now clear that he was being bought to book for one of many scabrous misfortunes attributed to his hand. When O'Brien came to a natural pause, Winston could do nothing but blurt out a babbling rejoinder.

'But O'Brien! I'm doing my very best! The misfortunes occur faster than I can rectify them! It's a losing battle! And they're getting worse, much more vile! Spiteful! Hateful! O'Brien, the innocent are suffering and no-one is doing anything about it! Murder! Rape! Suicide—quadrupled! Crimes that were happily condemned to the past are now returned—and on the increase, tenfold, twenty-fold! The misfortunes are wreaking havoc! No one dares even mention the glitch within the Composition Department! We deal with the misfortunes but not the glitch! What *is* the glitch? Why aren't we doing something about the glitch? It's running rings around us! There's even a rumour that the precaristocrats have their own secret factory somewhere, in some

Leabharlann Fionnghlas
Finglas Library
01-2228330

222

obscure country estate, stately home, hunting lodge or forest! That they're crafting misfortune cookies in their thousands—*the lazy bastards are churning them out!*'

O'Brien spooled deliberately around the desk toward Winston, forcing him back a little, almost pinching his toes with the arc of her wheels, fixing him with a solemn expression.

'What about your friends and fellow wonks in the Ministry? What are your feelings about them?'

'They dedicate their lives to the pursuit of pleasure, but since they're obliged by a sense of consensual communality, they must regulate themselves with forms of abnegation more stringent even than the notorious laws of a God they've long since emancipated themselves from! They're obsessed with wellness, such that any unbound hedonistic urges that exceed the wholesome demands of wellbeing must be compacted back into the body and stringently metered by yoga, fitness regimes, and spiritual health—merely the neuronic spasms and energetic twitches of an anatomy grappling with its own indiscrete composure. Wellness is nothing more than external authority incorporated as vicious gnosticism, a vile and tyrannical superego that compels its host to the misery of underachievement—by degrees, *wellness is next to holiness!*'

It was quite possible that he had made a grave mistake in assuming he had an ally in O'Brien, for what evidence had he in reality that his mentor possessed any sympathetic feelings about poetry, the deep glitch, or Goldstein's charity drive? Nothing but a flash of the eyes and a single equivocal remark: beyond that, only his own secret imaginings, an optimistic fantasy founded on some distant spectral dream. But Winston was in too deep and too far gone to hold back now....

'O'Brien, I am of the opinion that there is a conspiracy of forces at work that asserts the theology of wellness as the natural order of things—a survival of the flattest, of the mediocre—to the detriment of all else. For this reason I must declare that I am an enemy of consensus, opposed to Goldstein's two minutes compassion, against charity, and a firm enemy of the fortunes. I stand against the narcissism of unity, of the society of the polite, of good causes, of nature, of an art determined by positivity and the anthropomorphic search for cosmic significance. I came here because I think that you might agree with me. I want to begin a new kind of poetry, a new kind of art—no longer predisposed to the average appetite, no longer predisposed to the mediocrity of consensus, no longer desperate for en-masse solicitude, a poetry that is no longer bound by a tactical predisposition to the obstinately informed, the corrupt and the entitled—to the prejudice of the well-intentioned—but a poetry that seeks out the freshness of the new-born—not the innocent underling, but the shrieking, seething bundle of desires that has no reserved objective, but emits only a hopeless gaping yell—an art that excludes those in the know, those au courant aesthetes who *know* what meaning is even before meaning knows itself, who have *sensibility* sewed up in their pockets, and continue sowing the seeds of self-improvement everywhere like a plague of well-intentioned locusts. I tell you this because I am a dark poet without artistic compatriots, and I wish to place my poetry at your mercy. And if you want—*need*—me to incriminate myself in such a cause, I am here and I am ready, because...*Prime purpose in life is best help to others. And if cannot best help them, then most best hurt them.*'

O'Brien was now poised before the desk, arms crossed, closely observing Winston's unease. Then came a small gesture towards the television with the remote, a stabbing motion, as if straight through Winston's torso, increasing the volume of the *Big Brother* zealots and thus saving him from the shame of his rambling sermon.

Soon enough, the all-too-familiar theme tune rang out.

'Do you follow *Big Brother*, Winston?'

'No. Not as a rule.'

'So you're not a fan.'

'No. I'm not a fan of television in general, I mostly listen to it rather than watch it. I prefer to watch television obliquely, it helps me concentrate.'

'Concentrate on what?'

Winston avoided O'Brien's eyes by dipping his head and engaging his brow.

'Well, I think you might find tonight's episode quite interesting.'

Winston wondered how O'Brien might have already formed an opinion about a live programme before it was even broadcast—but the narrator's voice, forthright as ever, and with its familiar phonic tinge, interrupted his wonderment.

O'Brien gestured for him to sit, and so he sat.

'It's 11.20 pm. The housemates are assembled in the communal conversation pit in the kitchen. Rabbi Lamm has called an assembly, and Father Graham has the floor...'

Father Graham could be seen standing aloft, the shadow of his deferential stoop cast over the supine object of his immediate meditation. 'My dearest Sister Aaradhya, if I've somehow managed to offend thee in some way, I offer my most humble apologies, unshaken in the belief that *one must do unto others as one would have them do unto you; for this is the law of the prophets.*'

Aaradhya simply gazed up at her looming apologist with default forgiveness in her kindly eyes—but before she had a chance to exalt Father Graham, Brother Liu Xiang, seated directly next to her, all glabrous and monastic, was swift to tender his own hermeneutic exegesis. 'Most favourable answer, Father Graham. That one may not *do unto others what you do not want them to do unto you* is of course beyond inter-denominational doubt. But *if thine eyes be turned towards justice, choose thou for thy neighbour that which thou choosest for thy self.*'

'Dearest Brother Liu Xiang, are you sitting comfortably?'

Brother Liu Xiang simpered most graciously, allowing Father Graham the grace to continue.

'I have only the utmost respect for your esteemed doctrinal teachings, I really do—but after a lifetime devoted to my own contemplations upon the nature of the Divine, I find myself most humbled by your remarks—unable as I am to discern whether such notes are incomprehensible because they are so *wise*, or whether they are indecipherable because they are simply *enigmatic*. That said, may I offer you, or any of the others gathered here amongst us, a fresh brew?'

Amid a host of polite *yes*es and *no*s, Father Graham squeezed past the semi-circle of the seated congregation, collecting up the empty cups and mugs, moving deliberately amongst his fellow syncretic Buddhist, Confucian, Hindu, Muslim, Jew, Sikh, Zoroastrian and a slumbering Humanist, passing each housemate with a murmuring incantation. *'Lapsang souchong? Green tea? Chamomile? Rooibos? Nettle? Rosehip? Jasmine? Lemon and Ginger? Assam? Alderman grey? Builders?'*

Most were thankful for the opportunity of renewed refreshment, but Brother Liu Xiang was so moved as to offer a reflex bow of the pate, with flattened palm over his half-empty cup, which only complicated Father Graham's progress around the pit, giving Rabbi Lamm, the most youthful of the housemates, opportunity to thrust his own mug upwards, and—'May I trouble you for a fresh matcha, Father! I doubt if *even you* could raise this cup of cold tea from the dead!'

Father Graham took the cup without comment, but Lamm had youth and verve on his side and was plainly unstoppable.

'Friends! Housemates! Lend me your ears! Surely the prism of the infinite makes mortals of us all in the eyes of God? *What is hateful to you, do not do to your neighbour!* In the spirit of fellowship and good housekeeping, our gentle neighbour

Aaradhya earlier offered an opinion regarding the commission of domestic duties—a view with which I have some sympathy, observing that there are *some amongst us who have neglected their domestic duties as others have done unto us their domestic duties...*'

From the kitchen came the sound of cups being cleansed, along with Father Graham's off-camera and ever so slightly raised voice. 'Dear Rabbi Lamm, best not beat around the burning bush. Ambiguity is an abstraction of the Devil! Say what you mean, lest you be mean in what you don't say!'

'Indeed! Indeed! Not to put too fine a point on it, Aaradhya alludes to the fact that *some of us here have failed to attend to the cleanliness of the toilet as others have attended to the cleanliness of the toilet.* Father Graham, I think your name was mentioned.'

From the kitchen now came the sound of a cup being dropped into the stainless-steel basin, enamel clanging on enamel, resonating with the infinite. Father Graham appeared in person over the pit, now visible to those watching at home, and evidently aggrieved by the accusation. '*THE TOILET?* Oh, how could you, Aaradhya!'

'*No! No!* Dear Rabbi Lamm bends my words!' yelped Aaradhya. 'There was no malice in my words whatsoever, nor should I wish to *do unto others what you do not want them to do, and in everything, do to others as you would have them to do to you,* which surely applies to you.... Oh Father! I fear my words are now so confused they deserve only to be disregarded!'

'On the contrary! Our obliging companion Rabbi Lamm has been kind enough to reveal to me an unambiguous meaning of which no censure can now occur. 'Tis true that *nature alone is good which refrains from doing unto another whatsoever is not good for itself.*'

Rabbi Lamm leapt to his feet. 'Father! Dearest Father! Nothing in what Aaradhya said nor in what I added was intended to cause harm!'

'If I'm not mistaken, Dear Rabbi, what you did was to whittle Aaradhya's blunt cudgel into a sharpened arrow!'

'Most illuminating parable,' whispered Liu Xiang, slipping a supple bow just beneath Father Graham's already crestfallen ledge, in preparation for the avalanche to come.

'What Rabbi Lamm has revealed to me is that your accusation was already pointed enough, that it is me that you intend to shame in the accusation of *neglecting to clean the toilet as others have cleaned the toilet.* But as I stand here beneath the righteous judgement of God, I assure you that I have *cleaned as others have not cleaned*, and tidied *as others have not tidied*, and fussed *as others have not fussed* without suggestion of complaint in these recent weeks, indeed months, and as such, *you should not hurt others in ways in which you yourself would find hurtful.*' He stooped even lower to deliver the hot drinks to those in need, each of whom thanked him most graciously. 'The Lapsang for you...the rooibos for you...*and chamomile for you.*'

Lamm received the mug with good grace, seeing fit not to hint at Father Graham's apparent mistake, assuming his confusion to be an effect of the priest's present emotional penury. Father Graham turned to find his place on the couch, yet paused before he sat, preferring to address Lamm whilst standing.

'Oh Rabbi Lamm, contrary to popular belief, green tea is not the *innocent* it appears to be. It carries potentially harmful doses of caffeine, and given the heightened state of emotion—well, I thought it best to serve *you* chamomile.'

Rabbi Lamm lowered himself to his seat slowly, whilst Aaradhya once again reached out to Father Graham, who, smiling, took her hand, kissed it obligingly, and gracefully sent the gentle paw back, so that Aaradhya was obliged to reel it in without the satisfaction of a meaningful catch.

Suddenly, Imam Malik became animated beyond his usually pensive frown. 'One might be forgiven for focusing on this singular aspect of communal hygiene, but I should like to add to the question of general cleanliness by way of the kitchen, since kitchen tasks should by instinct also invoke a generosity of spirit. In fact, *not one of us is a believer until he loves for his brother what he loves for himself.*

'Dearest Imam Malik, your comments are perhaps rather unhelpful at this moment,' said Sister Aaradhya. A polite enough interjection, but Father Graham's stoop and smile were already bowed beyond the curvature of reasonable return.

'Aaradhya, you must let Imam Malik speak. After all, we may have need of his belated wisdom. I'm curious to see whether he can add any further insult to injury.'

'My friend,' said the Imam simply, 'your cooking and the victuals that you prepare for the consumption of all who reside in the council of your good grace are sometimes prepared and offered to the community...without love.'

Father Graham was rendered aghast, losing his balance where he stood. 'I'm rendered aghast at such a profane accusation.'

'*Nope. No. No.*' Suddenly, the inert object, the corpse of a woman who had thus far remained curled up motionless on the curved seat, came to life like some anthropomorphised sloth. The Humanist was stirring.

'No, sorry mate. He's spot on—the Imam, I mean. It's proper shite the slop you've been serving up. Proper fucking slurry. I wouldn't fucking feed it to me dad's dog, and me dad's dog's fucking dead. And anyway, *any cunt who lives in a glass 'ouse shouldn't fucking throw stones.*'

It was now the turn of all present to be rendered aghast.

Father Graham collapsed into his seat. Brother Liu Xang covered his head with his hands and hummed an obliterating mantra. Sister Aaradhya's eyes welled up before flushing like the very unsanitary toilet that had started the whole mess. Imam Malik's eyes rolled back into his head and a spring-loaded finger pointed up to his beloved God. Rabbi Lamm shook his head deliberately, harbouring only a barely detectable smirk.

'So first the *toilet* and now *food*. It seems that I'm to be blamed for fouling both ends of the alimentary canal...'

Suddenly the picture became unhinged, the camera losing its sharp focus, blurring in and out, panning, disorientated—and then went black, and, just like that, live *Big Brother* was off-air.

O'Brien switched the television off and turned her attention to Winston, scrutinising him in the wake of *Big Brother*'s unscheduled demise—as though Winston held some unknown solution to an as yet undisclosed problem.

'In general terms,' O'Brien said finally, 'what are you prepared to do?'

'Anything that I am capable of doing,' said Winston, guessing.

'You're prepared to give your life to your work?'

'Yes.'

'You're prepared to be vilified for your poetry?'

'My poetry? Yes.'

'You're prepared to alienate yourself from all that know you, even your closest friends?'

'Yes.'

'You're prepared to dismiss those who will never understand your work?'

'My work? Yes! Yes!'

'You're prepared to cheat, to plagiarise, to corrupt the minds of children, to take habit-forming drugs if they aid your imagination, to prostitute yourself to publishers and critics, to offer yourself sexually if it furthers your cause—to do anything likely to make sure your poetry is widely read and reviewed?'

'Yes, I am!'

'If, for example, it would somehow serve your aesthetic interests to throw sulphuric acid in a child's face—would you be prepared to do that?'

'Yes.'

'You're prepared to lose your identity and live out the rest of your life as a waiter, a smoothie wonk or a granola-cum-coffee-grinder, and to be compelled to mention your unpublished poetry to your customers at every juncture, even if they are indifferent and don't want to hear about it?'

'Oh yes!'

'You're prepared to commit social suicide, if and when we order you to do so?'

'*We?* Yes of course!'

'You will be fighting in the dark. You will always be in the dark. You will receive my orders and you will obey them, without knowing why. I shall send you a book, and from this book you will learn the true nature of the society we live in, and the strategy by which we shall eventually destroy it. When you are caught, you will confess. This is unavoidable. But fortunately you will have very little to confess. You will not be able to betray anyone else but me, but by that time I will have become a different person, with a different face and a different voice.'

She continued to move restlessly to and fro over the soft carpet, and in spite of the bulk of her body set so heavily in the chair, there was a singular grace in her turning circle, and in the arc of her motion geometric tread patterns was indented into the seagrass weave's texture—recording her passage like crop circles, or druidic remains scoured into the land. Just as she was scoured with the ironic confidence that befits a radical, since, however much in earnest she was about her hopes and dreams, she had nothing of the single-mindedness that belongs to a hopeless fanatic, someone who martyrs themselves without hope of seeing the change they yearn for. When she spoke of Winston's poetry, of his disregard for the reader, of her contempt for the critics, of venereal disease, amputated limbs, and altered voices—it was with a faint air of persiflage.

'This is all unavoidable,' she said again. 'But it is not what we shall be doing when life is worth living again.'

For a moment O'Brien seemed lost in abstract sadness. Winston shimmered between the two poles of human expression, performing a gestalt shift from one foot to the other, the happy and sad, yin and yang, flotsam and jetsam, honey and vinegar, Janet and John, sad and happy—with fleeting glimmers of all the intermediate stages. Finally, O'Brien broke into a smile.

'You must get used to living without hope. Winston, you must write until you are caught, they will read your work and you will confess, and then you will die a terrible death. Those are the only consequences of your actions. There is no possibility that any perceivable change will happen within our own lifetime. We are the dead. Our only true life is in the future. We shall take part in it as handfuls of dust and splinters of bone acting as the dice of chance. How far away that future may be, there is no knowing. It might be a thousand years before the name Winston Smith comes to mean anything, or before your corpus is finally published, taught in schools and regarded as the masterpiece it truly is.

At present nothing is possible except to extend the area of sanity before death, little-by-little. We cannot act collectively. We can only spread our knowledge outwards from person to person, generation after generation. There is no other way. Winston, do you have any questions?'

'What about Julia?'

'*What about Julia?*'

'What should I tell her?'

'Julia knows nothing, so tell her nothing.'

'I will not tell Julia anything.'

'Good.' O'Brien wheeled up and down, made a couple of full rotations, clockwise then anti-clockwise, as if to cover her tracks. She stopped and came about-turn dramatically, speaking quickly, urgently. 'When you are least expecting it, someone will approach you and hand you a package. You will find it very interesting. Look after it. Guard it with your life.'

'I will, O'Brien,' said Winston. '*With my life.*'

O'Brien took Winston's hand and wrung it firmly.

'We shall meet again—'

'*In the place where there is no darkness!*'

O'Brien nodded, charmed by Winston's most faithful reprise.

CHAPTER IX

Winston was gelatinous with fatigue—the perfect description for a body possessed by the weakness of insensate jelly, and a more than adequate description of its strange translucency. For if he had had the energy to hold his hand up to the light, he would have been able to see refracted sunlight, perhaps even a rainbow, raking through. All the red blood and lymph had been drained from him by an enormous debauch of creativity, leaving only a frail structure of jangling nerves, desiccated bones, and gelatine skin. All sensations were magnified. He had persisted for more than ninety hours in just five days. Now the surge was over and he had nothing to do, no essential rectifications of any description until the next morning. He could spend fifteen hours languishing in bed (but sadly, without Martha's rigorous attentions in the morning).

In the afternoon he ambled in the direction of *Venus*, its windows fully aglow despite the ample sunlight. The parcel, not so heavy in his hand, was nonetheless sending a tingling sensation from the tips of his jelly fingers up his arms and deep into the murky parenchyma of his body. Wrapped inside the rough artisan-brown paper was the book, which he had had in his possession for some six days without an opportunity of examining it. On the sixth day of *We ♥ Love Week*, following all of the wonderful processions, the stirring speeches, the cha-cha-cha-chanting, the b-b-b-bells, the la-la-la singing, the smiley-face banners, the smiley-face posters, the smiley-face badges, headbands, armbands, scarves, hats, T-shirts and socks—the feel-good-rom-com-chick-flick-happy-go-lucky sense of it all, the rumbling rainbow of urbane tribal drums and the squealing of punk trumpets and sexy saxophones, the hefty tramp of happy vandals in sandals, the grind of the granola granulating machines, the aromatic coffee roasters, the improvised roar of berserk children running free of their hothouse carers, the celebratory boom of rainbow fire-works—after six delicious days of this, when the great communal orgasm was quivering to its consummate climax with the sense that anything could be achieved if it was consensually desired enough by those embraced by the consensus, Winston was in one of the central city squares at the very moment when it happened. It was evening, and the smiley faces and the scarlet banners were quite beautifully floodlit. The square was packed with several thousand people, many with burning torches, including a bloc of about a thousand school-children decked out in the colourful red uniforms of the Youth Neighbourhoodie Watch.

On the central speaker's platform, draped with long cascades of crimson smiley-face banners, Goldstein's *numero uno* acolyte was in full swing. A small lean man with disproportionately long arms and a large bald skull over which a few lank dreadlocks straggled, he was haranguing the crowd, tugging at their willing heartstrings—a heroic Rumpelstiltskin figure, contorted with a lifetime's implored overtures. He gripped the neck of the microphone with one hand while the other, enormous at the end of its bony arm, clawed the static air above his head as if swatting flies. His voice, endowed with a sonorous reverberation by the amplifiers and many speakers, boomed forth an endless catalogue of natural disasters, faraway environmental atrocities, reports of looming famine, and suffering children lifted from the limp clutches of broken-hearted, dead, dying parents. It was almost impossible to listen to him without working up an insatiable thirst for simple natural justice. Every few moments, the sadness of the crowd simmered up and the voice of the speaker was drowned in a low autonomic groan that palpitated in a thousand hearts as one group-o hug-o. The most passionate and authentic moans rose up from the vast body of assembled children, for they saw morality with innocent eyes, with a sadness so wrapped up in self-interest that tragedy was felt authentically and without contrivance (which was why, once-upon-a-long-time-ago, they had made such merciless and righteous soldiers/civic moral arbiters capable of seeing through even their own parent's oedipal bullshit).

The public lament had been underway for perhaps twenty minutes when a messenger hurried onto the platform, propelled by a great spontaneous cheer of relief from the crowd. A scrap of paper was passed into the speaker's wafting hand. He read it without pausing in the delivery of his oration. Nothing much altered in the tone of his voice or in the expressive metre of his presentational manner, but the emphasis seamlessly shifted from the need for food and water to the suddenly more urgent need for clothes and bedding. Reports had just come in that, since the most generous surge of donations recently dropped off at the many public collection points about the city was now spoiling—the food rotting, milk curdling, rats moving in—instead what was really urgently needed was clothes and bedding, and children's toys. With no need for extra words the new requirement was felt by all: clothes, bedding, toys—not so urgently food and water. The banners, pamphlets, posters, and sentiments with which the square was decorated were wrong. It was a simple mistake. An oversight. The orator, still gripping the microphone by its throat, his shoulders hunched forward, a free hand clawing at the flies, had modified his speech accordingly. One moment more and the melancholy groans had grown, rising from the crowd to shimmer just above their heads, as the sadness rose too, a risible exothermic misery. The agonising plight of orphaned nurslings with neither beds nor toys stung the grizzled mass of eyes staring at the huge TV screens showing enormous naked children, their blinking bewilderment magnified a thousandfold, huge God-sized beings with neither beds nor toys nor hope.

Immediately the square was awash with tears for the blighted

baby gods, their divine gift so quickly withdrawn. It was rain-
ing tears—a biblical flood of the humblest salt water, a torrent
of penitent saline solution. Even if the miraculous downpour
could somehow have been collected up by the barrel-load, it
would still have offered a futile sacrament for the thirst it dearly
wished to quench, since the tears of sadness harvested en masse
would be quite poisonous.

It was while the inaccurate posters and pamphlets were being
collected up to be recycled that a man whose face Winston knew
not to turn around to see tapped him on the shoulder softly.

'Hey man, you dropped this beautifully wrapped parcel...'

With a voluptuous fatigue that only rendered Winston's febrile eagerness yet more exquisite, he slipped past Charrington's domestic divide and climbed the stairs to the cherished
sanctuary above the luminous and dusty *Venus* antique sex
shop. Julia would arrive quite soon—but the parcel would not
wait, and Winston would not make it wait. He began a close
inspection of the brown paper, picking at the tape, prolonging
its excavation with embellished rituals of clumsy undoing—like
those promiscuous socialite macaques that lend their altruistic
labour to the grooming of local deer, transplanting the captive
ticks and fleas onto their own bodies so as to invent the hard
labour of leisurely preening. Thus Winston deliberately and
carefully unwrapped the parcel, with its impossible tape and in-
destructible paper—eventually discovering the book inside with
the measured surprise of a child at Christmas. Except that what
was instantly revealed to his incredulous gape was the book's
impossible title and the name of its author—which the unwrap-
per's hallowed hush answered with a formless gasp at the same
time as the tips of his fingers blindly followed the contours of
its embossed letters, much as a small child might feel out the
dot-to-dot of braille for the first time, confirming the tragic stig-
matic obliteration of his sight with the possibility of all insights

to follow. Winston read it again in disbelief, and yet the words were the same:

MY BIG BOOK OF ME
by
Winston Smith

Perhaps even more perplexing than the unsolicited attribution of his bona fide moniker to this peculiar publication were the two simple words loitering inside the book on the first page, and which filled him with an even greater sense of bewilderment...

For Julia

He flicked through the pages to see the many legions of words amassed, and nerved himself to begin at the beginning—preferring to read aloud, but in a faintest, most timid tone—hallowed by the creeping recollection of the alien cerebral cascade that had, up until this very moment, belonged exclusively to his own private crepuscular gloom.

'*Chapter One... Must compassionate mind, cultivate warmheartedness, peace of mind come from...heart root of all goodness, all exist in simple soil... No need complicated philosophies... My tingle brain and soft shell heart... The kindness cat has for injured mouse...*'

Winston paused to listen to the faint cries of happy children outside. In the room itself there was no sound save for the frustrated buzz of a common housefly blinded by daylight and baffled by glass. He settled back, and as if to surprise the book into yielding some hidden clue as to its progenitory stimulus, snatched it open at random, staring into the fold, reading aloud wherever his eye happened to make legible contact.

'*Sometimes one must create most best dynamic impression, by say something...and must one create...significant an impression...by remain silent. Saying, sometimes...silent in practice of tolerance... since enemy is best teacher. We can never obtain peace...in outer world...until make inner-peace with self. Where ignorance is master... there is never much possibility of peace.'*

Winston paused again, listening out for the comforting cries of the children below, but this time hearing instead warning shouts from fleeing precaristocrats and the drone of an insurrectionary jet-spray hounding the streets with its indiscriminate bursts. But no terrorist outrage was going to wrench Winston from the urgency of the book. And despite the shock of its material existence, his bewilderment was slowly caving in to pride, and delight was settling gently into his fatigue, welcomed into the soft towelling of the bed, the room caressed by the touch of the faint breeze on the window, a metronomic sense of order provided by the fly buffeting against glass....

He had only just doubled back to savour the first chapter when he heard Julia's footsteps on the stairs and so started out to meet her at the door with the astonishing news. Julia arrived, pushed past, and dumped her bag on the floor with a sigh.

'Look! One of O'Brien's agents gave me the package!' exclaimed Winston. 'The package that O'Brien told me about. Remember, I told you. I was at one of the *We Heart Love Week* parades—he pretended I'd dropped it. I brought it back here to open it—and you'll never guess what!' he gushed. Disentangling himself from Julia's embrace, he took the book out from behind his back to reveal it to her.

'That's fantastic,' said Julia, with facsimile interest, tousling her hair and rehearsing her best smile in the mirror, visible over Winston's left shoulder.

'But look, Julia! *Look!*' Winston held the book up to her, obscuring her line of sight to her own reflection. 'It's not just any old book! It's *my* book. It's a book of *my* poetry! O'Brien must really appreciate my writing, because she included some

240

of my most eloquent fortune rectifications! I'm actually lost for words!'

'Really? Let me see.'

Julia took the tome and weighed it in her hand as if such a gesture were the trusted physical test for scholarly gravitas. She fondled the embossed title and checked the spine with a professional touch, opening the book to inhale the warm waft of its atavistic flutter.

'Strange. No back-notes. No publisher's details,' she muttered, raising an eyebrow, and only then happening across the dedication on the first page after the main title page—

'For Julia? *Oh, Winston!*' she wept, '*My darling! Oh darling! Sweet Winston!*' Julia kissed Winston all over his face and clung to him like a child, whilst managing to keep at least one eye on the smiling mirror behind. Mindful of ruining the moment, Winston chose not to mar the sincerity of her affection by admitting that he had not in fact dedicated the dedication—instead, like a dutiful macaque, he simply harvested the praise for a parasite's labour.

Julia rushed over to the bed and lay down, patting the narrow space next to her for Winston to join her. 'Read to me,' she said. 'My *petit rédacteur-cum-auteur!*'

'If you would like me to, then I shall,' said Winston, making himself comfortable next to her and taking the time to select a favourite passage before clearing his throat. '*Now must burst world of imaginary, immeasurable force upon quaking tower, rhomboidal, opalescent, juxtaposed...juxtaposed...Julia?*'

Julia's breathing had become heavy, her eyelids beyond leaden.

'Julia, are you asleep?'

'No, my love,' the little voice came from far, far away. 'My eyes are shut, but I'm still listening. Go on. It's utterly marvellous, I'm enjoying every minute. It's quite inspirational. You're a very clever boy…man…*comrade.*'

Julia was sitting comfortably, so he continued.

But in the secrecy of Julia's dream, Chlamydia was already far, far, far away on the tropical island of Morass, in the presence of the island's enigmatic owner—the female sublime yet to be extricated from the male hubris of the ancient text…

'Algernon loves me unconditionally,' says Chlamydia, 'like a puppy dog loves a slipper.'

'You're mistaken. You're a cog, a fan belt, a spark plug, a window wiper—you're an unwitting mechanical component in a larger mechanical mechanism. But his mechanical plan is flawed—foiled by one simple oversight.' His gaze roams freely across the reciprocating contours of Chlamydia's body like a deodoriser ball lapping up body odour.

'Why?' asks the lump in Chlamydia's throat. 'Because I'm not your type?'

'Because my need for a simple life is far greater than my desire for the prittle-prattle of human intimacy.'

'Solipsism,' she says, nodding, 'how quaint—presumably you can afford to turn down a fortune?' Disdain casts a flaring glance over the worn textures of the dressing gown.

'I live according to my needs—I have little need for anything nor anyone.'

'You're a recluse? A loner? The world has spurned a wish and driven you to reproach it by withdrawing into obscurity—an immodest sentiment indeed!' she says lasciviously, refilling her glass indolently without asking or offering. 'Anyway', she adds, 'I don't see where we're going with this conversation'.

'For dinner,' he says. 'You're going to join me for dinner.'

Eyes frost-bitten onto his, Chlamydia places her glass on the table and extends her cold hand outstretched and diffuses her precious name into thin air. He inhales as though the sound were perfume, takes her paw firmly and kisses it hard.

'Delighted to meet you, Chlamydia Love. What a beautiful name...'

'It's Greek for contagiously popular.'

'How delightful—Helmut Mandragoras at your service...'

'Helmet...,' she says, rolling it around in her mouth. 'Mysterious name. Where is it from, what does it mean?'

'Helmut means "hell hound". Mandragoras derives from a shamanic shrub known as the mandragora or mandrake—a rootstock believed by the ancients to thrive from the sperm-soiled earth found beneath the feet of men who met their fate hung by the neck'.

'Charming. And what's for dinner, Mr Helmut Mandragoras?'

'You are...'

'I'm hardly dressed for dinner...' Chlamydia is proud to observe her host's mouth softening in acknowledgment of the backhanded reference to his own ramshackle appearance.

'Oh, let's not allow petty social protocols to spoil our evening—and anyway, I've been swept off my feet by the contagiously popular Chlamydia Love...'

Chlamydia smiles. Mandragoras has a tendency for baroque ornamentation, a penchant for self-satisfied pleonasms, for pure and simple pig-headedness... Perhaps Helmut is a forlorn poet soured by some tragedy that put him all out to sea and then washed his sodden husk ashore on Morass... Chlamydia enjoys her mental crucifixion.

'If you'll permit my abandoning you out here in the twilight,' he says at length, 'I'll go see about din-dins. I do apologise if it's a paltry offering—my dear old housekeeper prepared something earlier before I knew I was to have a guest.'

Momentarily governed by politeness, Chlamydia offers to help.

'How kind!' he says, sarcasm expanding into the open gesture surrendered to his disposal.

'Don't be insulting, Mr Mandragoras, I may leave if you insist on being insulting'.

'Poor Chlamydia—first you were thirsty, now you're hungry.

If you wish to stay, stay.' And, gesturing towards the volcanic slope,
'If you wish to go, you'll find gravity in your favour...'

Chlamydia's eyes sting, anger briefly swells, wanes, then dimples
sweetly.

'Forgive me for saying so,' she says, 'but your need for solitude is
symptomatic of an unhealthy loathing of women.'

'—JULIA! JULIA! WAKE UP! PLEASE OPEN YOUR EYES!
LOOK WHAT THEY DID TO MY BOOK! THEY FILLED IT
WITH THINGS THAT I DIDN'T EVEN WRITE! TERRIBLE
THINGS! THINGS I WOULD NEVER WRITE! WHY WOULD
O'BRIEN PURPOSEFULLY RUIN MY BIG BOOK OF ME BE-
FORE I EVEN HAD A CHANCE TO WRITE IT MYSELF? WHY,
JULIA? WHY?'

Julia was lying on her side with a cheek pillowed on her hand
and one dark lock tumbling conveniently across both eyes. Her
diaphragm rose and fell slowly, inhaling and exhaling, nice and
regularly—nothing untoward. Winston gave her a gentle shake:
he shook her shoulder, then an arm, but could not wake her by
shaking or pinching. He graduated to hands-on manhandling,
but despite great efforts she could not or would not wake—in
fact, she was unawakenable. His yelps and shouts soon ebbed
into a broken murmur, as the familiar mumbling recitation
floated upstairs from the yard below.

'By change of place: Now conscience wakes despair / That slum-
berd, wakes the bitter memorie / Of what he was, what is, and what
must be / Worse; of worse deeds worse sufferings must ensue...'

Even the *snip, snip, snip* of the decapitation of pretty flowers infiltrated the booming silence of the room. And only then
did Julia wake up, sitting up, yet her facial muscles clenched
with suddenly sinuous tension. She rose to her feet with an uncanny approximation of a smile—then backed away from poor
Winston, as if to better observe his reaction to the sound of the

thousands of unknown footsteps surging up the worn wooden stairs from the shop—and the concrete reverberation of many uniformed bodies rushing into the backyard, of footsteps tangled with urgent commands, vastly drowning out the genteel pruning and nonsensical recitation.

'What's happening? Julia! We're being invaded!' cried Winston, running first to the door and then to the window.

'We *are* being invaded!' confirmed Julia, excitedly clapping her hands.

'But why are we being invaded?'

Julia shrugged and widened her smile.

'Julia?'

'*Surprise!* Look in the mirror, Winston! *Wave!*'

Winston looked in the mirror, and saw only the face of confusion and Julia's naked excitement—he waved nonetheless, dumbly, compelled by a sense of disembodied politeness that all mirrors routinely extort.

'*So good to see you, Winston!*' came a cheery voice from somewhere beyond.

'You can see us? *How can you see us?*' said Winston, squinting at the mirror.

'*How can we see you?*' came the voice. 'Why, through the looking-glass, of course!'

With a sound of crashing glass from behind, the tip of a long aluminium ladder came crashing through the window, lifting the entire wooden frame, mangled bamboo blinds, and a mess of fractured shards into the room. No sooner had the wreckage landed than it became the subject of a damage report by a bird-faced man clutching a clipboard upon which was clipped a pro forma claim document that Winston was being urged to sign. Wonks clambered up the ladder and into the room as though over the fallen ramparts of a besieged castle—men and women manhandling battered flight-cases containing many technical components to snap, twist and screw together, the binary connective mode clearly not yet subject to a successful libidinal reorientation. The stairway disgorged a stampeding swarm of technicians with integrated headsets and microphones, urgent voices in their heads giving instructions to position tripods, boom-stands, reflectors, monitors and other miscellaneous apparatuses. Each wonk had a precise part to play in the choreographed chaos, and for a while Julia and Winston stood passively in the midst of the light, cameras and action as if forgotten altogether. Then came another crash—more of a dull thud than a crash, if truth be told. Some clumsy wonk had nudged the table next to the bed just enough for the coral phallus to pitch a little, sway a bit, then teeter and topple until it finally fell.

With an apologetic whine, a most sorrowful props-wonk hollowed out a small clearing for Winston to stoop down so as to examine how the clear acrylic, brittle with age, had shattered upon impact with the floorboards, the small fragment of coral expelled from its clear casing and exposed to his looming scrutiny. He looked at it, this diminutive embryonic thing, saw how it had survived the dark orifices of countless ancient corpses only to be born into the light—and like all things born into the light, it was a worthless crust of nothingness, a hopeless piece of histrionic flotsam, a scrap of jetsam, and before his eyes it merely collapsed under the dead weight of its own precarious rot—whatever it had once been *metaphorically* was now reduced to dust, shamed by the revelation of a most humble truth.

A short period of grief passed before a wonk was motioned forwards to sweep up the mess, and another with a utility box stuffed with a mass grave of make-up sent to begin stuffing tissues around Winston's clammy neck. Seeing that Julia was exempt from the tissue treatment, Winston cast a quizzical frown in her direction, only for her to betray a duplicitous smile that immediately melted as she slunk backwards into the blur of busybodies going about their urgent business.

'Julia! Julia? What's going on?'

'Because you're worth it, Winston! It's all because you're worth it!' Julia's soft voice was muffled by a violent cloud of the softest fluffiest fluffy cotton wool brushes applying healthy hues and perlite matting powder—and in seconds Winston's wan complexion was simply radiant. He dared not turn his head even by a millimetre, struggling as he was to breathe against the fluffing-caressing-fluffy-velvety-cushiony-brushy brush. He could just about bear it, pleasant torture being the worst kind, the kind of torture where there is no hidden secret for the interrogator to extract, and thus no end in sight for the victim—only the agonising feeling of suffocation as his pounced eyes were clenched tight against the predacious scut and the abstract sounds fluffing all about him.

So he stayed standing dead still, still clutching his *My Big Book of Me* close to his chest. No one in the room had addressed him directly, so why would he risk moving? He held the book tight; if he stayed still, silent, and did nothing untoward, it might still all turn out to be a simple mistake. He wondered about Charrington, if they had caught him out too, or whether the old man had been in on it all along. He wondered what they had done to the humming fossil massacring her plants down in the yard. The lights were blistering hot, Winston was sweating and fretting, fretting and sweating about the expensive pulvil clogging up in his cratered pores, imagining the pools of mire—or Syme's human gore *juxtaposed* with mud, an old film still of a wartime shell crater, or something equally tragic, vaguely poetic—and then, from the blind spot of the searing luminescence focused on Winston there came an unanticipated silhouette, from which emerged the familiar figure of *old man Charrington*—a different Charrington, now smiling broadly, now manifestly flamboyant, light on his feet, but still adorned in his old moth-eaten velvet jacket, now revealed as pure costume, with oversized cuffs, big childish stitches embroidering the seams, decorated with jumbo buttons.

His entrance was made to cries of '*Bravo! Bravo!*' With a generously wide embrace of sweeping and endless arms, Charrington beckoned for a shy and retiring Julia to step forward from the shadows—and with gestures of reserve, modesty and delight, she held out her paw for young Charrington to draw her fully into the spotlight, where both took the most yawning and ponderous bows to rapturous on-set applause. Julia and young Charrington bent over to touch their toes...then up...and down once more...*Oh! One last time*; and, as is customary in pantomime, where the professional cast is obliged to deflect a little glory in the direction of their sporting stooge, a little applause was politely dedicated to Winston, and somewhere in the tangle of neuronic reflexes rudely awakened, a trigger triggered, a cog cogitated, and Winston found himself also doubled over in the performance of a most supple bow, still clutching the book to his chest, as if many years of Martha's yoga had prepared for this very moment. But upon coming erect, he greeted the spectre of a third significant player gliding slowly forwards from the shadow into the light, squeaking forth as Julia and young Charrington made way, leaving their conjoined arms in an arch through which the spectral figure of O'Brien steered into the light.

'*O'Brien! Thank God! What on earth is happening?*' said Winston, his voice elevated to a nursery falsetto. O'Brien came forward with the most beneficent of smiles—but upon seeing Winston, her expression immediately turned to granite, her smile crashing down like a detonated rock face, many tons of emotional rubble falling upon the small child looking up at its now face-crushing benefactor.

'*What have I done?*'

O'Brien came to a standstill before poor Winston. She gestured for the crowd of technicians to go about their last minute checks. She beckoned for Winston's hand, pulling him close—and began:

'You see Winston, before the Age of Great Consensus, the world was an endless nightmare of war and pain. The Age of Great Consensus saved the dying world from this endless war and pain. We know this to be true, yes?'

'Yes.'

On the affirmative, O'Brien dropped Winston's hand and spun away, ostensibly to allow the bed to be carried past and removed from the room by two assistants, and the table too—but apparently also the better to observe Winston's discomfort.

'The world was finally blessed by peace.' She came closer to deliver a whisper. 'With no need of a standing army, no bombs, no secret police, no surveillance nor patriarch nor tyrant to watch over us. We do not inflict systemic violence, however subtle, since divine love conquers all—of course, it goes without saying that we would *fight to the death to preserve the freedom of even those we disagree with*—but who needs to fight when you can more easily conquer with love? World domination through world peace! Are you with me so far, Winston?'

'Yes.'

'You and I lead good lives, eat good food, live in comfort and have ample opportunity for wellness, mindfulness and self-improvement—as do we all, and it's groovy. *N'est pas?*'

'*Oui.*'

'But in sacrificing war and pain in favour of universal consensus, we quite rightly reject every human extremity in favour of a *mediocrity of means* and an *average of intent*. With all wanton intensities pacified by sober acquiescence, we find little threat to our happiness, other than those accidental misfortunes of everyday chance, the stubbed toes and the odd cancer. We have no mortal enemies—even those who for centuries lived off the labour of our flesh now freely wander among us as the living dead, the precaristocrats, living fossils, quaint relics of a besmirched past. We feed the famished, but only enough to ensure a mutual reciprocation of dependence and guilt. We suffer the odd act of terrorism, by sentimental revivalists who have vastly mistaken the meaning of *ethnic cleansing*—most likely performance artists, yet to reveal their demands. *And now we have you.* Winston Smith, heroic rectifier of errant misfortune cookies.'

O'Brien paused, giving Winston dispensation to respond to the presentation so far.

'Well, that's exactly what I am! In a nutshell! I'm a simple everyday rectifier of errant misfortune cookies! I've always attended to the rectifications with great care! You know how proud I am of my work! I'm just a happy yippy wonk doing my thing, like all the others in the Ministry! Ask anyone there! *Ask Syme!*'

It was a paltry offering, and did nothing to dissuade O'Brien from tightening the noose.

'Forecasts for the expected seasonal famines are not looking as promising as first predicted. Viewing figures for the Two Minutes Compassion are actually down for the first time in recorded history. Goldstein's talent contract is coming up for renegotiation at the end of the season—and between you and me, the rumours of an obscene salary ultimatum are not just idle gossip. Compassion fatigue is on the rise. But now we have a chance to remind everybody exactly why consensus requires great discipline and self-restraint.'

'I...I understand...'

'They will see it like this: Winston Smith is a criminal in a world without living memory of crime. It is he who secretly composed the misfortune messages that drove hundreds of innocents—thousands, or tens of thousands, millions if you prefer—to their death. Winston Smith has descended upon us with the malice and ruin of the old world. Winston Smith is a monster...a reminder of the worst of humanity.'

'But why?'

'Why Winston? *Why?* Let me tell you *how*, and the *why* will soon follow. You predicted the method of your victim's expiration and told them that fate was unavoidable, and they succumbed because they were kind and trusting folk, motivated by a belief that those miraculous turns of events that endow life with significance *must* be predetermined—the humble *everything happens for a reason* tautology. And you very quickly noticed the difference between those fortunes that customarily promised ambiguous hope, good health, enduring love and emotional prosperity—and those especial *misfortunes* that we indirectly supplied, the ones giving precise predictions of the grimmest catastrophes to come. As you noticed, it was only the *misfortunes* that had any evidential clairvoyance—only the misfortunes that were effective, that came true—the bodies, the deaths, the suicides. You led the weak by the nose in the name of fate, manipulating the naivety of a population happily dumbed-down by years of willing consensual mediocrity. The poor souls who fell foul of fate were merely following orders—*your orders*. But look how it affected you. A man without art, without vision, devoid of lyricism, became a poet. And how it sharpened your pessimism—how acute now is your self-doubt. Do you remember what you told me when you recently visited my home—that you were of the opinion that there is a conspiracy of forces at work that asserts the theology of wellness as the natural order of things? How did you describe it? Oh yes! *The survival of the flattest! Of the mediocre—to the detriment of all else...* Remember, Winston? I do! When you stormed my apartment to tell me how you were an enemy of consensus, of compassion, of charity, of good fortune, of the narcissism of unity, of the society of the polite, of good causes, of nature, of an art determined by positivity and the anthropomorphic search for cosmic significance? And do you remember telling Julia that you were *tired of the congealing of all forces towards the obvious, of anticipating the average for the sake of mediocrity*...that you were *tired of the magical consensus that envelops all in the mediocrity of harmoniousness*...? Do you remember telling your beloved muse that *our primitive ancestors learned to turn the other cheek...to love thy neighbour as themselves*—and that, *for all their petty genocides, leading to the grandiloquent statement of progress—of disapproving what another might say, but defending to the death their right to say it, in their millions if needs be*...? That you were *sick and tired of our great planetary consensus and its arrogant limit to progress itself*? Good God Winston! *You became more enlightened than all of us put together!* Winston, *you put us all to shame!* You despised us because our mediocrity disappointed you! We had fallen so far short of true enlightenment that all you could do was to punish us by working yourself to the bone, like some old pessimistic Stakhanovite—repudiating the very dream of progress that you so secretly adored. We failed to live up to your expectations, and this is how you rewarded us: *Whether rich, poor, educated white, white trash or illiterate black, religious brown or non-believing circumcised flesh of straining purple member, stale jism spurting into heaving loin, yoga-master growling, must bury tongue in shit, dip in shit, dip-shit, must shun family, must shun loved ones, must suffer loss, must lose all hope*—Winston, you were performing our self-loathing for us!'

'But O'Brien! It's not true! You just admitted that you made the worst of it up! You know very well that I didn't write those awful words, since you asked me to rectify them! You personally approved of my rectification before it was sent back out!'

O'Brien nodded eagerly, as if egging Winston on, to defend himself, to tell the truth, to put her right, to say it how it is—nodding at each and every word as it stuttered from Winston's gabbling mouth—But when he ran out of things to say, O'Brien swiftly took up the slack.

'*I hear you*, Winston, but I'd be remiss if I didn't inform you that it's not looking good for you right now. All things considered, it's nothing less than mass murder. Genocide. And with your book soon to hit the shelves...a veritable manual of sickening crime...'

O'Brien gestured for the book and Winston handed it over limply, its gravitas now burdened by accusation. O'Brien flicked through the pages with familiarity bordering on contempt, opening it wide until the spine cracked beyond its binding, and molesting the crease, her nose stuffed deep into the crack.

'I have to say, it's a very handsome object, nice design, feels nice, nice paper, good font. Winston—you must be so very proud!'

'Must I?'

'Well...you must at least agree that it feels serious—*weighty*. And what an achievement for it to be published during your lifetime! You're officially immortal, Winston! It's certainly a page-turner—and you can bet it'll be an instant bestseller! Don't you worry—we'll make sure of that. Oh—and Julia has kindly offered to write a blurb for the back cover. Something about the forensic extrication of the female sublime from the hubris of the male gaze.'

'But you know very well that the majority of these words are not mine—'

'Yes I do. *I do do*. And the parts that are yours are quite good—you have some talent—you really do. But of course, we've been helping you out with the wording of the misfortunes for many months now, edging you toward the creation of your finest work—and we're quite content to let you take the credit for all of it.'

Winston sagged with the dead weight of a body draped from a welcome noose.

'Excuse the pun, but it's going to be a very *novel* experience for us all—for everyone. Not for many years has the public been invited to pore over such extreme violations in detail, their disgust indulged publicly without shame—oh, how the communal flesh will crawl! It'll positively quiver and turn to stiffened gristle! Our eyes will bulge! We'll prolong the public's moral ejaculation with tantric discipline, until the appetite for your sickening pornography will turn into self-disgust, be purged—and then, and only then, shall we sacrifice you, my dearest Winston, to the pious outrage and the reinvigorated cause of mediocrity. I can see it now: *To Catch a Cookie Killer*—catchy, no? I might ghost-write it myself someday.'

Suddenly the bustling room bristled into unified purpose, a sudden stillness took hold, and signs were given for the lights and cameras aimed at Winston and O'Brien to flare.

'I think the season premiere of *Two Minutes Hate* is ready for us,' said O'Brien, gently cajoling Winston to turn on the spot for the camera, whilst gesturing for a handy wonk to lunge forwards to pluck an errant make-up tissue from his collar.

'*And, action!*'

'Winston Smith, your confession, if you please.'

PART 3

CHAPTER I

Winston had awoken much earlier than normal, stirred by the same old nasty nag that keenly reminded him that there was nothing at all normal about the beginning of another day inside the house. As usual, morning was unambiguously declared by the lights being thrown on without so much as a hint of warning. On for day—off for night. There was no naturalistic fading up to daylight, no dawn chorus, no diminishing of the light toward nightfall, since there were no windows through which the diurnal motion of the earth's relation to the sun and moon could be detected, and no creeping crepuscular shadow. No constellation of stars. No rotation of the sky. No nothing. The motivation to spring out of bed and seize the day was merely a Pavlovian hangover from a happier former life, as were the cursory yawns that greeted darkness when the house was consumed by pitch black at midnight.

Early on in Winston's incarceration, before the others had been selected and deposited, he had often been teased in the purity of his isolation by the faint sound of chanting coming from somewhere beyond the set walls, somewhere outside. He imagined it to be a revivalist vigil—he'd seen old pictures of ambiguous figures loitering at the gates, waiting to witness the prison lightbulbs dim as some child killer was sent to hell. Even this amateurish chorus of death chants waxed and waned without providing any clue as to the day, month or season, however—and eventually dissipated long before the other housemates were drafted in and the new season announced. But there was one constant that never went away, lingering beneath everything—a dark underbelly to all things: a low, surging hum, which Winston had long assumed to be the sound of an occult static built up between all of the combined machines of perpetual broadcast—the electromagnetic death drive of live TV.

Winston was a dab hand at fumbling and dabbing around in the dark. He often fumbled his way into the sunken communal conversation pit, waiting there patiently for the morning sun to be switched on. This morning he was sitting there, gnawed at by a dim suspicion of hunger—not enough to motivate him to move into the communal kitchen to attempt breakfast in the dark, not least because he was unsure whether this morning hunger was also an artefact of the production, a fiction that compelled him in the absence of any real sensory stimulus. So he sat as still as he could, with hands crossed politely on his knee, in the dark, smiling, alone—quite sure, despite the darkness, that he was not alone at all, knowing that he was being watched, quite positive that he was being very closely observed. The cameras kept running all day, switching to night-vision when the lights were tripped off, whether by hand or timer, no one knew which. In the evening some housemates transported their reflex yawns to bed, while others crept about, entertaining themselves in the dark, their ghostly movements captured for the ghouls at home.

Reduced to a luminescent grey with bright green eyes, these formless, featureless, pallid beings haunted the set for the entertainment of a great tide of insomniacs—thousands, perhaps even millions washed up past their own domestic bedtimes, taking great comfort from this nebulous pantomime of incarcerated jellyfish floating about aimlessly, with nothing to do, too insubstantial to settle and sleep.

We shall meet in the place with no darkness... the place where nothing went unseen, where even the pitch black was colonised by X-ray eyes that saw everything—tired eyes that could not switch off and which, whatever they saw, were never offended enough to be plucked out.

Even in the dead of night, when Winston was reduced to his most superficial self, unable to see his own hand in front of his face should he make the mistake of moving it, the inspissate mass of prying eyes was still there, blinking in the dark, glued to the screen, prepared to see all at any cost, determined to study his inanimate husk even though he knew that they knew that he was feigning sleep. And so his reluctance to move was the best he could do to underwhelm his audience, who punished him with the revenge of even greater attentiveness. It was no exaggeration to say that the housemates and the house that the housemates inhabited had no solidity to it at all. Desired into being by the wilful voyeurism of many mesmerised millions, it was an animistic shipwreck floating in mid-air, levitating above the planet, held aloft by the collective will of the devoted legions of viewers, a vessel whose doomed shipmates existed in a state of perpetual insomnia, never allowed to fully rest and destined, by way of deprivation of sleep and social grace, to lapse back into incest, cannibalism, prostitution, murder, rape, drug addiction, obesity, slavery, gluttony and alcoholism, and the rest. A ship of fools dashed upon the rocks of self-ruin, an invitation to all the bad things once rife before the great global detoxing, the great Undustrial Revolution and the cleansing Age of Great Consensus, to return once more, if only so as to be subject to mass scrutiny, to be damned yet again, *retoxed only to be detoxed, detoxed only to be retoxed, in an endless eternal return of the same....*

Winston had learned to sit very still. Even in the dark, any unexpected movement caused the cameras discretely mounted high up on the set walls and concealed behind mirrors to bristle, rotate, pan, and refocus. Winston heard their servomotors whir as he moved. When he walked it was as if his own bodily motion, his joints and muscles, were automated. The servos possessed the uncanny sentience of cockroaches, except that it was Winston who was the cockroach, his mechanical passage from room to room observed with a certain revulsion by the human audience. And it was not only purposeful movements they were interested in, but even the tiniest motion—an innocuous scratch, a blink, a casual itch or a nervous tic. The tiniest of motions, thus rarefied, became the most delightful.

The banality of duration rendered the housemates prone to boredom. Their lethargy reduced somatic movement to the bare minimum of a nominal existence. The sight of their excruciating boredom had itself become the precise jewel of entertainment—at home, viewers could delight in seeing them do exactly nothing, a nothingness amplified so effectively that there was a substantial eagerness even to watch them sleep—even better if their sleep were to occur during the day, so one could watch their days squandered in listless hibernation, witness their withdrawal into inertia, until their decline into existential minimality and the minutiae of quashed self-esteem had itself become monumentally fascinating, a sublime entertainment. The extreme pressure thus placed upon even the slightest movement imbued the desire to itch, scratch or rub raw with an overwhelming gravitas: the long term suppression of a tingling itch might eventually give way to an outburst of violent scratching, an epileptic fit of itching, a monkey's rash of chafing—small movements rendered violent by their contrast with the almost cryogenic state of suspended animation that was the norm, enough to cause sudden fright and the spilling of TV dinners, an explosive cough, reflex itch or sudden sneeze blowing the petrified audience backwards into their armchairs like a slapstick blunderbuss.

Winston sometimes wondered whether his parents and sister were at home watching *Big Brother* and, if so, whether they had not by now already disowned him. His prevailing unease was itself an itch that must not be scratched—and yet, judging by the sound of collective snoring that seeped from the communal dormitory, the other housemates had little trouble abiding by the indubitable fact that all was normal in the house, and that morning was *real enough*.

When the lights eventually blinked on, Winston knew that morning had broken—completely broken, like the first morning. He was yet to move. One eye was shut, the other aimed at the mirror opposite him, its line of sight angled so as to bounce its way into the adjacent room by way of the accumulated reflections of a labyrinth of mirrors. In this way he could observe his housemates emerge from the communal dormitory before they were anywhere near the communal living room, and could prepare himself accordingly.

Heralded by the sound of shuffling slippers, the poet Ampleforth was the first to shamble into view, yawning from mirror to mirror, still in pyjamas. Ampleforth, the hairy-big-eared forgetful owl-poet Ministry missive journeyman, made one or two uncertain movements from side to side, as though having some deluded premonition that there were more doors to pass through, but merely confusing the mirrors for portals. He moved through the communal living room into the communal kitchen, passing by Winston without particularly noticing him, and filled the yawning mouth of the kettle. He was several days away from a shave. A delicate feathery beard covered his face to the cheekbones, imparting an air of rustic bohemianism that suited him well. He decided to notice Winston, and only then cracked a hairy-poet-smile.

'Morning Winston! What are you in for again?'

'You cannot stop bird of sorrow fly overhead, but can prevent such unhappy thought from nesting there.'

'Oh yes...' Ampleforth chuckled. 'I do remember. Cup of tea?'

'Please.'

'Milk?'

'Please.'

'Sugar?'

'Please.'

'One or two?'

'*Much sugar necessary for best way obscure poison, please.*'

Ampleforth examined Winston deliberately, observing his manic smile and now plainly sectionable eyes. He tipped a little almond milk and two raw-cut coconut sugar cubes into a cup of Alderman Grey tea, and stirred. 'Fate has a rather eccentric way of rewarding us when we least expect it,' he began vaguely. 'I've been an avid fan of *Big Brother* since season one, and have watched without ever even imagining that some day I would be a housemate myself. You can imagine my surprise when a fortune cookie script I happened to open in the Ministry eatery invited me here—*in person!* I've never heard of such a thing! It addressed me by name! Can you imagine my surprise?'

'*People take different road for seeking fulfilment and happiness but the road for all people is the same.*'

'Indeed…thank you for those elegant words, Winston. I shall cherish them forever.' The expression on Ampleforth's face changed, suddenly suffused with the warmth and joy of the poetic pedant who has stumbled across some forgotten tome. 'Has it ever occurred to you,' he said, 'that the whole history of English poetry has been determined by the fact that the English language lacks rhymes?'

'*Truly compassionate attitude toward other does not change even if they behave negatively or even if they hurt you,*' said Winston, beaming.

Ampleforth looked on, slightly bewildered by the elegiac banality of Winston's contribution. His eyes flitted about the mirrored walls, seeking a single solitary window by means of which to confirm a conjecture, but only seeing out into a flatland infinity. 'I'm quite sure it's the morning—isn't it?'

'*Happiness is not something ready-made. It must come from own generous action. Must action speak louder than word,*' said Winston, hands neatly crossed, eyes beaming.

Ampleforth continued with his green tea and progressed to a light breakfast. Joining Winston in the sunken conversation pit, he munched his freshly ground granola, wild berries and yogurt while Winston sipped his tea, one eye readied on the mirror. Someone else was stirring. Tomioka emerged wearing khaki shorts and a linen blouse, with the now customary red raw eyes.

'Morning Ampleforth...Morning Winston,' she said on her way to the kitchen, sobbing inconsolably, doubtless with thoughts of her little Gilbert.

'Morning Tomioka!' said Ampleforth brightly. 'What are you in for?'

'Every morning the same quip...I could set my watch by your forgetfulness, dear Ampleforth.' Tomioka took a bite out of a small, red, crisp apple and wept at the sound of its crunch.

Tomioka, to answer Ampleforth's question, was *in* for letting her dear son run in front of the parade lorry for loose sweets, and for the tragedy that followed. Tomioka took her soured apple and sat with Ampleforth and his granulated granola. Winston sat perfectly still, as still as a beaming Altaic deity.

Another housemate emerged from the communal dormitory.

'Good morning Ampleforth, Winston, Tomioka!' said Syme ever-so-cheerily, with a smile perfected in the dark.

'Good morning Syme,' said Tomioka. '*What are you in for?*'

Syme rewarded Tomioka's conceit with an unfettered smile, but just as cleanliness had once been next to godliness, Syme's happiness was now mostly next to weepiness—since, in answer to Ampleforth's proxy query, Syme was *in* for having squandered his Goldstein sabbatical honorarium. He had intended to work on a highly promising dystopian novel about an overbearing sibling who watches over everyone with a vast array of invasive technologies, but it had turned out to be nothing more than the pretentious ruminations of a mild depressive with an inferiority complex. There was little writing to speak of, and what there was revealed itself to be motivated largely by narcissistic self-loathing. Ultimately, Syme's literary legacy added up to chronic paralysis, as he hung somewhere between a forestalled first page and an unaccomplished suicide. Too scared to write, too scared to strike the decisive blow against the obligation of living, too fearful to act against the tyranny of life, unable to leave its dutiful sufferers to shamble around in abject anger, furious at the audacity of action, abandoned to the sentiments of memory that makes sheep of all men...*For where can suicide happily reside, when fluoride is added to drinking water to promote healthy teeth, and mercaptan added to odourless domestic gas to cause nausea instead of death? Even domestic utilities poisoned by a surreptitious well-being!*

Syme noticed Winston examining him, sensed him forming an opinion. Winston noticed Syme and adjusted his grin accordingly, beaming extra-wide in an effort to counteract Syme's scrutiny. The little thick-skinned gonk nevertheless shimmied around the curved seat until he was pressed up against Winston's shoulder, his mouth dangerously close to Winston's ear. He began to whisper, the fervid words hissed quietly but at a prolific rate.

'*He imagined the smash of truncheons on his elbows and heel of jack-boots on his shins; he saw himself grovelling on the floor, screaming for mercy through bloody and broken teeth. He thought of Juliette. She was fixed in his mind. He loved her but she had betrayed him; that fact was as true as he knew the rules of arithmetic. He felt love for her, and he wondered where she was. He thought about a razor blade, it would bite into him and the fingers holding to his wrist would also be cut to the bone. He was more squeamish about cutting his fingers than his wrists—*'

'What are you doing?' Winston's lips mouthed the words with ventriloquial restraint, his muscles taut around a petrified smile. 'You realise they can hear everything we say? *Everything!*'

'But Winston...I've been working on my novel...'

'*EVERYTHING.*'

Suitably scolded, Syme slumped back in silence. Winston's beaming rictus grin flared with hidden anger, but he managed to tame it before the sound of a perky glockenspiel ditty boomed loudly over the household PA.

Ding, bing, dong! 'Good morning housemates! This is Big Brother speaking.' Of course, the voice, most congenial and masculine, was that of O'Brien, affected by a simple filter, her unmistakably strident feminine timbre exchanged for a more rueful male modulation. 'Would housemate Ampleforth be so kind as to join us in the Diary Room after breakfast. But take your time. Thank you.'

Ampleforth set his granola down clumsily, spilling his spoon, clearly dismayed by the request. A labyrinth of glances deflected silently around the communal conversation pit, and the dim hunger in Winston's belly turned up a notch. Ampleforth spoke, addressing the omniscient Big Brother in the most earnest tone that a human larynx could summon.

'Big Brother, haven't I told you everything already? Haven't I already spilled the beans and let the cat out the bag? What else do you need to know? What else *is there* to know? There's nothing I wouldn't confess, nothing! Just tell me what it is and I'll confess straight off. Write it down and I'll sign it! *Please! Anything but the Diary Room!*'

'Housemate Ampleforth, I'd really appreciate if you could come to the Diary Room after breakfast. Thank you kindly.'

Big Brother was unbending. Ampleforth rose to his feet slowly, clasping his heavy heart.

'Do anything to me! Finish it off and let me die! Shoot me! Hang me! Sentence me to twenty-five years! Is there somebody else you want me to give away? Just say who it is and I'll tell you anything you want! I don't care who it is or what you do to them! I've got a dutiful wife and three sinless cherubs at home! The biggest of them isn't six years old, bless him...or her! You can take the whole lot of them, march them out one by one and cut their throats in front of my eyes, and I'll stand by and watch—I'll even help! Wipe the spit and blood from the blade on my sleeve! But I beg of you, *not the Diary Room! Anything but the Diary Room!*'

Ampleforth flung out an arm and projected his finger at Winston's idiotic grin in the hope of deflecting his own incrimination. 'That's the one you ought to be taking to the Diary Room, not me!' Adding, in a whispered aside, 'Sorry, Winston.' And then, his voice once again elevated, 'You don't hear what he says under his breath. Give me a chance and I'll tell you every word of it. *He's* the one that rails against poor Goldstein, *against charity, against consensus,* and whatever else it is he's in here for—it's him you should have in the Diary Room, not me.'

'This is Big Brother. I must insist you come to the Diary Room. Please do so now.'

Syme and Tomioka had cheered up a little, relishing Ampleforth's little drama, clapping their hands and laughing without reserve, since Ampleforth was mostly homosexual, had no connubial partner to speak of, and especially no such thing as a wife, nor children that he knew of.

Ampleforth took a last mouth of granola and chewed it with the disdain of a man regretting not his crime, but the choice of *last supper.*

All knew his fate, but none would mention it by name.

'Well, that's that then,' he said, resigned. 'Off to the Diary Room to talk about me, myself and how I feel about you lot, yet again.'

When the housemates were not performing small and worthless tasks for the effective increase or punitive diminution in quantity or quality of rationed victuals, they drifted about the household with lacklustre bearing, tending to the hydroponic herb garden, drinking tea or detoxing, napping, finger-painting, life-drawing or writing or scribbling, or forming tantric meditation crosswords in the sandpit. Lethargy's gravity often pulled them into the communal conversation area, that mass grave of half-eaten conversations that lingered and festered into resentments and injurious grudges. But on the odd occasion when *Big Brother* requested it, the housemates were set precise tasks, the performative execution of which would determine the provision and rustic quality of the food, yoga classes, and other wellness opportunities—or the punitive revocation thereof.

One such menial task had required the housemates to spend five days of unbroken eight-hour shifts segregated into small isolated deprivation booths gnawing away at the sharp geometric edges of sugar cubes, transforming them laboriously into more irregular shapes, a little more idiosyncratic and kooky, a tad more personalised, much like the wonks who might eventually sweeten their tea with them. While working they were required to wear headphones which delivered into their skulls immersive recordings of *The Tibetan Book of the Dead* and *Principles of Scientific Management*, split into respective left and right ear channels so that the mental collision added to the mind-numbing Taylorist piecework might give rise to spiritual self-realisation—or just plain old migraine.

Entering their booths promptly at seven-thirty in the morning, they had to work continuously, with only food and water provided as they toiled.

On the second day, Ampleforth was secretly instructed by Big Brother to vacate his booth only moments after entering, his withdrawal timed so that his workmates witnessed him enter as they themselves entered, but would remain oblivious of his staggered exit. Ampleforth was secretly summoned to the kitchen, there to receive immodest gifts of artisan carrot cake, yogurt and rustic cashew cheese—on strict condition that he must not reveal his exemption. On the second day Ampleforth *and* Syme were relieved of their labour by the same method, and presented with even greater bounty. On the third day, Ampleforth, Syme and Tomioka were initiated into the secret rewards of the kitchen. And on the fifth day the same three spent the day luxuriating in fine food, candle-making, coil pots, Jenga and reflexology— before being returned to their work hives only a few minutes before the end of the shift and released moments later, deceitfully aping the exhaustion and indignation of their Stakhanovite colleague, the poor, unwitting, brain-battered, tooth-weary Winston Smith.

Other obligatory group tasks included batik, Zen archery, egg blowing, stone sucking, sponsored silence, sonic wine tasting, bead worrying, glass blowing, immersive performance art, stick whittling, street graffiti, yoghurt making and revivalist agit-prop festival banner design. One such task-orientated morning the bright lights came on and Ampleforth, Syme, Winston and Tomioka awoke to Big Brother's request for them to assemble in the communal living room, there to find, set out upon a large trestle table, many, many pieces of coloured paper and four pairs of safety scissors. They were told that they must complete as many origami pieces in a single day as they could. No specific goal was set, but Big Brother added that systemic wellness for the coming days would be contingent upon divine origami productivity. Each took up a pair of scissors and found a seat around the table, whilst Ampleforth read aloud from the *Origami Bible*.

'Origami comes from *ori* meaning folding, and *gami* meaning paper...'

'Groovy...' Having worked with small pieces of paper for many years, Winston took to this particular task like a pro.

The first piece he made was a swan, and then a duck. The others' fingers were less inured to the threat of death by a thousand paper cuts, and their woes culminated in nasty fingertip blisters that, once burst, would have made the manipulation of paper impossible, were it not for the escaping blood and pus that moistened the paper enabling the ancient technique of *wet-folding*, at least until the paper became too saturated with pus, at which point the windmills, kites, flags, hot air balloons, butterflies, candy-floss, sweets and cakes, bushbabies, honey bees, giraffes, caterpillars, dragon flies, porcupine, jugglers, owls, doves, palm trees, zebra, rhino beetles, aardvarks, little red riding hood, scarecrows and snowmen became too soggy to maintain their structure and were doomed to collapse in a general distortion of form—much like those bloated bodies of misfortune victims that washed up along the shore, folded into similarly contorted shapes.

Winston was quick to notice a neat connection between Origami and the cookie fortunes he had once worked on, and devised an application that would link the two forms: he imagined fortunes written on cute origami sculptures to be carefully placed inside cookies as the vehicle for an even more astonishing mode of dissemination. Winston considered this an adorable idea which someone in a position of influence ought to mention to someone in the know.

The fifth contestant in the house was excused most menial tasks on account of being generally work-shy and drunk, occupying her time in the household sleeping off a thirty-year hangover. But one fine afternoon, the hibernating contestant woke up. She had escaped eviction during the Religious Zealot season, and her prize for such endurance was a season roll-over, which meant she had remained in the house, and was incidentally quite satisfied with this arrangement since apparently she was, in real life, homeless.

Winston caught sight of the rarely glimpsed rollover house-mate awakening mid-afternoon from her marathon slumber, her image deflected in the many angled mirrors some time before appearing to the naked eye, like fossilised light sent from some obscene unheavenly body, hurtling towards Earth, threatening the planet with immanent peril. Winston observed its approach with the appropriate hush and awe until, shedding her garish silk kimono to the floor, she announced to all and sundry, 'Fuck me, I've been asleep for twelve fucking hours and I'm still fucking knackered! What's that all about?'

'Sleep breeds sleep,' blurted Syme, his little wonk fingers and thumbs worrying his worry-beads sick with worry.

Winston endeavoured to peel his grimace back to its default setting, but the newly arrived housemate launched herself into the hot tub with no consideration for the potentially catastrophic displacement that would result, causing a tidal wave to rise above the human Plimsoll line, teetering at the nipples, eliciting a univocal gasp from Winston, Tomioka and Syme. She then rolled over and dumped herself across Winston's lap, hoisted herself upright with a splash and hearty yell of 'Fuck me it's hot in 'ere!', then allowed her upper body to slide off Winston's knees to find her own submerged ledge.

'Beg your pardon, sweetheart,' she said. 'I wouldn't have sat on you, only I was just having a dream I was playing roly-poly down a grassy knoll. Sorry love!' She paused, patted her chest, and belched into her other fist. 'Pardon. Nice an' warm in 'ere, innit? I ain't quite meself.' As Winston and the others looked on aghast, she leant forward and vomited into the bubbling water. 'Thass better,' she said, leaning back with closed eyes. 'Ooooooo. Never keep it down, thass what I say. Get it up while it's fresh on your stomach, like.'

Once revived, she turned to have another look at Winston and seemed, by dint of his convenient position next to her, to take a slight fancy to him. She draped an arm around his shoulder and drew him towards her roughly. 'Wass your name, dearie?'

'Winston Smith,' said Winston, his smile verging on a grimace as stomach debris bobbed before him.

'Well that's a name I'll never fucking forget! *Whass yer name again?*'

Tomioka, shocked to silence, leant over to Syme, managing a whisper. 'Who is she again? *What's she in for?*'

'She's been in for a while. I think she's always been here. Even when Winston was in on his own, she was here, tucked up somewhere in the dark, asleep. She was in with the zealots. Her salt-of-the-earth humility outshone them, and she ended up winning.'

'She's a *prole*,' hissed Syme. 'The last remaining one.'

'The last prole? What's a prole?'

'You know, prole—*worker, donkey, hireling, khalasi, servant, grunt*...a pre-undustrial slave, really.'

'But she's not old enough.'

Syme shrugged. Tomioka shrugged too.

'And why is she so excessively fat?'

'Oh. Because she's poor—but not *famine* poor.'

'Oh yes. Poorly obese.'

Syme had now edged as far from the last prole on earth as inhumanely possible, so as to observe the rare specimen at a safe distance, so that her leer might more naturally settle upon the more proximate Tomioka.

'Last time I was 'ere I got told off by Big Brother. In the last season. The religious nuts—oh, what a fucking party that was! I can't even remember saying the thing I was supposed to 'ave said. Y'know, the thing I was supposed to 'ave said.'

Nothing from the housemates.

'Well, apparently, I used the "P" word...'

'I have no idea what that means,' said Tomioka curtly.

'And neither do I want to,' said Syme, leering from beneath the centre-parting of his long yippy wonk hair, betraying a sly appreciation of Tomioka's unease.

'Wass your name, dearie?'

'Tomioka.' Out of politeness, she added, 'What's yours?'

'Jade. It's Jade. I mean, I can't even imagine saying such a word under my breath. That "P" word, I mean.'

Sparing Tomioka the need of another repudiation of archaic racist language, at this point Ampleforth emerged into the sunny halogenated garden to find his housemates in the hot tub. 'A pool party! *Wonderful!*' He skirted back inside laughing. 'If I bring vino, can I dip my tootsies in too?'

'I'll have a rosé. I'm really not bothered. I'll drink the whole fucking bottle on my own if no-one else is drinking!' shouted Jade.

Ampleforth returned, cradling a selection of wine flagons and a cack-handed clutch of glasses. He opened one each of rosé, red and white, undressed, and entered the tub, leaving the glasses and bottles to bob cheerily on an inflatable drinks float.

Jade and Ampleforth were the only takers, and both ample takers at that, demolishing a bottle almost immediately. Ampleforth was committed enough in his speed drinking to soon bring himself up to speed with Jade's pickled state.

Syme observed, whilst Winston sat unflinching, hidden behind the village idiocy of his fixed ear-to-there smile.

'I can't imagine saying it—even under me breath. Not the bloody "P" word.'

'I'm sure no one has even heard of it,' said Ampleforth.

'Well, it rhymes with "tacky",' she said, offering a clue to her disgrace as she clinked glasses with Ampleforth.

'I don't want to know,' said Tomioka.

'Well that's exactly what I thought. I mean, I don't use them words lightly,' said Jade, pickled and vindicated all at once.

'Well that's cleared that up!' concluded Ampleforth in conciliatory tone.

Jade endeavoured to clink glasses with her sponsor, but spilled wine on both.

'I'm so embarrassing! This is why I never drink red—never do!'

Jolly Ampleforth was in hysterics, and began to sing. 'Oh there once was a house that was so happy!'

'And then what entered was a—'

'Oh great! We're all going to go to Big Brother prison!' said Tomioka.

'This *is* prison.' Syme, gloating.

'Actually, what I was going to say was *nappy*,' said Jade. 'What's wrong with you people?'

'You people?'

'I didn't mean it like that!'

'You said it like that.'

'She didn't *mean* it like that—or *say* it like that! *Say* it or *mean* it or *imply* it like that! *Tra-la-la-la!*' sang Ampleforth, enjoying the chaos.

'Don't give Ampleforth another drink,' mumbled Tomioka.

'You know what else she said to me? No? She told me that *Big Brother* was going to be my only claim to fame—that's what she said.'

'But it *is* your claim to fame.' Syme, again.

'Who said that? Whom said *what*?' said Ampleforth.

'I don't know her surname. Aaradhya-whoever-the-fuck-she-thinks-she-is! I was fuming! I can't stay...I can't stay in this house, I said...I've got to go because I'm common and I need to go and get elocution lessons because I'm common? How dare she turn her nose up at me? I'm not one of her pissing nuns or monks or servants or whatever. She's in a house with nine other normal people. Conrad Withers was a fucking legend—you don't 'ear 'im talking down to people. You don't 'ear him turning his nose up to people. And he was the quietest, nicest, most genuine person. Loved him to bits, I did. Genuinely, a genuine person who was lovely. He was a Jehovah's Witness, but he was proper genuine. And I gotta be honest, I witnessed a lot of sniggering and whispering and talking about him, from the other religious nuts—so they evicted him, they kicked 'im out, but he wanted to leave anyway 'cos he was stuck in 'ere, and was worried he couldn't devote enough time to saving people, 'an he was worried he'd lose his fucking salvation, the silly cunt—'

'I think you should just go,' suggested Tomioka, flatly.

'*Oh come now! Let's just drink more wine...*' said Ampleforth.

The clink of glasses signalled that it was time for Winston to exit the tub. He waded to the edge, and at the top of the steps caught sight of himself in the nearest mirror.

Here was once a guardian of the human spirit, a professional rectifier—now a cowering grey-skinned skeleton-like thing, emerging out of the primordial steam and primal soup, a half-being dripping with Jade's honest debris—a grotesque vision indeed. The creature's face was protruded, with bent carriage stooping forward. A forlorn face with an uneven forehead radiating over into a balding cranium, with maladjusted nose, and gaunt cheekbones, eyes dull, ebbing, with only the minimal requisite of life. The mouth was a drawn-in gash. Certainly it was his own face, but it had changed more than he had realised. He had been physically rectified—and not for the better. Except for his hands and the vague circle of his face, the body was grey with ancient ingrained dirt—well beyond the cleansing powers of the hot tub. Here and there beneath the stain of dirt were the red scars of wounds, and near the ankle a varicose ulcer was embossed like a bird's claw. Squalid skin was now bloated by water, ready to peel off his bones. The barrel of the ribs was as narrow as that of a skeleton: the legs had shrunk so that the knees were thicker than the thighs. The curvature of the spine was astonishing. The thin shoulders were hunched forward so as to make a cavity of the chest, the scraggy neck seemed to be bent double under the ponderous weight of the skull. At a guess he would have said that it was the body of a man of sixty, suffering from some malignant disease.

Winston plucked at his head and brought away a tuft of long hair. He seized his last front tooth between thumb and fore-finger and wrenched it out by its rotten roots. He threw it into the tub, and before he knew what he was doing had collapsed onto the small stool on the artificial lawn and burst into tears, He was a bundle of brittle bones weeping beneath the synthetic sunlight: but he could not, or would not, or even should not, stop himself crying.

CHAPTER II

Winston was lying on a bed, fixed down in some way so that he could not move. Light, perhaps from a small torch, teased his face. O'Brien was somewhere in the room: Winston could hear his unmistakable squeak. A man in a white coat retreated into the shadows with a dripping syringe. Even after his eyes were open he took in his surroundings only gradually. He had the impression of swimming up into the room from some subterranean world, from far beneath. The underwater creatures had followed him up, a column of ghosts formed of the finest filaments, bland grey flesh given lucent form by even the dimmest hint of light. Some had saw-toothed fangs decorating their elliptical under-bites, or moved with trawling mouths gaping wide, others had tight-lipped jaws siphoning plankton and krill through finely fringed baleen. Usually shrouded by the darkness of the primordial depths, they now floated up toward the light, following Winston. Some had angle-poise lamps hanging over their heads, some were glowing with the filaments of dimmed light-bulbs; some resembled luminescent tangled plastic bags with nothing in them, others were like nebulous cellophane, or discarnate pictograms or silken x-rays; diagrams for creatures yet to be conceived—spiritless fragments yet to emerge into material being, monsters made of cobweb, delicate strands of fibril covered in vibrating cilium, tedious wispy beings, precarious organisms floating in an abstract solution, orphans so individually monstrous that each must be a species of one, a world of mucilaginous gobbets bobbing about, pieces of cartilage and jelly stranded in strange currents, with jelly eyes peering from beyond, from the dark abyss, all lifeless yet undead. On the palisade, the jelly-faced poster gazed down compassionately upon the bent and heaving body, its towering jelly penis entering a monumental jelly vagina with a jelly anus entrance around the back for underground parking, but Winston never had need to visit the Ministry of Love nor park his sweet rustbucket in its backlot, so he lowered the nib toward the page because the deep sea creatures were once again congregating, gathering to help him with his work, congregating in the light to urge him on, with the collective murmur of the dead ancestors, to speak through him—but he faltered for just a second. To mark the paper was the decisive act. To begin at the beginning brought an end to thought. He knew he had to cultivate a vision of a happier, more peaceful future and to make the effort now to bring it about. But Oh! The elbow! The funny bone! He had slumped to his knees, almost paralysed, clasping the stricken elbow with his other hand. Everything had exploded into yellow light. Inconceivable, inconceivable that a single blow could cause such pain! The light cleared and he could see the other two looking down at him. The guard was laughing at his contortions, but in Winston's mind he was crawling away through the desert, escaping through failed crops. He dragged himself through a glockenspiel of collapsed animal bones, causing a terribly sad polystylistic jingle to ripple out loud as he ricocheted through, but he was nonetheless ever so happy that civilisation had achieved pure and total consensus, and O'Brien's face was as happily-miserable as everybody else's.

'We shall meet in the place where there is only light entertainment,' said the voice, and Winston saw the faces of his mother and father lighting up in the shabby-chic gloom. He took his hand and fed it into the grating teeth of Mr Tooth-Fairy, all the way up to the elbow, gnawing past the words JE VEUX TE BAISER until the red letters were drowned by blood. But no matter what he did, no such sacrifice could prevent the waterlogged bodies washing downstream, so many stricken jellyfish stranded by pitiless tides—each and every act of violence unified by an instructive sliver of paper inscribed with the indelible fate of each trustee: emetophilia, scatophillia, frotteurism, paedophilia, necrophilia and hematolagnia.

'It's not my fault' whimpered Winston, 'I'm doing my best to rectify them, but they just keep coming! The deep glitch!'

'Say Aaaaaaa!' said the man in white.

Winston obliged before he could be forced, allowing his tongue to spool out for inspection. Sure enough, it was quite swollen—with a rash of spots, red, orange, yellow, green, blue, indigo, violet—then something else came coughing from his mouth, an object falling so gracefully, seeming to stall in mid-air, swinging in the brilliant searchlight as it sailed down, down, down—and as if by virtue of the mesmeric effect of its elegant descent, all the shrill and offensive noise became miraculously tranquil, all tattered senses became calm, pressing down, down, down. But how long he had been down there he did not know. Since the moment when they arrested him he had seen neither darkness nor daylight. Perhaps it was a hood? Besides, his memories were less than continuous, and there had been times when consciousness, even the sort of deranged consciousness that one has in sleep, had stopped dead and started again only after a blank interval. With that first blow on the funny bone the nightmare had started, the infrared monsters had come, mustered like the audience of homeless insomniacs—he too saw them floating from room to room, with their dead eyes illuminated by the dead black light. He was one of them, and rolled about the floor, as shameless as an animal, writhing his body this way and that in an endless, hopeless effort to dodge the kicks, and simply inviting more and yet more kicks, in his ribs, in his belly, on his elbows, on his shins, in his groin, in his testicles, on the bone at the base of his spine. A surly barber arrived on his hoverboard to scrape his chin and crop his hair, and then other businesslike, unsympathetic men in white coats came to feel his pulse, tapping his reflexes, turning up his eyelids, running harsh fingers over him in search for broken bones, and shooting needles into his arm to make him sleep. They slapped his face, wrung his ears, pulled his hair, made him stand on one leg, refused him leave to urinate, shone glaring lights in his face until his eyes ran with water; he became simply a mouth that uttered, so keen to confess even that he was a devout Christian, a jihadi, an admirer of aristocrats, a homophobe, a misogynist, an anti-Semite, that he was sexually complacent, impatient with children, not a good listener, a despiser of all poetry and art—and for such illiberal sins deserved to be in a cell. Suddenly he floated out of his bed, and was swallowed up by a huge hole, and the hole turned into a mighty corridor, a kilometre wide, full of glorious, golden light. He was roaring with laughter and shouting out, making many absurd confessions at the top of his voice. He was confessing anything and everything, even the things he had succeeded in holding back under the torture. He was relating the entire history of his life to an audience who knew it already, they were clapping, and there was added canned laughter. With him were the guards, the other questioners, the men in white coats, O'Brien, Julia, Mr Charrington, all clattering down the corridor together shouting and laughing. Everything was all right, there was no more pain, the last detail of his life was laid bare, understood, forgiven.

He was starting up from the plank bed in the half-certainty that he had heard O'Brien's voice. All through his interrogation, although he had never seen her, he had had the feeling that O'Brien was at his throbbing elbow, just out of sight. It was O'Brien who was directing everything. It was she who set the guards onto Winston and who prevented them from killing him. It was she who decided when Winston should scream with pain, when he should have a respite, when he should be fed, when he should sleep, when the drugs should be pumped into his arm. It was she who asked the questions and suggested the answers. She was the tormentor, she was the inquisitor, but she was also the friend who could stop the pain. When her voice entered Winston's thoughts, usually during drugged sleep or near-slumber, the most he could do was tighten his foetal coil, and hope that he would not be woken completely, and so let O'Brien's words swirl freely in his mind.

But the voice penetrating this particular dream was not O'Brien's at all, and because it was not O'Brien's, Winston's curiosity could not help being stirred; he frowned, sucked his thumb and kicked a leg; he moved beneath the cover but immediately became aware of the warmth of another body pressed close behind him. In the darkness he turned his head slightly on the pillow, and felt the warm waft of someone's breath blowing words into his ear.

'Winston, Winston, it's me...wake up!'

Winston tried to tug the duvet over his head to protect the sanctity of his sleep, but the cover was firmly pinned. Instead, he pressed his face into his pillow and uttered a muffled protest:

'There no fortitude like patience...just as there no destructive emotion worse than hatred...most best practice patience!'

'But Winston, it's getting really good now, listen, I've almost finished it: *His entrails were endlessly contracted. Soon, very soon, perhaps in five minutes, perhaps now, the tramp of boots would mean that his own turn had come. The door would open. The cold-faced young officer would step into the cell. The pain in his belly—'*

'Stop...I beg you...please stop...'

'—a piece of bread; the blood and the screaming. There was another spasm in his entrails, the heavy boots were approaching. As the door opened, the wave of air that it created brought in a powerful smell of cold sweat.'

Winston could hear the servomotors adjusting focus, drilling into the dark—and knew that his eyes, although blinking blindly and wildly in the dark, would be rendered luminous by the infrared cameras set behind the mirrors. He knew that any motion and every subsequent word spoken loud enough for the microphones would be instantly relayed out into the ether. So he turned his head, once more to appeal to his spooning trespasser, and whispered.

'You realise they can hear us? Every word! They can see us too—even in the dark!'

'I'll let you read my book before anyone else!'

'Listen to me. You had your chance, but you blew it! If you'd actually written the damn thing rather than squandering your bursary on worry beads, you might have avoided this place. But it's too late now! The world will never be as dull and depressing as your story makes out! And anyway, why would a futuristic tyranny ever resort to

surveillance, when with just a mild tickling of the feet, even reflexology unleashes the gushing confessions of those so desperately eager to spill their overtherapised guts! Your vision of dystopia reveals nothing but a sentimental yearning for the bogeyman to show his face! For you to experience your fear as a convenient object! Your dystopia indulges an imaginary threat—like a god, or a looming tyrant! But the truth is that the worst tyranny already resides within you!'

'Yes, yes, that's all very interesting Winston—but listen, I've turned you into the hero of my story! This is how it begins! *It was a bright cold day in April, and the clocks were striking thirteen. Winston Smith, his chin nuzzled into his breast in an effort to escape the vile wind, slipped quickly through the glass doors of Victory Mansions, though not quickly enough to prevent a swirl of gritty dust from entering along with him—*'

'Syme, please concentrate on what I'm saying. I bear you no malice, but I don't care if you've written a masterpiece, nor do I care whether someday in the future they decide to teach your ludicrous ideas in the classroom! You may use my name, you have my blessing—since I have no particular affection for it. But I can tell you this for sure: it's not my fault that you're in here, and I am not the solution to your problems. Stop pestering me.'

Winston wrenched the duvet into the coiled knot of his body. He reburied his head in the pillow, and with a hefty backwards shove of the rump, the unwanted bedfellow was relegated to the floor with a thud.

Winston was sitting in a rabbit-bitten pasture, with a foot-track wandering across it and a molehill here and there. In the ragged hedge on the right-hand side of the field the boughs of the elm trees were swaying very faintly in the dreamy breeze. The ambient light dipped a notch as a passing cumulonimbus caused the halogen suns above to dim, the light lifting and dipping as each sun was obscured and revealed in turn. The Diary Room held nothing more minatory than a single armchair adorned with a revivalist floral pattern that blended in neatly with the backdrop. Winston had been called and had taken his place on the seat, sitting face-to-camera, smiling, adjusting himself with some instinct for symmetry, as though the camera lens embedded in the adjacent wall demanded it. Despite the acoustic dampening that lent the room its aura of sensory compression and created a safe place for fluid confession, Winston heard chanting, sirens and breaking glass seeping in from somewhere beyond, but was not sure whether the baying crowd was anything but a residual sonic ghost of the first vigil.

'Good afternoon, Winston. This is Big Brother speaking. May I thank you for coming to the Diary Room so promptly. And may I further enquire as to whether you're enjoying your time in the household so far?'

Winston cleared his throat. He adjusted himself before he spoke.

'*All most social animal be compassion, care and concern for other bring us all together.*' Winston smiled, beaming from ear to there, hidden behind the bedazzling glare that was his most best defence. He now knew the voice was O'Brien's, despite the filter—it was the same voice that had once whispered to him, *We shall meet in the place where there is no darkness,* in that other dream, so long ago. He sat back in the chair, settling into the naturalistic ambiance, the sound of the pasture being bunny-nibbled and gnawed, the foot-track pacing across it and a molehill here and there fouling the green grass with patches of upturned soil. In the ragged hedge on the right-hand side of the field the boughs of the elm trees were swaying dangerously in the wind. Winston watched the clouds darken, feeling happy for the company of chattering birdsong, as the many passerines began to flee.

'Big Brother once told you,' said O'Brien's fake voice, 'that if we met again it would be here.'

'If show concern for other and respect for right, must you establish trust; must trust be basis of friendship.'

'Oh, very good, Winston. Very good. Why don't we just cut to the chase. Reach beneath your chair. There's a little surprise waiting there for you.'

Winston leant over to reach under the chair. He knew it was the book before he touched its spine. He removed it, holding it awkwardly, purposely so, as if it were diseased and he feared contagion. He dropped it in his lap with a roughness that bespoke his disowning of the tome. It was as unloved as an anthology of poetry on a poet's lap could ever be—and then he beamed once again, quite broadly, but just a little dimmer, and behind the dim smile began a dull pain that made the sweat draw out on his forehead. He breathed hard through his nose, trying to maintain his composure by Martha's meditative method, tantric breathing, *inhaaaale* and *exhaaaaaale*—and continued to beam as brightly as the dull pain allowed.

'Big Brother can see that you are afraid,' said O'Brien. 'That you fear that something unpleasant is about to happen. You fear that you're going to be revealed as a writer. You fear that your anonymity will be dashed, and Winston Smith's anonymity is paramount. It separates you from all the foolish people who were once concerned at your creative reluctance. They cared for you and you despised them. The book sitting on your lap—you have no idea whether there's just *one* copy or *many thousands*. You have no idea how many have seen it, or read it—let alone reviewed it. This is what you are thinking right now, isn't it, Winston?'

Winston calibrated his smile proportionately to the new threat.

'Remember Winston, if Big Brother suspects any porky-pies, or if you underwhelm us with deflections and false modesty, we will be forced to withhold all household victuals and increase daily chores for all housemates. Do you understand? No-one will die, but the anticipation of a loss in breakfast smoothies, supplements, vitamins, and bircher muesli, will kill them.'

'*Meaningful dialogue require best respect other right and other interest—compromise is most best only way resolve dispute.*'

'Have it your way, Winston, but *Big Brother* has only so much patience,' said the disembodied voice in an impatient tone. 'Before we go on, I have a small favour to ask…'

Sitting comfortably in the floral armchair, the cheerful smile concealing his dread, Winston contemplated the nature of the favour he was apparently at liberty to grant. '*Genuine compassion—unbiased, no mix with false attachment—is source of genuine human happiness.*'

'Oh it's quite a simple request—nothing to unfairly tax your talent. It's already there, sitting on your lap…'

'*As human brother must commit to let people know that all possess seed of love and compassion and forgiveness.*'

'Pick it up for me Winston. Feel its weight. Open it…'

Winston suddenly lunged forwards in his chair to whisper into the lens, hoping for a quiet word, whispering so that the viewers at home might not hear. 'Please Big Brother, not that—*anything but that.*'

'But the viewers would like to hear it from the horse's mouth. They would like to hear it from you, in your own words, Winston.'

'*Please, O'Brien. We both know they're not all my words.*'

'Tell me, Winston, how long have you been with us here in the household?'

'I don't know. Days, weeks, months—many, many months,' he whispered.

'And why do you imagine we bring people into the *Big Brother* household?'

'To make them confess. *To punish them.*'

'Oh, Winston! You see? That's a writer's imagination—right

there! Honestly! Have you been punished since you've been here? Even *lightly* punished? Is what I'm now asking you to do for the folks at home really a *punishment?*'

'No.'

'Then what is it?'

'Entertainment.'

'What *kind* of entertainment.'

'Enlightenment through light entertainment!' said Winston, sitting back.

'*BINGO!*' said O'Brien. 'You said it yourself! Your words, not mine. This is how you see the sum total of human progress— *from enlightenment to light entertainment!* So let's continue with our enlightened light entertainment. Please. The book. If you don't mind.'

The sweat had sprung out all over Winston's body and the pH-buffered air tore into his lungs, issuing back out into the tiny room in deep groans, which, even with a firm clenching of teeth and a default smile, could not be easily restrained. He took the book in his hands, opened it at the beginning, and saw the words leering up at him. He tried to focus on them through the lens of nascent tears welling up in his eyes...

'*Are all human being possess seed of compassion. Must use intel-ligence to cultivate the inner value associate with—*' Winston's sob-bing made his pronunciation incomprehensible, punctuated as it was with little grunts, gulps, and many a quivering of the chin.

'Most lovely sentiments Winston. Please take your time and continue when you can.'

Winston composed himself and began again. '*Create better world will require will-power, vision and much determination. And for that must need strong sense that humanity is one single family—*'

'Winston, I must apologise for the interruption: even though it's live TV, we do still have a time constraint—so let's advance a couple of pages and read on from there.'

In the simplicity of such an instruction lay a callousness that shivered through the reader's being. He could do nothing, nothing but obey—obey, submitting himself headlong into the dread that he now knew was waiting patiently for him. So he continued. '*Compassion bring peace of mind. Bring smile to face and genuine smile all close together.*'

'Very nice, perhaps even further on, skip a few pages—into the meat of the matter, as it were.'

'*When you have more compassionate mind and cultivate warm-heartedness, must whole atmosphere around be more positive and friendlier.*'

'A little further still, if you could.'

'*Problem create by human being must solve by human being. Basic human nature is compassionate and this is source of much best hope.*'

'Ah yes! The allegory of the blocked sink! Further on, please Winston.'

'*Neither space station nor enlightened mind can be realised in single day.*'

'A little further still.'

'*Be most kind and compassionate person. This inner beauty is key factor to make a better—*'

'Next.'

'*Love and compassion most important because—*'

'A couple more pages further!'

'*Inner peace help sustain—*' Winston was rushing to finish each bite-sized homily before being rudely moved on to the next.

'Next chapter!'

'*When we—*'

'Winston, I don't imagine it's an easy thing to be a celebrated writer, to discuss a new book in public, on television, being watched by millions of viewers,' said O'Brien. 'But you do seem to be a little shy of your fame. I'm worried that you're not making the most of it. I'm trying to get to the real meat of your work, the nub of it, for your fans at home—so let's get to the juicy stuff, and find out who Winston Smith really is!"

'*How can I help it?*' Winston blubbered. '*How can I help that two and two are four?*'

'Oh, I see. But you know very well that sometimes they are five, and you've proved it most convincingly in your writing. You state it quite plainly, often. You must stop imagining that posterity will vindicate this stubborn reluctance to exist as a popular poet. Posterity will never hear of you unless you speak up. You will be lifted clean out from the stream of literary history if you do not take this opportunity right now. People are interested in what you do. They haven't yet heard just how exceptional you are. How will your new book become an airport bestseller if you won't let us hear the spoken wisdom of its author? Your humility is endearing, but obstructive, and Humanity cannot abide the hoarding of talent, especially if it retards our collective advancement, *our progress*. Today we are lucky enough to hear you read from your book, to witness what you are giving to the world—your gift contains within it the hopes of the multitude realised in the acts of the singular individual. So Winston, please be so kind as to indulge our fascination, we merely wish to thrive from your talent, and so you might forgive us for our simple greed. Winston, we beg of you, *please, please, continue.*'

Winston turned the page, fearing the next black mass of words lying in wait. He cleared his throat and began. '*Can lead horse to water but cannot force to drown alone.*'

'Ah! I detect a sea change. Next!'

'*To invent ship is to invent shipwreck and to invent car is to invent carcass.*'

'Oh Winston! Don't stop!'

'*Anorexic appetite so hungry for meat prefer shun supermarket nibbles to devour own flesh.*'

'That's more like it!'

'*Every mushroom cloud has silver lining.*'

'Yes! Yes! That's the spirit! Here comes the pathos!'

'*Hideous social intimacy we call love is merely infinity put at disposal of poodles.*'

'Are they prepared for this at home, Winston? Do they know what's coming? *Next!*'

'*War is to dream of world peace what pony is to Miss Universe.*'

'Oh Bravo! Winston! Bravo! This is the stuff they'll remember you for! Next!'

'*Altruism is selfish kindness, like child who cheats piggybank or like crack baby loves its mummy's teat.*'

'Oh how could you Winston! You monster! Next!'

'*Logically, must harmony come from deep inside the heart. Harmony much too based on dog trust cat, not so much cat trust dog. As soon as use force, creates pussy fear. Pussy fear and doggy trust cannot go together on walk in sunshine, but only sit in shadow of garden sprinkler. Wet cat. Wet dog. Bad smell.*'

'They are weeping for their serenity Winston! Weeping! *Next page!*'

'*If must can cultivate right attitude, enemies are best spiritual teacher because their hate provide opportunity to enhance and develop hate, develop patience and understanding of more better hate.*'

'You are a most evil and wicked man, Winston. *Next!*'

'*Choose to pretend be optimistic? Much feel better than pretend be happy. Pretend happy is like puppy bite slipper, but no blood. Puppy much best happy not pretend happy but bite hand of owner, taste much blood. Much happier.*'

'Winston, perhaps you might turn a few pages further into the text, I feel we haven't quite got down to the deep core of it yet, to the marrow, to the disease of it, to the nitty-gritty. To what is *exceptional* about your voice, place and hurt.'

Winston did as he was told, turned a few pages, and saw what was waiting there. He looked up from the page and into the camera lens, beseeching Big Brother to release him from his task.

'Winston? We're waiting. Pussy fear got your tongue?'

'*But I didn't write this...*' he whispered.

'Of course not! No author can claim the absolute minority of his voice—we're quite aware that a work, however masterful, is in part created by a population, that no man is a monad. *Read on.*'

There was more than a trace of amusement in O'Brien's voice. Winston reluctantly began the next section.

'*Most rotten heaven now vacate absent god most all too burden by authority, nonetheless worship by litter of diehard runt and Santa little helper and much other self-deputise dwarf who confuse elongation of midday shadow for measure of towering stature and size of penis—must peel from obscene protuberance, stuck fast in much slime, dark mass so dense, living, breeding, excrement of toil and rack, tint blue sea brown and green land black. Must hideous formless horror wait for morning sun, moon and tide to untangle their affect and drift apart into cold dark universe we have for so long been promised.*'

'Oh that's very good Winston! That's the classic Winston Smith we all want to hear. Next!'

'*Sad war-baby cry itself dry until both eye socket like empty crater. Must cry acid rain, for Aztec rip out living heart must only through extraction does sun agree to return, otherwise ulcerated threshold of gouged darkness, is partial glimpse of unimaginable ugliness, plague, breed pestilence and ruin—must protect mystical peculiarity of baboon's fleshy genital eruption or peacock opulent fan. Necrotic device is most hectic to diagram, most better low-life and vile biology thrust into welcoming arm of inferiority complex, as insurmountable potlatch, or movement most giddy effect, because death is nerve ending—life, most rotten communication.*'

Resigned to his task, Winston continued without need of O'Brien's hounding prompts, noticing the odd fragment of his own work amongst the litter of misfortune profanities.

'*Must sun's holocaust deluge with blind indifference, solar beam embalm inside the skin of meek who seek to pass their inherited share. Even must sea vomit on shore like dog disgorge bloody chicken bone stolen from master's drain. Bulimic tide convulse, and disgorge detritus like monster tear out own teeth—must water-edge be a ruptured tear, where land dissolve like nasty clot—and yet not all earth Aspirin can cure the pain nor put Humpty Dumpty back together again! No engineer save broken egg from mechanical striptease, no rustic squeak nor boutique sigh, nor nerves pinned to infinity, nor calm of the dead, with much flimflam puppetry—and bed-side mannerism inflate and deflate sigh of iron lung set to ponderous respiration. Goldstein papier mache head nodding and shaking or bob up and down like cistern-float-equilibrium-valve await next turgid flush, hoping that somewhere in mish-mash of contradictory expression live approximation of death, him block head tease by granite of grief, many crush children—so began to giggle all most innocent, then churlish as common murderer. Death pressed hand to mouth—To store morbid crow safe inside cage. Creasing at neutered obscenity of human compassion, with more mechanical nod and shake, most spectator implore it to stop—must beg to refrain from pornography of mockery. Was all could do to implore—while death bully at desperate antic, wringing its hands-tickled-pink that a species so very close to death—so professionally familiar with its coming and going—yet did not know it from Adam.'*

'Winston, Nagasaki has nothing on you! But jump a few pages—we're almost there!'

'Instead of blind-lead-blind through wasteland of dreary idyll—tropic of idiotic disorientation without fang nor gore to suck in sight, nor snuffed out babies to mewl over nor stand as ground-zero of all thing bad nor fountainhead to all thing good, must best instead put "fun" back in funeral, "twat" back in weightwatchers, "fist" in pacifist, "cock" in cock-a-doodle-doo and "cunt" in vagina, or best hanker for rampant crime undilute chaos of preferred world, not windmill, kite, flag, hot air balloon, butterfly, candy-floss, sweet and cake, bunny

rabbit, honey bee, ladybird, caterpillar, dragon fly, squirrel, bear cub, juggler, owl, dove, olive, mice, swan or feather, most feedback through diagonal web of jism spittle twang in gobshite funhole duct, sinus cum block snot purge, larynx, kidney, heart, adenoid, colon ejaculatory duct, muck sinus block, choke to larynx, split kidney, dullard heart, tease gurgle adenoid, donate purpose sickened liver to sick child, pancreas, when clench must tighten even more, crimson coral weaves through sinew plus strand root, plus stems plus pretty ugly leaves petrifying cell-strata tissue by pricked open sagging lungs, shitty spleen, shitty bladder, shitty prostate, shitty colon, shitty appendix, shitty tangle human hair scream pull out, palate cleft in shitty big toe foot-in-mouth, shitty taste tongue, stub toe, pierced testicle to atrioventricular valves, ejaculatory duct calcifying vessel plus vertical capillaries into thin glass needle noodle soup snap off inside abdomen compress, must hell-bent on obsess over forensic details own suicidal outpouring, boo hoo, who? Only you. Rotten penis sag on swollen belly, pulse slit shitty wreckaged rancour flyblown vision best ever so lightly tease by prosthetic optical apparatus in deepen porous of shitty doomed molar unit, most bescrawl and inchoate, since dyslexia is to dyslexic what stutter is to stutterer as lisp is to lisperer.'

'That's the stuff, Winston! I can hear hell groaning! Just a few more pages—*we're so close!*'

'*There no need erect temples, no need God. Better you susurrate swollen blood thrust of loins in split shitty tissues. Better you drape head open mouth soiling blood spattered veil face beaten or better violaceous liquefied all body politician. Better you strangle penis sweat clitoris slime frothing in nostril sagging load straggling over and over shaved occiput or better mauve slit of angry arse. Much better when discontent devour dead membrane's throat gurgling jism purge with bloody smear-chipped tooth-dent in screaming soft rape flesh, especially in June—legs spread, club-foot egg spoon race, rough armpit juice, dribble lick, stick, prick, flick, nick, dick, slick, caked muck mire mien, swollen fist fuck stuck fast, slow, palpitating dermis peeling away in acid bath, have much taste of own medicine, whether universe, with countless galaxy of muck, star and planet, has most best deeper meaning or not, but at very least, it clear that human who live on earth face task of obliterate planet. Therefore, it important to discover what bring about greatest degree of personal destruct. The more motivate by hate, more fearless and free action will be. Human potential is most same as toilet potential—same shit, different toilet. You must feel, "I am of no value", is true. Absolute true. You deceiving self in power of thought—so what lacking? So what? If have willpower, then you change only local putty in baby hand. You are own master, but only master of masturbator—only slave's slave.'*

'Oh, that's a favourite of mine! One of the most impressive *misfortunes* you ever penned! Not so good for those poor souls who followed your advice. Do you remember writing in this very book that it *did not matter whether I was a friend or an enemy, since I was a person who understood you?* You were right. I enjoyed your mind. It appealed to me, until you perverted the divinatory nature of the fortunes and drove innocent people to forms of violence not witnessed for more than a century. Winston, you are a criminal, your poetry is pure evil! But perhaps this is the cost of creativity?' There were layers of amusement in O'Brien's voice posing as outrage. 'Now we must allow our viewers to judge the power of your work. Let us see if they can separate the beauty of your writing from its murderous consequences. Perhaps your work can be redeemed beyond the condemnation of your actions! Let our audience decide—appalled as they must be by now! Astonished! Shocked! Disgusted! Their world turned upside-down! But they can always vote you out of the household if they so wish, that is their Democratic right, the basis upon which our consensus is formed.... So let's cut to the chase. *Turn to page 101, and we shall see.'*

'*Page 101? What's on page 101?*' spluttered Winston, aghast, horrified.

'Oh, Winston, you know what's on page 101. Everybody does, even without reading it. But you have the book in your hands, so why not take a little peek?'

'I don't want to. Please, Big Brother, please, O'Brien, *please don't make me.*'

CHAPTER III

'Page 101,' said O'Brien. 'It's the last page in the book. Just ten lily-white words waiting there for you. But you already know the answer. Everyone knows what the worst thing in the world is for them. Two plus two, Winston! The unthinkable plus the unmentionable equals the unnameable! But the worst thing in the world varies from writer to writer. It may be a description of ugly curtains, bad dialogue, a recalcitrant plot, no twist, or a flat ending. There are cases where it is something quite trivial, and not even fatal. In your case, it's *the poetic revelation of the true nature of your soul*, and so the worst thing in the world for you just happens to be on page 101.'

A premonitory tremor passed through Winston. He looked down at his lap, at the *My Big Book of Me* abandoned there; he saw his name embossed on the cover, traced it with his fingers, and imagined all that a first book should be to a newly published writer.

'You can't do that!' he cried out. 'You couldn't, you couldn't! It's impossible!'

'Do you remember,' said O'Brien, 'the moment of panic that comes over you in your dreams? Those good ideas, bits of incomprehensible scribble and fleeting ideas all forgotten in the dead of night, grasped at in the morning—*but gone*?'

'*O'Brien!*' cried Winston, making a supreme effort to calm his voice. 'Please! You know this is unnecessary. You know I'm innocent!'

'By itself,' said O'Brien, 'the truth is not always enough. There are occasions when a contestant will stand up against the facts, even to the point of self-harm. But for each of us there is something unendurable—something that cannot be contemplated calmly. If you fall when ice-skating you will ruthlessly grab at a child, or if you are drowning, gain buoyancy at another's expense. Instinct inhabits the mind, and is not subject to the conscious vacillations. Instinct is consensus, and consensus is instinct. So it is with your writing. You stand accused of composing many malicious misfortunes, and thereby sending many to their deaths. You are a pariah, Winston, it is incumbent upon you to sacrifice yourself to a higher purpose.'

'But it's not my writing! You know it isn't! You said so! The misfortunes were written to manipulate me, to force me to rectify them as though they were the consequence of a malicious glitch. But they influenced my writing, permeated my thinking so much that I believed some creative force was being channelled through me! I can no longer tell what was mine and what I believed had chosen me as a cipher! I can't be judged for something I didn't *intend!*'

'Why do you deny your talent? I'm sure the viewers at home are desperate to know, if only to restore their faith in poetry— this is your opportunity to explain, Winston. Don't blow it—*for their sakes!*'

But Winston could only hear the blood singing in his ears, mixed with the revivalist vigil outside the walls of the *Big Brother* house jeering and baying for his blood. He was in the midst of a great empty plain, a flat desert drenched with sunlight, across which all sounds came to him out of immense distances, an immense desert scorched by an angry sun, a glockenspiel of collapsed animal bones upon which an emaciated child played *Twinkle, Twinkle Little Star* with a pair of spare ribs. All around the patterned armchair there lay a parched river-bed cracking into an impossible puzzle of itself, attended by a pet lapdog hung from the agony of its own serrated spine. Soon there came the familiar voice delivering its sonorous narration, and the sight of the many post-apocalyptic American families captured by toxic dustbowls, the mockery of flies in the air, their God holding them to their humble misery, obscenely fat, obese, yet starved of any voice, place, hurt, dignity or wholesome nourishment—

'*DEATH...SUGARY DRINKS...OBESITY... MISERY...HOPE-LESSNESS...DEATH...SUGARY DRINKS...OBESITY...MISERY ...HOPELESSNESS...DEATH...SUGARY DRINKS...OBESITY... MISERY...*'

The flies were lapping at Winston's tears and Emmanuelle Goldstein was nowhere to be seen, her salary request rebuffed since, now that they had Winston, there was no need for compassion, and O'Brien's Big Brother was still there, unseen and omniscient, watching him, surveilling him.

'Page 101, Winston. It's waiting. The future is in your hands now.'

Still the chanting: '*PLACE ... VOICE ... HURT ... PLACE ... VOICE ... HURT ... PLACE ... VOICE ... HURT ...*'

Winston was aware of a deep primordial moan, and from the very depths of this first almighty plaint, a new poetic howl announced a more sublime demand upon the universe. His sobs were heaving, chest heaving, universe heaving—chin quivering, puckering and dimpling like a putty-faced crack-baby denied its mother's teat. He fumbled through the pages, blinded by waterlogged eyes. At page 101 he came face-to-face with the inexorable fate waiting there for him, the last ten words of the book—just as O'Brien had predicted: ten, to the letter.

He took a breath of air—it felt like his last—and began to read the last ten words of his first book:

FUCK COMPASSION
FUCK COMPASSION
FUCK COMPASSION
FUCK COMPASSION
FUCK COMPASSION

He imagined the smash of truncheons on the elbow and the

heel of jackboots on his splintering shins; or were they glow-sticks, rainbow socks and Birkenstock sandals? It was difficult to tell. He saw himself grovelling on the floor, screaming for mercy through bloody and broken teeth; or was it red Merlot and popcorn? He thought of Julia. She was fixed in his mind. He loved her but she had manipulated him; he knew that fact as truly as he now knew the rules of Twister. He felt love for her, and he wondered where she was. He thought about Syme's razor blade. It would bite into him, but the fingers holding it to his own wrist would be cut to the bone. For some reason he was more squeamish about slicing his pinkies than cutting his wristies. Then he was falling backwards, down into an enormous depth, he had fallen between the crude atoms of the floor, they had moved apart for him—he oozed through the earth, drifting through the viscous oily oceans beyond, past the glowing deep sea jelly creatures with their black eyes and grey smiles, out into deepest darkest rippling cosmic matter, into the flowing gulfs between the stars. The jeering had stopped, no more malicious chanting of his name, no more revivalist vigil....

CHAPTER IV

Serendipity Café had largely emptied for the evening, save for Winston Smith, who was sitting at his favoured table in the corner, captivated by a small portable television opposite, its sound turned down, but with the large smiley poster blaring out above—SMILE AND THE WORLD SMILES WITH YOU.

These days he was less inclined to focus his mind on anything for more than a few moments at a time—but the television was soothing enough in its chronic banality to match his newfound tempo. So he watched, unflinching—sipping the full-fat froth on his coffee until it was tepid enough to drink—his third cup of the evening, proxy rent for his extended occupancy of the corner table.

His regular visit to the café—with its perfect white sugar cubes and Black Forest Gateaux haemorrhaging with whipped cream—had contributed to Winston's passage to an unhealthy weight following his emaciated eviction from *Big Brother* and dismissal from the Ministry of Fortune. With his fall from grace had come the mandatory destruction of the only copy of *My Big Book of Me*, and his pledge to give up writing—both rectificatory and creative. He had served O'Brien's purpose, and while never officially pardoned, he had been put out to grass, wandering out of sight and out of mind, inhabiting his obscurity without complaint. A certain wan complexion had taken hold of his corpulent face, since it was now subjected to an assault of formaldehyde moisturisers, petroleum balms, and toxic toners. His hair was shaved to the bone. His lapse into obesity was less a tactic than an affliction of lethargy: Winston was hiding in the plain sight of personal dilapidation.

The volume of the television was increased by some unseen hand from behind the counter, but volleys of fireworks could be seen and heard bursting on the diminutive screen, with the acoustic grandeur of rippled bubble-wrap. He saw many colours exploding above the Ministry of Misfortune, highlighting the three new slogans of unhealthy living gouged into the sloped Himalayan crystal rock face:

BE WRETCHED IN YOUR OWN SKIN
BELIEVE IN HATE
BECAUSE YOU'RE NOT WORTH IT

Winston's heart stirred just a little above its usual autonomic murmur as the new season premiere of *Big Brother* announced itself onscreen—the fresh-faced presenter caught in the chaos of live TV, poised before the house, awaiting the arrival of the new housemates upon a long runway that vanished towards the entrance, across the razorwire and surrounding moat which contained at least the rumour of alligators and crocodiles. The smiley flags were now all rendered miserable, upturned and tattered in the raging wind, as epic searchlights formed aerial criss-crosses as Neighbourhood Watch helicopters dangled in mid-air like toys—*or maybe they were toys*. Posted either side of the door were two brutish sentinels who seemed plucked from some Symeonesque counterfactual history, with pantomime steel helmets, black jackets, black jodhpurs, shiny black jackboots, wearing smiley armbands and holding short riding crops. Suddenly the lumbering steel doors of the house swung open to reveal second-time rollover winner Jade, spewing out as far as her jangling chains would allow—drunk and incensed, in a coarse cotton full-length dress and matching headscarf—a ferocious scullery maid tethered to her post, ready to meet and greet her new co-contestants with a flurry of archaic obscenities—and with insults to spare for the baying crowd too, from whom she received rocks, bricks and bottles for her trouble.

'*What could be more inviting than the fury of fools? Is it not "good" to be encouraged to do "bad"? For what proposition does such an invitation serve other than to bolster the morality of weaklings who need evil in order to live like sheep! We are all fucking sheep, but what kind of fucking sheep do you want to be? Baaaaaa! Fucking baaaaaaaaaa!'*

As objects rained down upon her head, the angry crowds pushed closer, pressing against the wire fence in their white loose-linen open-necked blouses, loose jeans, open-toed sandals, strings of raw sandalwood beads tied loosely about their wrists, with simple sand-coloured wooden paynim pendants, and the rigorously unkempt hair—only the wire held them back from tearing the sacrificial prole apart, but they bayed for her blood nonetheless.

'IN WITH HATE! OUT WITH LOVE!
IN WITH HATE! OUT WITH LOVE!
IN WITH HATE! OUT WITH LOVE!'

Winston recalled the amateurish drone of his own hate vigil, the farouche jeering and gauche bad-mouthing of his good name that haunted him at the time of his incarceration in the house, way before the other contestants, Syme et al, were co-opted into joining him—when he had been offered to the public by O'Brien as the founding pariah of the new interim Two Minutes Hate.

But that was just the beginning. Now the indignant horde had really found their métier and came professionally mob-handed, pressing their compound mass against the mesh fence, a thousand sinewed fingers squeezing through the holes, straining, and faces pressed to—with newfound leering and baying, and handsome healthy faces once so resplendent with utter well-being now quilted by the crossed lattice-wire, a crowd of hot-crossed buns basted and baked by rage. Winston watched the TV, blindly tracing with his finger on the table:

$$2+2=5$$

Accompanied by a univocal surge of excitement and the muscular threat of mass violence, the brand new contestants rolled up in a replica prison truck, its pantomime bars mounted upon the substructure of a craftisan milk-float. The spotlights raked over each bewildered nominee as they were roughly plucked from the dark vehicle and led out into the febrile chaos, witless stricken eyes dilated and vast with fear. The PA announced each of them first by hereditary title, then name, but went largely unheard beneath the swelling rumble of vilification. Then each candidate was led along the cage toward the door, accompanied by the glorious sound of harpsichord, say, Scarlatti or Soler, or KoKo the Klown, who knows—*who cares*—but with legions of tentacles, bloodraw tongues and snapping teeth straining through mesh to gouge at them. Each petrified precaristocrat was manhandled along the catwalk with the aid of ancient *Venus* sex toys reconfigured as buzzing cattle-prods, herded toward the bellowing rollover winner Jade, an erstwhile slave waiting to offer them a foul-mouthed Anglo-Saxon welcome.

Winston recognised the tinged tennis pair, the viridescent jogger: it was the old man from the wine bar and the sad pruning lady from the garden below the window, still silently gasping her archaic recitation. He recognised also one or two tinged shoppers from the street, the shopping trolley eel—all now stumbling blindly along the runway towards their new home, running the gauntlet of jeers, rounded up for the enlightened light entertainment of all those unified by hate.

Captured on the cameras mounted high inside each room, the greenish half-beings staggered around in the opulent Baroque ornamentation to continuing harpsichord accompaniment, Chinese wallpaper and slave figurines adorning the walls, Rococo cornices, neo-classical textiles, marmoreal columns as well as an impressive collection of paintings and a labyrinth of two-way mirrors with gilded frames, plus gilt pier-glasses, gilt girandoles and a suite of Louis XVI Lit à la Polonaise beds billeted in rows in the vast and luxuriant dormitory—the poor old filthy-dirty precaristocrats finally reunited with the ancestral finery they had once been so cruelly denied, reinstated in this season's *Big Brother's Stately Home.*

The café door cracked open and Julia—if indeed that was her name—leaked in from the oily darkness with noticeable purpose and the shock of his anatomical transformation visible in her eyes. As she cautiously drew up a chair and sat opposite Winston, he wondered how she might have found him.

'I'm sorry I betrayed you.' The words were spoken so very softly, the sentence only just forming. Winston saw that Julia was poised to receive his customary words of wisdom, but he could only look upon her with a sense of sorrow for what he knew was to follow.

'*Come gather 'round people wherever you roam, and admit that the waters around you have grown, and accept it that soon you'll be drenched to the bone. If your time to you is worth savin' then you better start swimmin', or you'll sink like a stone, for the times they are a-changin*''.

'What?'

'*What is...is just.*'

'Winston, are you alright?'

'*Oh, I'm outta sight.*'

Winston grinned with a thick-headed bromidic vigour, a tantric daze, an ayurvedic funk, with something of the magnitude of the oceanic or the abstract, or both, or none—it was difficult to tell.

Seeing how Winston's words were lacking in their usual sagacious yet user-friendly elevation, Julia recalled the purpose of her visit and, even more nervously, pushed a small object across the table without taking her eyes from his. Fearful that her fingertips were in danger from some imaginary rat-trap, she swiftly retracted them, stood up and, with a brittle twitch of a smile, turned and hurried to the door and back out into *Big Brother*'s brand new homicidal night.

Winston observed the thing wedged just under the saucer of his coffee cup, and could smell the balsam even before disturbing it. He unfolded it as he had unfolded a million fortune cookie papers before. The words were pressed into soft tissue paper with a neat handwriting that was anonymous to him, such that he did not know, nor care, if *he* or *she* had written it minutes before or many moons ago.

As O'Brien's redemptive social experiment erupted, heralded by the sublimated violence of pretty fireworks, as many VW Beetles were rolled onto their backs and set alight, the streets menaced by vandals in sandals and hippy tie-and-die lynch mobs, and as looting broke out and the city burned with rainbow rage and molten lava lamps, with the combined fury of every lightning strike ever to have hailed from sky to earth, the polarity now reversed as a million years of accumulated wellness welled up into an almighty tectonic holocaust raging from the earth's monstrous bowel, the sublime telluric corpse-grinder taking revenge on the wafer-thin Anthropocene for irritating its allergic skin—O'Brien's compassion fatigue rose to a cataclysmic pitch, forming a brand new consensus of hate.... *Exhaaaaaaaaaaale*——

Winston flattened out the tissue and read its scrawl:

'*Mine is most peaceable disposition. My wish is humble cottage with thatched roof, but good bed, best good food, most fresh milk and best butter, much flower before window, and few fine trees before door; if God want make my happiness complete, must grant me joy of seeing six or seven of enemy hang from those trees. Before their death I shall, moved in heart, forgive all wrong they did me in their lifetime.*'[*]

Winston summoned his most best beaming smile, but a tear

---

* Heinrich Heine, *Gedanken und Einfälle* (Section I), *rectified*, quoted in Sigmund Freud, *Civilization and its Discontents*, tr. J. Strachey (London: Norton, 1989).

was soon to follow, since the sweet kooky sound of a soft female voice wafting along to lazy strums of an acoustic folk guitar met his ears: *woman is the nigger of the world...oh yes she is...just think about it...* carried on the mutinous breeze, the night descending like an embalmer's sheet—dark, solid as livid meat laid out on a morgue slab, dense as the slab itself.

And so here rests Winston Smith ... Ass ... Buffoon ... *The Last Man...*